EMERALD WAVES OF PASSION

"I want to kiss you, Red. I want to kiss you in the worst way." And he suddenly realized it was true, for he'd thought of little else since that night of the storm when she'd been waiting for him to come home.

Prudence couldn't breathe, couldn't answer; she could only stare at the lips that were only inches away from her own and wonder what it would feel like to have them pressed against hers. She didn't have to wonder long, for suddenly Brock's lips descended, his mouth covering hers in masterful persuasion.

His tongue traced the softness of her lower lip, sending her stomach into a wild swirl. Then his mouth covered hers hungrily, searching, tasting, wanting, creating a need that centered deep within her, stirring the embers of her passion that had lain dormant these many years.

Also by Millie Criswell

Phantom Lover

Available from
HarperPaperbacks

Diamond in the Rough

⊱ MILLIE CRISWELL ⊰

HarperPaperbacks
A Division of HarperCollinsPublishers

This is a work of fiction. The characters, incidents, and dialogues are products of the author's imagination and are not to be construed as real. Any resemblance to actual events or persons, living or dead, is entirely coincidental.

HarperPaperbacks   *A Division of* HarperCollins*Publishers*
10 East 53rd Street, New York, N.Y. 10022

Cover illustration by Jean Monti

First printing: January 1994

Printed in the United States of America

HarperPaperbacks, HarperMonogram, and colophon are trademarks of HarperCollins*Publishers*

❖ 10 9 8 7 6 5 4 3 2 1

To Matt, who makes me proud to be his mother every single day of my life.

ACKNOWLEDGMENTS

I wish to thank Ken Alstad for his remarkable collection entitled *Savvy Sayin's*, from which I have quoted at the beginning of each chapter and throughout the book.

Also thanks to Phillip Ashton Rollins for his excellent reference book, *The Cowboy*, an indispensable guide to the Old West.

Last, I would like to thank my own indispensable, knowledgeable husband, Larry, for brainstorming the plot of this book with me and offering support and encouragement. And for saying, and truly believing, that *Diamond in the Rough* should be made into a Movie of the Week!

If Eve had been a ranchwoman,
she would never have tempted Adam with an apple.
She would have ordered him to make his [own] meal.

—Anthony Trollope, 1862

1

*Some cowboys got too much tumbleweed
in their blood to settle down.*

**Colorado Territory,
September 1875**

    Great. Just great! Brock Peters thought as the first roll of thunder echoed off the mountains of granite behind him. He looked up to find dark, ominous clouds, then dismounted and untied the leather thong that held his canvas slicker to the rear of the saddle. Just as he pulled on the slicker, the heavens opened up, spewing forth a shower of water.

    "Great. Just great!" he muttered, pulling down the brim of his black felt hat to ward off the steady downpour before remounting. The rain was falling in heavy sheets, and he could barely make out the thick stands of golden aspens in the distance.

Welcome to Colorado, he thought disgustedly. Why hadn't he stayed in Utah? At least it was dry in Utah. And that job tending bar hadn't been all that bad.

But he knew why he hadn't stayed. He never stayed in any one place too long. Not long enough to put down roots, anyway. Roots could strangle a man. And he liked being footloose and fancy free, with no one to care for, no extra baggage to carry.

With a shake of his head that sent droplets of water flying every which way, he heaved a thoroughly disgusted sigh and nudged his bay forward.

The town of Absolution looked like many others Brock had visited during his years of wandering. There was the prerequisite dry goods store, which looked to be doing a thriving business despite the unpleasant weather, and a tonsorial parlor, which reminded him that he hadn't shaved in over a week and sure could use a bath.

He sniffed. Yep. He needed one all right.

The hotel looked fairly decent, and he'd make arrangements for a room. But first he needed to get his horse situated, then find something to warm up his aching bones. Spying the Silver Slipper Saloon across the street from the hotel, he smiled. It was just what the doctor ordered.

"Come on, Willy. Let's get you a nice dry stall and a bag of oats. You deserve it after what we've just ridden through." The horse gave an impatient snort, tossing his head back as if agreeing with Brock.

"Howdy, mister," called a wiry little man as Brock stepped into the livery. "Name's Hank Brewster. What can I do for you? You look a mite drowned. You just ride through that storm?"

The answer seemed as obvious as the large nose on the inquisitive man's face, but Brock nodded patiently and smiled. "Yep. I'd appreciate it if you could give Willy here a good rubbing down and a bag of oats. He's as waterlogged as I am."

"Sure thing. How long you expectin' to stay? I can give you the weekly rate of five dollars. It's cheaper than a dollar a day."

Brock shook his head. He never knew how long he would remain in any one place, so it was always better to opt for the short-term arrangement. "Just charge me by the day. I haven't decided if I'm stayin' or not."

The proprietor rubbed his neck. "Well, that sounds sensible to me. There ain't a whole lot going on in Absolution. Since the silver dried up, the town's mostly made up of cattle ranchers and farmers. They're God-fearing folk, if you get my meanin'."

"That's reassuring," Brock said with just a hint of sarcasm, untying his bedroll before loosening Willy's cinch.

"Though we do have a bit of excitement here today. Folks is fixin' to punish young Mary Winslow down at the Town Hall. The reverend calls it a public humiliation. Mary up and got herself pregnant by the Fitzsimmons boy. 'Course, he denies it's his. Her old man kicked her out, and now the church elders are fixin' to set an example by her."

Deep lines bracketed Brock's mouth. He disliked injustices of any kind. His legal background always rose to the forefront when he was faced with wrongs against innocent people. And it didn't sound to him like this Mary Winslow was guilty of anything besides naiveté.

"How old is this Winslow woman?" he asked, noting the indifference on Hank Brewster's face as he rubbed his whiskered jaw.

"I 'spect about sixteen. Her ma died when she was born, and she was raised by that pitiful Wilbur Winslow. The man's drunk most of the time."

"Great. Just great," Brock mumbled, knowing there was no way he could avoid butting into something that wasn't his business. Damn!

"You say something, mister?"

"Yeah. Where'd you say this town meeting was going to be held?"

"In the Town Hall at the end of Main Street. You can't miss it. It sits right next to the church."

"How appropriate." Brock spun on his boot heel and headed for the door, inwardly cursing the pious, the righteous, who wore their religion like a banner.

"You fixin' to go and watch, mister?" Hank hurried after the stranger to hear his reply, but all he got was the heavy wooden door slammed in his face.

Moody Carstairs drowned his disappointment in yet another glass of whiskey. Pensioned off. Who would have believed it? Thirty-two years in the United States Cavalry. Thirty-two goddamned years, and he'd been pensioned off like an old horse put out to pasture. Not that he wasn't capable of staying on. He still had a few good years of service left in him. But the army was looking for younger men—West Point types who were eager for adventure and glory.

"Fifty's the magic number, Colonel Carstairs," explained the young upstart major who had come to Fort Garland to replace him, a slightly superior smile twisting his snotty-nosed face.

"They sent a boy to do a man's job," Moody slurred to no one in particular, though several of the Silver Slipper's patrons turned disgusted looks in his direction.

He supposed he deserved their scorn. He'd been drunk for three days running, four counting today. Well, it was just too damned bad if they didn't like it. A man deserved to get drunk when he reached the end of his career.

"I think you've had enough, old man," the beefy barkeep informed Moody, stepping to his table to pick up the bottle of whiskey.

Bleary eyes tried to focus on the giant. "Watch who you're calling *old man.*" Moody attempted to rise but fell back down on his seat, producing a chorus of laughter from the other patrons seated around the smoke-filled, noisy room. Even the tinny sound of the piano in the corner couldn't drown out their snickers.

Gripping him by the arm, the barkeep helped Moody to his feet and escorted him to the pair of swinging doors. "You're a disgrace to that uniform, old man," the barkeeper said. "Where'd you get it? Steal it from some dead soldier?"

Amid the laughter, Moody Carstairs felt himself being booted out of the saloon and into the muddy street. He tried to raise his head to refute the disparaging remarks, but the effort proved too dear and he passed out cold.

Reverend Ezekiel Entwhistle stood at the head of the room atop an old apple crate, waving his hands frantically to and fro as he addressed the congregation. He was garbed all in black, and Brock thought he resembled a vulture with his pointed head and hawklike nose.

The Town Hall was packed; he couldn't believe, as he stood near the rear door observing, how all these good, moral-minded folks could stand by and watch a young woman, whose only crime was getting herself with child, be publicly chastised.

The reverend began to shower down fire and brimstone. His voice boomed loud and clear, keeping time to the thunder that could still be heard in the distance, and Brock turned his attention back to what he was saying.

"A sin has been committed, brethren. How can we stand by and allow our town to be tainted by the immoral, the unholy?" The crowd murmured, "Amen," nodding solemnly in response.

"Bring in Mary Winslow," directed the man of the cloth. "And let no man or woman look upon her flesh, lest they be tainted by her sins as well."

Brock's brown eyes widened as the congregation bowed their heads and stared down at their shoes. But his mouth fell open when a frail-looking blond girl, who was at least eight months pregnant, walked up the aisle escorted by two stern-looking men.

Anger roiled through him. He clenched his fists, taking deep breaths to tamp it down when one of the men, the larger of the two, pushed roughly at Mary's back, almost causing her to stumble.

"Mary Winslow, what have you to say to this gathering?" Reverend Entwhistle inquired.

Defiance sparked in the girl's eyes, and she tilted up her chin defiantly, saying nothing. Brock watched her in admiration.

"Step up, then, and let all who look upon you know that God cannot abide sinners." The reverend grabbed Mary's arm, drawing her forward.

When the crowd began to jeer and toss out disparaging remarks, the young girl's eyes filled with tears, and something inside Brock snapped. His deep voice rang out from the rear of the room.

"Take your hands off that girl."

Everyone turned to find the stranger at the back of the room stepping forward to eat up the distance between him and Mary Winslow. The crowd began whispering and speculating, and several sharp, very loud gasps could be heard.

"Who are you to interfere, sir?" the reverend asked, clearly surprised by the intrusion. "This is a private matter concerning the citizens of Absolution and this young woman's father. It is Mr. Winslow's wish that this girl suffer public chastisement for her sins."

"Has this woman had a fair trial?"

The reverend's beady black eyes narrowed, and his voice was filled with annoyance when he demanded, "Leave us, sir. This is none of your concern."

Brock stepped forward until he was standing shoulder to shoulder with Mary Winslow, then grasped her elbow gently. "I'm taking this woman into protective custody." He turned toward the congregation. "Are you the judge and jury here?" he asked, impaling them with a look so fierce, so accusing, many turned away to stare sheepishly at the floor.

A red flush suffusing his face, Reverend Entwhistle raised a finger to point at the ceiling. "We have a higher Judge here."

"Mary," Brock whispered, edging toward the door, "we're leaving this place." She nodded mutely, her eyes wide with fright.

A hushed silence fell over the room, and all eyes were trained on the stranger who dared defy a man of God.

At the doorway, Brock paused and looked back. "I was under the impression that absolution meant forgiveness. That doesn't seem to be the case in this town."

Holding tight to Mary's hand, he pulled her out the door and into the rain-soaked street. The rain was still falling hard, and Brock removed his slicker, tossing it over Mary's head; he was rewarded with a grateful smile.

"Come on. My horse is at the livery. I'll take you home."

She pulled up short, balking like a mule about to cross a rushing river. "I can't go home, mister. My pa threw me out. He said if I was to come home, he would take a gun and shoot me. I ain't got no other family."

Brock winced at her forlorn expression. "Is there someone else in town who'll help? I can take you there instead."

She shook her head. "Nope. The Fitzsimmons fixed it so that nobody'll speak to me. They spread lies. Said I was a whore." Tears filled her eyes, and her hands went to her swollen belly. "But I ain't no whore. Bobby Fitzsimmons told me he loved me. Said we was goin' to be married.

"I tried to hide the fact that I was going to have his baby by letting out the seams of my dress. But my pa came into my room unexpected and saw me in my shift. It was his idea for the reverend to punish me. Said I shamed him in front of the whole town."

He would dearly love to get his hands around Bobby Fitzsimmons's horny throat, Brock thought, and Wilbur Winslow's vengeful one, too, for that matter. "Let's get to the livery. We'll decide what to do once we're out of this rain."

Soiled hay and wet horseflesh greeted the pair when they entered the barn a few minutes later. Brock glanced about but Hank Brewster was nowhere in sight, so he led the young woman to a hay bale, advising her to sit while they figured out what to do.

Mary looked small and lost, like somebody's kid sister. Her blond braids hung down her back like two thick gold ropes, emphasizing her youth, and Brock felt an unwanted surge of protectiveness wash over him.

"Look, Miss Winslow, it's going to be dark soon. I haven't secured a room at the hotel, and it's still raining harder than your Reverend Entwhistle's convictions. I want to help you, but I'm not sure I can."

Her voice grew pleading. "If you could just escort me to the ranch, I could get help there."

A rush of relief swept through Brock. So she did have kin after all. "I thought you said you had no family. Are you sure this ranch will take you in?"

"They ain't family. It's Miss Prudence's Rough and Ready Ranch for Unwed Mothers. Miss Prudence Daniels will take me in."

Dark eyebrows rose. "A ranch for unwed mothers? I've never heard of such a thing."

"It's true. The townsfolk don't cotton to Miss Prudence too much, 'cause she helps those that can't help themselves."

Brock heaved a sigh and yanked off his hat, slapping it against his thigh. Great. Just great! For a man who traveled with no baggage, Mary Winslow was turning out to be one major piece of luggage. "Where is this place?" he asked, settling the felt on his head once again.

Mary shrugged. "I don't rightly know. All I heard is that it's several miles from here. I ain't never had no call to go there before now." Her cheeks filled with color.

Hearing the barn door slam shut, Brock turned, relieved to see the proprietor. Hank seemed out of breath, as if he had just run a footrace, and he frowned when his eyes landed on Mary Winslow.

"You shouldn'ta brung her here, mister. I was over to the saloon and just heard what happened. The folks at the Town Hall are pretty riled up."

Brock wasn't the least bit surprised to hear that. He thought for sure that the good Christian folks of Absolution were going to string him up. It was probably time for their monthly crucifixion.

"As soon as I get directions to the Rough and Ready Ranch, we'll get out of your hair directly."

A shrill whistle flew out between Hank's thin lips. "You're fixin' to take her to Prudence Daniels?" He shook his head. "Mister, you are a glutton for punishment."

Mary cast the proprietor a disgruntled look, but Brock nodded absently in agreement, figuring that the man was probably right. He shrugged into his sheepskin jacket. "Do you know where it is? We're in a hurry."

After getting directions that left quite a bit to be desired, Brock handed over a hefty sum of money to the distrustful proprietor and rented a buckboard. Although Mary had assured him she could "ride like the wind, iff'n it weren't too windy," Brock didn't think it'd be a good idea for a woman in her condition to sit a horse. He hitched Willy to the wagon, then gathered his things together, placing them in the back of the buckboard with some additional items he'd purchased from the reluctant man.

The ranch was only about five or six miles outside of town. With luck they would make it before nightfall.

"Do you have any belongings we can gather, Mary?" he asked the young girl.

She shook her head sadly. "My pa sold off all of my ma's stuff to buy whiskey. All I got is this here dress. It's my nicest one, though it don't fit too well anymore."

He gazed down at the faded blue homespun and sighed. Well, at least she had shoes, he thought.

"Come on, then, let's make tracks. The sooner we can get out of this town, the sooner you'll be safe and warm at Miss Prudence Daniels's ranch."

The way Hank had described Miss Daniels, as "the meanest spinster this side of the Rockies," didn't make Brock feel any too confident about their reception.

According to the stableman, she had "a temper that would rival the devil's, and a tongue so sharp it could cut a man to ribbons at twenty paces."

"Great. Just great!" he muttered as they rode west toward the ranch.

The rain had let up a bit, but the road was a quagmire of mud. The wheels were continually getting stuck in the deep ruts, and Brock had to get off the wagon occasionally to coax Willy forward. And each and every time he waded through the thick silt, he wondered why in hell he hadn't minded his own business. He'd broken his own rule of not getting involved, and now he was paying the price.

"Mr. Peters," Mary called out, pointing, "look up ahead. There's something in the road."

Brock reined the horse to a halt, then turned to gaze down the road. Sure enough, there was something, or someone, in the middle of all that mud. A dappled-gray mare with a United States Cavalry saddle stood grazing nearby.

Could things get any worse?

With a cluck of his tongue, he urged Willy forward. They had gone only a short distance when Brock pulled the wagon to a halt, handed Mary the reins, and jumped down.

The man was lying facedown in the mud. He was dressed in the uniform of a cavalry officer, but he didn't look like any officer Brock had ever seen. When he turned the man over, he smelled whiskey on his breath and frowned.

"You goddamn fool!" he cursed, trying to lift him.

The drunk moaned, then opened his eyes. "I am, sir, quite the fool. And I thank you for stopping to assist me. It's more than I deserve."

"I'll say," Brock retorted. "You could have been killed, riding out in this storm as drunk as you are."

Moody Carstairs smiled. "Was. I find that lying in the mud in the pouring rain has a sobering effect on a body."

"Well, get up, then. You're blocking our way."

Moody gazed over at the wagon and noticed the young girl. He smiled kindly at Mary, but she blushed and turned away. "Your wife?"

"Not hardly," Brock replied. "She's a bit young for my taste. Now, if you'd be kind enough to remove yourself from the road . . ."

"I'd like to oblige you, Mr. . . . ." Moody paused expectantly.

"Brock Peters."

"Mr. Peters. I'm Colonel Martin Carstairs. My friends call me Moody. As I said, I'd like to oblige you, but I'm afraid that my fall has resulted in a broken bone. I can't seem to move my right leg."

Brock's eyes rolled toward the heavens, having just found out that things *could* get worse. Placing his hands on the leg the man claimed to have broken, he felt the separation of bone; Moody's howl split the silence, causing both Mary and Willy to start.

"It's broke all right. And I don't know a thing about setting broken bones." Brock sighed. "Guess you'll have to come with us."

The man's voice was threaded with pain. "And where might that be, Mr. Peters? I'm not entirely welcome in Absolution."

"Neither are we. We're heading for the Rough and Ready Ranch. Ever heard of it?"

Carstairs rubbed his grizzled cheek. "Can't say that I have."

"Miss Winslow has friends there," was all Brock

would admit to, receiving a grateful smile from the pregnant girl.

It took a few minutes, but Brock was finally able to get Moody loaded into the back of the wagon. Immobilizing the man's leg as best he could between the two saddles, he covered him with a blanket—not that it did much good; the blankets were soaked, like everything else he owned or wore—and tied the colonel's mare to the back of the wagon.

More baggage, he thought as he climbed aboard, and urged the horse forward with a snap of the reins. He shook his head in disgust. For a man who liked being footloose and fancy free, he sure as hell had one big load of baggage.

The first thing Brock noticed about the Daniels ranch was the sign. It hung lopsided on a piece of rope and was shot full of bullet holes. Mary hadn't exaggerated about the townsfolk not liking Prudence Daniels, he thought.

Maneuvering the wagon down the road leading to the main house, he observed acres of rolling green grass and white-faced Hereford cattle grazing contentedly. The landscape was dotted with aspens, birch, and spruce, and the snow-capped mountains in the distance served as an impressive backdrop. A small stream meandered through the property—an offshoot of the nearby Gunnison River, Brock deduced correctly.

"It's real purty here," Mary commented, trying to hide her nervousness as she fidgeted with the folds of her dress.

Brock glanced over his shoulder to find Moody Carstairs still asleep. "I think you're going to like living here." He'd often dreamed of having a place like this, but that was before—pain wrenched his gut—before Catherine and Joshua died. Eight years. Had it really been eight years? He pushed the disturbing memory to the back of his mind.

"You ever worked on a ranch, Mr. Peters? You never did say where you was from. You just sort of showed up, like a hero out of one of them dime novels I heard about."

Brock's laughter was self-derisive. Coward was more like it, he thought. He'd run away from his problems, not having the guts to stay and face the pain. "I'm originally from California, but I've lived just about everywhere, done just about everything there is to do. I've traveled quite a bit these past few years."

"I like having roots. I thought me and Bobby was going to settle down and put down roots, raise a family. I guess I was wrong." She stared down into her lap and grew quiet.

Brock patted Mary's hand comfortingly. "Don't give up on Bobby yet, Mary. He may just see the right of it and come around." And if he had to pound some sense into the boy himself, he would. Great God! he thought, shaking himself. He was beginning to sound like an overprotective father.

The sight of the ranch house halted their conversation. Expecting the usual log structure, Brock was surprised and impressed as he stared at the sprawling white two-story wooden house with the bright red shutters. It had a large porch that fronted the entire width of the house, and there were flowers growing along the edge of it—marigolds and chrysanthemums—which added sparks of color to the velvet green of the lawn. It was obvious Prudence Daniels took a great deal of pride in her home.

The sight of the house brought to mind another, with

a white picket fence and a profusion of dark red roses cascading over it. It had been his house—his and Catherine's and Josh's. It had been home.

"Well, ain't that just the purtiest house you ever seen?" Mary's face brightened with pleasure.

Brock swallowed and nodded absently, drawing Willy to a halt before handing her the reins. "Wait here and keep an eye on the colonel. I want to announce our arrival." And make sure that Mary and Moody would be welcome, he added silently.

Stepping onto the porch, he found an Indian seated on one of the cane rockers, whittling. The man's hair was long and snowy white, quite in contrast with his skin, which looked as wrinkled and tanned as a well-used saddle. He didn't look up until Brock cleared his throat, and when he did, suspicion was bright in his dark eyes.

"Is this the home of Prudence Daniels?" Brock asked. The man nodded slowly in response. "The Prudence Daniels who runs the home for unwed mothers?"

This time he got a grunt and decided the Indian was either mute, rude, or both. Not about to be dissuaded, he knocked on the door.

Another Indian answered, this one a woman—a short, rotund woman who couldn't have weighed less than a full-grown heifer. She had jet black hair that was fashioned into two long braids. Her dark eyes were kind, and unlike the man on the porch, she seemed friendly.

Could *this* be Prudence Daniels? he wondered. It didn't seem likely, but he smiled and asked anyway: "Miss Daniels?"

The woman covered her mouth and giggled, shaking her head. In a singsong voice she replied, "Miss Pru's upstairs. Come in. I fetch her."

Brock was escorted into the large front room. It was empty, and he felt relieved that he hadn't encountered any more pregnant ladies. One was quite enough to contend with at the moment.

It was nearly dark, and the kerosene lamps on the mantel had been lit. A cheery fire was blazing in the stone hearth, and he stepped toward it to warm himself.

The inside of the house reflected the same meticulous care as the outside. The whitewashed walls were spotless. The red-and-white gingham curtains hanging at the window looked freshly starched and ironed. The furniture was substantial—heavy wood and leather pieces that a man could sink down into after a hard day's work. But there were also attractive crocheted afghans and needlepoint pillows to soften the effect.

Catherine had loved doing needlework.

"May I help you?"

He turned at the sound of the feminine voice, his eyes widening in surprise. He didn't know what he was expecting Miss Prudence Daniels to look like, but it wasn't this freckle-faced redhead who didn't look much older than Mary. Dressed in yellow gingham, she was like a ray of warm sunshine, willowy as a slender birch with eyes as green as clover.

"Miss Daniels?"

She inclined her head. "I am. And what can I do for you? Hannah said you wanted to speak to me."

Removing his leather gloves, he stepped forward to shake her hand. As soon as their flesh touched, a shot of awareness jolted through him, causing him to pull away as if shocked.

"My name's Brock Peters. I've brought a young girl from town—Mary Winslow. She's pregnant and had nowhere else to go. She said I was to bring her here to you."

The woman's eyes hardened; her welcoming smile melted into a thin line. "I see. And where is this woman?"

Brock gestured with his head toward the window. "I wasn't sure if her information about this place was accurate, so I left her in the wagon. She's watching over Moody."

"Moody?" Her voice softened momentarily. "Is that this woman's husband?"

Brock shook his head. "No. He's a man we found on the road. His leg is broken. I didn't know what else to do with him, so I brought him here."

Prudence Daniels sized up the man before her and fought to keep her temper in check. Dressed in wet woolen pants, sheepskin jacket, and black felt hat, it was obvious he was a cowboy. Another reckless cowboy who'd gone and gotten a girl in trouble, then expected to dump her off like unnecessary baggage. It was always the same.

This man was attractive. With his dark curly hair and soft brown eyes, she could see why a woman would be foolish enough to give herself to him. Most likely he'd told her he loved her; they always said that.

"I'll have Hannah fetch your *friend*." The way she said the word made Brock take a step backward. "Indian Joe will see to Mr. Moody."

"It's Moody Carstairs, ma'am. He's a colonel in the cavalry."

Her eyebrow arched. "Is that so? And does this colonel have someone who'll come fetch him in the morning, Mr. Peters? We're running a home for unwed mothers, not an infirmary. I'm not equipped to handle injured army officers." Nor did she want a healthy man, broken bones or not, mingling with her ladies.

"I don't know anything about Moody, ma'am. We

just met. But I will pay for Miss Winslow's upkeep. She doesn't have any other means of support."

Prudence crossed her arms over her chest, and in a voice that could freeze a pond in the middle of July, she said, "And I guess, since you just happen to be the baby's father, it's the least you can do. Isn't that right, Mr. Peters?"

Brock's face whitened, even under the week's growth of beard. He was about to set the record straight when Mary burst into the room, running to his side and throwing her arms about his waist. She was shaking and frightened, and he could do no less than pat her head and try to comfort her.

"It's all right, Mary. This nice lady is going to take care of you." He smiled at Prudence Daniels, but she merely glared.

"But you won't leave? You won't leave just yet?" Mary implored.

"Of course not," Brock reassured her. "I'll wait until you're settled."

Mary was clinging to Brock Peters like a vine wrapped around the trunk of a tree, and it was all Prudence could do not to step forward and slap his handsome face. The pregnant woman wasn't a woman at all, but a mere girl who couldn't have been more than sixteen. And Brock Peters looked every bit of thirty-five. He should be ashamed, Prudence thought, robbing the cradle, then putting his own baby back into it.

For some reason she didn't recognize the young girl, which was odd, considering she knew most of the folks in town; she made a mental note to ask Mary why that was so.

"Why don't you have a seat on the sofa, Mr. Peters," Prudence suggested, her green eyes sparking fire. "I'll see to Mary's comfort and return momentarily. There are several things I'd like to discuss about your *friend.*"

Damn! There was that word again. She made it sound so sordid.

Brock began to pace the room as soon as Mary was ushered out. Maybe he should just leave—leave before he got himself any more entangled than he was already. It was obvious this Prudence Daniels thought he was responsible for Mary's predicament.

But he couldn't leave. He had promised Mary he would stay a while longer.

Recalling Prudence Daniels's accusing face—a face that would be downright pretty if she smiled—he cursed inwardly. As if he didn't already feel miserable enough, he recalled what the man from the livery had said: "She had a temper that could rival the devil's, and a tongue so sharp it could cut a man to ribbons at twenty paces."

Sinking down onto the sofa, he clutched his head in his hands and stared dejectedly at the floor. "Great. Just great," he mumbled, wishing he'd never heard of Absolution, Colorado, the Reverend Ezekiel Entwhistle, and most especially, "the meanest spinster this side of the Rockies"—Miss Prudence Daniels.

2

> *You kin cut your throat*
> *with a sharp tongue.*

"*Mr. Peters.* Mr. Peters!"

The voice grew louder and more insistent, drawing Brock's attention. He looked up to find Prudence Daniels hovering over him like an avenging angel. Her hands were splayed on lean hips; her face, rigid with indignation, could have been carved from granite.

He made to rise, but she motioned him back down, dragging over a cane bent rocker from the corner of the fireplace.

"Your friend Mary is resting," she confided, her voice filled with disdain. "She's quite overwrought by her ordeal, and I think it's best to let her rest in bed for the remainder of the day."

Which was of short duration, Brock observed, glancing out the window to find the sun setting into the horizon. "It's kind of you to look after her, Miss Daniels."

"Kindness has nothing to do with it, Mr. Peters. It's duty, plain and simple. I'll do my duty and I'll expect you to do yours."

There was no mistaking the challenge, and Brock's eyebrows rose in response to it, even as he heaved a deep sigh of frustration. He was tired and damp, and he sure as hell didn't have the energy to argue with this stubborn, opinionated woman. But he knew he had to set matters straight.

"Look, Miss Daniels, I know what you're thinking, but you're wrong. I'm not responsible for Mary's predicament. I'm just an acquaintance concerned for her welfare."

Prudence's eyes narrowed as she rocked back and forth, back and forth, trying to keep her anger in check. She knew he would deny the child was his. They always did. But for an instant she'd thought Brock Peters might be different. He was a mature man who seemed concerned about his friends. Obviously he wasn't concerned enough to stick around to raise the child of his unbridled lust. Men were only after one thing; Brock Peters was no different.

"It wouldn't be wise for you to leave just yet, Mr. Peters, if that is your intention. For some reason we shall abstain from mentioning, the *child* is quite attached to you." She let the word sink in, then continued, ignoring the way Brock Peters stiffened on his seat. "Mary might not be able to accept the betrayal . . . the realization of your departure," she amended at the hardening of his eyes. "I would strongly suggest that you remain at the ranch for a day or two, until she adjusts to her new life."

He nodded, twirling the brim of his hat round and round in his fingers while he studied the woman before him.

Prudence Daniels was full of hurt, that was for certain. She wore her pain like a hair shirt. Her opinions were as rigid as her spine, and arguing with her would do little good. He'd been a lawyer long enough to know when a judge and jury had made up their minds. And Prudence Daniels had declared him guilty as sin.

"I'll stay, but only for a day or two." At her nod of approval he added, "How is Colonel Carstairs?"

"The colonel is feeling very little pain at the moment," she confided, not bothering to mention that the brave cavalry officer had bellowed like a newborn calf, forcing the usually passive Hannah to threaten him with his scalp if he didn't shut up.

"We dosed him with laudanum after Hannah reset the bone and splinted his leg. You can look in on him in the morning."

Brock's stomach rumbled, sounding loud in the uncomfortable silence. "Sorry, ma'am, but I haven't eaten since last night." And then it had only been cold beans and beef jerky. It had been raining too hard to start a fire.

Prudence pushed herself to her feet. "You can bunk in with the hands tonight, Mr. Peters. I'll have Indian Joe show you the way. Tell my foreman, Mr. Stewart, that I approved it. As for the food, you'll have to make do with a couple of ham sandwiches and some leftover potato salad. I'm afraid we had our supper early. We always do on the Sabbath."

"That'll be fine, ma'am. I'm much obliged."

"You might as well be apprised, Mr. Peters, that I won't tolerate any drinking, cussing, or lewd behavior in front of my ladies. We have rules here at the R and R, and as long as you're staying here, I'll expect you to abide by them."

He wondered if he'd have to ask the puritanical spinster for permission to use the privy. Or maybe she considered *that* lewd behavior, too.

"Is that clear, Mr. Peters?" she pressed.

"Yes, sir! I mean . . . ma'am." He smirked at the resentment flaring briefly in her eyes.

Pulling her skirts close to her body so she wouldn't make contact with the insolent cowboy, Prudence preceded him out of the room, hoping upon hope that Brock Peters would be out of her life very soon. There was something about the self-assured cowboy she found very unsettling.

Brock was having similar thoughts as he followed the taciturn Indian out to the bunkhouse. He wanted nothing more than to ride hell-bent for leather away from the spinster.

Women like Prudence Daniels were nothing but trouble. They were mean-spirited man haters. And though she looked like an angel, with big green eyes and pouty lips that begged for a man's attention, she had the devil's own meanness flaming through her, and he had no intention of getting burned.

Having decided to leave after all, despite his assurances to Prudence Daniels to the contrary, Brock found himself up before the rooster's crow, dressed in dry, warm clothing, eager to saddle his horse and be on his way.

The night he'd passed in the Rough and Ready bunkhouse had been nothing short of unusual. The cowboys were a hairbreadth away from being considered a bunch of old men, save for the one they called "the boy," who couldn't have been more than seventeen and had the look of greenhorn all about him; all had been as quiet and uncommunicative as a roomful of worshipers at a prayer meeting.

Of course, what else could he expect? They'd been living under the watchful eyes of Prudence Daniels and her long list of edicts.

"You fixin' to head out today, mister?"

Brock paused in his efforts to retie his bedroll and turned to find a leathery-cheeked, blue-eyed man at his elbow. The man sported a bushy mustache that matched the snow white of his hair.

"Shorty Jenkins's the name," he said, holding out his hand. "Sorry we weren't more talkative last night, but Miss Prudence likes us to reflect of a Sunday evening. I guess we was doin' quite a bit of reflectin' when you come in."

Shrugging indifference, Brock introduced himself, then explained, "I'm just passing through. Did a favor for a friend. Now I'm headin' out."

The man looked about anxiously to make certain no one was in earshot, then lowered his voice. "We could always use another hand, iff'n you've got a mind to stay. A change of pasture sometimes makes the calf fatter." When Brock smiled, Shorty added, "The work's not too hard, and Hannah sets a mean table."

Brock had the feeling that Shorty Jenkins was admitting more than he was saying, but he didn't want to get any more involved in matters at the R and R than he was already. "I appreciate the offer, though I thought Stewart was ramrodding this outfit."

The man didn't bother to hide his dislike as his lips twisted into a sneer. "Stewart eased himself into the job like a colt dropped into a fresh mound of hay. Buck Taylor used to be foreman, till he got hisself killed ridin' the perimeter. In waltzes Stewart, pretty as all get out, totin' Buck's body into the barn one summer's afternoon, claimin' Buck was killed by some disgruntled Cheyenne." Shorty snorted his disbelief. "I seen men killed by the Cheyenne, and this weren't their work."

As Shorty followed Brock out the door and into the corral, Brock couldn't help but ask, "Why'd Miss Daniels hire him? Seems like she would have done some investigating."

"Oh, she investigated all right. Had that neighbor of hers, Jacob Morgan, assisting her." Shorty spit a stream of tobacco juice into the dirt. "He's the one that recommended Stewart. The man's on loan from the Bar J— Morgan's ranch. It adjoins ours to the south."

"What happens at the R and R doesn't have a thing to do with me, Shorty." Brock approached his horse, who waited patiently by the corral fence. "I'm not one to get involved in other people's problems." Involvement meant getting close, opening yourself up to hurt. He'd had enough of that over the years. "I keep my own counsel."

Shorty rubbed his chin, eyeing the stranger speculatively. "I can't fault you none for that, Peters. But sometimes always lookin' the other way gives a fella a powerful crick in the neck."

Just as Brock was about to reply to the sarcasm, he was interrupted by a loud commotion from the direction of the main house. Glancing toward the porch, he noticed Dave Stewart and Prudence Daniels in the midst of a shouting match. Prudence was flailing her hands at her foreman, shaking her head to the negative. She reminded Brock of a feisty little roan filly, with her red mane flying about her shoulders.

"Looks like Miss Pru's hotter'n one of them geysers in that Yellowstone Park. Sure looks like she's about to blow."

Tossing his saddle over the fence rail, Brock strode toward the house, Shorty following close on his heels.

At closer inspection, Brock had to admit that Shorty's observation was accurate. Calm and collected Prudence Daniels was redder in the face than a drunken cowboy.

"I told you if I caught you one more time near the women's quarters, Mr. Stewart, there would be hell to pay. The rules of this ranch are for everyone, including the likes of you."

A look of innocence was plastered on the foreman's face as he held out his hands beseechingly. "But, Miz Daniels, Louann asked me to walk out with her last evening. I didn't see the harm in it."

"The harm, Mr. Stewart, has already been done. There's a swollen belly to attest to that fact."

"Now wait just a gall-darn minute, little lady. You ain't going to hang that heifer's calf on me. I weren't even around when she done the deed. And she done the deed quite often. Louann's been with every cowboy 'tween here and Denver."

Although she hated to admit it, what Dave Stewart said was correct. Louann Jones was a whore by profession. Since her arrival in Absolution three years ago, she'd been turning tricks at Madam Eva's bordello. But whore or not, Prudence wasn't going to let the man off the hook that easily.

"Perhaps not, Mr. Stewart," she conceded, "but I doubt very much that your intentions are entirely honorable. Or are you telling me that you'd like to marry Louann?"

The cowboy paled under his black beard. "Hell no! Just 'cause we exchanged a few kisses in the moonlight don't mean I'm fixin' to marry that gal. Some man's already got his brand on her."

With hands on her hips, Prudence retorted with more venom than a rattler, "That's right, Mr. Stewart! Louann's already been marked for life. And she doesn't need any more problems with a randy cowpoke who would like nothing better than a free sample of her charms."

Shorty gasped. Brock stared openmouthed. And the rest of the hands, numbering three, who had gathered in the yard to hear the confrontation, braced themselves for the showdown.

"Whooey," Shorty whispered to Brock, "that woman's got a burr under her saddle this mornin'." He chuckled. "I do believe this ranch has seen the last of Dave Stewart."

Shorty was correct in his assumption, for not a moment later Dave retorted angrily, "You frustrated old spinster. You're just upset because no man will give you the time of day, with your lizard's tongue that lashes out at everybody." At Prudence's gasp of outrage, he smiled nastily. "I quit."

"Mr. Morgan will hear of your impertinence," Prudence threatened, her face nearly purple.

"I don't doubt it, Miz Daniels. By tomorrow the whole blamed territory is goin' to hear about it." With that assurance, he spun on his boot heel and headed for the bunkhouse.

Hearing the excited comments and whispers from the hands, Brock felt something akin to pity as he gazed at the stricken expression on Prudence Daniels's face. He turned toward Shorty. "Don't you think it might be wise to get these men back to work? I think Miss Daniels needs some time to get her composure corraled."

"Gotcha," Shorty retorted with a wink. "Why don't you go and see if she needs some help. She looks like a lost puppy standin' there on the porch like that."

Brock heaved a sigh, thinking that puppies were known to bite, but he took the old man's advice and stepped across the yard. When he reached the porch, he found Prudence slumped on the rocker, looking as if she'd just had the wind kicked out of her by an ornery mule.

"Mornin', Miss Daniels," Brock said, leaning his right shoulder casually against the porch post, noting that Prudence's cheeks had receded from bright red all the way back to ghostly white. "I couldn't help but overhear the confrontation you just had with your foreman. Is there anything I can do to help?"

Now why did he ask that? he wondered. He didn't really want to help. He didn't want to do anything but saddle Willy and be on his way. But there was a suspicious brightness in the young woman's eyes. And he didn't think Prudence Daniels was a woman given easily to tears.

Pushing herself to her feet, Prudence slipped her shaking hands into the pockets of her apron. To be castigated publicly was something she was used to. But to be vilified in front of her own people, accused of being mean-spirited, was not something she could easily dismiss.

"I'm sorry you had to witness such unpleasantness, Mr. Peters. Mr. Stewart and I have been butting heads for several weeks over a variety of things. I guess his action of last night was merely the straw that broke the camel's back. Or my temper, to be more truthful."

Brock pushed his hat back on his head. "If you don't mind my makin' an observation, Miss Daniels, I don't see how you're going to make do with the few men you've got left in your employ. You've got half the amount you need, and most are a little long in the tooth, if you get my meanin'." He doubted seriously if Shorty could take an all-day hitch in the saddle. "And that boy is greener than the pasture grass out yonder."

Prudence heaved a sigh. "Money's been tight, Mr. Peters. I had to let the younger men go earlier than usual this year." She always pared down her crew come November anyway. "With winter coming, I couldn't afford to keep on extra hands. I realize some of the boys are getting up in years, but those who are left have been with the R and R too long to let go. Most worked for my father before he died.

"As for William, well . . ." She shrugged. "He's Polly Fletcher's younger brother. He escorted her here from New York a few weeks ago. I couldn't very well turn him out."

"You're in a bit of a predicament, Miss Daniels."

Prudence studied the man. He was young and strong, as evidenced by the way his biceps bunched beneath his shirtsleeves. He obviously knew his way around a ranch; his knowledge of ranching matters proved that much. Although she hated to admit it, she could use some help. And Brock Peters, for all his shortcomings, filled the bill quite nicely. And perhaps if he remained, he would see the error of his ways where Mary was concerned.

"If you're truly sincere about helping, Mr. Peters, you could take over the foreman's job. It doesn't pay much, a dollar a day, but you'd get lodging and three square meals a day. Sundays are usually free, after church service, that is."

Brock's mouth gaped open, then he slammed it shut and shook his head. "I've done my share of herding cattle, Miss Peters. But I'm not in the market for a job . . . at least not in Absolution," he amended. "It smacks of puttin' down roots. And roots can strangle a man."

Known for her tenaciousness throughout six counties and beyond, Prudence merely nodded. "I can understand your reluctance, Mr. Peters. Under the present circumstances—with Mary, I mean, and your friend Moody Carstairs—you're probably better off to run away. Facing responsibility is never easy. I see the struggle on the faces of those young women I care for every single day."

Her barb hit closer to the mark than Brock cared to admit. His reasons for moving on were his own, and he was getting damned tired of everyone on this ranch taking him to task because of them—first Shorty, now Prudence Daniels. Just because a man liked to keep his own counsel, not get involved, was no reason to paint him yellow-bellied.

He heard the condemnation in Prudence Daniels's voice, saw the challenge in her emerald eyes, and it rankled. It rankled so much, he found himself saying, "You've got yourself a foreman, Miss Daniels. But it's only temporary. I want to make that quite clear. I'll stay until you can find a suitable replacement for Stewart. Preferably someone who's not likely to drop dead from old age."

For the first time since Brock entered the Rough and Ready Ranch, he saw the corners of Prudence's mouth twitch. He also saw the satisfaction in her eyes and knew that the willful woman had bested him. He just wasn't certain how.

Prudence held out her hand to seal the agreement and was immediately sorry. Brock Peters's skin felt hard and hot, and she felt an unwelcome tingle of awareness shoot up her arm. By the uncertain look in the cowboy's eyes, she could tell he felt it, too. Self-consciously she shoved her hand back into her apron pocket.

"Report to me after breakfast, Mr. Peters. I'll take you on a tour of the R and R, introduce you to the ladies under my protection, go over the rest of the rules."

His eyes widened. "You mean there're more rules than those you've already told me about?"

Prudence's smile gave the sun that was rising above the mountain peaks a run for its money in terms of brilliance, and Brock was taken aback by the transformation. "Indeed, Mr. Peters. We have barely scratched the surface."

She walked back into the house, slamming the door behind her, and Brock could only stare, stupefied at the audacity of the woman. Then he smiled. Prudence Daniels was one hell of a woman. And then he frowned, remembering that "hell" was an accurate term where she was concerned.

Shaking his head, he stalked back out to the corral to retrieve his saddle, guessing he wouldn't be going anywhere for a while. A short while, he amended.

Shorty hadn't been exaggerating about the cook's capabilities, Brock decided, patting his stomach in satisfaction. It had been a good while since he'd had a meal that delicious. Spicy sausage patties, thick slices of ham, fried potatoes and gravy, and the fluffiest biscuits this side of heaven. He sighed contentedly as he made his way to the rear of the house where Moody Carstairs had been put.

His appointment with Prudence had been postponed for an hour, so he thought it might be a good time to look in on the colonel and see how he was faring, especially after the way the Indian woman had sneered when asked about his whereabouts.

"Bluecoat in back room off kitchen," she had said, shaking her head and snorting in disgust before turning back toward the stove, leaving Brock to wonder just what kind of medical care the cavalry officer had received.

He entered the small room to find Moody propped up against a pile of pillows, staring morosely out the window. His leg had been splinted, just as Prudence had said, and was sticking out from under the covers, his long red underwear cut open to accommodate two sturdy pieces of birch that held his broken leg immobile. He looked a trifle feverish, but since Brock knew little about such matters, he couldn't be sure.

"Are you up to visitors, Colonel?"

Moody turned, and the look of relief on his face was laughable. "I thought it might be that damned Injun come to torture me again."

"I take it you're referring to Hannah?" Brock almost smiled at the way Moody retreated into his pillow at the mention of the housekeeper's name.

"Yes, that's her name. A more disagreeable woman I've yet to meet." He shrugged. "I guess I won't have to worry about her from here on out. Miss Daniels informed me this morning that Hannah has refused to treat me. Said I was too much trouble. Can you imagine that?" He was clearly indignant.

Brock pulled up a maple slat-backed chair and sat down. "Well, at least she fixed up your leg."

Moody wasn't impressed. "I felt for my scalp after I woke up, I can tell you that much. She cursed me in every heathen language she knew."

"How are you feeling?"

"As useless as a tit on a boar, and as old as the Grand Canyon."

Brock did smile that time. "That good, huh?"

"The prospect of lying helpless in this bed with that Indian in the same house gives me cause for concern. Not to mention her husband, who's about as gentle as a herd of stampeding buffalo. He almost broke my other leg when he hauled me up here."

"Did Miss Daniels say how long it will be before you can get up and on your feet?"

Moody shook his head. "She's sending me another nursemaid. Somebody by the name of Sarah. Someone who undoubtedly excels in various forms of torture."

Brock's voice held a note of censure. "You're lucky Miss Daniels took you in, Carstairs. She wasn't too pleased about it. Not with her group of unwed mothers in the house."

Moody's head jerked around, his eyes widening. "You mean . . ."

"She's got seven pregnant ladies living here, counting Mary, the girl I brought in yesterday. It seems this is a ranch for unwed mothers."

"Well, I'll be a son of a bitch. Is that how come you came to be here, bringing that young girl to the ranch?"

Brock briefly explained the situation between Mary Winslow and the good folks of Absolution.

Moody's face twisted in disgust. "That girl's but a child. Of course, having experienced the warmth of this town firsthand, I don't doubt for a minute that what you're telling me is the gospel truth." Nervously he plucked at the bedclothes with his fingers. "You fixin' to leave?"

Brock heaved a sigh. "Miss Daniels's foreman quit this morning. I foolishly said I'd help out until she could find a replacement."

Breathing deeply in relief, Moody smiled. There was safety in numbers. It was the first thing he'd learned upon entering the cavalry at the tender age of eighteen.

"Miss Daniels is a sight for these tired old eyes. I always did have a partiality toward redheads. They're high-spirited, like wild mustangs." Moody smiled wistfully.

Brock pushed himself to his feet. "High-spirited is an understatement. You obviously haven't been the recipient of Miss Daniels's wrath. She's as touchy as a teased snake. And as deadly, I warrant."

"Why you stayin', then?"

Brock's broad shoulders raised, then lowered. "That's the hell of it. I don't rightly know. Guess I'm just a sucker for lost causes."

"You'll be rewarded in your next life."

"If I live to survive this one," Brock mumbled, and headed for the door, ignoring Moody Carstairs's burst of laughter.

3

*Some folks are so soured on life
they can't get the acid
out of their systems.*

The layout of the ranch house was as unusual as the ranch itself, Brock noted as he followed Prudence from room to room.

The pine-paneled ranch office, located off the entry-way, was masculine and functional. A large oak desk filled the center of the room, with two comfortable-looking red-leather wing chairs positioned in front of it.

"I do most of the book work in here," Prudence explained, "as well as conduct most of the R and R's official business. This room is the lifeblood of this ranch." She smiled to herself, thinking of all the times she'd bounded in here with her sister, Clara, to pester her father while he worked. Those were good times, happy times, before . . . She swallowed the lump in her throat.

It was still difficult to think about Clara, although her sister had been dead nearly seven years. They'd been as close as any two sisters could be—two sides of the same coin, her father always joked.

Clara, two years older than Prudence, had been sister, mother, and best friend all rolled into one. And Prudence had been lonely without her, lonely enough to bring strangers into her home. And though the women had helped ease her loss, they could never take Clara's place, not completely. If only . . .

Brock noted the sadness on Prudence's face and knew she was thinking of someone she cared deeply about. There was a vulnerability about her at that moment that gave his heart a queer little lurch. He cleared his throat, needing to empty his mind of the woman whose problems he wanted no part of.

"The upkeep of this place must keep you pretty busy."

Prudence heaved a sigh, shutting the door, and her painful memories, behind her. "You don't know the half of it, Mr. Peters."

"Why don't you call me Brock, ma'am? Since we're going to be workin' together, I think it makes more sense."

She paused in the hallway and looked up at him. "I don't like familiarity, Mr. Peters. I find it's best to keep a business relationship formal." Familiarity led to intimacy, intimacy to ruination. And she had no intention of letting either into her life.

She continued down the long dark hall, and Brock could only stare at her retreating back and wonder what had made this woman so distrustful of everyone she came in contact with.

When they reached the door at the end of the hallway, Prudence stopped before it. "These are the women's quarters, Mr. Peters. You will find most of the women friendly, but there are a few who have no use for men. Please don't be offended if you are not greeted with open arms."

His eyebrow arched. After the welcome she'd given him he'd expected nothing less, but he refrained from saying so as he followed her into the large rectangular room.

It was an attractive room, but far more functional than the front parlor. A massive stone fireplace graced the far wall, and four mullioned windows, two on each wall, allowed plenty of light to enter. The room had obviously been added on to the original structure, Brock decided, noting the set of stairs nestled in the rear corner, which led to a second floor where the sleeping quarters were located.

Before the fireplace, seated at a long scarred maple worktable, were several of the ladies. They were of various ages and descriptions but possessed one common denominator: they were all pregnant.

"Ladies, I would like to introduce you to the new foreman of the R and R," Prudence said. "This is Mr. Peters. If you would stand when I introduce you, then perhaps Mr. Peters will be able to familiarize himself with your names and faces."

An attractive young woman with long flaxen hair stood first. There was nothing shy and retiring about her, and when she smiled there was a definite invitation on her lips. "I'm Louann," she said, appraising him with frank admiration. And then he knew that this was the same Louann who had gotten Dave Stewart in trouble.

Louann pointed to the frail-looking woman seated on her right. "And this little mouse who doesn't say a word is Laurel."

Prudence leaned over and whispered to Brock, "Laurel was raped by outlaws. The stagecoach she and her husband were on was robbed a few miles outside of town, and he was killed." Her voice caught momentarily. "They were newlyweds coming to Absolution to open a mercantile. Papers found in her reticule indicated as much. She hasn't spoken a word since she discovered herself with child. I took her in about two weeks ago. Her baby's due in the spring."

Brock, too choked up to speak as he stared at the dark-haired girl with the haunted eyes, merely nodded. He was relieved when the next woman, who introduced herself as Sarah Davenport, rose to her feet.

She was a handsome woman, a refined woman, as evidenced by her cultured speech and demure manner of dress. Her thick chestnut hair had been pulled back severely into a bun at the nape of her neck, and all Brock could think of was that Moody was going to be in for a big surprise when his new nursemaid showed up to take care of him.

"The others, Christey, Eliza, and Polly, are upstairs resting, along with Mary." Prudence's voice filled with condemnation again. "The women's sleeping quarters are off limits to all men on this ranch. No exceptions." She glared at him accusingly.

That pronouncement produced a rather loud giggle from Louann, who was never at a loss for words. "Miss Pru's protecting our chastity, Mr. Peters." She patted her swollen stomach. "And me six months gone. Ain't that a hoot?"

Prudence's frown was enough to make the young girl stare into her lap and Brock to swallow his smile.

"Get back to work, Louann. You've still not met your quota for the day."

It was then Brock noticed the piles of tanned leather on the table. Laurel's nimble fingers were weaving the thin rawhide strips into braids.

"We produce leather goods, Mr. Peters, to supplement our income. At the moment, the girls are weaving lariats to sell through the saddlery in town. We also produce fancy tooled boots, saddles, gloves, chaps, and a host of other items."

There was a wealth of pride in her voice, and Brock couldn't help but be impressed. "Very industrious."

"We're practical, Mr. Peters. The face of poverty is not a handsome one. It tends to make one practical. The R and R does not run enough cows to make cattle production profitable, so we fashion leather goods.

"The profits we make are divided amongst the women. A quarter of the money earned is used to defer operating expenses at the ranch, another quarter is for each individual woman to keep, and the remaining fifty percent is put into a fund for the women to use upon leaving the ranch. They're allowed to remain up to one year after the birth of their child, so the money serves as a stake to see them through rough times until they can find suitable employment."

She pulled the door shut, continuing to talk as she walked back down the hall toward the front parlor, and Brock found his admiration for this woman and her business acumen growing.

"Joe Two Toes does the tanning of the hides. He and Hannah taught me everything they knew about leather goods. The rest I learned from books, and from the various cowboys who worked at the R and R over the years. I, in turn, taught the other women."

"I'm impressed with your resourcefulness, Miss Daniels," Brock admitted upon entering the parlor. He took a seat next to her on the sofa. "Not many women would have been able to take so much responsibility upon their shoulders. And yours are not all that big."

A rush of color filled Prudence's cheeks, in stark

contrast with the white of the crisply starched cotton blouse she wore. "One does what one must to survive, Mr. Peters. Men are forever underestimating the abilities of women. Women are capable of surviving quite nicely without men."

She was a perfect example of that fact, having run the R and R's various enterprises for the past eight years by herself. And it was herself she counted on, depended upon, not some footloose cowboy who was apt to run off at the first sign of trouble.

For some reason he didn't quite understand, Prudence's independent streak annoyed Brock, as did her self-assured, detached manner. She was hard on a man's ego. And he wondered what it would take to ruffle this pretty bird's plumage.

"Surviving is merely existing, Miss Daniels. 'Man's love is of man's life a thing apart, 'tis woman's whole existence.'"

She recognized the quote from Byron and was momentarily taken aback by the fact that it came to his lips as easily as his cowboy vernacular; but she chose to ignore it.

"As I previously told you, there are rules which must be observed. Everyone who works at this ranch, save for Joe and Hannah, who worship their own deity, must attend church service on Sunday."

Great! Just great! He would get to rub shoulders with the God-fearing hypocrites of this town who called themselves Christians. "I was under the impression from what Mary said that you and yours aren't all that welcome in town."

Her chin came up and there was a spark of defiance in her eyes. "Nevertheless, we all attend church. It is our God-given right to do so. And though I am quite aware of what the citizens of Absolution think of me, I don't let it prevent me from going to town or to church."

He didn't doubt that for a moment, having observed a stubborn streak in her any mule would be proud to possess. "What else?"

"I don't abide liquor, except for medicinal purposes. Spirits erode a man's and woman's sensibilities until they are left dull and fatuous. Colonel Carstairs is a perfect example. He smelled of whiskey when you brought him here, and I don't doubt that it was his predilection for alcohol that brought him to this end."

"I hesitate to bring this up, Miss Daniels, but most men aren't of such high moral fiber as you. Am I to keep the men from going into town to take their ease?"

Her cheeks grew pink again, but her direct look didn't waver. "I'm quite aware of men's needs, Mr. Peters. I have seven women to attest to them. Obviously, what the men do on their day off, or on an evening, is of no concern to me. I take it you are inquiring for yourself as well?"

Why was it that Prudence Daniels made him feel like an errant schoolboy who'd just been taken to task for sticking some girl's braid in the inkwell? He was a grown man, for God's sake. A man who had needs, and she might as well be apprised of that fact now.

He leaned forward until they were practically nose to nose. "I've got needs same as any other man, Miss Daniels. And unless you're offering to satisfy those needs here at the R and R, then I'll damn well be taking them to town."

She gasped and jumped to her feet, clenching her fists. "How dare you!"

"Me?" He stood, shaking his head in disbelief. "You're the one who makes so many goddamn rules a man can't breathe or take a piss, if he's a mind to."

Another gasp, much louder this time.

"Men are men, Miss Daniels. I don't profess to be so

righteous or upstanding that the smell of lilac in a woman's hair doesn't turn my insides to butter. Or when I see the curve of a plump breast against a cotton blouse, I don't want to run my hand over it to see if it's really as soft as it looks." His gaze dropped to her bosom, then back up to see the look of mortification on her face.

"I'm a God-fearing man. And I guess I've got just about as many morals as the next person. But I'm flesh and blood, Miss Daniels. And I'm not likely to apologize for that." He strode toward the door and paused when he reached it, looking back.

"The name's Brock, Miss Daniels. I've got a few rules of my own, and that's one of them. Be sure you remember it."

Watching him slam out the door, Prudence felt her cheeks ignite into flame once again; she placed her hand over her heart to still its erratic beating.

Never in her whole life had she been spoken to in such a rude, familiar manner! Taking several deep breaths to calm herself, she was immediately assaulted by the scent of lilac water.

Lilac! Her hands went to her cheeks and she plopped down on the sofa, the *whoosh*ing sound of the cushion mimicking her own deflated composure.

He'd been talking about her. Great merciful heavens! Brock Peters had been talking about her.

Sarah Davenport eased open the door to Moody Carstairs's room and stepped inside silently. Only a request from Prudence could have made her swallow her misgivings about entering the room of a complete stranger—a man, no less.

The man in question appeared to be sleeping, and she

was greatly tempted just to tiptoe out and close the door behind her.

But she couldn't. Prudence had asked her to care for this man, to help nurse him back to health. And it was the least she could do, considering all that Pru Daniels had done for her.

Gathering a washcloth and basin from the marble-topped washstand, she took a seat on the chair next to the bed and waited for the man to awaken so she could perform his morning ablutions. He needed a shave, she thought, observing the gray stubble on his cheeks and chin, but she hadn't thought to bring a straight razor with her.

The injured man was sleeping fitfully. His skin appeared flushed, and she wondered if he was feverish. She placed gentle fingers on his forehead; he was hot.

"Martha, is that you? Martha?" His hand came up to grasp hers, and he held it to his cheek. "I'm sorry, Martha. I should never have brought you to this godforsaken place. Can you ever forgive me?"

Whoever this Martha was held a powerful grip on his memory. Sarah knew what it felt like to be haunted by dreams of those you loved.

"Of course I forgive you," she heard herself reply.

That seemed to quiet him for the moment, and he relaxed his grip on her hand. She dipped the cloth into the cooling water and sponged his face and forehead with it; for several minutes she bathed him, wiping his arms, his chest, grateful that he was unconscious and couldn't watch her perform such an intimate task.

When she was finished, she stood and crossed to the window, opening it a crack to let out the noxious odors of the sickroom.

Slowly Moody opened his eyes to find an angel bathed in the golden glow of the morning sun. Was he dead? he wondered. Surely no mortal woman could be so lovely as the one standing near the window. The sunlight streaming in illuminated her flawless complexion and slightly upturned nose.

"Mornin'," he managed, but it sounded more like a croak than a salutation.

Sarah turned toward the bed to find her patient wide awake and smiling. He was quite pleasing to look at, she decided, and not nearly as old as she thought, despite the gray sprinkled generously throughout his brown hair.

Suddenly flustered by her wayward observations, she cleared her throat. "Good morning, I'm Sarah Davenport. Miss Daniels has asked me to take over your nursing duties."

"I thought you were an angel come to take me to the Great Beyond."

Sarah's cheeks flushed, but she smiled nonetheless. "I'm hardly an angel, Colonel Carstairs, as evidenced by this growing mound beneath my skirts." Teaching had made her practical, if not painfully honest. Too honest sometimes, she thought as she gauged his surprised expression.

He attempted to push himself to a sitting position, and she moved forward to help him adjust his pillows.

"Well, now, there's nothing lovelier than a woman who's carrying a child. There's a special glow she gets in her cheeks that's sweet as clover honey and as bright as a sun-dappled stream." He'd always regretted that he and Martha'd never had any children.

"You are quite the poet, Colonel," Sarah said, shaking her head at his outrageous comment. "One doesn't usually find such a poetic heart in the guise of a cavalry officer."

"Please sit," Moody urged, pointing to the chair beside the bed. Noting her hesitation, he added, "I'm hardly in a position to do you harm, Miss Sarah, and it's been horribly lonely in this little room." Though solitude had been preferable to the company of the Ute housekeeper and her nasty disposition.

"Very well, but only for a moment. I have other duties to perform. We all pitch in with the chores here at the ranch. And it's my turn to gather the eggs."

"Miss Daniels seems to run a tight post," Moody commented, remembering Brock's angry recitation of the spinster's set of rules.

"Prudence has a lot of responsibility for one so young," Sarah offered by way of explanation. In the six weeks she'd been at the ranch, Sarah found that people tended to judge the young proprietress rather unfairly. Sarah had detected a loneliness, a quiet despair, in Prudence that neither she nor any of the other women had been able to salve with friendship or advice.

"You're hardly much older, Miss Sarah," Moody pointed out.

"I'm past my prime, Colonel, and a good deal older than Prudence." Vanity kept her from admitting that she'd be thirty-six years of age in a few months.

"Age is merely a matter of the mind, my dear Miss Sarah. I'm fifty, but I hardly think I'm past my prime, though the United States Cavalry didn't agree with me. They've pensioned me off, like some old, useless army mule."

She heard the hurt in his voice and was saddened by it. The colonel was still a vital man, despite his years. His flesh was firm, or firmer, than that of many men years younger, and she'd felt the muscles of his chest and arms when she'd sponged him off.

That memory brought a rush of color to her cheeks, and she covered her embarrassment by saying, "The army was obviously in error, Colonel. Except for your present infirmity, you appear to be quite fit."

Moody smiled, and there was a twinkle in his eye that hadn't been there for quite some time. "I think we're going to get along just splendidly, Miss Sarah. Are you going to finish my bath now? I was quite enjoying your tender touch a while ago."

Sarah Davenport's cheeks turned various shades of crimson before she jumped to her feet. "I . . . I really must be going, Colonel Carstairs." She moved toward the door, unwilling to look at him. "I shall return later to bring you your dinner." With that she scurried out of the room, shutting the door firmly behind her.

Yep, Moody thought, smiling happily to himself. He was still in his prime. He might be gettin' long in years, but his horns hadn't been sawed off yet.

Later that same evening, the women of the R and R huddled about the massive stone fireplace of the great room and listened while Prudence performed her evening ritual of reading aloud from the Bible.

"'Thou shalt love the Lord thy God with all thy heart, and with all thy soul, and with all thy might.'"

"Do you think God still loves us, even though we sinned, Miss Pru?" Polly interrupted, taking another bite of her second slice of Hannah's apple-walnut pie.

Removing her spectacles, which she used only for reading, Prudence smiled patiently at the girl sitting at her feet. Polly was stuffing her face as if there were no tomorrow, though Prudence had warned her she would make her delivery more difficult by gaining too much weight.

"God loves even sinners, Polly. But He has a difficult time with those of us who practice gluttony." She leveled an accusing look at Polly, who was just about to take another bite of pie. Embarrassed, the young girl set down her fork.

"I'm sorry, Miss Pru. I know you said I needed to watch my weight, but I'm just so ravenously hungry all the time."

"Madam Eva, who ran the brothel where I used to work, was like that," Louann counseled, toying with the ribbons of her red satin wrapper. "Eva claimed she had to eat 'cause she wasn't satisfying herself in a sexual way anymore."

"Really, Louann!" Sarah chastised, noting the tears that sprang quickly to Polly's eyes. "Sometimes you say the most thoughtless things."

"I didn't say it," Louann protested in wide-eyed innocence. "It was Madam Eva, I tell you."

"Shall we continue, ladies?" Prudence suggested, observing the raven-haired woman standing alone by the window. She frowned—not at the bantering that continued among the women; she was used to that—but because Christey Baker's morose behavior worried her.

Christey's husband had dropped her off on his way to Nebraska to stake his claim on a farm, vowing to return in a month's time. But it had been three, and Samuel Baker had still not come to collect his pregnant wife.

"Would you like to read the next verse, Christey? I don't think Samuel will be arriving this late of an evening."

The sullen woman shook her head, her hand going absently to her slightly protruding stomach. "No, ma'am. I'd just prefer to stare out the window, if you don't mind." There was such sadness, such utter despair, in the young woman's voice that Prudence thought it best to let the matter drop.

"Well, I can think of better things to do than read

Bible verses," Louann insisted. "Why don't we talk about that new foreman of Miss Pru's? He sure is a looker."

"Leave it to you, Louann, to always talk about men," Polly remarked, making a face at her.

Across the room, Eliza Dobbyns caught the mortified look on Prudence's face and smiled knowingly. Obviously the new foreman must be quite handsome to bring such a flush to Prudence's cheeks. She was not usually affected by such things.

Oh, to be young again, Eliza thought, a wistful smile lifting the corners of her mouth as she stared down at the knitting in her lap. She'd once been the belle of Caroline County in her home state of Virginia. Until that bastard husband of hers, Simon Dobbyns, had dragged her west in search of gold.

Simon hadn't found the gold he'd searched for, but he had found a way to make himself rich by selling overpriced supplies to the miners. And he'd also found himself a young mistress. Eliza had found them in bed together on the very day she'd returned home from the doctor with the exciting news that she was pregnant with their first child. That had been three months ago.

"Eliza, are you feeling all right?" Sarah pressed, alarmed by the sudden pallor on the older woman's face. Pregnancy at any age was difficult enough, but to a woman well past forty, it was nothing short of brutal.

"I'm fine." Eliza smiled reassuringly. "And I'd love to hear more about this mysterious foreman we've hired on."

Prudence Daniels's face was beginning to match her hair. "Mr. Peters is only here temporarily." And a more infuriating man she had yet to meet. "Unlike Louann, I hadn't noticed Mr. Peters's physical attributes," she lied, hoping her blush would be attributed to the heat of the fire. "But I do know that beauty is only skin deep and folks should judge a body on what's inside, not what's out."

"I don't doubt Mr. Peters has some pretty interesting stuff inside those britches he wears." Louann's quip brought a chorus of ribald laughter to the room; even Christey smiled at the remark, though her cheeks were burning.

Prudence was grateful that Mary was still confined to her bed. She didn't think the young girl would appreciate her lover being discussed in such an offhand manner.

Before Prudence could chastise Louann for her comment, a knock sounded at the front door. Knowing that Hannah had retired for the evening, Prudence pushed herself to her feet.

"If that's Mr. Peters," Louann teased, "don't forget to check on what he's got on the inside."

Slamming the door behind her before Louann could make another outrageous comment, Prudence stifled her annoyance and went to answer the summons.

It was with no small amount of consternation that Prudence opened the door to find Brock on the other side, bringing each and every one of Louann's lewd comments to mind as she stared at the handsome cowboy. And for the life of her, she couldn't keep her eyes from drifting to the area below his belt. Fortunately his sheepskin jacket prevented her from satisfying her curiosity.

"Sorry to bother you, Miss Prudence, but I was wondering if you might have a spare blanket I could use. The bunkhouse ain't exactly snug, and I'm freezing my. . . ."

The thought was left unsaid, but Prudence's eyes drifted down again and a strange thundering began in her chest. "Of . . . of course, Mr. Pet—" At the warning look he flashed her, she amended, "Brock," though it galled her to do so. "Come in. I'll just be a moment. I have to run upstairs to fetch it."

The sight of Prudence's derriere as it swung provocatively up the stairs was too interesting for Brock to let go of, and he found himself trailing after her, like a horse being led on a lead rope.

He stood in the doorway of her bedroom to find her bent over a blanket chest made of rich red mahogany. "That's a mighty fine"—his gaze shifted from her rear to the chest— "piece . . . of furniture."

Prudence reared up so quickly, she banged her head against the lid of the chest. "Stuff and thunderation!" She rubbed the top of her head, rising to her feet. "What are you doing up here, Mr. Peters? I thought I left instructions for you to remain downstairs." Men were not allowed upstairs. She'd made that rule perfectly clear already. Why, she had never once, in her entire life, had a man present in her bedroom, save for her father. And that didn't count.

Brock's gaze slid briefly to the big brass bed with the fluffy blue quilted counterpane, to the white batiste nightgown that hung casually over the bedpost. "That's an awfully big bed for a little girl like you." He grinned at her embarrassment.

Prudence flung the woolen blanket at him, feeling the heat of her anger creeping up her neck. "Here is your blanket. Now I'd suggest you get back out to the bunkhouse where you belong."

"Your cheeks are almost the same color as your hair. Did you know that . . . Red?" The nickname came easily to his lips. Red. It fit much more appropriately than Prudence.

A thousand vile epithets suddenly formulated in Prudence's mind, but she took a deep breath and abstained from uttering any of them.

"Please refrain from calling me that awful nickname.

You may call me Miss Daniels, or Prudence, if you like. But nothing else."

Red indeed!

Lifting the blanket to his nose, Brock inhaled deeply. Instead of the mothball scent he was expecting, he detected another. "Lilac," he murmured, his gaze raking over her suggestively, bringing another scarlet stain to the spinster's cheeks. "I guess I'll have sweet dreams tonight." He winked, delighting in how easy it was to tease her. "Good night, Red. See you in the morning."

Prudence, too flustered to form an adequate retort, stared openmouthed at the now empty doorway, unable to believe the audacity of the man she had hired as her foreman.

Well, tomorrow she would just put Brock Peters in his place and fire him, she decided, folding her arms firmly over her chest.

But she knew that she wouldn't.

She couldn't.

She needed the audacious cowboy.

And that thought infuriated her even more.

4

*Jus' cause a man ain't yet had a chance to steal
don't mean he's honest.*

The screen door banged loudly and Prudence
jumped, spilling the hot milk she poured from the old
enamel pot into her mug.

"Stuff and thunderation!" She cursed herself for her
clumsiness, mindful of the fact that she was still tired
from a fitful night's sleep. Turning to stare at the door
she saw the reason for her sleeplessness amble into the
kitchen, and her eyes narrowed.

"Mornin', ma'am," Brock said cheerfully. "You're up
early."

Prudence didn't need to be reminded of the obvious.
It was as inky dark outside as the bottom of a well. The
cowboy's infuriating grin as he handed her the bor-
rowed blanket made the hackles rise on the nape of her
neck.

"Thanks for the loan. I slept snug as a woolly worm."

He removed his jacket and hat, hanging them on the hook by the door. His hair curled damply about the nape of his neck, glistening like obsidian in the glow of the kerosene lamp. The clean, fresh smell of his shaving soap made her achingly aware of his masculinity, and her throat suddenly went dry, making it difficult to speak.

"You're . . . you're quite welcome, Mr. . . ." She stopped in midsentence, tossing the woolen throw onto the chair, annoyed that she'd been aware of him as a man. He was an employee, she told herself. Nothing more.

At Brock's lingering gaze, Prudence suddenly grew aware of her improper attire and clutched the edges of her flannel robe together. She looked a fright! Her hair always curled up tighter than a buckboard spring during the night, and she hadn't taken the time to brush it out this morning.

She looked damned appealing, Brock thought, with her hair springing every which way and that soft flannel robe revealing far more than it concealed, especially to a man with his vivid imagination. She hadn't taken the time to put on her slippers, and her small pink toes peeked out from beneath the hem of her robe.

"Was there something you needed?" Prudence asked, eager to escape Brock's presence. They were very much alone in the early morning silence. The girls still slept soundly in their wing of the house. Colonel Carstairs, though nearby, was hardly in any condition to render assistance. Hannah wouldn't arrive for half an hour yet. She backed away from the admiration she saw reflected in his gaze, stubbing her toe on the kitchen table.

"Stuff and thunderation!" she cursed again, sitting herself down at the table and grabbing her throbbing toe, blinking back tears that sprang to her eyes.

"Here, let me look at it," Brock offered, kneeling down to grab hold of her foot, which was as small and dainty as the rest of her.

She gasped as the feel of his hands on her bare flesh sent tingles of awareness shooting up her legs, and she tried to pull free. "Mr. Peters, unhand me!" she demanded, feeling her face flame. He ignored her request, continuing to massage her toe with a thoroughness she found infuriating . . . and exciting.

"It's no more than I'd do for an injured horse, ma'am," he said, finally releasing her. "There's no need to thank me." With an irksome grin, he turned toward the stove to put on a pot of coffee.

As soon as his back was turned, Prudence leapt off the chair, unmindful of the toe that still throbbed, and hopped her way out of the kitchen and upstairs to dress. There was no way she was going to give Brock Peters the opportunity to molest her further.

Seating himself at the table, Brock stared at the empty chair and smiled thoughtfully to himself. Prudence Daniels was quite an enigma. She might be tough as old shoe leather on the outside, but she was damned soft and vulnerable on the inside.

Hobbling into her room, Prudence headed straight for the nightstand, filling the porcelain basin with cold water. She splashed water over her burning face, trying to cool the effect Brock's touch had on her body.

He was certainly no gentleman! she thought, touching her foot with such familiarity. She sat on the chair near the fire, grasping her foot, remembering . . . and her heart began throbbing as wildly as her toe.

She was certainly no lady! For no lady would be experiencing these strange sensations that were coursing through her body.

What on earth had come over her?

Brock Peters, that's what.

Silently she cursed him and herself, hating the way he'd made her feel—alive, womanly.

No good could come of feelings like that. Clara had confided how breathless and giddy Billy Preston had made her feel. She'd let down her guard, given in to all those delicious, heady sensations. And where had it gotten her? Pregnant, that's where.

No man, no matter how handsome, no matter how charming, would get to her like that, Prudence vowed. Her guard was up, and up it was going to stay.

By the time Prudence reentered the kitchen, the rest of the men had joined Brock, and Hannah was bent over the cast-iron cookstove, fixing flapjacks. The smell of frying bacon lingered in the air, as did the aroma of freshly brewed coffee, teasing Prudence's stomach into restlessness.

"Mornin', Miss Pru," the men said in unison—all but Brock, who grinned, saying, "Mornin', Red. How's the toe?"

Turning as florid as the gingham tablecloth, Prudence attempted to ignore Will's and Slim's questioning glances and the definite amusement on Shorty's and Burt's faces. "Good morning, gentlemen," she replied, purposely ignoring the chair that Brock held out for her and taking a seat next to Will instead. Her action produced more whispers and snide looks from the men.

Pretending not to notice the slight, Brock slid in next to Shorty. "Do we need to wait for the other ladies?"

"Naw," Slim Robbins replied, "they'll eat later, after we clear out. Ain't that right, Miss Pru?"

Slim's speech was slow, like his mind, but Prudence found him harmless and his honesty refreshing. He had a child's way about him that was open and forthright, and she guessed he didn't know enough to be devious or cruel.

She smiled at the tall, lanky cowboy. "Quite right, Mr. Robbins. The ladies will eat after you have begun your work for the day." Turning to Brock, she explained, "We only eat Sunday dinner together, Mr. Peters. The ladies seem to prefer it that way."

Brock doubted that very much. From what he had observed, the women were eager for a little male company. It was most likely another of the spinster's irksome rules.

"We're fixin' to string fence along the south pasture today, Miss Pru," Shorty explained, pausing to take a sip of his coffee. "Once we get the rest of the barbed wire in place, that should cut down on the number of head we're losin'."

Prudence listened to Shorty's explanation, nodding absently. She hoped she was doing the right thing by stringing barbed-wire fencing. The R and R had had open range for as long as she could remember, but the increasing number of cattle that had disappeared had forced the necessity of trying out Mr. Glidden's newly patented invention.

"Mr. Morgan wasn't too pleased when he heard about our decision to fence, Mr. Jenkins."

Brock's ears perked up at the mention of Jacob Morgan, and he didn't miss the animosity coloring Shorty's words when he mentioned the Bar J's owner.

"I don't doubt it, ma'am. Jacob Morgan's had access to our land for a good while now. You know your pa never allowed Morgan's cattle to cross over into our pas-

ture. In drought years there's hardly enough grass for
our own herd."

"I'm certain Jacob . . . I mean, Mr. Morgan"—she
blushed at Brock's raised brow—"had a perfectly good
reason to trespass on R and R range, Mr. Jenkins."

Shorty stood, pushing back his chair. "I'm sure he
did, ma'am. A very good reason."

Brock and the rest of the men soon departed, leaving
Prudence to wonder what Shorty had meant by his
remarks. She was further confused when Hannah,
who'd been silent as a shadow up till now, paused in
clearing the table to point her finger at Prudence's
chest.

"For wise woman, you don't have such good eye-
sight. We must open eyes to see what is before us."

"What is that supposed to mean?"

But Hannah only shrugged and turned her back on
Prudence, preparing another bowl of batter for the next
round of diners, leaving Prudence more confused than
ever.

"This section of fence has been cut, Mr. Peters,"
young Will announced, his face reddening as he
addressed the new foreman.

Swinging down off his horse, Brock frowned over the
top of Will's head at the sight of the cut barbed wire.
"Great! Just great!" What the hell had he gotten himself
into, a goddamn range war?

The boy looked up from his position on the ground
where his horse had unseated him. "I'm sure I'll do
better next time, Mr. Peters," he said, mistaking the
direction of Brock's anger. "I haven't had much practice
riding."

Brock heaved a sigh and turned his attention back to

the tenderfoot. "Get up, Will, and go fetch Shorty. Tell him that we need to restring this section of fence."

He watched the boy approach the sorrel mare warily and shook his head. "If that horse thinks you're scared, boy, she's going to toss you on your rump every time you get on her back. You've got to show her who's boss.

"Don't grab the pommel like that. That's the way girls ride. That's better," he said when Will let go to hold on to the reins. "Now don't pull back on the reins so tight. This horse only needs a gentle tug to let her know which way you want her to go." Brock demonstrated, laying the reins gently against the horse's neck.

The blond boy smiled gratefully, and Brock was reminded, just for a second, of another boy who used to smile at him like that.

Is this the way, Pa? Josh's voice surrounded him, as did the image of his small trusting face and bright blue eyes, so like his mother's.

Shaking off the memory, Brock said, "Go on, now, and do what I told you. And keep your butt in that saddle."

He watched the lad ride off, and a great wave of sadness washed over him. "Josh," he whispered.

"Company's comin', Prudence," Eliza announced, gazing out the parlor window to see a spanking new buggy coming up the road. "Looks like Mr. Morgan has come to pay a call." She couldn't keep the aversion out of her voice, but if Prudence noticed, she made no mention of it.

At the window, Prudence followed Eliza's gaze and groaned in dismay. "Good heavens!" She smoothed down the skirt of her soiled gown. "I'm quite a mess. I wasn't expecting company."

"You look just fine, dear. I'm sure Mr. Morgan won't even notice that spot of lemon oil on your apron."

Prudence ripped off the offending garment and handed it to Eliza. "Does my hair look like a tornado's passed through it?"

"That man's far too old for you, dear. Jacob Morgan is fifty if he's a day. I don't know why you get yourself in such a dither when he comes to call."

"I am not in a dither. Jacob and I are just friends. You know perfectly well that folks around here are not exactly cordial to me. Jacob is the exception. He's been as good a friend as I could ever hope to have." And if she were honest with herself, she'd admit that she found his attentions flattering.

"Hmph! Well, he's too much like my Simon for me to consider him anything but an opportunist. I'll be in the great room if you need me. I promised Mary I'd teach her how to knit."

Mention of Mary, who was up and about and feeling much better, brought to mind the very odd fact that the young woman had not once asked for Brock. Prudence found it extremely curious, considering the couple's present circumstances and the fact that Mary was about to have his baby.

At the sound of the door knocker thoughts of Mary flew out the window. Prudence hurried to answer it.

"Why, Jacob Morgan, what a nice surprise," she said, staring at the tall, robust man before her. He was a striking individual in his black broadcloth suit and string tie. He fairly filled the door frame with his imposing size. He had a ready, friendly smile to greet her.

"Afternoon, Prudence. You're looking quite lovely today." His gaze roamed over her appreciatively, bringing a soft blush to her cheeks.

She shook her head, ushering him inside. "I look just

awful and you know it, Jacob. I was polishing furniture when I saw you drive up. I probably smell like lemon oil."

He sniffed the air in an exaggerated manner. "You smell like lilac. And that's a fact," he said in his usual authoritative way. He took a seat on the sofa, while Prudence opted for the rocker.

"May I offer you some refreshment? Hannah has just baked a batch of oatmeal cookies."

"Thank you, but no, honey." He patted his paunch. "I'm afraid I've indulged a bit too much these past months as it is."

Prudence gritted her teeth at the endearment. It sounded like some lurid tag on a saloon girl, and she hated it. She had a perfectly good name. Why on earth didn't anyone choose to use it?

Red. Brock's nickname surfaced, and she felt her cheeks flush. Quickly she turned her attention back to Jacob's conversation.

"I suspect I've gained a few pounds."

Now that he mentioned it, she did notice the increased girth around his middle. And there also seemed to be a few more gray hairs to mingle in with the black ones. Even his mustache, which was spiked with silver, showed signs of aging.

"Was there something you wanted to discuss with me, Jacob? You don't usually pay a social call in the middle of the week."

"It's about Dave Stewart. I was quite surprised when he told me you two had a falling-out." His voice filled with concern. "This place is too much for a little gal like you to run alone. Why don't you give up this foolishness about running a home for unwed mothers?" He leaned forward, reaching for her hand. "I've told you before, Prudence honey, I'd like nothing better than to make you my wife."

Noting the sincerity in his hazel eyes, and unwilling to hurt his feelings, Prudence rose to her feet, eager to put a halt to this topic of conversation. They'd had this same discussion many times over the years. And although she was flattered by his proposal—the only one she was likely to receive—she couldn't accept it for a multitude of reasons: she valued her independence; she loved her ranch and her pregnant ladies; and she didn't love Jacob Morgan.

"Your offer touches me deeply, Jacob. But I'm not ready to make a commitment. I have a responsibility to the women in my charge."

"Prudence honey," he said, stepping up behind her to place his hands gently upon her shoulders, turning her toward him, "I only want what's best for you. Your father was my friend. Cody would have expected me to look out for his little girl."

"I—"

"I hope I'm not interrupting."

The door slammed shut. Prudence turned to find Brock walking into the room, and the expression on his face was anything but cordial as he glared at the Bar J's owner. Guiltily she pulled out of Jacob's embrace.

"Brock!" she said breathlessly, quickly recovering her aplomb. "Please come in and meet our neighbor, Jacob Morgan." Looking at Jacob, she explained, "Brock is my new foreman."

There was a moment's hesitation before Jacob held out his hand in greeting, but Brock didn't miss it or the slight thinning of the man's lips as Prudence made the introductions.

"Mr. Morgan," Brock said with a nod of his head. "Sorry to interrupt. I'll come back when it's more convenient."

"No need, Peters. I was just leaving. Prudence and I are finished with our discussion . . . for the time being."

He bent over to graze her cheek with a kiss, and Brock found his hands balling into fists.

After Morgan had taken his leave, Brock leveled his gaze on Prudence's flushed face. Whether it was flushed with guilt or adoration, he couldn't tell, which irritated him even more. "Sorry to have interrupted you and your *friend.*" He made the word sound every bit as insulting as she had that first day when she'd inferred a relationship between him and Mary. The shoe was on the other foot now; let's see how well it fit.

It was pinching. Her furious expression told him that much.

"Mr. Morgan and I are old friends," she explained, hoping to wipe the sneer off his face.

Removing his hat, he brushed impatient fingers through his hair. "Well, your friend has been grazing his cattle on your pasture. We found fifteen head on R and R property, as well as a section of cut fence. Do you think your *friend* had anything to do with that?"

"Don't be ridiculous. Jacob Morgan owns one of the largest cattle ranches in Colorado. Why on earth would he want to graze on Rough and Ready range? That doesn't make a lick of sense."

"There's a lot that doesn't make sense when it comes to the doin's of cattle barons, if that's what Morgan fancies himself to be. The land they own is never enough. They want more and more. They want it all."

She looked at him as if he were quite insane. "That's preposterous! Jacob was a good friend of my father's. He's the only one in these parts who has been kind enough to help me."

"Like providing you with Dave Stewart for a foreman?"

"I admit Mr. Stewart wouldn't have been my first

choice. But after Buck was killed, he stayed on to help. Jacob arranged everything."

"How neighborly of him."

She missed the sarcasm and nodded in agreement. "Yes, it was. Jacob would never do anything to hurt me. He's"—she blushed a deep crimson—"he's asked me to marry him."

Disgusted with the pleasure he thought he saw on her face, Brock plopped his hat back on his head and spun on his heel. "Well, isn't that just great."

Stepping outside onto the porch, Brock sucked in a deep breath of crisp autumn air to tamp down his temper. *Damn, foolish woman!* he thought disgustedly, knocking the flat of his hand against the porch post. Though he wasn't sure whom he was more mad at: Prudence or himself. He had no right to feel protective toward her, to care if she wasted her time on a bastard like Morgan. But he did. And that was the hell of it.

"Mr. Peters."

He looked over his shoulder to find Mary perched on the edge of the rocker. She looked rested and not altogether unhappy. And she had on a different dress from the one he'd brought her in.

"Hello, Mary," Brock said, smiling as he tipped his hat to her. "How are you feeling? Better, I hope."

"Much. Thanks to you and Miss Daniels. She's an angel of mercy."

Brock held his tongue at the comparison, but the word *devil* was perched precariously on the edge of it.

"She gave me this dress," Mary went on, quite unaware of Brock's resentment, smoothing down the folds of the pink wool gown that had been altered to accommodate her increased girth. "It's the nicest one I've ever owned."

"Miss Daniels is a very . . . generous person," he conceded. She was certainly generous with her narrow-minded opinions and her long list of rules.

"I was happy to hear that you'll be stayin' on for a spell, Mr. Peters. This is a real nice place to put down roots, don't you think?"

"I'm only staying temporarily, Mary, until Miss Daniels can find another foreman. Then I'll be moving on."

Disappointment flared in her bright blue eyes. "Oh, I'm sorry to hear that."

"You mustn't fret. You'll make friends soon enough."

Her face brightened. "I already have. Eliza's teachin' me how to knit so's I can make something purty for the baby. And Louann's been giving me all kinds of tips on how to handle a man."

I just bet! Brock thought, swallowing his smile.

"I know she's a whore, but she's still nice to me, even if she makes her livin' on her back. Leastways, that's what Polly says."

Brock turned at the choking sound to find red-faced Will Fletcher standing right behind him.

"You're lying! My sister would never say such a crude thing. She's a *lady*," Will accused, staring daggers at the woman on the porch. The way he said the word implied Mary was not, bringing tears to the young girl's eyes.

"Here, now!" Brock said, noting the distressed look on Mary's face. He grabbed Will by the scruff of his shirt. "They'll be no talk like that, boy. You'd best apologize to this young woman. It's never proper to call a lady a liar."

"But she said stuff about my sister. That's not proper, either, is it, Mr. Peters?"

"Mary only repeated something your sister said. We call that hearsay in a court of law, but here we call it gossip." His point was well taken, bringing a bright blush to Mary's cheeks.

"I didn't mean to carry tales, Mr. Peters." She looked up at Will. "I'm sorry for what I said."

Will shrugged, staring down at the dusty toes of his boots. "That's all right. No harm done. Would you like to come out to the barn to see the new litter of kittens?" he offered as an olive branch.

A look of excitement crossed Mary's face, and she made to rise, then sank back down and wagged her head, her voice filled with disappointment. "I can't. I promised Miss Daniels I wouldn't venture farther than this porch. I'm going to have a baby, you see."

Will's cheeks crimsoned, his eyes widening as his gaze traveled to the large swell of Mary's belly.

"Why don't you fetch one or two of the kittens and bring them back here, Will?" Brock suggested, hoping to spare the boy further embarrassment. "That way Mary can see them without tiring herself out."

"Oh, would you?" she asked, clapping her hands together in childish delight.

Will tried to act nonchalant, but Brock could see he was as eager to share his excitement over the kittens with Mary as she was to see them.

"I guess," Will responded, hoping he didn't sound too anxious. Then he dashed across the yard at break-neck speed.

"Promise you won't stay out too long, Mary," Brock cautioned. "We wouldn't want Miss Daniels to get upset at either one of us."

Mary's eyes rounded. "Are you scared of her, too, Mr. Peters? I thought I was the only one." She blushed. "I mean, Miss Daniels is nice and all, but she's got a quick temper."

Brock nodded gravely. "Terrified. The woman scares me out of my wits." But it wasn't her temper that had him full of unease.

Neither Mary nor Brock noticed the red-haired woman, who had just arrived and was staring at them from the office window, or the small smile tugging the corners of her mouth as she listened to their exchange.

5

*A lot of folks would do more prayin'
if they could find a soft spot for their knees.*

"*Must you hit* every rut in the road, Mr. Jenkins?" Eliza yelled from the rear of the wagon. "I swear, you've nary missed a one since we've begun this god-awful trip."

Shorty stared over his shoulder, his eyes narrowing as he took in the sharp-tongued woman. "If you think you can do better, why don't you come up here and drive this wagon yourself, ma'am?"

Brock and Prudence exchanged amused glances, then Prudence reached over and patted Eliza's hand. "We're almost to town, Eliza. It'll only be a few more minutes."

"Hmph! I feel like a sack of flour loaded back here in the rear of this wagon. I don't see why we couldn't have brought the buggy."

"The buggy's not big enough for all of us to travel in, Mrs. Dobbyns," Brock explained, leaning his arms on his knees. While Burt and Slim followed on horseback, the rest of the party—except for Sarah, who'd stayed behind to tend Moody, and Mary, who Prudence said was too near her time to ride in the wagon—were crammed into the rear of the buckboard, like pickles in a jar.

"None of us is too comfortable"—he'd lost feeling in his legs twenty minutes ago—"and I think Shorty's doing the best he can to avoid the ruts."

Eliza's cheeks grew pink. "I do apologize for my caterwauling, Mr. Peters. I'm just out of sorts today. The thought of attending another one of Reverend Entwhistle's sermons has me sorely vexed. The man is a self-inflated bag of wind."

Prudence bit her lower lip to keep from laughing at Eliza's opinion, for it directly mirrored her own. The reverend was as pompous and boring an individual as she'd ever had the displeasure to meet. And the fact that he looked down his long, beaklike nose at her and the girls didn't endear him to her in any way.

"What about me?" Louann protested, stabbing herself in the chest with her index finger. "He's always talking about sinning and whoring. And he looks straight at me with those beady eyes of his. I bet he's made a few trips to Madam Eva's when he didn't think anyone was looking."

"That will be quite enough, Louann," Prudence interjected, drawing her shawl more tightly about her to ward off the early morning chill. "Though the reverend's religious beliefs leave something to be desired, he's still a man of the cloth, and we must respect that fact. It is God's word we're going to hear, anyway, not Reverend Entwhistle's."

*　　　*　　　*

It might have been God's word they'd gone to hear, but it was the righteous little reverend who'd kept them pinned to the back of their seats for the past forty minutes.

Brock squirmed restlessly, hands folded across his chest, as his attention strayed to the woman seated in the row in front of him. Prudence's mass of red curls were stuffed up under a green velvet bonnet, and he could smell the scent of lilac she wore. He thought of sweet green clover, as green as her eyes, and white fluffy clouds, as soft as her skin looked to be, and . . .

"That man ain't likely to shut his trap anytime soon," Shorty whispered, nudging Brock in the ribs, interrupting his pleasant daydream. "I sure would like to mosey on down to the saloon and wet my whistle."

Prudence turned in annoyance, glaring at Brock and Shorty. "Ssh! This is the Sabbath, gentlemen. It's time to reflect upon our shortcomings." And her accusing look said they had an abundance to reflect upon.

Leaning forward until his lips were practically touching Prudence's ear, Brock whispered, "I'm reflecting on my stomach, Red. It's as empty as your Reverend Entwhistle's head."

Outrage shone clearly on Prudence's face before she turned back to listen to the rest of the sermon. Brock just smiled, pleased that he'd been able to provoke the bossy beauty. It was time she learned that when it came to verbal sparring, he was a master. He hadn't been the most successful attorney in Sacramento for nothing.

He closed his eyes, his thoughts drifting back to the bustling state capital of California. Sacramento had been booming when Brock practiced law there. He'd been a damn good trial lawyer and moderately successful. And he'd finally been able to buy Catherine the white clapboard house with the picket fence that she'd dreamed of. He had even been able to put money away toward Josh's college education.

After years of struggle and sacrifice, Brock had finally achieved his lifelong goal of combining a successful career with a family. Catherine had presented him with the son he'd always wanted, and they'd talked about having another.

But those plans were never realized. The cholera epidemic that swept through the town had killed them, along with his family.

Clutching the pair of crutches that Joe Two Toes had made, Sarah entered Moody's room to find him staring morosely toward the window. She knew how difficult it was for such an active man to be confined to bed, which is why she had asked Joe to fashion the crutches, much to the old Indian's annoyance.

"Good afternoon, Colonel," she said. The sudden pleasure that entered his eyes when he saw her made butterflies dance in her stomach. "I hope I'm not disturbing you."

"I welcome the diversion, Miss Sarah. I'm close to losing my mind, lying in this bed for hours on end. I fear I'm going to become one with it soon."

"I thought as much, which is why I've brought you these." She placed the crutches within his reach, watching his eyes widen in surprise, then soften in appreciation.

"You're a woman after my own heart, Miss Sarah. Thank you, my dear."

She blushed, stammering, "You're . . . you're quite welcome, Colonel."

"Why don't you call me Moody, or Martin, if you like? That's my real name."

Smiling softly, she reached for the woolen robe at the foot of the bed that once belonged to Cody Daniels and handed it to him. "Would you like to try out your new crutches, Martin?" She tested his name on her lips and found that it came quite easily.

He looked as pleased as a child with a new toy on Christmas morning. "Indeed. Nothing would give me more pleasure." He winked at her suggestively. "Well, almost nothing."

Shaking her head, her cheeks softly flushed, she approached the bed and assisted him into his robe. Once he had managed to fasten the sash, she held out the crutches while he scooted himself to the edge of the mattress, lifting his injured leg carefully.

"Now you must be very careful. If you fall, you could do a great deal of damage to yourself."

"If you would permit me to lean on you, Miss Sarah, I think I can manage to upright myself."

Even with Sarah's help there were a few moments of struggle, but Moody finally managed to get to his feet, bracing himself on the oak crutches when he did. He tested their strength, and once satisfied that they were strong enough to hold his weight, he took a few steps.

"Don't overdo the first time," Sarah cautioned, noting the strain on his face. "You've lost a lot of your strength and muscle lying in that bed. You need to proceed cautiously."

Ignoring her advice, he made his way to the window, looking out to find the sun glistening off the colorful leaves of red and gold that garlanded the trees. Smiling, he sighed in contentment, staring at the azure sky as if seeing it for the very first time.

"It's funny how much you miss the small things when they're taken away from you."

Sarah bit the inside of her cheek to keep from crying

and thought of James Brockton, the father of her unborn child. James had never really been taken from her; she'd never had the right to possess him in the first place. He was married and the father of one of her students in the Denver school where she'd taught the last fifteen years. Even knowing of James's prior commitments hadn't been enough to prevent her from falling head over heels in love, to deter her from having an illicit affair with him.

Tenderly she placed her hands over her belly, stroking the protruding mound, which had just recently begun to show signs of life. She had paid the supreme price for her folly. When James had found out she was pregnant, he and his family had left Denver in the middle of the night, leaving her to deal with her problem alone.

"My dear, are you all right?" Moody's voice was laced with concern. "You look quite pale." Trying hurriedly to cross the room to comfort Sarah, Moody put too much weight on his right side and began to topple over.

Fortunately Sarah, having noticed his foolish but sweet heroics, anticipated the fall and rushed forward to hold him steady. With her hands securely about his waist, she led him back to the bed and helped him to sit.

Nearly out of breath, Moody needed to take a moment before he could speak. "You really are an angel, Miss Sarah." He reached for her hand and kissed it.

Uncomfortable with the praise she knew she didn't deserve, Sarah pulled her hand from his grasp. "I'm anything but, Colonel, and if you knew everything about me, you'd know that I'm just a stupid woman who performed a stupid act. And now I'm paying the price for that stupidity."

Before Moody could respond, Sarah rushed to the door and disappeared down the hall, leaving Moody to wonder who the *stupid* man was who had broken Sarah Davenport's heart.

After the church service, the congregation spilled out onto the front lawn. Most everyone in town knew everyone else, so there was the usual gossiping—the men called it "catching up on business"—exchanging of recipes, and the expected commentary on how uplifting the good reverend's sermon was.

Of course, the ladies and gents of the R and R were not included in the general camaraderie going on around them. Shorty and the rest of the cowboys, who already knew what to expect, wasted no time in heading toward the saloon for a little libation, gambling, and other amusements, despite the fact it was Sunday.

Though the reverend and his band of followers had done their best to rid the town of such dens of vice and corruption as the Silver Slipper Saloon and Madam Eva's bordello, they'd been unsuccessful.

Absolution, for all its morality, had its roots in silver. Once as wild and corrupt as Dodge City or Abilene, it had grown sedate over the years. But there were still enough old-timers, enough cattlemen and cowboys, who resisted the church's edict to shut down the saloon and brothel on Sundays. So despite the good reverend's threat of eternal damnation, the establishments had remained open.

While the hands headed over to the saloon to seek their pleasures, Brock remained behind, riding herd over the females, who showed no obvious distress at being slighted by the God-fearing folk of Absolution. He guessed they were used to it by now, especially Louann, whose previous occupation had already made her an outcast of polite society.

Still, it bothered Brock to see the womenfolk of Absolution turn up their noses at Prudence and her brood. They'd even gone so far as to move their skirts out of the way when the pregnant women walked by, so as not to be tainted by contact with them.

"Ladies," Brock said, touching the brim of his hat with his forefinger, "would you care to accompany me on a stroll down Main Street? I'd be willing to treat for some refreshment, perhaps a slice of pie at the Blue Willow Restaurant."

Prudence, who'd been doing a thorough inspection of her gloves to avoid facing the unkind looks of Mrs. Childs and Mrs. Lowery, looked up at Brock and smiled gratefully.

"Your offer is most considerate, Brock. Ladies," she said, turning to face the other women, "shall we go get some pie and coffee?"

The general consensus was yes, except for Louann, who begged to visit her former friends at Madam Eva's. Promising to be back in thirty minutes, she disappeared down one of the side streets, while the others walked down the wooden sidewalk toward the restaurant.

They hadn't gone but a few feet when two men, one stocky and middle-aged, the other a boy about eighteen, began to laugh and point their fingers at the group of women.

"Look, Pa, it's that woman who runs the ranch. The one Mary run off to."

Recognizing Bobby Fitzsimmons immediately, Prudence tensed and her lips thinned in displeasure, but she kept walking, hoping Brock would do the same. She had no intention of becoming a spectacle this afternoon, and the Fitzsimmons were known troublemakers.

Brock halted in midstride, glaring at the younger of the two men. "Is that the Fitzsimmons boy?" he asked, his hands clenching into fists as he stared at the tall, huskily built lad.

"Why, yes, it is," Eliza offered, making Prudence groan inwardly. "He's quite the ruffian, or so I'm told."

"You the one that took that whore Mary Winslow in?" Frank Fitzsimmons asked, pointing an accusing finger at Prudence. "You should be ashamed bringing these trollops to town, parading them in front of our womenfolk."

Prudence noted the exact moment Brock's temper snapped. Having heard his crude curses, she watched in dismay as he stepped off the sidewalk and stopped directly in front of Frank.

"I think you owe these ladies an apology, Mr. Fitzsimmons. I heard what you said, and I don't think it was very gentlemanly of you."

Scratching his belly as if he were infested with lice, which Brock thought was a likely possibility, Frank said, "Is that right?" He looked at his boy and chuckled. "Hear that, Bobby? This cowboy don't like the way I talk to his whores."

Without warning, Brock lunged, smashing his fist into Frank Fitzsimmons's face, bloodying his nose and knocking the man to the ground. This brought a collective gasp from the women standing on the sidewalk, who stared slack-jawed and wide-eyed.

"I think you owe these ladies an apology," Brock repeated, hands on hips, straddling the man's legs.

"Get up, Pa, and wallop him good," Bobby encouraged, trying to pull his father to his feet.

Brock's smile was sinister. "Yes, do get up, Mr. Fitzsimmons. I'd be more than happy to accommodate any sort of retribution you have in mind."

By this time a crowd had gathered, but rather than the mortification Prudence expected to feel, she was elated that Brock had come to the defense of her ladies.

"Well, well, if it ain't Frank Fitzsimmons," Louann said snidely, joining the rest of the onlookers. "You still owe me for the last time, Frank. Guess I'll have to have Mr. Peters collect it for me."

Louann's comments brought chuckles and snorts of derision from the onlookers, making Frank Fitzsimmons's face about the color of the blood dripping from his nose, which looked suspiciously broken.

Wiping the blood from his face with the back of his sleeve, Frank shook his head. "I don't have no call to fight with you, mister. I reckon I was out of line about what I said to the ladies. I'm sorry."

"Pa!" Bobby wailed, shaking his head in disbelief.

Brock turned on the father of Mary's child. "I don't know what sweet Mary saw in you, boy, but love sure as hell must be blind. You're nothing but a horny little bastard who ought to have the shit kicked out of him from here to next Sunday. Pardon, ladies," he said, looking over his shoulder at Prudence and her brood. And to Bobby: "You ever come near Mary Winslow again, and you'll think the beating I gave your father was a love tap."

Ignoring the two pairs of hostile brown eyes boring into his back, Brock made his way to the sidewalk. He held out his arms to Prudence and Eliza. "Ladies, our pie awaits."

The crowd on the sidewalk parted like Moses dividing the Red Sea, allowing Brock and his ladies to continue on to the restaurant.

Prudence, who was still trying to digest everything she'd heard this afternoon, including the accusation that Bobby might actually be the father of Mary's child, walked on silently, wondering if she had completely misjudged Brock Peters. And wondering, if that were true, what she was going to do about it.

*   *   *

The night air was brisk. The wind howled mournfully as it ruffled the aspen and oak leaves, and Brock turned up the collar of his sheepskin jacket as he walked away from the bunkhouse.

He needed some time to himself. Having had to relate the events of this afternoon at least five times over, thanks to Louann's effusive praise at dinner, he found himself growing restless and thought a walk about the yard might ease his unsettled mood.

Heading toward the massive oak tree silhouetted in the distance by the light of a full moon, he paused at the top of a slight rise. Before him stood the Daniels cemetery. Fenced off in whitewashed pine, the tombstones stood solemnly, white marble against the black velvet night.

They drew him forward and he stopped, bending down to read the first inscription: *Here lies Cody Daniels, beloved husband of Abigail, father of Prudence and Clara. Born February 1, 1800—Died April 22, 1867.*

Prudence's father, Brock thought, pushing himself to his feet, noting how well cared for the graves were. There were three altogether, he noted, reading the other two inscriptions for Abigail and Clara Daniels.

These were the family Prudence grieved for, and he knew what that was all about. His family had been gone for eight long years. Time was supposed to heal all wounds, but it didn't. He still missed the two of them so damn much. He kicked at the ground with the toe of his boot. It wasn't fair. It wasn't right that he had been allowed to survive, while God had taken his good and beautiful wife and child. Josh had only been six years old.

Guilt consumed him, as it always did when he thought of how Catherine and Josh had fallen prey to the disease while he'd been in San Francisco, defending a worthless bastard who'd been put on trial for murdering his entire family.

The irony of it was that it hadn't even been his case. He'd gone to San Francisco as a favor to his father and had returned to Sacramento to find Josh dead and Catherine dying.

Brock had kept constant vigil by Catherine's bedside for three days, praying to God to spare her life, imploring the Almighty to take him, too. But God hadn't seen fit to do either.

Catherine had died in his arms, and the day after her funeral he had packed his belongings, closed up the house, and left, blaming God, the law profession, but mostly himself.

"Catherine," he whispered, the name drifting on the wind to be carried to the woman who stood watching at the edge of the fenced-in area.

Prudence's heart ached at the mournful sound of it. She recognized the pain well, for it lived within her own heart and mind. She had come to the cemetery to grieve, not expecting to find another tortured soul. "Hello," she called out softly.

Brock turned, surprised by the sight of Prudence standing by the fence. He swallowed with some difficulty, stepping toward her. "I hope you don't mind. I was just out for a walk and found myself here," he explained.

She drew her shawl more tightly about her against the biting wind, which whipped her skirts about her legs. "I don't mind. I often come here at night. I find it gives me peace to talk with my family. I miss them. Not so much my mother, I never had a chance to know her. She died when I was born. But Papa and Clara . . ."

"Was Clara your sister?"

Prudence nodded. "She died several years ago, shortly after my father."

"I'm sorry. Was she sick?"

"Sick?" She shook her head, her voice filled with sadness. "Sick in her heart, perhaps. But, no, not sick from a disease. She died in childbirth." The light of understanding entered Brock's eyes, and Prudence recognized the pity in them, the compassion.

"Is that why you started this ranch? For Clara?"

Prudence sighed. "For Clara and other women just like her. Women who were discarded after their usefulness had been served."

Her voice grew bitter. "The cowboy who got Clara pregnant worked for my father. Billy Preston was his name. A handsomer man I've yet to meet. He could charm the skin off a rattlesnake when he put his mind to it. He charmed my sister instead. Clara fell in love with him, gave herself to him. When she got pregnant, he took off for parts unknown. We never heard from him again."

That explained a lot, Brock thought, observing the pain, the bitterness, on Prudence's face. "Is that why you've never married?"

She could feel her cheeks grow warm. "Partly." And partly because no one had ever asked her, she confessed silently. Cody Daniels, for all his well-meaning ways, had been overly protective of his two daughters. He'd intimidated most of the young men who'd come to call, with promises of retribution if they so much as laid a hand on his daughters.

Her father had kept a tight rein on everything at the R and R, including Prudence and Clara; and Prudence supposed it was the reason Clara, who possessed a streak of independence and stubbornness, had rebelled and gotten herself in trouble.

Prudence had been the dutiful one, which is why the R and R had been left to her upon her father's death. She'd always looked up to Cody, accepted his word as the gospel truth, and only after Clara's death had she come to realize that perhaps he had done his children a grave injustice. But by then it was too late. The suitors, save for Jacob, had grown few and far between, none wishing to marry a woman with such unorthodox views as Prudence possessed.

Brock touched Prudence's shoulder. "Are you all right? You seem a million miles away."

Realizing her mind had wandered, Prudence apologized, then replied, "To answer your question as to why I've never married, the truth is I've never been able to trust a man after what Billy did to Clara. Clara died in childbirth, but she died inside long before God took her."

"Not all men are like Billy Preston, Prudence. There are some good, honest individuals who stand behind their deeds."

"Are there?" She shrugged. "You'd have a hard time proving that by me and those young women in there." She tilted her head toward the house. "Most found out the hard way that their man couldn't be counted on when the going got rough. It's a painful lesson to learn."

"And you thought I was one of those men when I brought Mary here? A worthless cowboy who'd come to drop off his excess baggage?"

She had the grace to blush. "It appears I've misjudged you. I spoke with Mary after we returned home today, and she told me about Bobby Fitzsimmons. I'm sorry."

"Things aren't always what they seem."

"Perhaps," she conceded, "but they are nine times out of ten. You were the exception."

He grinned. "I am rather unique. One of a kind, so to speak." He made her smile, and for some reason that made him glad.

"I admit that you're different from most cowboys."

"Handsomer? Smarter?" Her laughter sent ripples of pleasure coursing down his spine.

"More conceited, that's for sure. But tell me, why have you never settled down? Why are you so determined to remain footloose?"

Pain entered the brown eyes. "I was married once." I loved once, cared once, but no more. It hurt too damn much to lose those who meant the world to you.

Before Prudence had a chance to question Brock further about his startling revelation, a frantic shout split the stillness.

"Prudence, come quick!"

Brock and Prudence exchanged worried glances. "It's Sarah," Prudence said. "Something's happened." Lifting her skirts, she began to run toward the house, Brock keeping pace with her.

"Prudence!" Sarah's voice rang out again. "It's Mary. She's going to have her baby."

"I'm coming," Prudence shouted. Then to Brock, "Lord have mercy. I wasn't expecting Mary to have that child for at least two more weeks."

When they reached the porch, Brock stopped short. "Let me know what happens. I'll be in the bunkhouse."

"You'll be no such place, except right here in this house. Mary's quite attached to you, Brock. It might comfort her to know that you're close by."

He doubted that. He'd been scared witless when Josh had been born. His own mother had kicked him out of the house in annoyance. "I'm not much good at these types of things," he insisted. The sound of a woman's labor was something he didn't care to experience again.

"I think more men should hear the screams of child-birth," she said as if reading his mind. "It might make them think with their brain instead of another part of their anatomy."

She left Brock staring wide-eyed and cursing mildly under his breath.

6

*The food on some ranches might be
a mite weak-tastin',
but the coffee's strong enough
to bring up the average.*

Brock interrupted his pacing long enough to pour himself a glass of brandy. Miraculously, he'd found the bottle in a curio cabinet in the front room, where he'd been cooling his heels the last two hours. And Prudence Daniels's edicts or not, he was going to drink it.

The liquor went down smooth and warm, and it almost took the edge off the horrible screams coming from the other end of the house.

Almost. Nothing could ever wipe them out completely. Mary, for all her small size, had one powerful set of lungs. And she'd used them unmercifully.

"If Miss Pru catches you, Brock, there's going to be hell to pay."

Brock turned to find Shorty stepping into the room. He was smiling, glancing at the bottle of brandy Brock held as he shed his jacket and tossed it onto the red leather wing chair.

The old man's warning didn't deter Brock, who gulped down the rest of the fiery brew. "Listening to that caterwauling is hell, Shorty." Suddenly, as if remembering something, Brock's forehead wrinkled in confusion. "What're you doing here? I thought you'd be fast asleep by now."

Shorty eyed the bottle of brandy with such longing, Brock was finally obliged to find another glass and pour him a drink.

"Hannah brought out the news about Mary's baby before she turned in," Shorty said, sipping the amber liquid. "She don't help with the birthin's. Says the screaming makes her crazy."

Hannah was smarter than she looked, Brock decided. "Who's in there doing the deliverin', then?"

"Miss Pru. She's been doin' it since her sister up and died. Guess she told you about that?"

"Some. But didn't they call in a doctor from town?"

Shorty shook his head. "Miss Pru won't hear of it. She won't let a doctor come within ten feet of this place. 'Twas a doctor caused her sister to die, or so she says. Of course, 'tweren't the same one we got now. Doc Smithson seems a capable sort, when he ain't imbibin' too freely."

"So Prudence has taken the responsibility of these women's deliveries upon herself?" Brock shook his head in disbelief. "She's got more courage than most."

Shorty joined Brock in his pacing. "She's read more medical books than most doctors. Her office is filled with 'em. And she subscribes to those medical journals to keep current on things."

Just as Brock was digesting all this startling information, Polly burst into the room, red-faced and breathless. "We need to know your name, Mr. Peters. The one in the middle, I mean."

Brock and Shorty exchanged confused glances, then Brock replied, "It's Jonathan. But why?"

"Got to get back," was all the plump girl said before spinning on her heel and disappearing into the hallway.

"Hey," Shorty said. "Do you hear something? It's suddenly grown quiet."

Brock listened, and sure enough, there was no more screaming. "What do you make of it? You don't suppose something has happened to Mary?" His stomach knotted in fear. The thought of that young girl slipping out of life before she had a chance to live it was unconscionable to him.

Shorty smoothed down his mustache with his thumb and forefinger. "'Pears to me that the young miss might've up and had her baby."

Shorty's prediction was proved correct when a moment later a baby's piercing cry split the silence, followed a few minutes after that by the arrival of Prudence, who carried a small bundle in her arms. Prudence's face was drawn with exhaustion, but she was flushed with excitement and smiling in delight.

"Meet Brock Jonathan Winslow, gentlemen," she announced, stepping farther into the room. "A more handsome child I've yet to see."

Brock's mouth fell open, then snapped shut. "Brock Jonathan?"

She nodded. "Mary's going to call him BJ. She says it suits him better. I'm inclined to agree."

"Well, shoot me a-runnin'! That little gal up and named her baby after you, Brock, and you didn't even have to do the deed. If that don't beat all!" Shorty said.

As if the thought of having a child named after him weren't earth-shattering enough, the sight of Prudence holding that small bit of humanity was enough to knock Brock's socks off. And he didn't like the way it was making him feel, all funny inside, like he'd just eaten a whole crate of green tomatoes.

"How's Mary doing?" he asked, eager to take his mind off the Madonna-like vision before him.

Prudence smiled. "Splendidly. Mary's young and healthy. I don't anticipate any problems."

"Glad to hear it."

Her eyes drifted down to the glass in Brock's hand and she shook her head, hiding her smile when Shorty thrust his glass behind his back. "I should scold you boys for drinking my medicinal brandy, but I won't. From the looks on your faces, my guess is you needed it. I haven't met a man yet who was any good in a real crisis."

"Well, now," Shorty argued, looking a mite put out, "that might be true about babies, but get me around a herd of cattle stuck in a raging river and I'll come through every time."

Brock looked completely dazed, and Prudence almost laughed. "Would you like to see the baby, Brock? After all, he is your namesake."

The question roused Brock from his stupor and he stepped forward, peeling back the blue receiving blanket. BJ's mouth was rooting at Prudence's breast, and Brock found himself staring at her lush mounds rather than at the downy-haired infant. And though it was the most indecent of thoughts, he couldn't help wondering what it would be like to be in BJ Winslow's place.

Whether it was from the baby's innocent quest for food or the realization that Brock was staring at her breasts with intense concentration, Prudence's nipples hardened into two stiff peaks. She looked up to find that

Brock had noticed, and her cheeks reddened as a rush of heat filled them.

"I'd better get the baby back to his mother," she said, turning away to hide her confusion. She'd never reacted to a man's gaze like that before, and she'd certainly never experienced any such emotion with Jacob. And he fairly devoured her with his eyes every chance he got. What on earth was the matter with her?

Brock watched Prudence depart, not liking the direction his thoughts were taking. As if those thoughts were transparent as glass, he heard Shorty remark, "Miss Prudence is prettier than a red heifer in a flower bed. Yep, she's quite a woman. It's going to take a strong man to bring that filly to heel."

Brock shrugged, doing his best to appear disinterested. "I pity the man who sets out to break her. He'll have scars when she's done with him."

Shorty laughed, patting Brock on the back as they walked out the door. "The man that always straddles the fence usually has a sore crotch, boy."

Jacob Morgan eased back in the tufted-leather swivel chair behind his desk, blowing smoke rings from his cigar into the air, studying the bearded cowboy who sat in front of him.

Dave Stewart was a big disappointment, a very big disappointment. He'd let his lust for that whore Louann jeopardize everything Jacob had been working years to accomplish. He'd up and quit and now Jacob had no one to keep him apprised of the goin's-on at the R and R.

"You've let me down, Stewart. I thought you were a man I could count on."

Dave wiped his sweaty palms on his pant legs and

swallowed nervously. "I am, Mr. Morgan. Miz Prudence just wouldn't listen to reason."

"I paid you to oversee things at the R and R, not to screw Louann Jones. I should cut off that miserable appendage you call a cock and stuff it into your mouth."

Dave swallowed so hard this time, his Adam's apple bulged as prominently as his eyes, and he covered his crotch as inconspicuously as he could with his hat.

"But I won't. I've decided to give you another chance. This new foreman of Prudence's, Brock Peters, is going to have to be watched. I don't want him interfering in our plans."

"Just give me the word, boss. I'll be happy to take him out, just like I did with Buck."

Morgan grimaced. "That was messy, Stewart, very messy. I was told the man looked like a gutted pig when you got through with him." He had never instructed his bloodthirsty foreman to kill Buck—only to frighten him off. Murder wasn't his style. He preferred using his wits to get what he wanted, and he wanted Prudence Daniels's land.

His own didn't have enough water to sustain the amount of cattle he wanted to run, but the R and R did. It had its own damn river. And water to a cattleman was far more precious than gold or silver.

"Indians can be ruthless, boss," Dave said, smiling as if they were sharing a great secret.

Jacob ignored him. "How many head are we running on R and R range? Did you get that last row of fence cut like you were told?"

"We had nearly a hundred head grazing the south pasture, but the R and R cowboys forced 'em back over the line and restrung the fence."

Morgan's beefy hands came down to slap the top of his walnut desk so loudly, Stewart jumped. "Goddammit! You're a worthless sonofabitch! I won't allow that goddamn barbed wire to be strung. Do you understand me, Stewart? I want it cut. And I want you to keep cutting it, until they get tired of restringing it. We've always had open range here in this valley."

He shook his head. "I don't know what's gotten into Prudence. She's too independent by far. It's all this talk of women's rights. Damn crock of shit, if you ask me."

Dave stood. "Yes, sir, Mr. Morgan. I understand. But . . ." He scratched his head. "How we goin' to keep those men from restringing the fence?"

With a look of loathing, Morgan replied, "I'm sure you'll think of something, Stewart, but no more killing. And in the meantime, I'll step up my efforts to woo Miss Prudence to the altar. I may even have to compromise her to get her there." The thought was not at all displeasing. He'd often wondered what lay beneath all that prim and proper starchiness the red-haired spinster wore like armor.

Dave's eyes widened, for he knew damn well that Miss Arabella, Mr. Morgan's mistress, wasn't likely to stand for that. Even if she did have the biggest set of tits this side of the Mississippi, she still had the meanest temper he'd ever seen. Miss Arabella's temper made Miz Prudence's seem tame by comparison.

"What're you looking so sick about, Stewart? You're as pale as a mewly kitten."

"It's Miss Arabella, boss. She ain't goin' to like what you're planning."

At the sound of his mistress's name, Jacob leaned back in his chair, heaving a sigh of frustration. Bella was definitely going to be a problem. The voluptuous Widow Potts fancied herself the next Mrs. Morgan. If she discovered what he was planning with Prudence, she'd cut off his balls and feed them to those two Russian wolfhounds she kept as pets, and she wouldn't think twice about doing so.

Yes, Bella was definitely going to be a problem.

Moody looked proud as a peacock as he propelled himself toward the kitchen table on his new crutches. He pulled up short at the sight of Hannah, who had tossed down her spoon and was pointing an accusing finger at him, a look of intense dislike on her face.

"I no cook if the bluecoat sits at my table," Hannah declared.

Prudence smiled at Moody apologetically. "Now, Hannah, be reasonable," she said, holding out her hands in supplication to the rotund cook. "Colonel Carstairs has been eating your food for weeks now. I see no difference if he eats it here or in his room."

Hannah shook her head, crossing her beefy arms over her chest. "Bluecoats kill many of my people. I no cook for them."

Feeling extremely uncomfortable that he'd been the cause of such distress, Moody said, "That's quite all right, Miss Prudence. I can go back to my room and wait for my meal."

"Absolutely not! You'll do no such thing." She turned toward the stubborn Indian woman and said, "Very well, Hannah, that leaves me no choice but to prepare breakfast myself this morning."

Hannah's eyes widened in dismay, but she didn't back down; instead she stormed out of the kitchen, slamming the door behind her.

Unaware of the disturbance, Brock and the rest of the cowboys walked in a few minutes later. Brock caught sight of the colonel and grinned.

"Well, Moody, you're finally up. It's about time," he teased. "Good morning, Red." He winked at Prudence, who glared in response.

"Where's breakfast?" Shorty asked, sniffing the air. "I'm hungry enough to eat the south end of a north-bound polecat."

"I'm afraid breakfast will be a little late. Hannah has decided not to cook," Prudence explained, approaching the cookstove. "I guess I'll do the honors." The fire in the box had already been started, and she began to slice the ham that had been left out on the counter.

Shorty, Burt, and Slim exchanged horrified looks before slinking down onto their chairs. Brock and Will, oblivious of their concerns, sat down as well.

"You need help with that chair, Colonel?" Brock asked Moody as he approached the table.

With the end of his crutch, Moody pulled back on the chair leg and eased himself into it with a satisfied smile. "I've been practicing with Sarah."

Brock's eyebrow arched. "Is that a fact?" He reached for the pot of coffee on the table, pouring Moody a cup.

"I'm sorry about the Indian woman, Miss Prudence. I wouldn't have come to the table this morning if I'd known it was going to create a problem."

"What's going on?" Brock asked, watching as Prudence bent over the cookstove to put some bread into the oven to toast. In fact, he was so intent on her behind, he burned his tongue. "Damn!" he cursed, covering his mouth.

"Joe and Hannah harbor ill will toward the cavalry, I'm afraid. Though they're Ute, they lived with the Cheyenne for a time. Joe's aunt married into the tribe, and they often visited her." Which was an oddity, considering the Utes and Cheyenne were at war most of the time. But Ouray, chief of the Ute tribe, was well respected, even by the Cheyenne, and he happened to be Joe's uncle.

"Joe and Hannah were at Sand Creek back in sixty-four when the massacre took place."

Will's eyes brightened with curiosity and excitement. "A real Indian massacre?"

The cowboys looked uneasy as they stared down into their empty plates; no one was proud of what had taken place at Sand Creek. Fingers and breasts had been cut off of the women and kept as souvenirs, dead squaws had been raped in relays, and toddling children had been used for target practice.

It was a shame no white man could ever live down.

"I wasn't part of Colonel Chivington's command," Moody explained, "but what was related to me made my stomach turn. I'm not sure that the breakfast table is a suitable place to tell the tale, lad."

Will's voice took on a pleading note. "Please, Colonel Carstairs, I won't get sick. I promise."

Prudence wished she could give such an assurance. The story of the senseless slaughter of over five hundred Indians, two-thirds of whom had been women and children, made her sick to her stomach every time she heard it.

"I concur with Colonel Carstairs, Will. Let's leave the telling of it for another time." She turned back to crack a dozen eggs into the blue splatterware mixing bowl.

"Aww, jeez."

"How are you doing with that horse, boy?" Brock asked, trying to take Will's mind off of Sand Creek. "Have you convinced her who's in charge?"

Will's chest puffed out with pride. "Yes, sir! That horse knows who's the boss, and that's a fact, Mr. Peters."

Prudence brought two platters of sliced ham and the bowl of scrambled eggs to the table, setting them down before the men. "Hope you're hungry. I made quite a bit."

"What's burning?" Slim asked, wrinkling up his nose in disgust as billows of smoke poured forth from the oven.

"Oh, my!" Prudence exclaimed, rushing toward the stove. She opened the oven door, coughing and waving her hand, shaking her head in dismay at the sight of the charred bread. "I'm afraid the toast is burned."

"Probably a blessin'," Shorty remarked under his breath, trying to catch hold of the runny eggs that dripped off his fork.

"Hey," Burt said, "this ham ain't been cooked. It's cold as a slab of marble."

Brock had to agree, after tasting the eggs and ham, that the meal was a disaster. Perhaps they should insist Moody stay in his room. At this rate they were all going to starve to death.

"I'm not much of a cook," Prudence confessed. "Hannah's always been around to do the cooking, and I never found the need to learn."

"Now don't you worry about a thing, Miss Prudence," Moody assured the crestfallen woman. "This meal is just fine. Why, I can't remember when I've had eggs this good. They taste just like my mother used to make them."

Had his father died of food poisoning? Brock wanted to ask, but he refrained after seeing the grateful expression on Prudence's face. "It's not too bad," he finally admitted, making Shorty choke on his coffee.

"Guess I'll be headin' out to the barn," the old man stated, pushing back his chair.

The other cowboys followed suit, mumbling their thanks before heading out the door, until only Moody, Brock, and Prudence remained.

As she stared at the unappetizing meal, Prudence heaved a sigh. "I'm better at keeping the books than at cooking."

Brock grinned and leaned back in his chair, folding his hands over his stomach. "It's nice to hear you admit that you're not perfect, Red. I was beginning to think you were."

Her eyes narrowed. "I doubt you'd recognize perfection if it slapped you alongside the head, Mr. Peters."

"Don't be too sure about that. I recognized some pretty perfect specimens last night." He winked, and her cheeks blossomed with color.

Being a romantic at heart, Moody witnessed the exchange with something more than casual interest. Unless he missed his guess, something very special was unfolding right before his eyes. He just wondered how long it was going to take the spinster and the cowboy to figure out what it was.

Arabella Potts was one of the wealthiest women in Absolution. Her husband, Henry, who'd been the town undertaker, had died unexpectedly of measles three years before, leaving her comfortably well off. So comfortable, in fact, she'd become the town's foremost society matron.

No party was given without consulting Arabella Potts about the guest list, no town function planned that she wasn't involved in from start to finish. And today was no exception.

The reigning queens of Absolution society, Mrs. Townsend, Mrs. Childs, and Mrs. Lowery, were seated in the front parlor of Arabella's exquisitely furnished Victorian-style house—the only one of its kind in Absolution—sharing a pot of tea and a plate of scones.

The odor of formaldehyde still lingered in the air—Henry had used part of the house for his mortuary—but no one was ever impolite enough to mention it.

While enjoying their refreshment, the ladies discussed the upcoming harvest ball, one of the town's biggest charity events, second only to the annual Fourth of July celebration.

Patting the sides of her neatly coiffed ebony hair, Arabella wrinkled her nose in disgust at the last suggestion Caroline Townsend had put forth.

"Apple bobbing is so, so provincial, Caroline. Don't you agree, ladies?" She turned to the two other women, pleased to find them nodding their heads in agreement. Her question had been merely a courtesy, for no one ever argued with Arabella Potts about anything.

Caroline's flaccid cheeks grew pink as she wiped her gloved hands nervously against the skirt of her black bombazine gown. "But, of course, you know best, Arabella. You're the one who has lived in the East. I'm sure you know what's proper."

These silly fools had actually bought her story that she and Henry had arrived in Absolution from Boston, when in fact they had come from their home state of Arkansas, with stops in San Francisco and Denver along the way. Enough time had elapsed between Little Rock and Absolution that not a trace of their cracker heritage had lingered upon their arrival in the backward community. It had been so easy to dupe these culture-starved biddies, it was downright pathetic.

Arabella patted Caroline's hand and smiled condescendingly. "One cannot expect to learn overnight what is not inbred, my dear."

"So what do you suggest, Arabella?" Livinia Childs asked, stuffing another dainty tea sandwich—her fourth—into her mouth.

Catching sight of her maid in the doorway, Arabella waved her hand airily. "I really can't think right now. I have the most dreadful headache." She pressed her forefingers to her temples. "If we could reconvene tomorrow, perhaps I could come up with some other suggestions."

Her maid had just given her the signal that Jacob Morgan had arrived, via the back door, and was waiting for her upstairs. She had to get rid of these women, and fast. It wouldn't do for them to discover that the refined Widow Potts kept a wealthy lover in her bed.

With the usual polite commiserations, the ladies soon departed, and Arabella breathed a sigh of relief before hurrying up the stairs.

Checking her reflection in the beveled mirror that graced the wall at the top, she smiled in satisfaction. At thirty-eight, she was still an attractive woman. The blue satin dress brought out the color of her eyes, molding the generous proportions Jacob found so appealing.

She bit her lips to redden them, running her tongue over them in anticipation. She turned toward her bedroom door to find her two wolfhounds guarding the entrance protectively.

Opening the door, she allowed the dogs to enter. When they spotted Jacob lying stark naked in the center of her lace-canopied bed, they growled.

"Holy cowshit, Bella!" Jacob exclaimed, pushing himself back against the headboard. "Why the hell did you let those two monsters in? You know they hate me."

Smiling, Arabella began to unbutton her gown. "I find it exciting to have them watch us, darling. They bring out the voyeur in me."

"Yeah, well, the only thing they bring out in me is hives. I think I'm allergic to the goddamn things." He began to scratch his arms, then his chest.

Completely naked, Arabella strode to the bed, lifting

her breasts as if offering a treat. "What can I do to make my little boy feel better, darling?" she asked.

It was a game they often played—one of many Bella found wildly erotic. She was a very sensual woman, and Jacob had proven to be an exciting, inventive lover. Far superior to that dunce of a dead husband of hers. Henry couldn't have ignited a fire with a crate of dynamite in his pants.

Jacob's excited growl matched those of the dogs, who landed on the bed at the same time Arabella landed on Jacob.

"Holy cowshit!" was all Jacob had time to say before Arabella silenced him with the sweetest pacifier he'd ever tasted.

7

*Having a jealous wife means
if you come home with a hair on your coat,
you'd better have the horse to match.*

Prudence rose from her chair and crossed to the kitchen window, the peas she'd been shelling left behind on the table, forgotten in the wrath of the storm.

Rubbing the heel of her hand against the pane to remove the condensation, she peered out. The rain lashed hard against the glass, the wind twisting the branches of the nearby oak into grotesque shapes, while its angry howl made her arms prickle with gooseflesh.

"Polly and Louann should have waited until this rain let up before going out to the barn. The pigs could've waited till morning to be fed," she said to Sarah, chafing her arms.

Sarah, who had volunteered to cook dinner in the face of Hannah's continued stubbornness, looked up from the pot of stew she was stirring. Wiping her perspiring forehead with the edge of her apron, she turned to face Prudence. "Now you know Polly promised Will she'd feed for him. He was so intent on accompanying Mr. Peters into town for supplies."

Prudence worried her lower lip over the fact that Brock and Will had been gone for several hours. "I hope they'll be all right. It's nearly dark, and this rain could very well turn to sleet if the temperature continues to drop."

Sarah didn't miss the concern in Prudence's voice and smiled knowingly. Whether Prudence admitted it or not, she cared about what happened to Brock Peters. And that was a good sign—a very good sign. As far as she was concerned, Prudence was too young and pretty to shut herself away from life and love, which is what she'd been doing the last few years.

"I'm sure they'll be fine, Pru. Martin told me that Mr. Peters has loads of common sense. If the storm worsens, they'll most likely spend the night in town."

For a fleeting moment, Prudence wondered whom Brock would be spending the night with. After all, he had told her that he wouldn't hesitate to have his needs taken care of. And for some reason she dared not question, that idea didn't sit well with her. She pushed the disturbing thought away.

"How is Colonel Carstairs? He's not overdoing it, is he?" As much as she liked the friendly cavalry officer, she wanted him gone as soon as possible. His presence was proving too disruptive to the household. And not only with Hannah, she decided, eyeing Sarah speculatively.

"He probably is." Sarah frowned in exasperation. "He balks at taking his afternoon naps. Though I insisted that he take one today."

"You like Colonel Carstairs, don't you, Sarah?" The schoolteacher's cheeks grew pink, but Prudence couldn't tell if it was a genuine blush or the steam rising from the boiling stew that caused the reaction.

"He's a very nice gentleman."

"They all are at first." Prudence sat back at the table and began shelling peas again, remembering how kind Billy had been to Clara when they'd first met.

Knowing she was not about to crack Prudence's hard-shelled opinion of men, Sarah changed the subject. "There's something I've been wanting to discuss with you, Pru. I guess now is as good a time as any."

Prudence dropped the peas back into the bowl and glanced up. "About Colonel Carstairs?"

"Heavens, no!" Sarah said, a little too emphatically. "It's about Polly."

"Polly? What's wrong? Aren't the rooming arrangements working out?"

Prudence had placed the young girl in the same room with Sarah, hoping Sarah would be able to ease the painful separation between Polly and her folks back east. Will had confessed that his sister was homesick for her mother, and Prudence had felt that Sarah, with all her mothering instincts, would make an excellent surrogate.

Sarah shook her head. "It's not that. We get along just fine. Polly's a very warm and loving child."

"Then what?"

"I'm not positive that what I suspect is correct"—she paused—"I don't believe Polly is pregnant."

The green eyes widened in disbelief. "Not pregnant? But why would she come here? Polly misses her parents dreadfully."

"I think Polly has convinced herself that she is going to have a baby. I think it's what doctors call a hysterical pregnancy."

Prudence nodded solemnly. "Yes, I've read about that in my medical journals." It was often referred to as a phantom pregnancy and was usually seen in women who were either very desirous of having a child or who sought to avoid one. These women exhibited many, or all, of the same symptoms as those women who were pregnant, but their symptoms usually disappeared when they were hypnotized or asleep.

"It's difficult to tell, of course, because of Polly's weight, but I've seen her undressed and she doesn't look all that different from the day she arrived six weeks ago. And at night when she's asleep, her belly flattens out like a pancake. It's very odd."

"I suppose I could examine her, but she's so shy, I don't want to embarrass her. And she's so taken with Mary's baby. I'm not sure if she'll be relieved or devastated if she finds out she's not with child."

Having the same concerns, Sarah cautioned prudent action. "I think we should wait a few more weeks. Polly has adjusted to all of us. And Will seems happy, especially now that Mr. Peters has arrived."

And Will had also developed an attachment to Mary and her baby, Prudence thought. That was going to be another problem if Polly had to leave.

What else could go wrong?

Just then Louann and Polly burst through the doorway, their cheeks glowing red from the cold. "It's starting to sleet," they announced in unison, stripping out of their damp coats and hanging them on the coat rack to dry.

What else could go wrong? Prudence heaved a sigh, realizing she should have known better than to ask such a question. It was the law of nature: If things could get worse, they usually did.

*   *   *

Brock glanced out the storefront window of Miller's Mercantile, then up at the regulator clock on the wall. What was keeping Will? He had told the boy to meet him back at the general store at four o'clock, and it was nearly four-thirty.

"Do you think that's going to be it, Mr. Peters?" the portly proprietor asked, loading several more tins of peaches into a box that was already filled with tobacco, baking powder, and tooth soap. "Miss Daniels don't have much more credit on the ledger," he stated bluntly.

Brock's eyes darkened. "Don't worry about the bill, Mr. Miller. I'll be paying cash for what I buy today."

A graying eyebrow rose in speculation. "Is that a fact? You and Miss Daniels good friends or something?"

Brock didn't like the sly smile on the flaccid-cheeked face and leaned across the counter to grasp the proprietor's shirtfront. His voice was as frigid as the sleeting rain outside when he said, "I don't like what you're implying, Miller. I'm Miss Daniels's foreman, nothing more. And if I hear you spreading gossip to the contrary, I'm going to come back here and rearrange that flab on your face. Do I make myself clear?"

George Miller swallowed and nodded emphatically. He'd seen what this man had done to Frank Fitzsimmons, and he didn't want no trouble barking at his door. "Yes, sir, Mr. Peters. I weren't implying a thing. I think Miss Daniels is a fine lady. I used to wait on her pa when old Cody was alive."

Brock released him with a shove. "Well, if that's the case, why do you treat her like she has the plague? Everyone in this town seems to dislike her."

"It ain't Prudence we dislike, but the fact that she runs that ranch for those women. The ladies of this town find it offensive. They think it's immoral, or some such. The reverend cautioned us about associating with sinners."

Brock could see that he was going to have to have another talk with that pious piss-ant of a preacher. "What's immoral is being narrow-minded and mean," Brock replied. He glanced at the clock once again. Damn! Where had Will gone to?

He looked out the window at the darkening sky. They needed to be getting home, and quickly. It was nearly dark, and the way the sleet was falling, the going would be slow and treacherous.

A moment later the bell over the door tinkled. Brock turned, his eyes widening to find Will, wet and bedraggled, entering the store. Both of Will's eyes had been blackened, and his upper lip was bleeding. It was obvious he'd been in a fistfight. But with whom? To his knowledge, Will didn't know a soul in these parts, except for the hands at the R and R.

From the back pocket of his pants he retrieved a handkerchief and stepped forward to hand it to Will. "You all right, boy?"

Bobbing his head up and down, Will pressed the cloth to his lip. "I know you're not going to believe this, Mr. Peters, but I won."

There was such immense pride in his voice when he made the statement that George Miller burst into laughter, his fat belly shaking like a mound of mint jelly. "You sure as hell could've fooled me, young fella. I'd hate to see what the other guy looks like."

Will forced a smile to his lips, then winced, licking at the blood with his tongue. "I ran into Bobby Fitzsimmons down at the saddlery, when I was dropping off those belts and gloves like you told me to, Mr. Peters."

Brock laid a comforting hand on the boy's shoulder, a measure of pride surging through him. "Do you want to tell me about it?"

"Fitzsimmons was spouting off about Mary, and how he had taken advantage of her. He thought it was a big joke, sayin' how gullible she'd been to think he'd fall in love with a dirt-poor, drunk farmer's daughter. He made everyone laugh at her."

Will's face grew florid, almost matching the anger on Brock's as he related the incident. "I punched him hard, Mr. Peters. I think I might have broken his nose . . . at least I hope so. They all said Bobby was going to beat my brains out. But he didn't. I whipped him good."

Wrapping his arm about the boy's shoulder, Brock smiled and gave him a gentle hug. "You done good, Will. I'm proud of you."

Will's smile was so full of genuine affection, it brought a lump to Brock's throat. Trying to swallow past it, he said, "Let's go home, boy. Miss Prudence will be waitin' supper on us."

But supper had long since passed. And everyone except Prudence, who kept vigil in the front room, had retired.

"Where are they?" she asked herself for the hundredth time, pacing back and forth across the brightly colored rag rug. She glanced at the beehive clock on the mantel, then crossed to the window and looked out again.

Sleet pelted the glass, making it difficult to see past the blackness. Sighing in frustration, she turned toward the fire, holding out her hands to warm herself.

She was most likely worrying for nothing. Brock was probably tucked safe and warm in some soiled dove's bed. Will, too, for that matter. She'd heard Brock say to Shorty that it was time Will had a *proper* male education. It didn't take a genius to figure out what that meant.

She frowned. Why should she worry? They were probably having themselves a grand old time. But she did. She was worried sick. And she hated herself for it.

Caring too much causes pain. She had counseled that very thing countless times to her ladies, cautioning them to be circumspect in their feelings toward men.

Clara had cared. And loved. And died. And Prudence was never going to forget that fact. Not even for a man who seemed kind and gentle. Whose smile warmed her heart. Whose laughter sent chills up and down her spine. Whose very nearness made her ache for the impossible dream—the very lie that consumed a woman: that love was forevermore.

The sound of hoofbeats, muffled by the rain, sounded in the yard. Forgetting all her convictions she had just made, Prudence rushed to the window again. With her hands cupped against the glass, she could make out shadows in the distance.

They were home! Brock had returned.

Her heart soared with unwelcome joy, and she took a deep breath, trying to get her emotions in check, wiping her now sweating palms on the skirt of her green wool shirtwaist. A moment later the front door banged open. She couldn't help herself: she moved into the hallway. The sight of Brock, dripping wet, ice frozen to his hair and lashes, brought a lump of relief to her throat.

"Brock!" she cried, rushing forward, stopping just short of throwing herself into his arms. "I was worried about you . . . and Will. Is he all right?"

Hanging his hat and coat on the hall tree, Brock looked up and nodded, removing his boots. "Will's fine, Red. We both are. Thanks for asking." She blushed then, a deep crimson that brought a strange ache to Brock's chest.

It had been a long time since a woman had waited and worried over him. A very long time. And he found that he missed the feeling of being important to someone.

Not liking where his thoughts were trailing, he quipped, "I'm so hungry I could even eat your cooking, Red."

She smiled. "You won't have to. There's plenty of Sarah's stew left over from supper. But first come in by the fireplace and warm up. You look half-frozen."

Brock's fingers tingled like a thousand pinpricks when he held his hands to the flames. He was more than half-frozen. Another hour out in that weather and he and Will would have qualified for igloos.

Will's horse had stumbled and pulled up lame, and they'd had to walk the remaining few miles home. And as slippery and frozen as the ground had become, they'd been like turtles skating on waxed glass.

"Did Will go to bed?" Prudence asked, trying to fill the awkward silence that had suddenly developed between them.

Brock nodded. "He was as hungry as me, but too tired to eat. I hauled him over to the bunkhouse before coming in."

"I thought perhaps you would stay in town." Unable to meet the knowing look that suddenly flared in his eyes, she turned to stare into the flames of the fire.

The firelight added more color to her already glowing cheeks, making the red highlights of her hair shimmer. She was achingly lovely, and he had never been more aware of her as a woman than right now. He realized that he wanted to kiss her—to hold her in his arms. And he hadn't felt that way about a woman in a very long time. Not since Catherine.

He'd had his share of whores to ease the pain of his loneliness over the years, but he'd never let any woman get close to him. And the fact that Prudence was making him think otherwise scared the hell out of him. He didn't want to feel that way about anyone. Not ever again.

"You thought I was going to spend the night with one of the whores in town?" he asked, wondering if it was jealousy or prudishness that motivated her curiosity. "Being with a whore usually doesn't require an entire night."

"I . . ." His bluntness threw her off guard, and she found herself at a loss for words. But only momentarily. "Well, did you?" The grin on his face made her wish she had kept her big mouth shut. Why on earth had she asked such a thing? It was none of her business whom he slept with. Though she doubted he did much sleeping.

"Did I what, Red? You already know I didn't spend the night, so you must be asking whether or not I frequented one of the whores."

"I'd best get to heating up your supper," she said, and started to walk away.

"Red," he called, stopping her in her tracks. "Thanks

for caring about my welfare." He'd let her sort it out if
he was talking about the whores or the storm.

Without looking back, she kept on walking, and
Brock found himself wondering again what it would be
like to kiss Miss Prudence Daniels. And he was fairly
certain that it wasn't going to be that long before he
found out.

8

*Life is one man gettin' hugged
for sneakin' a kiss 'n another gettin' slapped.*

Seven large pumpkins—soon to be jack-o'-lanterns—stood proudly in the center of the long work-table in the great room.

The storm had made attending church an impossibility today, much to Prudence's dismay. But it was nothing compared to the alarm she felt over Brock's suggestion that the hired hands and the ladies get together for a little Sunday afternoon pumpkin-cutting contest.

With Halloween a few weeks away, he had explained, and the weather not conducive to outdoor activity, the contest would be the perfect solution to alleviate everyone's boredom.

Gazing at Brock out of the corner of her eye as he went about the room dividing everyone up into teams, Prudence wondered how he had talked her into such a ridiculous activity. Of course, not everyone felt as she did, judging by the excited expressions on their faces.

"Will, why don't you and Mary form a team?" Brock suggested, winking at the young boy who came to stand behind Mary's chair. Will's bruises were finally fading, and Brock couldn't help but notice how much he had filled out in the last few weeks; the boy was turning into a man.

"Slim, I think you and Laurel might work well together."

"Brock, I'm not sure about that," Prudence said in a voice filled with concern, stopping the gentle giant in his tracks. But when she gazed at Laurel, she saw acceptance rather than fear on her face. "On second thought, I think it will be just fine." Perhaps this would be a first step in bringing Laurel out of her self-imposed cocoon of silence.

Eliza and Shorty paired up, as did Louann and Polly, Burt and Christey. Sarah had gone to fetch Moody, and they would form another team. That only left her and Brock.

Prudence's gaze slid to her foreman, and she found Brock's soft brown eyes upon her. There was mischief in them, and something else she dared not question, and it brought a soft blush to her cheeks.

"Red, why don't you come here and sit down by me?" He patted the space next to him. "Jack-o'-lanterns have always been my forté."

Not wanting to be a spoilsport with everyone staring at her expectantly, she did as he suggested and soon found their forced proximity most uncomfortable.

There was little room around the table, so she couldn't prevent their shoulders from touching. She also couldn't help but smell the spicy scent of Brock's cologne, the pungent aroma of leather from the vest he wore, and it made her very aware and extremely nervous. Her insides were churning harder than a paddle through thick cream, and she didn't know if she'd be able to keep her thoughts on the task at hand. How could she possibly hold a carving knife when her hands were sweating so profusely?

"Hello, everyone," Moody called out in greeting, hobbling into the room, giving Prudence an excuse to focus on something other than the width of Brock's shoulders. Sarah followed close on his heels, looking like a protective mother hen.

"Are you sure you can stand the competition, folks? I used to be quite skilled at this as a child," Moody bragged, easing himself onto a chair.

"Hear that, Red?" Brock said, nudging her arm. "The gauntlet's been laid down. Let's show old Moody what kind of stuff we're made of."

"Here now. Watch who you're callin' old, my boy. These crutches make a pretty decent set of weapons."

A chorus of laughter rang out, then Burt asked, "What's the prize for winning this contest, anyway? No one ever told me."

"It's a day off from chores," Will explained excitedly. "Whoever is judged to have carved the best jack-o'-lantern gets to take the entire day off from his chores." The sandy-haired cowboy seemed impressed by the news.

"Is that so?" Prudence asked, turning to stare at Brock, accusation bright in her eyes. "And who, might I ask, suggested such a thing?"

"Guilty as charged, Red," Brock replied with a wink, turning her insides to butter once more.

"Well, who's going to be the judge?" Polly wanted to know. "If we're all participating, there's no one to be impartial."

"Hannah and Joe have volunteered to do the judging, after much cajoling and a tin of Bull Durham tobacco," Brock said.

Moody made a noise under his breath that sounded like a curse. "Well, there go my chances. Perhaps Sarah should choose another partner."

"I'll do no such thing!" Sarah's response was so vehement, all heads turned to stare at the schoolteacher, while Moody sat there grinning like a cat with a full bowl of cream.

Brock shook his head. "There's no need. Hannah has decided to forgive you for your sins, Moody. And she's going to resume her cooking chores as of this evening's supper."

A loud cheer went up, followed by an enthusiastic round of applause.

"I'm not sure whether or not I should feel insulted," Sarah said in mock affront.

"Well, I know I should," Prudence added. This produced another round of laughter, and quite suddenly Prudence realized that it had been a long time since she had enjoyed herself so much.

"You're spilling seeds all over the floor, you silly old man," Eliza said to Shorty, her lips pursed in displeasure. "Honestly, Mr. Jenkins, you don't have a lick of common sense. You're supposed to put the seeds into the large bowl so we can roast them later."

Shorty didn't utter the nasty retort everyone was expecting. Instead he leaned over and whispered something in Eliza's ear, which made the woman gasp and turn beet red. Nobody heard what he said, but it was enough to put a self-satisfied smirk on Shorty's face and bring a youthful twinkle to Eliza's eyes.

After the group finished carving, Indian Joe and Hannah

walked around the table, studying the pumpkins with no small amount of disapproval.

"These bad medicine," Joe pronounced, staring at Brock's with an intensity that made Prudence slightly nervous. The pumpkin did resemble the Indian ever so slightly; and Joe, whom she knew to be very proud, would not take kindly to being made fun of. "Hmph!" he said, before crossing his arms and moving on. Prudence released the breath she hadn't known she was holding.

When Hannah saw Moody's pumpkin she couldn't help but giggle, for the jack-o'-lantern's eyes were crossed and his mouth held only one sharp tooth.

"Well, who would have believed it?" Moody whispered to Sarah after Hannah was out of earshot. "I think she actually liked my creation. Perhaps I'll name it after her."

Her eyes filling with alarm, Sarah grabbed his arm, saying in her best schoolmarm voice, "You'll do no such thing, Martin Carstairs, unless you want to do the cooking from now on."

"With you by my side, Sarah my dear, it wouldn't be such a chore."

Sarah felt intense heat rise from the tips of her toes to her face and center somewhere below her thickened waist. Way below her waist.

Huddled within the confines of her father's old sheepskin jacket, a pair of leather mule-eared boots on her feet, Prudence ventured out into the frigid night air, hoping a little exercise would assuage the restlessness she'd been feeling since the afternoon.

The sleet had stopped, but the temperature was way below freezing; and as she exhaled, she could see her own breath cloud before her face. Carefully, so as not to slip on the icy surface, she placed one foot in front of the other, crunching her way across the yard in the direction of the graveyard.

Before she could reach her destination, her name was called and she halted, peering into the darkness to find Brock's large form silhouetted against the barn. In a moment he was beside her, grasping her elbow.

"Red, for chrissake! What the hell are you doing out here all alone? You could fall and kill yourself."

Pleased by his concern, but angered by his high-handedness, Prudence's words were sharper than she intended. "I can take care of myself. I've been taking walks in the evening for a number of years."

"Well, that just shows me that you can't take care of yourself, because no one in their right mind would be out on a night like this. It's freezing, in case you hadn't noticed."

"You're out here," she pointed out.

"I was on my way to the barn to check on Will's mare. He's been worried sick about her, and I didn't want him out in this weather, so I volunteered to go."

Her anger melted as quickly as ice in August. "That was very considerate of you." Her voice softened. "Can I help? I know a little bit about horses."

"Hold on to my arm," he instructed. "I'll guide you along."

"Don't be ridiculous," she said, annoyed by his pro-tectiveness. She marched off on her own and hadn't gone five steps when her feet began to give way. Before her behind could connect with the icy ground, Brock was behind her, catching her against him. He lifted her into his arms, despite her vigorous protests, and carried her the rest of the way to the barn.

"Open the door," he instructed.

She crossed her arms over her chest in a gesture of defiance. "Put me down and you can do it yourself." His nearness wreaked havoc within her, and she wanted only to distance herself from him.

He heaved a frustrated sigh. It was colder than a witch's tit and she was arguing with him about opening the damn door. "You are without a doubt the most stubborn woman I have ever met. Now open the door."

His tone of voice was so commanding, so imperious, that despite her desire to thwart him, she did as he bade her. But when they reached the warm interior of the barn, he still did not release her. Instead he carried her to a stack of hay bales and seated himself, cradling her in his lap.

The barn smelled of horse, leather, and alfalfa hay— all comforting, familiar scents. But Prudence felt anything but comfortable.

"Release me at once," she insisted, trying to wiggle out of his grasp. But he only tightened his hold.

"What are you scared of, Red? Haven't you ever been held in a man's arms before?"

Hackles rose at the nape of her neck. "Of course I have." It had only been Jacob, but she wasn't about to admit that to him.

He nuzzled her neck, and she felt goose bumps sprout over her neck, arms, and every other conceivable place on her body.

"You smell good, Red, like lilacs in springtime. I'll never smell another lilac without thinking of you."

A lump formed in her throat and she quit struggling. No one, including Jacob, had ever said such a sweet thing to her before. She took a deep breath to calm her erratic heartbeat.

"I might be stubborn," she admitted, "but you're just the same. You like having your own way."

He grinned, tweaking the end of her nose, thinking that he'd sure like to have his way right now. "That's true," he admitted, settling her more comfortably against him. The feel of her soft buttocks pressing against his groin was pure torture. But it was sweet torture.

"If you hadn't been so contrary, I wouldn't have gotten my dander up. You do tend to bring out the worst in a man."

She nodded in agreement, deciding that Brock was probably right. Her father had always told her that stubbornness and defiance were unattractive traits for a woman to possess. And though she'd done her best to stifle her natural inclinations when Papa was alive, they'd risen to the top anyway—like cream. Papa had been correct: her defiance toward society's rules of decorum had made her anathema in her own community—a community where she had grown up, gone to school, had friends.

That was the one thing she'd missed about being ostracized—not being able to socialize anymore. Today's festivities had made that loss painfully obvious, bringing to mind how much fun she'd had.

"I really enjoyed myself today, Brock. Your idea for the pumpkin-carving contest was a good one."

Her admission surprised Brock, for he'd thought sure, even though she seemed to be having a good time, that she would take him to task for corrupting her pregnant ladies.

"I think everyone did."

The lantern hanging on the wooden beam illuminated the animation on her face. "I was so surprised about Laurel. Why, I actually saw her smile a time or two today." Prudence smiled happily in recollection. "I've despaired of ever seeing such a thing."

"Perhaps it's more than fear that haunts Laurel. Have you ever considered that she might be lonely?"

Prudence bit her lower lip, taking a moment to ponder the comment. "I hadn't thought of that. We've all tried to befriend her, make her feel like part of the family."

"Laurel was married. And although newly wed, I'm sure she had already established a close relationship with her husband. Men and women can be friends, Red. Perhaps Laurel misses the male friendship and companionship that her dead husband provided."

That was the one thing he'd missed the most after Catherine died. They'd been best friends. He could tell her anything, bare his soul; she'd always been there for him, always listened, encouraged, supported him when he needed a boost. And he missed that relationship.

"Do you think that's why she didn't mind when Slim helped her gather the eggs?"

Prudence's question brought his attention back to her. "Slim's a gentle man. I'm sure Laurel senses that about him. He seems quite taken with her. I'd venture to say that because of his slowness, he never really had a lady friend before."

"Perhaps I need to rethink some things," she admitted.

Turning her toward him, Brock tightened his hold and drew her close to his chest. He gazed into eyes that were cautious but curious, feeling himself being pulled under an emerald wave of passion.

"I want to kiss you, Red. I want to kiss you in the worst way." And he suddenly realized it was true, for he'd thought of little else since the night of the storm when she'd been waiting for him to come home.

Prudence couldn't breathe, couldn't answer; she could only stare at the lips that were inches from her own, wonder what it would feel like to have them pressed against hers. She didn't have to wonder long, for suddenly Brock's lips descended, his mouth covering hers in masterful persuasion.

His tongue traced the softness of her lower lip, sending her stomach into a wild swirl. Then his mouth covered hers hungrily, searching, tasting, wanting, creating a need that centered deep within her, stirring the embers of a passion that had lain dormant many years.

Prudence was shocked by her own response, by the fact that she hungered as he seemed to hunger. She couldn't control the hands that crept around his neck, the fingers that toyed with the soft curls at his nape, the soft moan of pleasure that escaped from her throat when his tongue plunged deeply, then retreated, over and over again.

When he lifted his head to stare into her eyes, she stared back as if dazed. Never before had she felt so all-consumed, so on fire, and it terrified her.

Rearing back like a skittish filly, she braced her arms against his chest to distance herself from him, shaking her head in denial.

Brock saw confusion and passion on her face, but he wasn't about to feel guilty. It was time Prudence Daniels owned up to being a woman. "I wish I could say I was sorry, Red, but I'm not. I've been wanting to do that since the first day I laid eyes on you."

She swallowed, and her senses began to clear. "Kisses are merely impulsive acts," she said, trying to rationalize her behavior. "I guess it's only human nature to act impulsively and irrationally upon occasion." Her throaty whisper sounded strange to her ears.

He grinned and set her from him, sliding her off his lap onto the bale of hay. "If you believe that, then you are more naive than I thought. Kissin' is purely pleasurable,

Red. Kissin' and touching and making love. If it's impulsive and irrational, then what's wrong with that? You know what they say about the best laid schemes. . . ."

She was angry now, standing on her feet, glaring at him in that righteous way he found so appealing. "And what do they say about consequences? About facing responsibility for one's action?" she asked.

"Your name's not Clara, and mine's not Billy—it's Brock. Why don't you try to remember that?" He turned then, walking away toward the rear of the barn, leaving Prudence to stare openmouthed after him.

When she realized that he'd gotten the last word, and that he had no intention of coming back, she kicked at the hay bale, wishing it was his head, and stormed out of the barn, her temper providing the heat for her nippy walk back to the house. All she could think about upon entering the ranch house was rushing upstairs to her room, sinking into her warm bed, and pulling the comforter over her head to try to block out the humiliating episode that had just occurred. But as her foot hit the bottom tread of the stairs, a small voice called out to her, and she turned to find Mary coming toward her. She was cradling BJ to her breast.

"Miss Pru, is something the matter? Your face is all red and you look plumb awful."

Prudence took a deep breath. "No, nothing," she lied. She stepped forward to gaze at the baby who slept so peacefully in his mother's arms, feeling like a hypocrite because of all the times she had lectured Mary and the others on the evils of the flesh.

"I'm just a little cold. I took a walk. My face must be chapped from the wind." Much to her relief, Mary seemed to accept the story at face value.

"I couldn't sleep. BJ was fretful and I just got him settled down a few minutes ago."

Sensing that the young woman wanted to talk, Prudence suggested, "Why don't we go into the parlor and have a cup of hot chocolate? Hannah usually leaves some for me on the stove. I'll go fetch it."

Prudence hurried to get the chocolate while Mary settled herself on the rocker, and the scene that welcomed Prudence upon her return brought a lump to her throat.

Mother and child rocked contentedly by the fire; both appeared to be asleep. It was the picture of innocence, of purity. And it made Prudence yearn for things she hadn't thought of in a long time. Things like a husband, a child, a family to call her own.

She shook herself, placing the wooden tray on the table next to the rocker quietly, so as not to waken them. She was just being fanciful—foolish. Just because she had exchanged a few kisses with a man who was practically a stranger didn't mean she should forget everything she believed in, had preached to others.

Love was a lie, and the proof of that was sitting right before her. No matter what lustful feelings she might have for Brock, she must never forget that he was a man.

And men took what they wanted and left.

That would never happen to her, she decided. Not ever.

"Oh, my darling . . . oh, my darling . . . oh, my darling Clementine. You are lost and gone forever, dreadful sorry, Clementine. . . ."

Prudence paused in the doorway of the kitchen, smiling at the sight of Brock cradling BJ against his chest, crooning softly to him in the early morning quiet. She stood staring, unable to believe the incongruous sight of the tall, tough cowboy holding the small, fragile infant. But then she remembered that Brock was really a very gentle person inside, not at all like the rough-tough image he sometimes portrayed, and it made her eyes mist. Convictions, she decided, were often difficult to keep.

He was gazing down at the baby with a faraway look in his eyes, as though he were seeing someone else. And then she remembered the name he'd called out at the cemetery. *Catherine.* Had Catherine been his wife? Had she died in childbirth?

The thought of Brock loving someone else brought a sharp pain to her chest, though she didn't know why, and she took a deep breath to quell it.

"Good morning," she said, interrupting his unorthodox lullaby in midverse. Brock's cheeks reddened in mortification, reminding her of a small boy who'd just been caught with his hand in the cookie jar. "I see Mary has convinced you to tend BJ this morning."

"Mary's out feeding the chickens and gathering the eggs. I told her I'd mind BJ until she returned," he said. What he didn't say was how he relished the chance to hold a baby in his arms again, to feel BJ's small, trusting hand wrap around his finger, to smell the sweet talc scent of his body . . . to remember.

"You seem very comfortable holding the child. Most men would be all thumbs." Pain flashed in his eyes, and she wished she could call back her words.

"It's a natural instinct, I guess," he said with a shrug, not wanting to discuss Josh's death with anyone, especially someone he knew would understand. Needing to throw her off base, he added flippantly, "Sort of like kissing." His ploy worked; Prudence blushed a deep crimson.

"It's very ungentlemanly of you to bring that up. Please refrain from doing so again. It was a mistake, and I'll take full responsibility for it."

The baby stirred, and Brock lifted him over his shoulder, patting him gently on the back. "You take full responsibility for just about everything, don't you, Red?"

"I asked you not to call me by that hideous nickname," she reminded him.

"You can ask all you want, Red. I usually do what I want, when I want, to whom I want. And I don't like being told otherwise."

Her hands balled into fists. "You are an infuriating, stubborn, mulish, son of a—"

"Tsk, tsk, tsk. Let's remember there's a baby present. Besides"—he grinned—"mulish and stubborn are rather redundant, don't you think?"

With a look that could intimidate a mountain lion, Prudence spun on her heel and disappeared into the larder; she returned a moment later, carrying a slab of bacon under her arm and a handful of potatoes.

Brock grimaced. "Please tell me you are not going to cook again this morning! I promise to shut up." Jesus! It had taken days for his stomach to quiet down after the last episode of her cooking.

She smiled nastily. "If I thought shutting you up was that easy, Mr. Peters, I would threaten to cook for you every day."

"There are other ways of shutting me up, Red. Ways that are much more enjoyable." He stared meaningfully at her lips, which were soft and full and immensely kissable, as last night had proven.

The cast-iron frying pan banged against the cookstove with such force, it jolted BJ awake, and he began to cry loudly.

"Now see what you've gone and done," Brock accused angrily, rising from the chair. He began to walk back and forth across the kitchen floor, trying to comfort the frightened child. "I'll have you know it took me thirty minutes to get this baby to sleep."

She spun around, braced for battle, her green eyes flashing fire. "And I'll have you know, *Mr. Peters,* that I don't appreciate your making such . . . such improper remarks. And if you do so again, I'll be forced to take this frying pan and bring it down upon your very thick skull."

At that moment Moody entered the kitchen, propping himself on his crutches as he stood in the doorway. He stared first at Brock, who looked angrier than a stallion in a corral full of pregnant mares, then at Prudence, who was doing a credible impression of a fire-breathing dragon.

"Is there a problem?" he asked.

"No!" came the reply, loudly and succinctly, from the couple who stared daggers at each other across the room.

A graying brow arched up, and he smiled. "That's good. I'd hate to think that you two were having a spat." At the furious looks they directed at him, Moody threw back his head and roared with laughter.

9

A good friend is one who tells you your faults in private.

"*I will not* attend the harvest ball and that's final!" Prudence declared, crossing her arms firmly over her chest.

"But Miss Prudence," Louann wailed, "we ain't been to town in weeks 'cause of the weather, and we ain't had much fun to speak of." Not wanting to appear ungrateful, and unwilling to meet Prudence's furious gaze, Louann stared down at her feet.

"Please, Miss Prudence," Mary implored, tossing Brock a sly smile. "Me and Will was lookin' forward to going. He said he would even teach me how to dance."

Brock leaned against the mantel in the great room and smiled to himself in satisfaction. He knew if he broached the subject of the ball in front of the women, Prudence wouldn't stand a chance. He could see by the uncertain expression on her face that she was weakening.

The harvest ball would be the perfect opportunity to get Prudence and her brood assimilated back into Absolution society, something he felt they would all benefit from, especially Prudence, who needed more out of life than worrying about a ranch and a bunch of pregnant ladies.

"It doesn't seem like it would do much harm, Pru," Sarah added, feeling guilty at the hurt expression Prudence threw at her.

Prudence heaved a sigh as she looked at each individual woman. Christey had already volunteered to stay with Mary's baby, so she couldn't even use that for an excuse not to go. And Eliza, who she thought sure would take her part, had been most enthusiastic about attending the ball. Of course, ever since the pumpkin-carving contest, she'd been making cow eyes at Shorty Jenkins.

What on earth was this ranch coming to? she wondered. And then she turned to stare at Brock, who she knew was at the center of all her problems, and her frown deepened.

He was smiling smugly at her, as he'd been doing since that awful fight they'd had in the kitchen two days ago, and she wanted to slap the superior look right off his face. But she couldn't. It was bad enough Moody had witnessed her show of temper; she wasn't about to give the others fodder for gossip.

Staring out the window, she caught sight of the sun and sighed again. Even the weather had conspired against her. Perhaps they'd have a full-blown snowstorm by tomorrow, and the ball would be canceled.

"Well, Red, have you come to a decision?" Brock prompted. "There's going to be some mighty disappointed ladies and gents if your answer is no."

"I can't believe everyone wants to be subjected to

ridicule and snide remarks. I'm sure I don't have to explain to all of you"—she gestured wide with her hand—"that the townsfolk are not going to be happy that you're there."

"Since when have you let that stop you, Miss Prudence?" Shorty asked. "You usually look straight through those old biddies."

"I'm not concerned for myself, but for the others." But that wasn't entirely true, and she could see by the look of disbelief on Brock's face that he knew it. Coward! he shouted silently at her. But it wasn't easy being the center of scorn and controversy. It was one thing to go into town for supplies and to attend church. But it was quite another to go just because of some frivolous barn dance.

And that's all it was! Arabella Potts could call it a harvest ball if she wanted. But it was nothing more than a stupid barn dance.

The expectancy in the air grew thick, while Prudence turned once again to stare out the window. Brock looked at Mary and Will and winked, catching sight of Eliza's blush as Shorty whispered something in her ear. Who would have thought it? Shorty and Eliza? But the old man had been as feisty as a calf in clover, to use one of Shorty's own expressions.

Brock shook his head. If he didn't know it was autumn, he'd swear every man in this room suffered from spring fever. He had to admit, it was getting to be downright contagious. Thoughts of Prudence had occupied his mind of late. In fact, since that night he'd kissed her, he could think of little else except doing it again. Except, of course, those nights when he'd lie in bed and mentally strip off every piece of her clothing, then make passionate love to her. God, it was sweet torture!

His gaze lingered on her, and he heaved a discontented sigh. Was she a witch? Had she cast some type of spell over him?

"I guess we'll go," Prudence finally said, and the collective sigh of relief interrupted Brock's lurid thoughts. "But if there's any trouble"—she narrowed her eyes at the hands—"any at all, we're turning around and coming home. Is that clear?"

Everyone said it was, and then all the men filed out to finish up their chores before supper.

That was another thing that had changed since Brock had come to the R and R. The men and women were now taking their meals together, Prudence having been outvoted eleven to one in favor of the change.

Noting that Brock still lingered by the door, Prudence stepped across the room to confront him. "Are you satisfied that you've caused a mutiny among my own people?"

Definitely a witch! he concluded.

Unwilling to speak in front of the others, Brock grasped her by the arm, and hauled her into the front room, away from prying eyes and inquisitive ears. "You might think you know what's right for those women, Red," he said, "but you don't. They don't want to be isolated like they've got some disease. They need to feel normal, wanted." She started to protest, but he held up his hand. "You can preach all you want about staying away from the wickedness of men, or whatever it is you spout." She blushed, so he guessed he was near the mark. "I'm just saying that these women are women, no matter if they're pregnant. And women want men, and vice versa. There's nothing you can do to change that. It's a fact of nature. And the way God intended."

Tears stung behind her lashes, but she refused to let Brock see that he'd hurt her feelings. "Everything was fine until you came here. None of the women wanted to be around the men. They all obeyed the rules."

He sighed and led her by the hand to the sofa. "I'm not faulting you for what you've attempted to do for these women. But you must know that people have instincts."

"Like animals, you mean!"

"You know what your problem is, Red? You haven't been kissed nearly enough. If you'd been made love to, you wouldn't be making those kinds of remarks."

Gasping, she turned as red as her hair. "You are the most . . ."

But she never finished her sentence, because Brock pulled her toward him, wrapped his arms about her, and planted a kiss upon her lips. When she resisted he increased the pressure, thrusting his tongue into her mouth until he felt her acquiescence. He kissed her long and hard and then released her, smiling into her dazed face before standing to take his leave.

"Women are a lot like horses, Red. They need a firm but gentle hand to take the orneriness out of them." He strode toward the door, but the sound of Prudence's very loud expletive made him turn just in time to see a heavy vase sailing straight at him. He ducked, and it crashed into the wall directly over his head.

"What the hell did you go and do that for?"

Breathing heavily, her nostrils flaring, she shouted, "Next time, you randy stallion, I'm going to aim a lot lower! And you're going to find yourself gelded and put out to pasture."

Prudence's hair had come loose from the coil at the back of her neck, and it lay about her shoulders all wild and untamed, just like her behavior at the moment. And Brock wondered what it would be like to have all that pent-up fury, that wildness, unleashed in his bed.

"You sure are pretty when you're mad, Red," he said, grinning.

"*Ooooh!*" she screeched, just before the second piece of pottery hit the wall.

Fortunately Brock had already taken his leave.

The barn where the dance was being held stood at the south end of town. Music and laughter drifted out into the street as the Daniels wagon pulled up in front of it.

The sky was black satin, studded with stars that glittered like diamonds, sparkling prettily like the excitement dancing in Louann's eyes.

"Oh!" she exclaimed. "They're playing 'Buffalo Gals.' I just love dancing to that."

"What makes you so sure you're going to be asked, Louann? Don't forget, you're pregnant and don't look nearly as desirable as you used to," Polly pointed out, a smug smile creasing her face.

Fluffing her hair, which she had left long to drape around her shoulders, Louann replied, "I look better on a bad day than you could ever hope to look on your best day."

"Well . . ."

"Let's stop this bickering right now, girls," Prudence warned in a stern voice, "or we'll be turning this buckboard around and heading home. I didn't want to come to this dance in the first place. I hope you'll both remember that." And she hadn't changed her mind, despite the fact that Sarah had talked her into wearing her pretty green wool dress with the white lace collar and cuffs. Her Christmas dress, Hannah called it.

Setting the brake, Brock jumped down to help Prudence off, while the other hands assisted the rest of the ladies. His eyes roamed over her appreciatively, taking in the new gown and cape he hadn't seen before. "You look mighty fetching tonight, Red. Green is definitely your color."

"Thank you," she replied, unwilling to return the compliment, though he looked equally as fine. Garbed in snug black pants that molded his muscular thighs, a light blue shirt with a bright red bandanna tied around his neck, and a black leather vest, he exuded masculinity, but she was not about to admit that to him, or herself.

They entered the crowded barn and went unnoticed at first, giving Prudence time to take in her surroundings. She had to admit that the ladies of Absolution had outdone themselves with the decorations. Bright orange streamers hung from the wooden rafters and crisscrossed the window. Bales of hay were stacked along the far wall, displaying dozens of carved jack-o'-lanterns the town's children had made. Prizes would be awarded later, she knew, for she'd had the good fortune to win one once, in another lifetime.

"Would you care for something to drink, Red?" Brock asked, helping her off with her cape and draping it over a hay bale designated for that purpose.

The refreshment table, which was really two sawhorses with a board stretched between them that had been covered with a sheet, was laden with all kinds of goodies—cakes, pies, and doughnuts of every type imaginable and three large bowls of punch.

She wagged her head, tapping her toe in time to the music, in spite of her determination not to have a good time. But Brock noticed. "Why don't we dance? It's been a while, but I've been told I'm pretty good."

"I don't . . ."

At her hesitation, he added, "All the other ladies are dancing."

And then she saw that he was right. Mary was sashaying about with Will—rather clumsily, but nevertheless sashaying—Eliza was dancing with Shorty and looking like she were in seventh heaven, and even Laurel, who was standing next to Slim, was clapping her hands and smiling. Sarah, wearing her protective mother hen look, was seated next to Moody.

"You're not scared, are you? Scared of what people might say?"

She was scared all right. Scared of being held close in his arms, scared of the tumult of emotions he raised in her breast, scared of giving in to the desire he made her feel. But she wasn't going to admit that to him.

Tilting up her chin, she said, "People have been talking about me for years. Why should I let their opinions matter now?"

"Because my guess is that you've never been here in the arms of a man before." He clasped her around the waist possessively. "But I guess there's a first time for everything."

To avoid a scene, she allowed him to lead her out on the dance floor. "I have danced with other men before, I'll have you know." True, they were mostly friends of her father's—but she had danced.

"Well, that suitor of yours, Jacob Morgan, appears to be occupied this evening."

She glanced across the room, her eyes widening in surprise to find Jacob in the arms of Arabella Potts. Arabella was an attractive widow—full-blown, was how the fashion magazines described her figure—and she couldn't help but notice what a handsome couple they made. She hadn't known they were even acquainted. But then she didn't venture into town all that often.

And it was really none of her business whom Jacob called upon. After all, they weren't affianced. But she had to admit, the thought of losing her one and only suitor was a bit disconcerting, which is why she replied, "Mrs. Potts is a widow, and I'm sure Jacob is merely being polite in asking her to dance."

"I'm sure," Brock said, pulling the naive woman into his chest and twirling her around and around. Prudence could think whatever she wanted to about Morgan, but he'd seen where Arabella Potts's hand had strayed, and it had put a pretty huge grin on old Jacob's face.

The feel of Brock's arm around her waist, his hand grasping hers, made Prudence feel all giddy inside. Her stomach kept fluttering like butterfly wings each time he drew her close, and gooseflesh covered her arms and neck when he bent over to whisper something in her ear, his warm breath tickling her lobe like a feather.

Why did he have this effect on her? He was only a man—an infuriating one at that—and she didn't even like men. At least that's what she'd been telling herself all these years. And she prayed to the holy Father in heaven that she hadn't been lying to herself.

When the dance ended and the music stopped, the whispering began. It became so loud, it was like a drone in a beehive.

"I knew we shouldn't have come," Prudence said to Sarah. They were standing next to the refreshment table, enjoying a glass of punch, while Brock visited with Moody. "These people don't want us here."

"Maybe so, Pru. But everyone has been polite so far. And we have as much right to enjoy ourselves as they do. Maybe they'll change their opinion of us, if they see that we're no different from them."

Before Prudence could respond, Jacob walked up behind her and tapped her on the shoulder.

"Why, Prudence, honey, I didn't expect to see you

here tonight. If I'd known you wanted to come, I'd have invited you myself."

Prudence returned his smile and wondered why he hadn't. "You remember Sarah Davenport, don't you, Jacob?"

"But, of course!" He leaned over to kiss Sarah's hand, and the gesture alerted Moody, who scowled deeply at the man.

"Who the hell is that?" Moody whispered to Brock. "He reminds me of a goddamned predatory wolf."

A wolf in sheep's clothing, Brock said silently, having had similar thoughts himself. "That's Prudence's neighbor, Jacob Morgan. He owns the Bar J."

Moody nodded knowingly. "So, he's the one?"

"I see Shorty's wasted no time in your education."

"What's being done about him? It won't be much longer till I can sit a horse again, then I'll be able to help out."

Brock's eyes narrowed as he watched Jacob escort Prudence onto the dance floor. "Red likes him—trusts him. And that makes matters worse. We tried to tell her he was playing her dirty, but she didn't believe us."

"He seems quite taken with her, but that big-busted woman in the blue satin dress don't seem to take kindly to it."

Brock glanced over at Arabella Potts, who was staring at Morgan as though she wanted to rip out his throat. He smiled. "It seems Mr. Morgan has a few secrets he hasn't shared with his widowed friend. I bet she has no idea that he's asked Prudence to marry him."

Moody's eyes widened in disbelief. "Marry! Shit! You're not going to allow that to happen, are you?"

Brock shrugged. "There's not much I can do. I'm just the foreman. And Prudence is a grown woman." And he had no claim on her heart.

A disgusted snort flew out. "Miss Pru might be all woman on the outside, but I'd venture a guess that she's just a little girl within. Her marrying that varmint would be like tossing a lamb into a fox's lair."

"I didn't say she was going to marry him. I just said he had asked her."

"For all Prudence's staunch beliefs and lectures to these pregnant women on the unfaithfulness of men, I'd venture a guess that she's never even been with a man. I can spot a virgin quicker than I can spit. And she's definitely a ripe plum for some old farmer like Morgan to pluck."

The thought of Morgan with his greedy hands all over Prudence's satiny-soft body was enough to make Brock's hands clench into fists. There was no way in hell he was going to allow that conniving, stealing sonofabitch to pick any unblemished fruit. Not as long as he had a breath left in him.

"By that nasty expression on your face, Brock, I would say that you're thinking of doing a little fruit picking of your own."

Brock shook his head. "Prudence Daniels is not someone to dally with. She's a woman made for the long run. Getting tangled up with her would mean putting down roots. And you know how I feel about that."

"A shallow-rooted tree doesn't survive long, Brock. Pretty soon it withers and dries up inside till there's nothing left but a hollow trunk. I know you're scared of commitment, of being hurt again, but maybe it's time to put your past behind you. I was devastated when Martha died, but life goes on."

"You should take your own advice, Colonel." Brock glanced over at Sarah, who was smiling prettily and waving at Mary, who was dancing again with Will. "I don't see you sinking your taproot down in Sarah Davenport's forest."

Moody threw back his head and laughed so hard that tears came to his eyes. "By God, boy, I should thrash you good for that comment. But I won't. Because it just so happens that I've been giving that idea some very hefty consideration." Suddenly he frowned with uncertainty. "I'm just not sure Sarah would want to hitch herself to an old cart like me."

"Women were put on the face of this earth to bedevil a man." Brock's eyes followed Prudence's every movement, narrowing when Morgan's hand moved below her waist. *That dirty old bastard!*

"Yes, my boy, that's true," Moody agreed, smiling. "But I, for one, would not want to live on this earth without them. They've got some pretty angelic parts, after all."

Brock's eyes traveled from Prudence's face, down her neck, to the fullness of her breasts, then lower, and he sighed in frustration. Angelic was an understatement!

Damn the woman! Why did it have to be that hardnosed, opinionated, man-hating spinster he wanted?

"I hate to admit this, but I had a delightful time," Prudence confessed, whispering so as not to wake the tired bunch in the back of the wagon. "I haven't danced so much in years."

Brock scowled and clucked his tongue to urge the horses into a trot. They were only a short distance from the ranch, and he was tired and eager to get into his bunk. And he was in no mood to hear what a wonderful time Prudence had in the arms of Jacob Morgan. She'd danced practically every dance with him.

"I never realized Jacob was such an accomplished dancer. Why, to think we actually won a prize . . ." She shook her head, clutching the ceramic figurine of the dancing girl in her hand and smiling to herself. "Did you have a good time?"

"Great! Just great!" he retorted with no small amount of sarcasm.

Prudence huddled deeper into her cloak, unconsciously snuggling closer to Brock to get warm. It didn't escape his notice, and he groaned aloud.

"I'm sorry. Is something the matter? You don't seem to be your usual . . . self this evening." She'd been about to say "annoying" but thought better of it. After all, they had just spent a pleasant evening together. Why spoil it by arguing?

He was going to answer that there was definitely something the matter, but before he could respond, frantic shouts came toward them out of the darkness.

Burt pulled up alongside the buckboard, gasping and trying to catch his breath. "Hurry, Brock, hurry. The bunkhouse is on fire!"

Prudence screamed, then covered her mouth.

"Jesus!" Brock swore and urged the horses into a gallop. "Hang on back there," he yelled to his passengers, who were now wide awake and full of questions that went unanswered.

As they neared the ranch house they could see orange flames shooting into the sky. The dry timbers of the old bunkhouse had gone up like kindling, making Brock wonder how the fire could have started. They'd been careful to extinguish the lanterns before leaving for the dance.

Grabbing Brock's forearm, Prudence asked, her eyes wide with fright, "Do you suppose Hannah and Joe are all right? Their cabin sits only a few yards away from the bunkhouse."

Brock was saved from answering when Shorty yelled out, "Indian Joe's about as smart an Injun as ever I seen,

Miss Pru. Don't you worry now. Him and that squaw are goin' to be right as rain."

Which is what they could use 'long about now, Prudence thought as the raging inferno came into view. It was obvious they weren't going to be able to save the old building, which was now completely engulfed in flames. But they needed to prevent the fire from spreading to the main house.

Pulling the wagon to a halt, Brock issued orders for Shorty to help the women and Moody into the house, then join him out at the bunkhouse. Moody protested vehemently that he could be of help, but Brock overrode him.

"I'll change my clothes and come, too," Prudence offered, unwilling to let the men take such a risk on her behalf.

"No!" Brock was emphatic. "You'll stay inside with the women. Prepare some food or something. Maybe bandages. We might need doctoring when we're through." When he saw she was about to protest, he added, "Please, Red. Just do as I say this once without an argument."

She nodded, and he disappeared around the side of the house.

The waiting became unbearable. At least Joe and Hannah were all right, and Prudence gave a silent prayer of thanks to the Almighty for that. The wind had changed, shifting to fan the flames in the opposite direction, and their log cabin had been spared.

Sarah joined her in the kitchen, where she was in the midst of fixing sandwiches. At least it occupied her time, she thought, even if her creations weren't the most edible in the world.

"Everyone is bedded down," Sarah said. "Even Martin, and that was no small chore. I finally had to put some laudanum into his hot chocolate. He's going to hate me in the morning."

Prudence smiled halfheartedly at the distraught woman. "When it comes to you, Sarah, I don't think the colonel has hate on his mind." Ignoring the woman's blush, she added, "Why don't you go on up to bed? I can handle things from here on out."

Rubbing the small of her back, Sarah sighed wearily. "Are you sure? I hate to leave you in the midst of all this chaos."

Prudence was as eager as anyone to climb into bed. It had been a long, worrisome night. She had already donned her nightgown and robe, and as soon as the men returned safely, she had every intention of turning in. But she knew she wouldn't be able to sleep a wink as long as Brock and the others were still out there fighting the fire.

"They can't be much longer. Will was in a few minutes ago to say that the fire was almost out. And you have the baby to think about. After all, you had a tiring evening. You need to rest."

"What about you? You take care of everyone else, never giving a thought to your own needs."

Piling the sandwiches on the plate, Prudence replied, "My needs are few, Sarah. I'm not pregnant, so I don't require as much rest."

"It was your emotional health I was questioning. You never take time for yourself. Never give yourself a chance to just relax."

"But I had fun tonight. I relaxed."

"Did you? I saw the way you hovered over everyone, making sure no one was overdoing. And every time you were on the dance floor with Mr. Morgan, I saw your gaze drift over to Martin and Brock, like you were making sure they were all right, too."

Prudence busied herself with getting the rest of the food together. There was no way she was going to explain why Brock's activities had occupied the better part of her evening. They'd only danced the one time, and she'd been obsessed with knowing if there was someone else he wanted to spend his time with besides her. But Jacob had kept her so busy, she had lost track of him as the evening progressed.

She changed the subject to the weather, and Sarah, losing interest in the conversation, made her excuses and went off to bed, leaving Prudence to wait alone.

Sarah hadn't been gone but a few minutes when the back door flew open, emitting a blast of cold air, and Brock entered, assisted by Shorty. Both men were covered with soot from head to toe, and Brock was holding his side, his face etched in pain.

"Brock's been hurt, Miss Pru. I think you'd better take a look at him."

10

*A year of nursin' don't equal
a day of sweetheart.*

Choking back a frightened cry, Prudence rushed forward, helping Brock onto the chair despite his protests that he was perfectly all right.

"Me and the others are going to bunk down at Injun Joe's tonight," Shorty informed her. "He said we could sleep on the floor. I figured it was best if Brock stayed here so's you could tend him proper."

Prudence swallowed hard at the idea of Brock staying in the house with her. "But where will I put him? Colonel Carstairs is already asleep, and there's only one bed in his room."

"Never mind," Brock said wearily, starting to rise. He sure as hell wasn't going to stay where he wasn't wanted. And he could see from the horrified expression on Prudence's face that she thought the idea smacked of impropriety. "I can make do out in the barn."

The barn! But it was freezing outside, Prudence thought, suddenly feeling guilty that she'd put her own fears before an injured man's needs.

With a heavy hand, Shorty pushed Brock back down on the chair, and the look he cast Prudence made her feel smaller than the lowliest ant. "Ain't your pa's room available, Miss Pru?"

Panic assailed her. Her father's room was right next door to hers. In fact, there was a connecting door between them. But, seeing the reproachful look on Shorty's face, she knew she had no choice. Reluctantly she inclined her head. "Of course, how stupid of me. You can go on now, Mr. Jenkins. I can tend Mr. Peters by myself."

"Don't you need help hauling him up the stairs?" Shorty's concern became sidetracked when he eyed the plate of sandwiches on the table. "Mind if I take these with me?"

"Take them. And don't worry about Mr. Peters, he'll be in good hands."

Brock winked at Shorty, and the old man knew it was time to take his leave. "Gotcha."

"You sure this isn't going to be an imposition, Red?" Brock allowed her to help him out of the chair. "You didn't seem too crazy about the idea."

Noting the singed fabric of his vest and shirt, she wagged her head absently, wondering how serious his injuries were beneath them. "I was merely taken off guard. I shouldn't have given you the impression that you weren't welcome," she said, placing her arm around his waist to guide him out of the kitchen and into the hallway.

"Hell, Red," he said, forcing a smile, though his injuries were starting to pain him, "I knew I wasn't welcome from the first day I stepped onto this place."

His barb hit too close to home. "Grab the banister," she ordered rather sharply, adding as an afterthought, "Please."

Her original welcome had been something less than cordial, she thought guiltily, thanking her lucky stars her father hadn't been here to witness it. Cody Daniels had been a stickler for hospitality. No man in need had ever been turned away from the R and R without a decent meal or a chance to earn a day's wages.

"Sometimes I can be a bit harsh," she admitted when they'd reached the top of the stairs.

It was the closest thing to an apology he was likely to get from her, so he just nodded, and allowed her to guide him into her father's old bedroom.

The room, filled with massive pieces of oak furniture, smelled musty from lack of use. A big black leather chair stood beside the hearth, and Brock longed to sink onto it.

"Sit here on the bed," Prudence instructed. And when he did, she helped him remove his vest and began to unbutton his shirt. "We'll need to clean your wounds. Burns can get infected quite easily."

She bit her lower lip in concentration as she worked the bone buttons through the holes, then her eyes widened as they took in his naked chest. Hadn't she ever seen a man undressed before? he wondered. But he already knew the answer: Prudence Daniels was as pure and untouched as the first snowfall of the season. Was she as cold?

Prudence gazed at the mass of muscles, the soft furring of hairs on his chest, and felt her mouth go dry. He was even more handsome without his clothes on, she thought, feeling her face warm. The burns on his chest weren't serious, thank goodness. She supposed the leather vest had something to do with that.

Fetching the basin of water off the washstand, she rinsed out the rag and, as gently as she could, washed the grime off his face.

"You've got a gentle touch, Red. I was beginning to wonder if there was anything gentle about you."

His words caused her blush to deepen, but she kept on rinsing the rag, wiping it over his face until all the soot had been washed away.

"I don't believe anyone has washed my face since I was knee high to a grasshopper," he continued, trying to keep his mind off the lush breasts that were close enough to touch. The smell of lilac drifted over him, and he longed to press his lips against the white flesh of her neck that was exposed to his view.

Green eyes locked with brown, and they stared at each other, noting the pent-up hunger reflected in each other's eyes.

"I . . . must fetch the salve," Prudence said hurriedly, needing desperately to put distance between them. "I'll only be a moment."

She ran out the door, and Brock watched her go, heaving a deep sigh of frustration. Dammit, but he wanted her! Wanted her in the worst way. He felt his need rising, pressing painfully against his pants, and he tried to focus on other things.

There was a painting hanging on the wall next to the bureau that looked an awful lot like Prudence, except for the fact that the woman's hair was brown, not red. A Winchester rifle leaned against the corner of the fireplace, as if waiting for Cody Daniels's return.

Prudence came back a moment later, carrying the salve and some gauze; and it looked as if she'd rinsed her face in the bathroom sink before returning, because the front of her nightgown, where her robe had gaped open, was all wet.

Her breasts stood out more plainly than before, and he couldn't seem to take his eyes off their soft roundness as she leaned forward to smooth the salve over his burns with gentle fingers.

The feel of Brock's warm flesh beneath her fingertips did crazy things to Prudence's insides. Her heart pounded so loudly in her ears, it could probably be heard clear over in the next county, she decided. When her knuckles accidentally brushed his nipples, and she heard his sharp intake of breath, she pulled back her hand, reaching quickly for the gauze to wrap around his chest.

"That should keep your burns from getting infected," she stated once she'd finished. She started to turn away, but Brock grabbed her wrist, preventing her escape.

"Red, don't leave just yet. I haven't had a chance to thank you properly."

The glimmer in his eyes told her exactly what kind of "thank you" Brock had in mind, and it frightened and excited her all at the same time. She was so startled when he pulled her down next to him on the bed, she didn't protest.

"I'm sorry we weren't able to save the bunkhouse."

It wasn't what she had expected him to say, and it touched her in some strange way. "I know that you and the others did all you could, and I thank you for it."

He reached out to toy with the red curls covering her breast. "You've got such lovely hair, Red, like curls of fire. It was the first thing I noticed about you."

His voice was mesmerizing, seductive, and she fought against its pull. "It's an unruly mess most of the time. I've always envied girls like Louann, who have straight, silky hair."

"I wouldn't trade Louann's hair for yours," he said, leaning into her as he brought the curls to his nose. "You smell so good, Red." He nuzzled her neck and ear, running his tongue over her flesh. "And taste so good, too."

"Brock . . ." It was all she had time to say before his lips closed over her mouth. He drew her down on the bed, half covering her body with his own. And all she could think of was that this was wrong, so very wrong. But she didn't have the strength of will, or the desire, to fight him.

Giving in to her own hunger, she kissed him back with a passion she didn't know existed, moving her hands over the taut muscles of his back. And when his tongue pressed for entry, she opened to allow him in, joining hers in a sensual mating act.

Every nerve ending in her body was on fire. His hands moved up to cup her breasts, but she didn't protest. Instead she pushed the aching globes into his palms, wishing the material that separated his hands from her flesh would disappear.

Her wish was granted a moment later when her robe was undone, as were the tiny pearl buttons of her batiste nightgown. She could feel the warm flesh of his chest, his bandage, pressing into her breasts and stomach. Soon his fingers were urging her sensitive nipples into rigid peaks, and a moan of desire escaped her lips.

"I want you, Red. I want you in the worst way."

His admission brought a flood of wetness to the apex of her thighs and a dull throbbing that seemed to intensify as his mouth closed over first one pink peak, then the other. He suckled, as a child might nurse at his mother's breast, and the sensation was unlike anything she'd ever experienced before; she felt her defenses weakening.

He was fully on top of her now, pressing himself against the throbbing mound of her womanhood. She couldn't prevent herself from arching up to meet him.

Wanting something . . . something . . . But not knowing what.

"Brock," she cried out as he drew up her nightgown and moved his hand up the inside of her thigh.

His mouth seemed to be everywhere at once—on her lips, her neck, her breasts, her stomach. She became mindless with desire, all senses centered on that forbidden area between her legs.

The feel of Brock's fingers as they trailed up her legs, up her thighs, brought her sanity back in the space of a heartbeat.

My God! What was she doing?

"Brock," she said, moving her head from side to side. But he mistook her refusal for passion and moved to separate her thighs, insinuating his hand in the moist nest of curls between her legs.

It was almost her undoing. With all the willpower she possessed, she cried out in a hoarse whisper, "Stop! Please stop!"

It took a moment for her plea to register, but when it did, Brock's hands stilled. He gazed into her passion-filled eyes and saw the fear. "Don't be afraid," he reassured her, kissing her gently. "I want to make love to you."

Wide-eyed, she shook her head in denial. "No! No! Let me up."

Realizing that she was frightened and not about to acquiesce, Brock rolled off her with a frustrated sigh, watching in dismay as Prudence bounded to her feet, clutching the edges of her nightgown together.

"I won't apologize, Red, because I know, and you know, that you want me. You're just too damned afraid, too stubborn, to admit it."

She shook her head. "No. It was all a mistake."

"Maybe so. But your pump's been primed, and you're

not going to be satisfied until that well of passion you've got stored up inside you comes gushing out."

She gasped. "That's disgusting!" she said with as much dignity as she could muster. "Just because you're as randy as a rooster in a henhouse doesn't mean I'm the same. I merely allowed the excitement of the evening to overtake my good judgment." She could see by his knowing smile that he didn't believe a word she'd said, which was understandable; she barely believed them herself.

"It was excitement, all right, that overtook you— but it wasn't your judgment that was affected. I'd say it was something centered a whole lot lower than your brain."

Her mouth had been hanging open, and she snapped it shut. Spinning on her heel, she stormed out of the room, slamming the door behind her.

With his burns throbbing, and his manhood crying out for release, Brock felt as miserable as a eunuch in a whorehouse as he stared dejectedly at the door.

Damn the woman for denying herself and him!

He'd had a taste of her now, and it wasn't likely that he was going to be satisfied until he had his fill. And he had a powerful hunger where Prudence Daniels was concerned.

Prudence leaned heavily against the door of her bedroom, cupping her burning cheeks in her hands, taking deep breaths, trying to get herself under control.

She rushed over to the connecting door and propped a chair beneath the brass handle—whether to keep Brock out or herself in, she wasn't certain—then crossed to the fire.

The flames had died down to embers, and she tossed

another log onto the grate, watching as the fire accepted it greedily and spurted to life.

What had happened? she wondered, heaving a deep, discontented sigh. How could she have forgotten herself so completely? And with a man she knew was only a temporary fixture in her life!

She had made herself a vow years ago that what had happened to Clara would never happen to her. And now she had almost given herself the same way. She shook her head at the realization of what could have happened had she acted on impulse.

She could have gotten pregnant. She could have ended up alone and despondent like Clara. She could have ended up dead. The brief moment of pleasure in Brock's arms wouldn't be worth the pain she would have to endure afterward.

Closing her eyes, she pictured Clara as she had seen her that last time, struggling to bring forth the child from her womb, screaming out in pain for the man who had deserted them both.

Tears sprang forth freely as she remembered the utter helplessness she'd felt, the anger and frustration at not being able to help her sister survive the ordeal of childbirth. The baby had been a breech birth; but, of course, she hadn't known that then. She'd only known that her sister had died because the doctor had convinced her that Clara needed to be bled—that the excess blood in her body was swelling her internal organs, preventing the child from coming out. And being ignorant, and trusting a man she assumed knew more than she did, she'd allowed the doctor to proceed despite Clara's anguished cries, despite the fact that his treatment made no sense to her.

Nothing about Clara's death made sense to her. Not why Billy Preston had left. Not why the doctor had been unable to save Clara. Not why she'd been foolish enough to allow the quack to practice his incompetency in the first place.

Why? That was the question. But, of course, there was no answer. Only guilt. Mounds and mounds of guilt. And hate. And distrust that lingered to this day.

She swung about to stare at the connecting door again. If only she could allow herself to believe that Brock would be different. If only Clara hadn't died and Billy hadn't left. But Clara had died. And Billy had left. And Prudence was no longer capable of allowing herself to trust anyone again.

Your name's not Clara and mine's not Billy.

Brock's words came back to haunt her, and she found herself crying anew for everything that had come and gone—for that which would never be.

11

*If you want to stay single,
look for a perfect woman.*

"*Why do you suppose* Miss Pru's been so touchy these past few days?" Mary asked Louann. They were seated in the great room, putting the finishing touches on some saddles they were stitching. "She about took my head off when I asked her about Mr. Peters's burns."

"I suspect it has something to do with Mr. Peters living inside this house."

"'Cause they don't like each other?" Mary grew instantly concerned. Mr. Peters and Miss Pru were two of her most favorite people. They just had to like each other.

Louann shook her head, a knowing look on her face as she drew the big needle through the leather. "'Cause they do. It has something to do with opposites attractin'."

Excitement lit the blue eyes. "Wouldn't it be wonderful if they was to get together? Miss Pru wouldn't be so lonely if that happened, and Mr. Peters is the nicest man I know."

Reaching over to fetch BJ out of his cradle, Louann cuddled the fussy baby to her breast, kissing the top of his downy head. "Miss Pru don't cotton to men much. Maybe she had some bad experience when she was younger. I seen whores who hated the very sight of men, but who laid with 'em anyways to earn a livin'."

"Are you goin' to hate your baby because it came from some man you don't even know?"

Louann's face softened as she stared down at BJ. "I never realized how much I wanted this baby I'm carryin'. At first I didn't much care. But after I felt her kick and move about, she became a real living thing. I'm just dyin' to get to the birthin' part, so's I can hold her like I'm holding this little precious bundle of yours."

From the look of Louann's belly that wouldn't be long, Mary decided, fastening the silver concha to the saddle skirt. She was as ripe as a plump tomato ready to fall from the bush.

"Even though I don't have a man, I wouldn't trade BJ for anything. He's my whole life now."

"What about Will?" Louann asked, a teasing smile on her lips. "He seems mighty taken with you and the baby."

The young girl blushed prettily. "Will's a kind man, but I'm not rushin' into anything again. Miss Pru says I need to gain a little more maturity before I make an important decision like marryin'. Besides, Will ain't asked me yet."

"Well, I envy you." Louann's words surprised Mary, and her eyes widened. "You're young and pretty, and you've got your whole life ahead of you."

"You're young and pretty, too," Mary insisted, not wanting her friend to be unhappy.

"That's true. But I'm used goods. No decent man would ever want to settle down with me. Men want women like me for only one thing. My future's already been decided."

"Then you're going back to Madam Eva's after your baby's born?" A horrified look crossed Mary's face. She couldn't imagine BJ residing in a place like Madam Eva's bordello. She might have sinned with Bobby Fitzsimmons, but she weren't no sinner. Not like the girls at Madam Eva's.

Seeing the stricken look on her friend's face, Mary blushed guiltily. Louann might be a whore, but she weren't no sinner, neither. She added quickly, "I mean, there's probably other kinds of jobs you can get."

"I gots to do what's best for the babe, Mary. How else would I support her iff'n I don't go back? I don't have no other skills. I never learned my letters. My cookin' is worse than Miss Pru's. And I ain't never learned to operate one of them Singer sewing machines."

Mary wrapped a comforting arm about Louann's shoulders. "Don't you worry none about that right now," she said, sounding years older than sixteen. "There'll be plenty of time to sort things out once that baby comes. I put a lot of faith in the Lord. He ain't never let me down yet. Why, look how He sent Mr. Peters to save me from that evil Reverend Entwhistle. I tell you, he'll come through for you, too."

"Do you really think so?" There was a wealth of hope in the question, though Louann had given up counting on miracles a long time ago. She'd been at the ranch nearly six months, and it was the first time in her life that she felt truly respectable.

"Didn't I just say so?"

Louann nodded, Mary smiled confidently, and both women resumed their work.

A few miles away, Jacob paced nervously across the wooden planks of his study. He'd received a note from Arabella that morning saying she was fixin' to call on him in the afternoon.

He frowned, pulling out his pocket watch and glancing at the time. She never came out to the ranch unless it was an emergency or unless she was so horny she couldn't stand not having him a moment longer. He'd like to think it was the latter; but knowing Bella's penchant for control, he doubted she was that needful. No, it had to be something else. And he had the sinking feeling he knew what it was.

Arabella stood waiting on the front porch of the sprawling ranch house and shook her head, her face screwing up in disgust. After she married Jacob she would make some changes around here. The paint was peeling in several places, and a shutter was hanging lopsided. Honestly, for a man who prided himself on his appearance, you'd think Jacob Morgan would take better care of his house.

The door opened and Jacob stood there, smiling, but she could tell that he was nervous as hell. He had that look on his face when the wolfhounds were in the same room, like he was going to get his balls bit off. She smiled confidently. That was not out of the realm of possibility this afternoon.

"Jacob." She presented her cheek to him as she rushed past in a flurry of taffeta and lace on her way to the parlor.

Jacob hurried after her. "I'm stunned by your visit, honey. I thought we'd decided to meet at your place again."

She peeled the leather gloves from her hands, slapping them against her hand, and her blue eyes narrowed into slits as she studied Jacob's nervous demeanor. *A guilty man runs when no one's chasin' him.* Henry's saying came to mind.

"Don't 'honey' me, Jacob Morgan. I want some answers, and I want them now."

He swallowed nervously, mopping his brow with his handkerchief. There wasn't a man alive who could intimidate Jacob Morgan, but Arabella Potts was a whole different matter.

"Answers? Answers about what, Bella?" he asked innocently.

She walked up to him and grabbed his crotch, squeezing his member none too gently. "If I thought this little rascal had been playing me false, Jacob, I'd be mighty upset."

Instantly his manhood stood at attention, pulsing painfully as she tightened her grip, and his voice rose an octave when he said, "Now you know that just isn't true, honey. I've got eyes for no woman but you."

She squeezed harder, making him wince. "Not even Prudence Daniels? I saw the way you were hanging all over her the night of the ball. Why, it was downright insulting the way you ignored me."

"Now, Bella," he cajoled, reaching for the hand that was bringing tears to his eyes, lifting it to his lips for a kiss, "you know I don't care a thing about Prudence Daniels. I was her daddy's friend. I promised old Cody I'd look out for her, that's all."

"And that's why you danced with her all night?" A thin eyebrow arched, and there was a note of disbelief in her voice.

"I was just being neighborly. Makin' sure that the rest of the town didn't treat her rude, like they usually do."

Arabella mulled over his explanation, finally deciding it made sense. She'd never understood why the towns-folk had it in for Prudence Daniels. As far as she was concerned, the woman was doing everyone a favor by taking in all those unfortunates no one else wanted.

And she thought Miss Daniels to be a fairly coura-geous woman to stand up for what she believed in. It was something they had in common. But she wasn't going to let the attractive spinster come between her and Jacob. She had her mind set on marrying the overweight bachelor, and by all that was holy, she would.

"I believe I would like a glass of sherry, Jacob."

He smiled in relief and turned toward the sideboard to get it. "Coming right up."

"Darling," she said, staring at the bulge in his crotch, "it's already up. Let's not waste it. Upstairs, Jacob." She removed a black velvet cloak to reveal a gown that barely covered her ample assets.

His eyes rooted on her pendulous globes, Jacob licked his lips in anticipation. Obediently he followed behind Arabella as though she had a magnet stuck in her bustle.

Arabella smiled as she climbed the stairs. Men were so predictable, and so much like babies. Give them a little sugar, a little tit, and they'd be content for days.

Polly sobbed into her hands, and Prudence and Sarah stood by helplessly, knowing there was little they could do to ease her grief.

"I'm sorry, Polly," Prudence said, patting the young

woman on the back to comfort her. "But my examination reveals that you're not going to have a baby."

The young girl's face was streaked with tears, and her lower lip quivered. "But I wanted one just like Mary's. I didn't at first, but now I do."

"Love, be reasonable," Sarah said, sitting on the bed next to the distraught young woman, grasping her hand. "You should be happy you don't have to bring a child into this world. It's hard enough for a woman to survive alone, harder yet when she has a wee one to care for." She patted her own stomach absently and sighed.

"It's because I ate too much, isn't it? I killed my own baby." Polly's sobs grew louder.

"Polly Fletcher, I've never heard such a ridiculous thing," Prudence reprimanded, her voice firm. "I'm telling you that you were never pregnant to begin with. You told me yourself how scared you and your beau were after you consummated your attraction for each other."

"We made love, Miss Pru," Polly said, thinking she needed to explain. After all, Miss Pru was a spinster.

"Yes, I know. And you were scared, weren't you? Scared you might get pregnant?" At Polly's nod, Prudence added, "Sometimes fear can make a body think otherwise. Your body just happened to think you were."

"Are you real sure, Miss Pru? There's no way you could be wrong?"

Prudence shook her head. "No, I'm not wrong. But like Sarah says, you should be happy. You can go home to your mama and papa."

Polly's face finally brightened. "I can, can't I? And I don't have to bring disgrace upon them."

"That's correct. You'll—"

"Red! Red!" Brock's voice screamed up the stairwell,

and Prudence halted in midsentence, coloring to match the nickname she abhorred.

"Good heavens!" Sarah said, her hand flying to her throat. "He sounds fit to be tied."

He'd sounded that way for the past two days, but Prudence wasn't about to reveal why. "Stay with Polly a while longer, Sarah. I'll go down and see what Mr. Peters wants." She knew what he wanted, but she wasn't about to give it to him.

"Red, come on down here, or I'm coming up to that goddamned sanctuary of yours."

Prudence stuck her head out the door and glowered at the infuriating man standing at the bottom of the stairs. "I'm coming, and this had better be important." She rushed down the steps, her eyes glittering in anger. "I'll have you know, Brock Peters, I happen to be quite busy at the moment."

When she reached the bottom step, Brock thrust a soiled rag in her direction; it smelled distinctly of kerosene.

"We were clearing away the debris, getting ready to rebuild the bunkhouse, when we found this among the ashes. The bunkhouse fire was no accident. Someone set it deliberately."

She stared at the rag in disbelief. "But who would do such a thing? Why would anyone want to hurt my cowhands?"

Her refusal to face the obvious angered him. "I doubt you'd want to know what I think."

"You're not going to tell me that Jacob is responsible for this!" She sighed in exasperation, shaking her head. "Really, Brock, just because you didn't like me dancing with him."

"What?!" He tipped back his hat, his eyes darkening in anger. "Don't flatter yourself," he said, and she colored fiercely. "What you do, and who you see, are your business. I couldn't care less."

That hurt, and she willed back the tears that sprang to her eyes. "I just meant that I know you don't like Jacob. I wasn't implying that you were jealous. One would have to have a heart to experience that emotion. And I don't believe you do."

He stiffened, knowing part of what she said was true. His heart had been shattered a long time ago by the death of his wife and son. But even with so great a loss, he wasn't as bitterly wounded as Prudence.

"At least mine isn't walled off by a protective barrier so thick no one could ever penetrate it."

"And you're saying mine is?" She but did her best to hide her rage.

"I'm saying that you're afraid to feel, afraid to let yourself go, afraid someone might actually penetrate that wall you've built around yourself. Well, you needn't worry, Miss Daniels. I don't have the time, or the desire, to scale a fortress so mighty."

Grabbing the rag out of her hand, he spun on his boot heel and left the room. Prudence stared after him with the sinking feeling that maybe her heart wasn't as protected as he might think.

The buggy bumped along the rutted road, and Sarah reveled in the warmth of the afternoon sun against her face. It felt glorious to be outdoors again, especially when she had such a wonderful companion. She glanced over at Martin.

"Are you sure your leg is not paining you too much, Martin? I wouldn't want to be the cause of any discomfort." He'd been off his crutches only for a day, and she feared he would overdo and reinjure himself.

Moody glimpsed the concern on Sarah's face and his heart swelled. He'd never thought to meet someone as lovely, as kind and generous, as his Martha, but he had. Sarah Davenport had brought sunshine back into his gloomy existence, and he thought Martha would heartily approve.

"My dear, you could never bring me discomfort. My leg has healed up quite nicely. Hannah gave me her stamp of approval only this morning." And she hadn't even cursed at him; they were definitely making progress.

"What about you?" he asked, bringing a blush to her cheeks. "Are you and the baby all right? You're not too cold, are you? We can turn back if you are." Although he dreaded the thought. He loved having Sarah all to himself, if only for a little while.

Reflexively her hands covered her abdomen, and she smiled. "Yes, we're fine. Though I wish the time would hurry along. February can't come soon enough to suit me."

"You should never wish time away, Sarah. Soon it's all gone and there's nothing left but memories to live on."

"Memories don't always have to be bad." Although her recent ones left something to be desired, she admitted to herself. "Surely you had a rich and fulfilling life."

He nodded. "My best years in the army were spent at Fort Garland. Martha, that was my wife, and I arrived there shortly after it opened back in . . ." He thought a moment. "'Twas fifty-eight, I think. The third infantry opened the fort to guard the route over the Sangre de Cristo pass from the Indians.

"Those were glorious times. I loved being in charge. I loved the challenge of what each day would bring. Even after Martha died, I still had my work to keep me going." His voice grew bitter. "Now, they've taken that away from me, too."

She pressed her gloved hand on his forearm. "Usually when something is taken away, something else turns up in its place."

Moody pulled the buggy to a halt beneath a stand of quivering aspens and turned to face her. A white-winged lark bunting dipped its wing as it soared by. "I hope I'm what's turned up in your life, Sarah."

"Martin . . ."

Placing his fingertips across her lips, he shook his head. "You don't have to say anything. I realize we haven't known each other long. And that you're a lot younger than me."

"Martin,"—she shook her head—"it isn't that."

"Let me finish, before I chicken out and never say what I want to say. I'm in love with you, Sarah. I haven't felt this way about a woman since I met and married my beloved Martha, God rest her soul. I want to marry you, become a father to your child."

Tears filled Sarah's eyes; she swallowed past the lump in her throat. "But you don't know anything about me. Why would you want to marry a woman who is carrying another man's child? A woman who has sinned in the eyes of the Lord?"

"We've all sinned at one time or another, my dear. I don't have enough years left to expound on all my shortcomings. When I look at you, all I see is goodness and beauty." He took her hand and brought it to his lips for a kiss. "You're that angel who stood in my room that first day I woke up."

"Oh, Martin, if only that were true. Don't you see, I'm no angel, I'm soiled goods. I had an affair with a married man—the father of one of my students. I'm a fallen woman—an unwed mother." She said the last with such derision, he wanted to pull her into his arms and protect her from the rest of the world.

"It takes two to make a child, Sarah. And I'd venture to say that the man you gave yourself to knew exactly what the consequences of his actions were. He was already married. You were not. I think you're being too hard on yourself."

She patted his cheek. "I don't deserve anyone as fine as you, Martin. You're too good for me."

"I've been a drunk the last few years of my life, but I haven't touched a drop since I've been here. I haven't felt the need for alcohol, and I owe that to you. There's not a soul alive who doesn't carry a past with them. It's what makes life interesting, I guess. Don't judge me too harshly, but most of all, don't judge yourself. That's the Creator's job, despite what Reverend Entwhistle preaches."

She smiled at that. "He really is a horrid little man, isn't he?"

"I love it when you smile." He squeezed her hand gently. "Say that you'll think about what I've proposed. Give me some hope to live on and a reason to stay."

The thought of his leaving sent shards of pain into her heart; she nodded. "I promise I'll give it serious consideration."

And she would. She'd never met anyone quite like Martin Carstairs before, and she wasn't likely to ever again. His proposal had taken her off guard, giving her volumes to think about.

"And would you also consider allowing me to kiss you?"

She colored fiercely, her hands starting to sweat, and nodded again.

Without a moment's hesitation, Moody drew Sarah

into his arms and pressed his lips gently to hers. His kiss was almost reverent, and as sweet as the man himself, and Sarah felt a tingle go all the way down to the tips of her toes.

"I love you, Sarah." He whispered the sentiment that shone brightly in his eyes.

Sarah, whose heart had risen clear up to her throat, swallowed the lump resting there and smiled through her tears.

I love you, too, Martin, she replied silently.

12

*Every town has a couple with
the same likes and dislikes:
they like to fight and hate each other.*

Prudence walked quickly across the yard in the direction of the barn, and Brock set aside his hammer to watch her. He'd purposely kept his distance from her the past few days, knowing to do otherwise might result in a confrontation neither of them wanted or was ready to handle.

He still craved her. Dreamed about her at night as he tossed and turned in his bed, knowing that she rested just on the other side of the wall. Sometimes he could hear her moving about, and he wondered if she was restless, too—if she ever thought about him. But in the mornings, when she riddled him with frosty bullets, he knew it was only wishful thinking on his part.

Prudence Daniels wasn't ready for a man. And as much as he wanted her in the way a man always wants a woman, he wasn't ready to lay his heart at her feet and let her stomp all over it with her dainty high-topped shoes. A woman like Prudence could do a powerful lot of damage to a man's heart.

As she drew nearer, he nodded in greeting. "Where are you headed, Red? You've got your Sunday-go-to-meetin' clothes on and it's only Wednesday."

Having thought Brock had gone to check on the new fencing he and the boys had strung yesterday, Prudence sighed in frustration. She wanted to avoid another confrontation with him. The last one had left her devastated, and she was in no mood for the verbal sparring he seemed to enjoy so much.

"I'm on my way to town," she explained. "I need to check on the mail and pick up a few things at the mercantile."

"Is that a fact?" He frowned at her. "Well, you're not going by yourself. Not after this bunkhouse was purposely set afire." He stared at the new frame they'd put up, wondering if winter would hold off long enough to allow them to complete the job of rebuilding. He was as anxious to move out of the house as Prudence was to have him gone.

"I am perfectly capable of going to town by myself. You are making much too much out of a fire that was most likely only an accident. You see villains at every turn. I'm not going to run scared. Besides, I have nothing anyone else would want."

He gazed at the porcelain beauty of her skin, at her lush curves and slim hips, and couldn't contain the naughty grin that spread across his face. "I wouldn't say that, Red."

She stiffened in indignation. "Must you reduce everything to your base instincts, Mr. Peters?" She turned away and entered the barn, only to find Brock following after her.

The buggy was ready and waiting for her, as she had instructed Slim this morning, and, climbing aboard, she breathed a sigh of relief. She had every intention of making this trip to town, with or without the imperious foreman's blessing.

She settled herself against the leather seat and reached for the reins, but Brock grabbed them out of her hand.

"Maybe I didn't make myself clear, Red. You are not driving this buggy into town by yourself. Now scoot over. I'm coming with you."

"That is not . . ." Noting the determined glint in his eyes, she swallowed her objection, took a deep breath, and moved over, cursing him under her breath. The man was impossibly stubborn. She knew from past experience it would do little good to argue with him. He was a born meddler. A mule-headed, interfering—

"Glad you decided to be sensible," he said, interrupting her silent diatribe. "After we clear up the little mystery of the fire, and find out who's been stealing your cows, then you may return to your former activities. But until then, you'll be cautious and follow my directions."

Her voice shook with anger. "You are the foreman here, Brock, not my keeper. I didn't hire you to ride roughshod over me."

"You might own this ranch, little lady, and be able to intimidate everyone else on it, but I am in charge now, and you'll do as I say."

"And if I fire you?"

He grinned and slapped the reins to urge the horses forward. "You're stuck with me now, Red. Better get used to it."

That was the trouble, she thought, she already had.

* * *

After agreeing to meet Brock in front of the post office in an hour, Prudence went about her business. She visited the dressmaker's, where she ordered two new shirtwaists; dropped off some tooled belts at the saddlery; and stopped at the mercantile for thread, writing paper, and an odd assortment of presents for the ladies.

It had become a tradition of sorts, each time she went into town, to bring back a gift for each lady. The presents were usually small and inexpensive, but the amount of pleasure they gave couldn't be measured monetarily.

For Mary she purchased two yards of white linen to make diapers for BJ. Louann would receive a length of blue velvet ribbon for her hair; Sarah, a bar of lavender soap. A new Beadle's dime novel awaited Christey—the bloodier the better, which always surprised Prudence— while Eliza would receive a skein of red yarn to finish the blanket she was knitting. Laurel had a penchant for sweets, so Prudence had bought two ropes of licorice. And for Polly, who would be leaving as soon as her parents responded to the letter she'd sent, she would give some pretty pink stationery, so the young girl could write regularly.

Thanking Mr. Miller, who seemed unusually helpful and friendly, Prudence headed for the post office to collect her mail. She was expecting a new edition of the *Western Journal of Medicine and Surgery*, as well as a few back issues of the Denver newspaper, the *Rocky Mountain News*. The editor, William Byers, always dished out the most informative bits of information on ranching. And since Absolution's newspaper offices had burned down over a year ago, the *News* was her only link to what was going on in the outside world.

When she entered the small wooden building, the first person she saw was Reverend Entwhistle, and she did her best not to groan aloud. He was garbed in his usual black: fitting, she supposed, since it matched the color of his soul.

"Good morning, Reverend . . . Mr. Younger." She smiled at the elderly postmaster. "I've come to collect my mail." The old man nodded and began to riffle through the stacks of correspondence while she waited impatiently and endured the reverend's scrutiny.

"Still subscribing to all those medical journals, Miss Daniels?" he asked, his voice filled with disdain. "Your heathenish practices do not find favor with the Lord, I'll have you know."

Since he had let her know many times over, Prudence only nodded. One confrontation a day was all she could stomach, and thanks to Brock she'd already had hers.

"Here you are, miss." The postmaster handed her a thick bundle of magazines, newspapers, and letters.

Gathering them in her arms, Prudence offered her thanks and reached into her reticule to retrieve her reading glasses. She always perused the mail before leaving to make certain it was all addressed to her. Despite the thickness of Mr. Younger's spectacles, the old postmaster invariably made mistakes in distributing the mail. And it was an awful nuisance to ride all the way back into town to return misdirected correspondence.

"I heard you and those women attended the harvest ball a few weeks back."

She looked up to find the reverend hovering over her left shoulder like a vulture waiting to pounce on its prey. He smelled of pomade and clove, and Prudence vowed it was the most unpleasant combination of odors she'd ever encountered.

Despite her determination to remain aloof, anger shook her voice when she said, "I believe this is still a free country, Reverend. Is there a problem?"

The door opened, emitting a cold blast of air, but Prudence was too intent on defending herself to notice that Brock had entered.

Great! Just great! Brock thought when he saw whom Prudence was arguing with. When he heard Entwhistle's disparaging remark, his hands balled into fists. It was time to administer a little frontier justice to the piss-ant preacher, he decided.

"Obviously, young woman," Entwhistle continued, "you don't realize what kind of trouble you bring to the good Christians of this town by flaunting those . . . those miscreants before us. Sinners, every one, and you the worst of the lot for allowing them to reside under your roof. You give succor to the wicked, Miss Daniels. That makes you wicked, too."

In a voice as cold and hard as the gun strapped to his thigh, Brock warned, "That's enough, Reverend, or I'll be forced to take you out into the street and whip some manners into that miserable hide of yours."

Gasping, Prudence turned to find Brock standing just inside the doorway. A large measure of relief washed over her. Although she hated to admit it, it was nice having someone else to fight her battles for a change.

"You!" Entwhistle's eyes rounded in surprise as he pointed a long bony finger at Brock in accusation. "You are the sinner who interrupted my prayer meeting."

Brock snorted in disbelief. "Prayer meeting! Ha! That's rich. More like a lynching party, wouldn't you say, Reverend? Or do you enjoy humiliating little girls?" Brock stepped forward, and the reverend retreated, wringing his hands nervously. "I didn't like what you said to Miss Daniels, Entwhistle," Brock continued. "If anyone in this town is wicked, it's you."

Pulling himself up to his full five feet, four inches, Ezekiel Entwhistle gasped aloud. "How dare you speak to me like that, you . . . you ruffian? I am a man of God. If you do not respect me, you do not respect the Lord our God."

Prudence watched the pulse in Brock's neck throb menacingly, and a measure of alarm darted through her. He was close to blowing a short fuse, and she thought they'd better leave before he did something they'd both be sorry for. But when she cautioned reason, he merely glared at her and told her to be quiet.

Brock stepped forward and grabbed the reverend by the front of his coat. "Let's get something straight, Entwhistle. You are not, in any way, shape, or form, a representative of the God I know. The God I know is merciful and kind. He doesn't pick on innocent women or children, and He sure as hell would never pick a narrow-minded, cruel despot like you to deliver His word." Taking hold of a handful of Entwhistle's pant seat, Brock ushered him out the door, then tossed the good reverend outside onto his belly.

"Next time, you hypocrite, I'll pull out that tongue of yours so you can't use it on anyone again."

Back in the post office, he nodded to the very startled postmaster, grasped Prudence's hand, and hauled her out the door to the waiting buggy, ignoring the hysterics of the man lying facedown in the dirt.

"Get in. We're leaving."

Knowing better than to argue, Prudence climbed aboard, tossing her purchases in the rear compartment.

She removed her spectacles, which were slightly askew, and shoved them back into her reticule.

"Now do you see why I didn't want you venturing into town by yourself?" Brock asked when they were finally on the outskirts of town.

She glanced at him out of the corner of her eye and noticed for the first time that he'd gotten a shave at the tonsorial parlor. It had been worth every bit of the twenty-five cents he'd paid, she decided, for his skin looked as smooth as satin, and she longed to reach out and run her hand over his cheek.

But she didn't.

Instead she thrust her hands into her lap. "Although I appreciate what you did for me, Brock, I can handle the reverend. I've been doing it for years."

Rather than the argument she was expecting, Brock glanced up at the sky and shook his head in disgust. The morning sun was gone, replaced by thick, heavy clouds that warned of rain or snow.

"I don't like the looks of that sky. We'd best hurry."

They rode several miles in silence, Prudence not daring to voice her fears when the sky continued to darken ominously. Finally, unable to restrain herself a moment longer, she said, "I think a snowstorm is coming in." The wind picked up then, lending credence to her words.

"Great! Just great!" Brock said as the first flakes of snow started falling. "We're as far from town as we are from the ranch. We'll never be able to outrun this."

Prudence nodded in agreement; she'd seen more than one blizzard in her lifetime. They came in like the wrath of God, bringing strong gusts of wind, usually accompanied by heavy, blinding amounts of snowfall. They had to find shelter and fast.

"There's a deserted cabin not far from here," she

shouted to be heard above the roar of the wind. "It's the old McCanless place. I haven't been by there in years, but I think the cabin is still standing." At least she prayed it was. Being stranded in the middle of a blizzard was a truly horrifying thought, equaled only by the disturbing realization that she would be stranded inside a deserted cabin with Brock Peters.

Swallowing her fears, she indicated that Brock should turn off the main road. They followed a narrow path she knew would lead them to the McCanless homestead.

Prudence had visited the McCanless place many times with her father, often stopping on their way home from town to drop off food and clothing. Matthew McCanless had been a poor excuse for a rancher, but Cody Daniels had called him friend. And friends didn't go without when Cody was around to help.

The roof of the buggy sagged under the weight of the snow that accumulated rapidly. Shading her eyes from the blowing white powder, Prudence peered out the side of the buggy, pointing at the log structure in the distance.

"There," she shouted, "up ahead. Do you see it?" She waited anxiously while Brock stared at the horizon, giving a silent prayer of thanks when at last he nodded.

A few minutes later they arrived at the cabin, and while Brock left to unhitch the horse and install him in the lean-to that abutted the cabin, Prudence hurried inside to get a fire started.

There was wood stacked in the corner, for which she silently thanked Eleanor McCanless. Matthew's wife had always taken scrupulous care to have everything at the ready. Even the cabin, which hadn't been lived in for years, was fairly clean and neat, though the blue calico curtains at the window were faded and dusty from age, as was the old quilt on the bed. And there were dust motes hovering in every corner.

"Eleanor, you always were an amazing woman," Prudence said, looking through the hanging cupboard for provisions. She smiled at the sight of six jars of peaches, two tins of evaporated milk, and a bag of beans. Well, at least they wouldn't starve, and there was no telling how long they would have to stay here.

She frowned at the unsettling thought and walked back to the hearth to poke at the fire. It was blazing quite nicely now, and she held out her hands to warm them, turning to stare over her shoulder when the door banged open.

His arms filled with the provisions he'd purchased in town, Brock entered. He was covered with snow from head to foot, and she rushed forward to slam the door shut behind him.

"Looks like you did a good job of starting the fire, Red," he said, dropping the foodstuffs onto the old wooden table. "Not only will we not freeze to death, but we won't starve, either." He hung his heavy sheepskin jacket over the back of a chair near the fire to dry it, instructing Prudence to do the same with her wool coat.

"There's already six inches of snow piled up out there, and it's my guess there's a lot more on the way."

"What about the girls?" she asked, suddenly anxious. "What if there are complications? What if Louann's baby comes early? Or BJ gets sick? Or—"

"Will you relax? Hannah is there to see to their needs, not to mention Moody, Shorty, and the rest of the hands. The women will be well taken care of. It's you I'm worried about." He gazed down at her sodden dress and shoes and frowned. "I want you to strip out of those wet clothes. You'll catch pneumonia if you don't."

She knew he was right, but she wasn't about to disrobe and walk about the cabin stark naked. As if he could read her mind, he said, "Pull that quilt off the bed and wrap yourself in it. Then come sit by the fire and warm up."

"Don't you ever get tired of ordering me around?" His smile sent her pulse racing.

"I'll keep my back turned while you undress. Then you can do the same for me."

While he faced the fire, Prudence stripped out of her wet dress and shoes in record time, covering herself with the heavy quilt while she removed her petticoat, chemise, and drawers. When she was completely naked under the quilt, she gathered up her clothes and brought them to the fire, draping them over a chair.

"You can look now. I'm decent."

Although she had the quilt wrapped around her shoulders Indian style, Brock couldn't get over the thought that she was deliciously naked under it. She might be decent, but his thoughts were anything but.

"I'll get undressed and join you," he said.

Sitting down in front of the fire, Prudence stared into the crackling flames; she listened to the howl of the wind outside, trying not to concentrate on the sound of Brock's boots as they hit the floor, followed by his belt and pants.

Would he take *everything* off? she wondered. And what would it feel like to be totally naked, sitting next to a man who was also totally naked? Of course, they both had on their quilts, but underneath . . . Naked was naked, no matter how you looked at it, she decided.

Prudence got her answer a moment later when a pair of red drawers were slung over the chair next to her underclothing.

He was naked! She wrapped the quilt more closely

about her, hoping the flush suffusing her body would be attributed to the heat of the fire.

Brock joined her on the floor, wiggling his toes at the fire, and she thought it was quite an intimate thing to see a man without his socks on. His calves were hairy and muscular and much whiter than his arms and face, as if they hadn't seen the sun in a while.

"My toes feel like icicles," he said, startling her out of her improper thoughts. "How about yours?"

"They're fine."

"I can rub them if they're not. No sense in getting frostbite."

"No!" she objected a bit too vehemently, remembering the last time he'd performed that exquisite torture. "They're perfectly fine. Splendid, even." How could they not be, when her blood was hotter than Hades and rushing through her veins like molten lava?

He grinned. "I bet this is the first time you've ever been completely naked with a man."

"I am not naked," she insisted. "I have a quilt covering me. Which is more than I can say for you." His blanket covered only the lower half of his body, leaving his chest, arms, and legs completely bare. "You're likely to be the one who gets sick."

The warmth of the fire added to her embarrassment, bringing a bright pink stain to her cheeks, and Brock had physically to restrain himself from drawing her into his arms and kissing her soundly on the lips. His thoughts were quickly communicated to the area below his waist, and he covered his lap with his hands to hide his reaction. She'd probably run out into the blizzard if she knew what he was thinking.

"How long do you think we're going to have to stay here?" she asked, uncomfortable with his silence. Her gaze followed the shrug of his broad shoulders, and she swallowed hard.

"That's difficult to say. It would be suicide to leave before the storm abates. And even when it does, it could be days before we can make our way out of here." At her look of dismay, he patted her shoulder. "Don't worry. We have enough to eat. And that bed in the corner is big enough for the both of us."

13

*A fickle woman and a good-shootin' man
are apt to hurt someone.*

"The both . . . !" She practically choked on her words, and her eyes grew wide as saucers. "Are you insane? You must be, if you think we are going to share that bed." She could barely bring herself to look at it. What was once an innocuous piece of furniture had suddenly turned into a lair of seduction.

"You won't be so outraged a few hours from now when the temperature drops and there are icicles hanging from your breath," Brock reminded her. "It's colder than a witch's tit outside right now. What do you think it's going to be like tonight when the temperature drops?"

She felt so hot, she doubted she would need any additional warmth to get her through the night. "It wouldn't be proper for us to sleep in the same bed," she insisted. "You'll just have to use the floor."

"The floor!" His look was incredulous. "Now who's nuts? If I sleep on the floor, I'll be frozen dead by morning. I know you don't cotton to me much, Red, but do you really want to be responsible for my death?"

"But we're not married!"

"Since when are you so concerned about convention? You've done everything but slap propriety right in the face."

"That's different! What I've done doesn't concern my welfare, but the welfare of others."

"Well, this concerns mine, and we're sleeping in that goddamn bed together. And if you give me any more arguments, I'll strap you into it."

She gasped and pulled her blanket about her, as if it could offer protection from this deranged, determined man. "You wouldn't dare!" But she knew he would; the sinister smile on his face told her that much.

"Why don't you rustle us up something to eat? I'm starved." He must be, Brock thought, if he was actually considering eating another one of Prudence's horrendous meals.

Starved for more than food, no doubt, Prudence decided. But food was all he was going to get. If he thought to seduce her once he got her into that bed, he had another think coming. She had an iron will when she needed to. And boy, she thought, staring at the erotic glimmer in his eyes, she needed to now.

They dined on peaches and cornmeal mush that was weevily but tasted good nonetheless. After supper they made small talk by the fire, Prudence finding that the more questions she asked, the longer she could prolong the inevitable of crawling into bed with Brock.

"And do you think we'll be needing to bring in the

herd this winter? With the snow and all, they might not survive."

He smiled inwardly at her transparent tactics. Having been born on a ranch, he was fairly certain that Prudence knew cattle could survive on the grama grass that grew on the range. "They'll survive. As I'm sure you're already aware, they'll just dig down through the snow to get to the grass. Herefords are very resilient animals. Isn't that why you chose the breed in the first place?"

"Of course," she faltered, wishing she knew what else to talk about. They could discuss their pasts, but that seemed too personal, and she didn't want them becoming any more personal than they already were.

After throwing a few more logs onto the fire, Brock pushed himself to his feet. "I think it's time we turned in. It's dark out, and I see no reason for us to stay up. And we might be able to make our way out of here by tomorrow."

"And"—her voice wavered— "if we can't?"

"Come on, Red, don't get weepy on me now. You've lived out here long enough to know about survival and making the best of bad situations. You're a woman of the West, not some sissy eastern gal who can't hold up her own." His words had the desired effect when her spine stiffened and she pushed herself to her feet.

Turning various shades of crimson, Prudence stared down at the floor. Woman of the West or not, she had certain needs to attend to before bed. "What . . . ? I mean . . . where do we . . . ?"

Understanding dawned, and Brock smiled. "Relieve ourselves?" At her nod, he replied, "I'm intending to open that door and . . ." He left the explanation unsaid. "I guess you're in a bit of a predicament." He scratched his chin, looking about the cabin, and his eyes landed on the empty peach jar. He handed it to her. "Hope your aim's as good as mine."

"You're awful!" But she couldn't help the smile that suddenly crossed her lips. "And where am I supposed to perform this feat?" The one-room cabin was small, and with Brock in it, it was getting smaller by the minute.

He walked to the door. "I'm sure you'll figure that out for yourself."

She did in record time, though she was mortified to think he could hear everything she was doing. Unsure of what to do with the jar once she'd finished, she left it on the floor in the corner and hurried to the bed, hoping he wouldn't trip over it.

Upon reaching the bed, Brock said, "Close your eyes if you're squeamish. I'm going to remove this blanket and lay it atop the both of us. It'll be warmer that way."

Her eyes widened. "But you'll be naked!"

"But warm." He raised a rakish brow at her.

He dropped the blanket, and she shut her eyes, scooting as far across the bed as she could without falling off, holding the quilt tightly about her, not caring that she wasn't sharing her cover. She'd be damned if she'd sleep in the nude with him. It was one thing to sleep in the same bed, quite another to do it buck naked!

When they were both nestled under the covers, he leaned over to blow out the candle and the room was plunged into darkness, save for the flickering firelight that danced across the ceiling.

"Good night, Red. Pleasant dreams."

There was silence, except for her even breathing, and Brock smiled. Poor Red. This was really quite an experience for her. She was in bed with a man she hardly knew, didn't like, and couldn't possibly want.

He, on the other hand, liked her more than he cared

to admit, and he wanted her more than he knew was reasonable for a man in his position. Damn! Just the thought of making love to her made him stiff as a board.

Prudence's soft snores soon filled the room, and Brock frowned. She was asleep! Obviously, she wasn't as bothered by sharing a bed as he was. Heaving a frustrated sigh, he wondered how he always got himself into such predicaments.

She rolled over on her side, inches from where he lay, and her hand came out of the covers to fall across his chest, her innocent touch searing his skin.

Great! Just great! The woman was definitely going to be the death of him yet. He might as well have slept on the damned floor. It couldn't have been any more torturous than what he was going through now.

On that thought, he closed his eyes, but sleep was a long time in coming.

Prudence snuggled closer to the warmth. Feeling gloriously content, she wondered if Hannah had come into her room to put another log onto the fire.

Cocking an eye open, she noticed a large male body lying next to her. She was scrunched up against it, her arm draped across his naked chest.

Oh, my God! Brock!

And then it all came back to her: where she was . . . whom she was with.

The second thing she noticed was that her quilt had come undone during the night and her breasts were pressed into Brock's arm. Feeling intense heat flush her body, and not entirely sure it was caused by embarrassment, she inched away as carefully as she could so as not to waken him.

Thank God he was still asleep. What would she have

done if he had awakened first and found her naked body pressed against his? Most likely he'd have considered it an invitation. And who could have blamed him, as wanton as she looked?

Wicked. Isn't that what Reverend Entwhistle had called her? Well, she guessed she was. No decent woman would be caught in such a compromising position. And no decent woman would relish the opportunity to study a man in his altogether. But that's exactly what she was doing.

Her eyes drifted over his face. His cheeks were stubbled with beard, making him look somewhat rakish. His chest was lightly furred, and she reached out to trace a finger over it. Soft. It was as soft as BJ's behind.

The blanket had slipped below his belly button, and she could see the swirl of hair there, too. Was it as soft? she wondered, then chastised herself for such impure thoughts. The skin below his waist was much paler than his chest, indicating that he'd often worked without his shirt on.

The blanket below his waist suddenly tented, and her eyes widened in surprise until she heard that soft, familiar chuckle that instantly turned her face florid.

"Mornin', Red. Did you sleep well?" He sure as hell hadn't, but he wasn't going to admit that to her.

"Yes, thank you."

The quilt was wrapped around her breasts, exposing her shoulders and neck to his view. Her hair curled about them riotously, and he itched to grab a handful of it. "Don't you know it isn't proper to stare at a naked man first thing in the morning?"

Despite her best efforts not to, her gaze drifted down below his waist again—the blanket was lifted up a good seven inches—then back up to his face. He was grinning at her like a hyena.

"I wasn't staring. I was merely curious to see if you were awake, that's all."

"You were curious all right, but not about my sleeping habits." At her gasp, he threw back the covers. "You'd best close your eyes. I need to throw some wood on the fire."

She did, but she managed to chance a peek at his firmly muscled buttocks and thighs before squeezing her eyes shut. What on earth had come over her?

"You didn't peek, now, did you?" he asked, rushing back to the bed. The mattress dipped under his weight as he got back in. Prudence shook her head so vigorously, he knew immediately that she was lying. "That's good. I wouldn't want to shock your ladylike sensibilities."

"Don't you think we should get up?" Prudence glanced out the window and saw there was no rush. Snow was piled next to the glass, all but obscuring the view.

"We won't be going anywhere today, Red." He smiled wickedly. "It's been a good while since I've spent a lazy day in bed with a beautiful woman."

His compliment made her feel all fuzzy inside. "I guess we should remain here until the room warms up." Which was occurring rapidly. *She* certainly felt warm.

He turned onto his side, leaning his head on his palm, and with his right hand reached out to curl her hair around his finger. "You sure have pretty hair." His finger trailed down to touch her naked shoulder. "And your skin is soft and white as cream." His eyes darkened. "I wonder if it tastes as sweet."

She swallowed. "Brock, you mustn't." But her protest was only halfhearted, and he knew it; he leaned over to place a kiss directly over her heart.

"Mmmm. Sweet. Just as I thought."

She should pull back, she knew, but she remembered the way his lips had made her feel the last time he'd kissed her. She desperately wanted to feel that way again. Tentatively she placed her lips against his, and the moment they touched, she knew she had made a terrible mistake, for that tender touch made her want more.

He deepened the kiss, plunging his tongue inside the soft recesses of her mouth, exploring, searching, making the blood pound in her brain. The quilted barrier was soon removed, and Brock's lips traveled down her neck to her breasts, drawing the stiffened peaks into his mouth.

Not content to suckle there, he kissed her belly, all the while stroking the sensitive flesh of her inner thighs, urging her legs open, moving lower and lower to taste the sweetness of her, then back up to settle on her breasts once more.

Prudence was mindless with desire. The feel of his lips, his tongue, bathing every inch of her was exquisite torture. She could feel her resistance slipping, receding with every warm caress. Her breathing grew labored; her heart thundered in her ears. "Oh, God!" she cried out, finally realizing that she was about to surrender.

She didn't know what brought reality crashing back down on her. Maybe it was the loud crackle of the logs or the cry of the wind that sounded so lonely, so mournful, reminding her of what life would be like once Brock was gone.

She pushed at his chest, rolling out from beneath him. "I can't. I'm sorry."

"Goddammit, Red," Brock said, taking deep, uneven breaths, "you can't keep torturing me, leading me on, then stopping at the last minute. I never figured you for a tease."

She drew the blanket around her once more, staring at the painful evidence of Brock's desire, knowing what she had done was wrong. "I'm not a tease. I'm just inexperienced when it comes to this sort of thing. And I'm afraid I let myself get carried away by your kisses."

"Why can't you let yourself go? Why must you ruin what could be a beautiful moment between us? I want you, Red. I need you more than you will ever know."

She shook her head, unwilling to let his words persuade her. "No! I won't ruin my life for a beautiful moment. Moments are fleeting. They slip away, melting into memories, leaving you with nothing."

Her lower lip was quivering, as though she were about to cry, and her eyes were filling with tears. Great! Just great! He was as hard as a goddamn icicle, and she was going to make him feel even worse by crying. He hated it when a woman cried. He could stand almost anything but that.

He wrapped the blanket around himself and climbed out of bed to cross to the fireplace. He picked up his pants and shirt and felt a measure of relief. At least their clothes were dry. Thank God for small favors.

"Here's your clothes," he said, tossing them at her. They landed unceremoniously on the bed. "Get dressed. I'm not staying in this cabin with you one more minute than I have to."

She sniffed. "But the storm!"

His voice was as cold as his eyes when he said, "I don't give a goddamn about the storm. I'd rather perish out there in the elements than suffer another night at your hands. There's an expression the cowboys use: 'Man is the only animal that can be skinned more'n once.' This makes two for me, Red. I'm not about to go for a third."

14

*When a cowboy's too old to set a bad example,
he hands out good advice.*

"*You are one* crazy son of a bitch!"

Perched on the snow-covered roof of the bunkhouse, driving nails into it as if there were no tomorrow, Brock glanced down to find Shorty yelling up at him. The old man's face was chapped red from the cold, and he was staring up at Brock as if he were deranged.

Which he probably was, Brock thought. But Prudence Daniels was enough to drive any sane man nuts. He'd be damned if he'd spend one night longer than necessary under the same roof with her. Not after that little episode in the cabin. And he'd told her as much just as soon as they'd gotten home.

True to his word, he'd come out at first light the following day to work on the bunkhouse, and the day after that, and this morning was no exception.

"It's not snowing that hard anymore, Shorty. And I

need the exercise. All those women under one roof make me crazy."

Shorty chuckled. "Come on down and have some coffee. I brung you out a hot cup." He lifted the tin cup toward Brock enticingly.

Brock swung down from the rafters, landing in the soft snow. "Thanks," he said once he'd righted himself. He reached for the steaming mug. "Don't mind if I do."

"You sure been acting mighty queer since you and Miss Pru got yourselves stuck in that blizzard. There's been a powerful lot of speculatin' about what went on."

"Not a damn thing went on!"

A knowing look entered the old man's eyes. "Well, now, that do explain a few things."

"Don't stick your nose into matters that don't concern you, old man. There's nothing between me and Red."

Shorty took a sip of his coffee. "Well, maybe that's so and maybe it isn't. But Eliza says otherwise. She says Miss Prudence has been moping about the house. Says she's off her feed."

Brock shrugged. "Sounds to me like she's sick."

"Yep. Sounds like that to me, too. Only I don't think there's a cure for what ails her."

"Oh, there's a cure all right. She's just not woman enough to take it."

"Miss Pru's led a sheltered life. Leastways, she did before her pa died. The sun rose and set on those two gals for Cody Daniels. He was protective of 'em. Too much so, if you ask me. They never had the opportunity to socialize proper like they should have. I suspect it's why Clara got herself into trouble with the first man that paid her some attention. Billy was a charmer."

"So Prudence tells me." Brock sipped thoughtfully on his coffee, warming his hands against the hot cup.

"A woman like Prudence needs a firm but gentle hand. She's like a skittish filly who don't want to be ridden." The cowboy heaved a deep sigh. "Can't say as I blame her none. Not after what happened to her sister. A woman's got a right to be leery of drifters."

"If this discussion is going to be long-winded, then I suggest we go inside the bunkhouse. There might not be any walls, but there's a semblance of a roof, and it'll keep the snow off us." Stepping into the half-finished structure, Brock pulled up two kegs of nails and they sat down.

"You know I ain't the interfering type," Shorty continued as if Brock had never spoken, and Brock's eyes rolled heavenward. "But I hate to see two young people like yourselves acting plumb foolish."

"Just because you been sparkin' Eliza Dobbyns doesn't make you the foremost authority on romance, Shorty."

Pulling a pouch of Bull Durham tobacco and a prayer book of papers out of his coat pocket, Shorty commenced rolling himself a cigarette. "I admit that old gal's got my interest up. She ain't like no other woman I ever met. Why"—he smiled to himself—"her voice is like sweet maple syrup. I could sit and listen to her talk for hours."

Which Brock was sure he'd done, knowing Eliza's penchant for talking. When a hen cackles, she's either layin' or lyin'. He thought about repeating the saying but doubted Shorty would appreciate hearing it.

"Maybe you should pay formal court to her, then," Brock suggested. He was only teasing, but he could see by the grave expression on Shorty's face that the old man had already given the matter serious consideration.

"I ain't told another living soul about this, so I'd appreciate it if you'd keep my counsel." Brock indicated he would, and Shorty continued, "When I was a boy I done had the mumps. Doc told my ma that I'd never be able to have young'ns. None of the women of my acquaintance ever found themselves in the family way, if you get my drift, so I think he musta been tellin' the truth. I've always had a hankerin' to have me a child. Marrying up with Eliza would kill two birds with one stone, so to speak."

Shorty's revelation came as a complete surprise to Brock. He'd figured the old codger was too set in his ways to be thinking about matrimony. Especially with a citified southern woman like Eliza Dobbyns. The two had never gotten along; in fact, they seemed to dislike each other.

Maybe opposites did attract, Brock thought, inhaling a whiff of Shorty's tobacco smoke. Suddenly Prudence's image rose to mind, and he frowned, swallowing it with a sip of strong, hot coffee.

"Do you love her?" he asked the cowboy. "It wouldn't be fair to marry the woman just for the child."

Shorty rubbed his chin, pondering the question. "Well now, maybe I do and maybe I don't. I don't rightly know the truth of that yet. A man don't have thoughts about women till he's thirty-five. Afore then, all he's got is feelin's. A man my age looks for companionship—a body to keep him warm on a cold night. I ain't sure if what I feel for Eliza is love, but I sure do like her well enough. And that's a start.

"Most young folks nowadays rush into things, never becoming friends before they become lovers. There's a lot more to marriage than weddin' and beddin'. A man needs to be able to talk to his wife outside of the bedroom, iff'n you get my meaning."

Brock sighed, wondering how they ever got on such a touchy subject. Talking of marriage inevitably brought Catherine to mind. And though thoughts of her had become less painful, more nostalgic, the agony of his loss would never disappear completely. But it was receding. He guessed he had Red to thank for that, though he wasn't sure he wanted to.

Red. What the hell was he going to do about that woman? She was an itch that needed scratchin'. But trying to satisfy that itch was like tryin' to scratch your ear with your elbow.

Prudence moaned softly, clutching Brock's head to her chest as his lips surrounded her pebble-hard nipples. Her head lolled from side to side as his lips trailed down her breasts, her stomach, his tongue flicking at her navel, then moving lower, ever lower, until the apex of her thighs flooded with desire, and her legs opened to receive the pulsing hardness of his manhood.

"Brock," she whispered, clutching the pillow to her as the clock on the mantel gonged six. Reluctantly she opened her eyes, groaning aloud as she stared at the clock, realizing that she was quite alone in her bed. It had been a dream. Another awful dream.

Throwing back the heavy quilt, Prudence hopped out of bed. This was the fourth day in a row she had overslept. And dreamed. She cursed Brock Peters under her breath for being the cause of her sleeplessness.

She shrugged on her wrapper, pausing to take a quick glance in the mirror as she headed for the door. The vision that greeted her brought a scowl to her lips. Dark circles rimmed her eyes, and her hair looked lackluster.

Your pump's been primed, Red.

Brock's taunting words came to mind, infuriating her. Childishly she stuck out her tongue at the annoying image before slamming out of the room.

Down the hallway, she yanked open the bathroom door—and gasped aloud. Brock stood inside, dripping wet and naked as the day he was born. Instantly a warm tingling feeling suffused her entire body.

"Don't you even bother to knock?" He grabbed a towel and wrapped it around his waist.

"I'm . . . I'm sorry. I thought you'd be gone by now."

"I overslept," was all he said. But the furious expression on his face brought a satisfied smile to her own. Apparently she wasn't the only one suffering.

"So did I. I was up late reading."

"Uh huh. Right."

She could tell he didn't believe a word she said, and it aggravated her. "If you're done in the bathroom, I'd like to use it. Jacob is coming to call today, and I need to make myself presentable."

He closed the space between them until his chest was practically touching her nose. "Well, don't forget to put on your protective armor, Red. I fear your friend has ulterior motives where you're concerned." What man wouldn't? She was damn desirable.

The scent of Brock's spicy shaving soap was making her weak-kneed, and she swallowed with some difficulty. "Don't compare Jacob to yourself, Brock. Not all men are randy lechers. I'll have you know that Jacob has always been a perfect gentleman."

He threw back his head and laughed. "I wouldn't trust him as far as I could spit. And spittin's never been my strong suit."

"You're wrong!" She pushed him out the door, even though the feel of his warm skin beneath her hands was making her crazy with desire.

"Just remember what I said," he shouted through the closed portal. "Keep your distance from Morgan."

Covering her face, Prudence took several deep

breaths. She was shaking, physically shaking. And throbbing! Her nipples were pebble hard and aching.

Damn Brock for making her feel this way!

Hastily she filled the porcelain tub with cold water, then sank into it. "Damn . . . damn . . . you . . . Brock Pe-Pe-ters!" she stuttered, the icy water turning her toes blue. "Damn you . . . you . . . to . . . hell!"

Jacob stared at the woman seated next to him on the sofa, and a deep frown punctuated his stony features. Prudence seemed different somehow. She looked the same in the familiar white starched blouse and navy serge skirt, but something was different. She was nervous, self-conscious. And he didn't like what that might imply.

He'd heard in great detail about her overnight stay at the old McCanless place. Everyone in town, including Bella, had gone to great pains to inform him that Prudence had spent the night in a deserted cabin with her foreman.

You couldn't keep a thing like that quiet in a town like Absolution. Prudence and Peters had been spotted leaving town, then Doc Smithson had seen them turn off the road, heading in the direction of the McCanless place. Old Doc figured they'd taken shelter there and said he would have followed them, except he knew Trudy Morehouse's baby was due any day and he needed to get back to town. More'n likely the old coot didn't have an adequate supply of whiskey with him, Jacob thought, hating the idea of Prudence and her foreman left alone all night to do God knew what.

Peters. That bastard! He'd probably plowed Prudence's fertile field and tasted all of her virginal sweetness. And it didn't set well—no, it didn't set well at all.

If Prudence Daniels was to be his wife, he wanted fresh goods, not used. He wanted to be her first, goddammit!

Maybe the rumors weren't true, he mused. Maybe he'd still be the first to land in the honey pot. His smile was predatory as he rubbed his sweaty palms against his pant legs, studying the fullness of her breasts, which were not as large as Bella's but adequate nonetheless. There was only one foolproof way to find out if Prudence Daniels was still a virgin, and he aimed to satisfy more than his curiosity.

"Would you care for more coffee, Jacob? Perhaps another sweet roll?" Prudence had never seen Jacob so distracted before and wondered if there might be a problem at the Bar J. Before she could ask, he set down his cup and saucer and scooted closer to her.

"It's not coffee or sweet rolls I've got a craving for, honey."

Prudence's eyes widened in surprise, then her gaze drifted down to Jacob's lips. They were full lips, almost pouty, and she'd never kissed a man with a mustache before. Maybe she'd find that Jacob's kisses were just as exciting as Brock's. Maybe if she let him kiss her the way she knew he wanted to, she'd discover that her attraction to Brock was purely physical, and not the deeper emotional bond she feared she was forming for the footloose cowboy.

Leaning toward him, she placed her hand quite daringly on his knee. With the invitation issued, Jacob wasted no time in capturing Prudence's lips.

Nothing. She felt nothing. No spark. No warm, snuggly feeling, as when she kissed Brock. Dismayed by what that meant, she attempted to pull out of Jacob's embrace, but her action merely caused him to tighten his hold.

"Honey . . . honey," he whispered, nuzzling her neck with wet, sloppy kisses.

She felt overwhelmed with revulsion. "Stop, Jacob! Release me at once."

Her pleas fell on deaf ears, as Jacob smiled in that self-assured manner of his. "You don't mean that, honey. Once we're married I'll give you such pleasure you'll think you've died and gone to heaven."

She shook her head in denial, but he captured it in his hands, bringing her mouth to his once again. Bile rose in her throat as his thick tongue thrust inside her mouth. She fought desperately, but her actions seemed only to excite him.

Oh, dear God, what have I done?

It was the middle of the day. No one was at home, save for Laurel. And Prudence knew with certainty that she was going to be raped in her very own parlor.

Scream! her mind shouted when his hand moved up to cup her breast, his thumb flicking lightly over her nipple. *Scream!*

Suddenly frantic screams ripped through the air, but they weren't hers.

In the next moment Jacob released her, and she thanked God silently, taking huge gulps of air. Once she'd regained her composure, she reached back and slapped Jacob Morgan soundly across his face. "How dare you take such liberties!" she accused, vaulting to her feet.

"Now, Prudence, honey." He rubbed at his burning face. For a gently reared woman, she certainly packed a wallop.

The screaming continued, and Prudence suddenly realized it was coming from the great room. She rushed toward the sound, and much to her dismay Jacob followed close on her heels like a shadow.

She pulled up short at the sight of Laurel standing on top of the table screaming at the top of her lungs. Prudence didn't know whether she was more surprised by the sound coming from the young woman's throat or by the fact that Slim Robbins hadn't ridden into town with the others and was attempting to coax the frightened woman off the table.

"I'm sorry, Miss Pru," the cowboy said, a chagrined look on his face. "I didn't mean to scare Miss Laurel. I only wanted to kiss her. Was that wrong?"

The poor man looked twice as distraught as poor Laurel, and Prudence had a hard time mustering any anger toward him.

"That's what you get for hiring dimwits, and taking in mental cases who belong in lunatic asylums," Jacob said from behind her.

Having forgotten for the moment that he was there, Prudence whirled on him, a feral look on her face. "Get out, Jacob. You've worn out your welcome here."

"Now, Prudence, you don't mean that."

"I'm pretty sure she does, Morgan," came a deep voice from the doorway.

Wonderful! Prudence thought as Brock stepped farther into the room. His unwelcome arrival had just made her day complete. "I can handle this, Brock."

He shrugged, leaning casually against the door frame as if he had all the time in the world and no intention of leaving; there was a lethal look in his eyes that Prudence found chilling.

She turned toward Jacob, and the nasty look on his face almost kept her from uttering, "Please leave, Jacob, before I am forced to have you thrown off this ranch."

Brock grinned and received a scathing look of his own.

The hazel eyes hardened, narrowing into thin slits.

"I'll go, but we're not through yet, Prudence. Not by a long shot. You'll be sorry you treated an old friend so shabbily."

"Is that a threat, Morgan?" Brock asked, his hand going to his gun belt.

"I am not without influence in this town. You will all soon find that out." He stormed out of the room, then a moment later the front door banged loudly behind him.

Laurel's screams finally subsided to whimpers, and she allowed Prudence to help her off the table. "Go up to your room, Laurel. I'll join you in a moment," Prudence directed, relieved when the young girl didn't argue. Laurel climbed halfway up the stairs, then paused to toss Slim a wave and sweet smile before continuing.

"I didn't mean no harm, Miss Pru," Slim reiterated, a thoroughly confused look on his face. "I just wanted to give Miss Laurel a peck on the cheek. My mama always gave me one when I was sad, and Miss Laurel seemed awful sad today."

Heaving a disgusted sigh, Prudence stabbed an accusing look at Brock that said quite plainly, "I told you this would happen."

"I'll talk to Slim. Explain to him about Laurel." When Prudence nodded and made to leave, Brock added, "But that doesn't mean this was all a mistake. Laurel's screams prove that much. She's finally expressing her emotions."

Prudence hated it when Brock was logical, for it usually meant he was right. Just as he'd been right about Jacob's ulterior motives. Of course, she had no intention of telling him so; the man was infuriatingly arrogant as it was.

"You really should get your medical degree, Brock. You seem to be so knowledgeable about the human condition," Prudence flung out before beginning to climb the stairs.

"If I thought all my patients would look like you, Red, I wouldn't hesitate. I can give a mean examination when I've a mind to."

She gasped and turned to face his grin, then purpled and hurried the rest of the way up the stairs.

"You know, Slim," Brock began, wrapping his arm about the cowboy's broad shoulders, "only a fool argues with a skunk, a mule, or a woman. I must be all kinds of a fool." For more reasons than one, he thought.

15

*Many things are possible if
you cinch your attention to them.*

    Outside, the snow began to fall again with renewed vigor, icing the frozen landscape. But inside the cozy dining room, the fire in the hearth crackled cheerfully, and an air of excitement prevailed around the walnut table, warming the inhabitants.

Moody and Sarah exchanged secret smiles, then Moody pushed back his chair from the table and stood, clearing his throat. All eyes turned on him. "I'd like to make an announcement," he said, brushing nervously at the blue uniform jacket, which Sarah had insisted he wear for the auspicious occasion. "Since Polly is fixin' to leave us tomorrow"—he smiled warmly at the young woman—"Sarah and I thought her going-away party would be an appropriate time to share some news with all of you."

An excited buzz started around the table, and Brock

gazed at Prudence to gauge her reaction. It was no secret what Moody was about to announce—Moody and Sarah had been mooning over each other for weeks—but he wasn't certain Prudence had been astute enough to pick up on the couple's feelings for each other. Brock's attention reverted back to Moody.

"I have the pleasure of announcing that Miss Sarah Davenport has done me the very great honor of consenting to become my wife." He leaned toward Sarah, who sat to his right smiling radiantly, and kissed her tenderly on the cheek.

Stunned, Prudence stared wide-eyed at the happy couple; then, realizing that everyone was looking at her for approval, she smiled and rose, kissing them both on the cheek. "Congratulations, you two! I'm very happy for you." And she was, she realized, though she was still quite surprised. She knew Sarah and Moody were enamored of each other, but she hadn't thought their infatuation would lead them to the altar.

"You old coot," Brock said, slapping Moody on the back. "How on earth did you talk such an intelligent woman into becoming your wife?" He kissed Sarah on the cheek, making her blush.

Everyone laughed except Polly, who burst into tears. "I'm going to miss the wedding," she wailed, sobbing into her hands.

"Now, Poll," her brother said, wrapping his arm around her shoulders, "just think, you'll be back home with Mom and Dad, spending Christmas just like you wanted."

"But you won't be with me, Will." She stared accusingly at her brother, then at Mary, who studied her food self-consciously.

"Oh, Polly, hush," Louann ordered between bites of ham. "You're spoiling Sarah's moment."

Biting her quivering lower lip, Polly pushed back her chair and ran from the room, and Sarah leveled such a withering look at Louann, it made the woman lean back in her chair.

When Prudence made to rise, Will motioned her back down. "I'll go, Miss Pru. After all, Polly is still my responsibility."

Sitting back down on his seat, Moody flushed slightly. "I'm sorry to have upset Polly. It wasn't my intention."

"She'll be fine, Colonel," Prudence assured him. "Polly's just saddened by her imminent departure. By tomorrow morning the excitement of leaving will make her forget all her unhappiness of the moment."

"Are you sure? I can go up and speak to her," Sarah offered, staring anxiously at the now empty seat across from her.

Brock shook his head. "I think we should let Will handle this. Those two still have some things to sort out between them."

Later, after everyone had retired for the night, Will sought Brock out in the kitchen, where he was preparing himself a snack before bedtime.

"Can I talk to you, Mr. Peters?"

Having just fashioned two large ham sandwiches, Brock pushed one across the table toward Will. "Sure, son. Come sit down and have a sandwich. Problems are always easier to solve on a full stomach."

"But we just ate a little while ago." Will stared at the large concoction only briefly before sitting down and digging in, making Brock wonder if the young boy was appeasing his appetite for the same reason Brock was: lack of sex. In Will's case, he decided, it was more likely because he was a growing boy.

A growing man, he amended. Will was turning into a fine young man. He'd put on at least fifteen pounds in the last couple of months, and the weight had turned into muscle, not flab.

"What do you want to talk about, Will?" he asked, taking a bite of his sandwich, then washing it down with a gulp of cold milk.

"Do you think it was bad of me, not wanting to accompany my sister home? Do you think I'm letting her down?"

Brock studied the anguish on Will's face and wished he could ease his torment; the transition from boyhood to manhood was often difficult, he knew. "Is that what Polly said?"

The young man shrugged. "Pretty much. She said I loved Mary more than her, and that family should come first before all else."

"And do you love Mary, Will?" Brock smiled inwardly as the young man's face flushed bright red.

"Yes, sir!" Will nodded enthusiastically. "Mary and BJ are the most important things in the world to me. I'm not saying that Polly isn't important, because she is. But I want to marry Mary one day, have a family with her. I just couldn't leave to go back home, Mr. Peters. I love living out west. Cattle ranching has opened up whole new vistas for me."

"But what about your family? Won't they be upset? Prudence said your pa wanted you to become a lawyer like him." Which sounded all too familiar, Brock thought. It was the very reason he'd chosen the profession himself.

He had followed in his father's footsteps to a point. But Calvin Peters had counseled the rich, defended the privileged, who'd always found their way around the law, while Brock had chosen to represent those who found themselves victimized by the very people his father defended. Theirs had been an uneasy relationship, and Brock had always regretted not mending fences with his father before he died.

"That's true, Mr. Peters." Brock's attention returned to what the young man was saying. "But I'm not like Dad. He's content to live in the city. He likes the finer things—museums, book recitals." Will wrinkled his nose. "I want adventure. I want to make my own mark in the world—be my own man, like you did."

What would Will say if Brock told him that he was a lawyer just like his father? he wondered. Would Brock be knocked off that pedestal Will had seen fit to place him on?

"There comes a time in every man's life when he's got to make his own decisions. They're not always the right ones, but when a man makes a decision, he's got to live with the consequences and know that he did what his conscience dictated."

"And do you think my decision not to go back to New York was the right one?"

Brock knew how easy it would be to give Will the reassurance he sought. But he also knew that it wouldn't be fair to Will in the long run. "Only you can know that, son."

The boy's face fell. "I was afraid you'd say something like that. Miss Prudence says you're so logical it's downright irritating."

Brock threw back his head and laughed. "Oh, she did, did she?"

Will nodded. "She told Mary that you were bossy and opinionated and liked to give advice. But that your advice was usually correct, and it was annoying in the extreme. I believe those were her very words."

A dark eyebrow arched. "Annoying, huh? Anything else?"

The young man's face reddened. "Well . . . it was most likely just women talk, but Mary said that Miss Pru confided that"—the boy's blush deepened—"that you had muscles in places she hadn't even thought about, and that your toes were attractive for a man." The latter was said in a rush of breath.

Brock stared at his booted feet, then up at Will's scarlet face. Well, well, it seemed Miss Daniels had been doing a fair amount of thinking about his anatomy. He smiled wickedly, wondering what other body parts of his she'd been contemplating.

"You won't tell Miss Pru what I said, will you, Mr. Peters? If Mary found out I'd told, after she swore me to secrecy, she'd skin me alive."

Brock smiled. "I won't tell, Will. But tell me this— you're not afraid of that little gal, are you?"

"I reckon." The youthful shoulders sagged in what almost could be described as a resigned gesture, and Brock noticed that Will's speech was taking on more and more of a western twang; it hadn't taken the boy long to adapt to his new environment.

"That's what comes of being in love, Mr. Peters. I'm sure you'll agree, you being in love with Miss Pru and all."

The chair Brock had been tottering back on came crashing forward with a resounding thud. "Love? Prudence Daniels?"

There was such disbelief, such utter shock, on the foreman's face, Will's forehead wrinkled in confusion. "Well, aren't you? Sure seems like you two have been sparkin' to me."

Sparkin'! Hell, they had a regular goddamn raging inferno going, Brock thought.

But love?

He had no answer for the boy. How could he? He'd never thought of Red in those terms before. Love to him was always Catherine and Josh.

But Red?

Loving Red meant betraying Catherine's memory. They'd vowed long ago to love and cherish only each other. How then could he allow himself to think in those terms with another woman?

Will cleared his throat impatiently, and Brock heaved an audible sigh. Great! Just great! The confessor had been turned into the confessee.

The best defense is a powerful offense. He'd learned those words of wisdom in a courtroom.

He turned on Will and in his best lawyer's voice said, "Don't you know it's not polite to question your elders, son? Some might think it rude." He almost felt guilty at the embarrassed flush suffusing the young man's cheeks, but he wasn't about to let Will continue this line of questioning.

"Sorry, Mr. Peters," Will said hurriedly, making his way to the door. "Guess I'll be turning in now. Good night."

"Good night, Will. Sleep tight."

He sure as hell wasn't going to.

He had a lot of thinking to do, thanks to Will's innocent question. He didn't know what kind of answer he was bound to come up with, and that scared the living hell out of him!

"I sure do appreciate your helping me out with these pies, Christey." Prudence dipped her hands in flour before picking up the pile of sticky dough. "I can't believe Thanksgiving is already upon us." Tomorrow, to be exact, and they had hours more preparation to do.

"I don't mind, Miss Prudence. It gives me something to do other than worry about Samuel." Her eyes filled with tears, as they did each and every time she thought about her husband, which was often. "I'm much better at baking than at sewing those belts and chaps. I don't have the talent like the others."

"You mustn't underestimate your abilities, Christey. Your work is quite satisfactory," Prudence advised, patting the dough into a smooth round.

"Thank you, ma'am. But I'd still rather be cooking and baking for my man. I loved keeping house and doing all the chores most women find tedious. It always gave me a sense of accomplishment." She smiled wistfully. "Why, I don't think there's a better feeling than pulling fresh loaves of bread out of the oven and realizing that you'd accomplished it all on your own." When Prudence's face fell, Christey added quickly, "You shouldn't fret about your cooking, Miss Prudence. You've learned a lot. Why, that dinner you prepared the other evening was quite good."

Prudence smiled in satisfaction. The ham had been quite succulent, the yams glazed to perfection. If only she'd remembered to put the yeast in the bread. "There's a lot more to this cooking than meets the eye," she stated. "But I told Hannah that I wanted her to teach me everything she knew, and I'm learning." If the method worked for tanning hides, why not cooking? she'd reasoned.

"Don't overwork your pie dough, Miss Prudence," Christey cautioned, turning a practiced eye on the lump of dough that was quickly drying out under Prudence's unskilled hands. "Pie dough takes a light, gentle touch. If you knead it too much, you're going to make it tough as old shoe leather. It's not like tanning hides into leather."

Observing how Christey handled the dough, Prudence imitated her motions and noted that it did make the dough easier to handle. "It's hard to believe that Polly's been gone a week. It's always sad when one of my girls leaves."

"Don't you want more out of life than taking care of other people's children? I mean," Christey explained, noting the crestfallen expression on the older woman's face, "don't you want young'ns of your own? It's a comfort knowing that even if Samuel never returns, I'll always have part of him with me."

"I've never given children a lot of thought. I guess I've always had someone else's around to care for and love." And having children meant having a husband. And that meant putting her trust in a man.

Christey patted her swollen abdomen, and Prudence felt a momentary twinge of envy. What would it be like, she wondered, to have children of her own? Brown-haired, brown-eyed children with dirty faces and impish grins?

Realizing whom those children were starting to resemble, Prudence slapped at the pie dough with such viciousness, Christey was forced to remark, "Goodness gracious, Miss Prudence! You are slapping that pie dough silly."

Prudence stared down at the horrible mess she'd made of all her hard work and felt like crying. But she didn't. Instead she poked two holes for eyes, indented a mouth and nose, then made a fist, and smashed her hand into the soft pile of dough, seeing Brock's face each and every time she connected with it. She felt immeasurably better.

But not for long, for not five minutes later Brock

sauntered into the sunlit kitchen, carrying the largest turkey she'd ever laid eyes on. It must have weighed a least thirty pounds. And it was completely cleaned.

Brock heaved the large bird onto the table. "Here's your Thanksgiving dinner," he said, smiling at the impressed looks on both women's faces. Prudence was probably surprised that he'd gone ahead and cleaned the thing. But after hearing from Hannah that Prudence was going to lend a hand in the preparation of the holiday meal, he wasn't going to leave it to chance that she wouldn't remove all the pin feathers. There was nothing worse than a mouth full of feathers . . . except for turkey that wasn't properly cooked. He grimaced at the memory of the last chicken dinner she'd prepared; the chicken had been raw. Raw! Hell! It had been downright bloody!

"It's a lovely bird," Prudence remarked, eyeing the oven door and wondering if it was going to fit. She hadn't the vaguest notion how long it would take to cook.

"I'd best go and check on BJ," Christey announced. "I promised Mary I'd look in on him while she's helping Will muck out the stalls."

Prudence frowned in dismay at the announcement. She had no desire to be alone with Brock. Things always seemed to happen when they were left alone together.

As if Brock could read her mind, he smiled knowingly at her. "What's the matter, Red? Does it make you nervous to be alone with me? It should, you know. There's still a lot of unresolved business between us."

She felt her cheeks grow warm and wiped her hands matter-of-factly on her apron. "I don't know what you're talking about, but then I rarely do."

"Oh, I think you do," he said, running his finger down her cheek. "You can't deny that there's something between us. And though you've done your best to fight it, it's not going to go away." His finger trailed down her neck, and he could feel the pulse beating there. "Why do you deny it?"

Her eyes were drawn to his hands, and she remembered how they had felt caressing her body. She fought to catch her breath, unwilling to let Brock know how his touch affected her. She dared not show her weakness. A weak woman could fall easily into a man's clutches, as she had done already on two separate occasions.

Noting the ardent look in his eyes, she stepped back from the table. Her heart beat a loud cadence in her ears, drumming the breath right out of her. After a moment she said, "Thank you for the turkey. I'm sure it will satisfy everyone's hunger."

His voice grew low and incredibly seductive. "You know there's only one thing that's going to appease my hunger, Red. And there'll be no substitute for it."

Her nipples hardened under his gaze, despite her best efforts to remain coolly detached. "Please, you mustn't speak so. What if someone were to hear you?"

With a shrug of his shoulders, he reached for a couple of the sugared apple slices in the bowl. "So? I doubt it's a secret that there's something between us. The temperature in a room rises at least ten degrees when we're in it together."

That was the gospel truth, but she'd rather be burned at the stake than admit it. "Don't you have chores to do or something? Surely the cattle need tending." She watched as he licked the sticky sugar and cinnamon off his fingers, and a fluttering began low in her stomach.

"Nope." He smiled at her disappointment. "Slim and Burt are out checking the herd." They'd found six head of dead cattle yesterday, but he wasn't going to reveal that now and ruin Red's holiday. He'd given the cowboys orders to shoot first and ask questions later. Rustling was serious enough, but killing another rancher's cows was the lowliest thing a man could do. And it fit Jacob Morgan's methods like a glove.

"Will's cleaning the stalls, and Shorty, with Eliza's help, has gone to town to fetch some odds and ends for Hannah. Speaking of which"—he looked about the kitchen—"where is the talented woman? I've been looking forward to eating her Thanksgiving dinner for weeks."

Prudence wasn't quite sure how to break the news to him, or to any of the others, for that matter. "Hannah's come down with a cold. Joe said she was coughing something terrible last night. I doubt she'll be up to cooking tomorrow's dinner."

Brock paled, and Prudence did her best not to feel offended. But it was difficult, considering the grimace of disgust on his face.

"You don't mean. . . ?"

"I'm fixing dinner, with help from Christey and Sarah. I'm sure everything will be quite delicious." Actually, delicious might have been a slight exaggeration; at this point she'd settle for edible.

"No offense, Red, since I know you've been taking some lessons, but don't you think a big holiday dinner is a little bit out of your league? It hasn't been that long since you learned to make toast without burning it. And your last batch of bread tasted like concrete."

She stiffened. "That's a rotten thing to say. Can I help it if my talents lie elsewhere?"

Noting the hurt look in her eyes, Brock reached out and caressed her cheek tenderly. "Love, your talents lie in the bedroom, not in the kitchen. And when you're ready for your next lesson, you just let me know. I'd be happy to teach you everything, and I've already discovered you're a quick learner. Contrary to popular opinion, the way to a man's heart is not through his stomach."

He kissed her lightly on the lips, and then he was gone, leaving Prudence stunned by the realization that she suddenly had a penchant for higher education, and the only teacher she wanted was Brock Peters.

16

*Close friends are folks who've sopped gravy
out'n the same skillet.*

Brock eyed the turkey with apprehension. It
certainly looked edible. But was it? Glancing over at
Shorty and Slim, he saw that they were having similar
thoughts. Unfortunately Prudence's cooking reputation
preceded her.

"The table looks just beautiful, Miss Prudence,"
Moody stated, giving Brock a sly wink. "I think you've
truly outdone yourself."

Brock had to hand it to Moody. He sure knew the
right thing to say at the right time. And judging by
the pleased expression on Red's face, he'd said
exactly the right thing.

In all fairness to Red, the table did look quite nice.
A pristine white cloth covered the wood, and delicate
china plates with tiny pink rosebuds—ones Brock had
never seen before—were placed next to sparkling

crystal goblets. The Danielses' family heirlooms, he surmised.

The blessing was said silently, and Brock prayed that the golden brown turkey gracing the center of the table would taste as good as it looked. Looks could definitely be deceiving when it came to Red's cooking, he knew.

"Would you mind doing the honors, Brock?" Prudence asked, handing him the bone-handled carving knife.

Brock's hand trembled when he set the knife against the bird, but a smile of great relief broadened his mouth when he sank the knife into the turkey and found it was cooked to perfection. Clear white juices trickled out, and the smell of the sage stuffing wafted up to make his mouth water.

"Looks like a winner, Red." Prudence's smile was so ebullient, it nearly made him drop his utensils.

After everyone was served, and they'd had their fill of candied yams, buttered peas, mashed potatoes and gravy, and rolls so light and fluffy they could pass for clouds, Prudence and Sarah went into the kitchen to fetch the pies and coffee.

"I'm going to have a hard time deciding which kind to eat," Burt confessed shyly. "Pumpkin's always been my favorite, but when Will told me about the apple, well . . ."

"We made eight pies, Burt, so I'm certain if you'd like to have a slice of each, Miss Prudence won't mind a bit," Christey assured him.

Before Burt could reply, a knock sounded at the door and everyone at the table glanced at each other with puzzled expressions on their faces.

"I wonder who that could be?" Eliza frowned. "You wouldn't think we'd be getting callers in the middle of a holiday meal."

Brock's thoughts flew to Jacob Morgan, and his hand tightened reflexively on the knife. Maybe the bastard had come to make amends. They hadn't seen him since Prudence threw him off the ranch, but he'd left his calling card—dead cattle—a number of times.

Pushing back her chair, Christey rose to her feet. "I'll go see. Perhaps Indian Joe needs something for Hannah."

Christey left the room just as Sarah and Prudence entered from the opposite direction, carrying large silver trays with four pies each on them. Burt and Slim jumped up to take the sweet-smelling concoctions from their hands.

Brock's chest swelled with pride as he gazed at the bounty before them. Prudence and the others had done themselves proud. The meal had been delicious, and the pies looked equally delectable. Nutmeg and cinnamon wafted through the air, filling his senses with memories of holidays past, making him forget his anger of moments ago.

"Red, I might have to change my mind about the way to a man's heart," he said, reaching for a piece of apple pie. "Like I said, you're a quick learner, and your cooking shows it."

Prudence blushed at Brock's underlying reference to yesterday's conversation. "Thank you. But I didn't do it all by myself."

He winked. "It usually takes at least two."

Before Prudence could comment, a loud scream erupted from the hallway. Brock and Shorty jumped up simultaneously and rushed out to find an unconscious Christey Baker in the arms of a redheaded stranger, who was covered from head to foot with snow.

Brock's eyebrows lifted, then understanding dawned and he smiled. "Samuel Baker, I presume?" He held out his hand, then withdrew it when he realized the man's hands were full of his wife, who had fainted at the sight of him.

"Well, I'll be hog-tied to a bare-assed mule," Shorty said to no one in particular.

"I'm Sam Baker." The farmer smiled ruefully. "I'm afraid my unexpected arrival was a bit too much for my wife. I hope I haven't endangered her life."

"She'll be just fine, Mr. Baker," said Prudence, who had just stepped into the hallway. "Please bring her into the parlor and set her down on the sofa."

Sarah fetched a cold compress, and in a few moments Christey opened her eyes to find her husband and Prudence leaning over her. "So it wasn't a dream?" she said, her eyes filling with tears as she held out her arms to her husband. "Oh, Samuel, where on earth have you been for so long? I'd almost given up on you."

Shorty nudged Brock in the ribs and shook his head. "Ain't it just like a woman to chastise a man before he's had a proper greeting?"

"You hush up, Mortimer Jenkins, or I'll be forced to give you a piece of my mind," Eliza said from behind them, her lips pursed in displeasure.

"Mortimer?" Brock mouthed, chuckling as the old man's face turned a sickly shade of gray.

Shorty shot Brock a scathing look, then whispered, "I told you not to call me that in mixed company, Eliza," before dragging his loquacious lady friend from the room.

"We'll leave you two to get reacquainted," Prudence said to the happy couple. "There's plenty of Thanksgiving turkey to eat, Mr. Baker, and you're welcome to join us at the table." Samuel Baker stared at his wife so lovingly, Prudence had difficulty swallowing past the lump in her throat.

The young couple looked so much in love, even Brock was having a difficult time hiding his emotions. He reached for Prudence's hand and led her back out into the hallway, shutting the parlor door behind him to give them privacy. Once he had Prudence alone, he turned her toward him. "Seeing their reunion made me realize how much we all have to be thankful for. I just wanted to tell you, Red, that you did a wonderful job with the meal. I'm very proud of you."

Prudence didn't know what to say. She wasn't used to this side of Brock's character. She was definitely used to his teasing, and even his bawdy comments, but his heartfelt words had taken her completely off guard, and she didn't know quite how to respond.

Before her mind could tell her that what she was about to do was extremely foolish, she tipped up on her toes and kissed Brock softly on the cheek, before making a mad dash back to the dining room.

Brock reached up to touch his cheek, and then a grin the size of the Grand Canyon split his face. Yep, he thought, Red was full of surprises tonight.

"I didn't expect to be gone this long," Samuel advised those members of the household still seated around the dining room table. He took a bite of pumpkin pie, then smiled in satisfaction. "Mighty fine pie, ma'am," he said to Prudence, who beamed with pleasure. She'd prepared the pumpkin pie filling all by herself, even remembering to remove the seeds from the pumpkin before setting it to boil.

Seated next to him, Christey glowed with happiness as she stared at her husband. "It was well worth the wait, knowing you came back unharmed and all in one piece, Samuel. I had terrible nightmares worrying about what might have detained you."

"Christey never gave up hope that you'd come, Mr. Baker," Prudence said. "She kept constant vigil at the window, sure in the knowledge that one day you'd be coming up the walk. I guess she was right."

"What was the hold-up, if you don't mind my asking?" Moody inquired. "There hasn't been any problems with Indians, has there?"

Samuel shook his head. "No, nothing like that. I had difficulty convincing the land office that the section of land I claimed was mine. An immigrant couple from Norway, who couldn't speak a word of English, were convinced that I was squatting on their land. It seems some unscrupulous land salesman had been selling off pieces of land that were already sold. It was a very difficult situation, with them not being able to understand, and I dared not leave for fear that once I was gone, they'd move onto the property and claim it for their own."

"Has it all been resolved, then?" Brock asked, wondering if he should offer any legal counsel.

Sam nodded. "The land's ours, all legal and proper. The immigrants finally gave up and staked out another claim. Mr. Burrows, the land agent, finally gave me clear title and a deed." He smiled proudly, patting his chest pocket. "The farm is ours now. And although it isn't much yet, it's going to be ripe with wheat one day."

"Samuel has always wanted to be a farmer," Christey confided with an abundance of pride in her voice. "His father wanted him to run the family barbershop back in Phoenix, but Sam said no, he wanted to farm. So we decided to move ourselves to a place we knew crops would grow. You can't grow much of anything except cactus in Arizona." She smiled sweetly at her husband, patting his hand. "It was the right choice for all of us. Our baby is going to be born in Nebraska on Baker land."

"When will you have to leave?" Prudence's voice filled with sadness. First Polly and now Christey. All her chicks were leaving the nest. "I hope you'll be able to stay on and rest for a few days, Mr. Baker."

"No, ma'am." He shook his head. "I'm sorry, we can't. I don't want to be gone any longer than necessary. Christey and I will be leaving at first light for Denver. There's a train heading east, leaving at noon, day after tomorrow, and we're going to be on it."

"Goodness, I—"

"Miss Pru," Louann interrupted, clutching her middle, "I think I had a bit too much Thanksgiving celebrating. I don't feel too well."

Alarmed by the sudden pallor on the young woman's face, Prudence rose to her feet to assist Louann out of her chair. She wrapped a comforting arm around her shoulders. "If you'll excuse me, I'll get Louann settled down for the night. I fear she's had one too many pieces of pie."

"I know the feeling," Moody said, rubbing his stomach. "I'm as stuffed as a mounted deer head."

Sarah smiled affectionately at her fiancé. "You really did overindulge this evening, Martin."

"That's what the holidays are for. Speaking of indulgence"—he turned toward Samuel, his blue eyes twinkling—"Sarah has prepared the room off the kitchen for you and Christey tonight. I thought you might appreciate a little privacy, this being your first night home." He chuckled as Christey's cheeks turned bright red. "I'll take the couch in the parlor tonight."

"That's mighty generous of you, Colonel Carstairs," Sam said, unable to disguise the eagerness in his voice. "Are you sure?"

"Couldn't be more sure. But call me Moody. I'm no longer in the cavalry. I've been put out to pasture."

"Now, Martin," Sarah scolded, "I thought we agreed there'd be no more talk like that."

Moody winked, forcing a smile to his lips. "I meant to say that I'm enjoying the heck out of my retirement."

"Speaking of which, I guess Christey and I will be taking you up on your offer." The tall, redheaded farmer grabbed his wife's hand and practically yanked her out of the chair in his haste to depart. "Hope we'll see you all in the morning."

Brock had his doubts that Samuel and Christey would be in any shape to leave too early, judging by the gleam in Sam's eyes, but he refrained from saying so. Not wishing to play third wheel to Moody and Sarah's cozy situation, Brock excused himself and headed up to bed, leaving the newly affianced couple alone.

Coming up behind Sarah as she began to place the soiled dishes onto the silver trays, Moody wrapped his arms about her rounded tummy, nudging her neck with his lips. "Brock is a very astute individual. I guess he knew that we wanted to be alone."

She reached up to caress his cheek. "We've only a few more weeks till Christmas, Martin, then we'll be wed. I'm as anxious as you to consummate what we feel for each other." In truth it had been all she'd been thinking about for weeks. She guessed she really was a fallen woman.

Turning her toward him, Moody gazed tenderly into her eyes, which reflected the same passion he felt. "We don't need to wait, Sarah. I'm sleeping in the parlor tonight. And there's a cozy fire blazing in the hearth. We could spend a nice romantic evening together."

"Martin!" she chastised, but her heart was suddenly pounding at the idea. She shook her head. "We couldn't possibly. What if someone were to wander in?" But, oh, the thought was wicked and exciting!

"That isn't likely. Everyone but us has gone to bed. And I assure you, Christey and her husband will be too occupied to pay us any mind." He kissed her softly on the lips, tightening his hold. "I want you for my own, Sarah. I want to be one with you."

Her heart ached with love for him. "It's what I've wanted since the first moment I laid eyes on you, Martin Carstairs." She placed her hand in his, taking a deep breath. "Lead on, Colonel," she said, her smile suddenly seductive. "Tonight we'll both have much to be thankful for."

Upstairs in the women's wing, Prudence sat on the edge of Louann's bed, sponging the blond woman's face. "How are you feeling? Are the pains in your stomach any better?"

She'd consulted *Dr. Chase's Practical Recipes* for treatment of dyspepsia and had ended up giving Louann a glass of sweet cream laced with brandy, which seemed to have quieted the cramping. If Louann's condition was more serious than a mere tummy ache, she didn't want to mask the symptoms by giving her anything stronger.

"A little. It don't seem to be hurting as much right now." Tears welled in Louann's eyes. "I ain't goin' to lose my baby, am I, Miss Pru? I don't think I could stand it if I did. I know I said at first that I didn't want this child, but I swear to God, I do. You don't think He will punish me by takin' it, do you?"

Prudence brushed the silken strands of hair away from the distraught woman's face. "Hush now. You mustn't talk so. God is merciful. He doesn't punish for things we say, or do, in a moment of weakness."

"But Reverend Entwhistle . . ."

"Is a horse's behind."

Prudence's uncharacteristic comment brought a small smile to Louann's lips, before she said, "I'm glad you think so, too."

"You must close your eyes and get some sleep. You and the baby both need to rest. I'll stay until you fall asleep, then I'll check on you in the morning."

Louann reached for Prudence's hand and brought it to her lips for a kiss. "You're the kindest woman I ever met, Miss Pru. My mama once told me that diamonds start out as ugly, colorless pieces of coal, but that when you get off all the layers and get down to the core, they shine and sparkle as prettily as stars, 'cause all their beauty that's been hidden beneath the surface comes up to the top. You're like that, Miss Pru. A diamond in the rough, they call it. Your true beauty is hidden, but it sparkles brighter than anyone else's I know."

Prudence's throat filled with tears, and it took her a moment to regain her composure. "I think that's the nicest thing anyone has ever said to me, Louann. I thank you from the bottom of my heart."

"If I hadn'ta been a whore, Miss Pru, I would've wanted to be good and kind like you." Louann closed her eyes then, and Prudence waited a few minutes to be sure she had fallen asleep.

When Louann's breathing grew deep and even, she rose and tiptoed out of the large room, glancing at Mary, Laurel, and Eliza, who were sound asleep. As she passed Christey's room she smiled, thinking of the joyful reunion she was having with her husband. She then spied Sarah's empty bed and was immediately filled with guilt. Sarah, bless her heart, had stayed downstairs to clean up the mess.

Vowing to rectify that situation immediately, she hurried down the steps and into the hallway, making her way toward the kitchen. When she reached the parlor door, she noticed it was shut. Odd, she thought, sure that she had left it open. She began purposefully to walk toward it, then pulled up short at the sound of voices.

The woman was giggling, and Prudence recognized the voice immediately as Sarah's. Well, she didn't need to guess who the man was. Obviously Sarah and Moody had decided to celebrate their wedding night a little ahead of schedule.

Hearing the passionate words they exchanged brought an emptiness to Prudence's heart. It seemed everyone but her had someone to love.

Tiptoeing away from the door as quietly as she could, she made her way up the stairs. When she passed Brock's door, she paused, wishing she had the courage to take her happiness where she could find it, knowing that it lay on the other side of the door with Brock.

Her hand reached out to touch the brass knob, and it lingered there a moment while her heart and mind warred for supremacy. Her mind won, and she drew it back, cursing herself for being all kinds of a fool.

But as she entered her cold, empty room, she wasn't sure if she was being foolish for having thought of lying with Brock in the first place or for not acting on her impulse to do so. Heaving a weary sigh, she went to bed.

17

If you got a choice, be brave.

Things were going to get awfully quiet around the house now that Polly and Christey were both gone, Prudence thought, staring morosely out the parlor window. Probably every bit as quiet as it was today, she decided, watching Sarah being helped into the old wooden sleigh by Moody, followed by Eliza, Mary, and Laurel.

The girls were sleigh riding into town with the hired hands, then staying to have dinner at the Blue Willow Restaurant. They'd been excited as schoolgirls about their adventure, promising that they wouldn't be arriving home until late in the evening.

The snow had finally stopped, but the sky still looked as gray as Prudence's mood. Sighing discontentedly, she wiped at the condensation that formed on the cold pane of glass.

Everyone had gone to have fun, except her . . . and

Louann, of course, who still rested upstairs in bed, showing little sign of improvement. And there was Brock, who had turned down the offer for a free dinner from Moody, opting instead to work on the interior of the bunkhouse.

She shook her head, unable to comprehend what could be so important about finishing that stupid bunkhouse. The man spent every waking moment out there! Perhaps he just didn't like her company. That thought made her even more depressed, and she found herself tracing her name on the glass, then his, linking them together. She stared at the writing, then smiled at her foolishness. *Prudence + Brock*, she had written, just like the old school rhyme.

"Morning, Red. What're you writing?" Brock asked, stepping into the warm room and stripping off his gloves.

Prudence gasped, horrified to have been caught at such a childish pursuit, and quickly obliterated their names before turning to face him. "Why, nothing," she answered, an air of innocence on her face. "What brings you in? It's hard to believe you've actually stopped working on the bunkhouse. It seems to be your greatest pleasure in life of late."

"One of the few I'm privy to," he retorted before crossing the room to warm his hands by the fire. "The snow's stopped, but the temperature's dropped again. I guess I'm getting old. I can't take the cold like I used to."

"Would you like some coffee? I was just about to have some." She indicated the ceramic pot on the table. Actually, the thought of having her coffee alone had been too depressing, and she'd intended to dump the entire pot into the sink, but now she wouldn't have to.

He nodded. "How come you didn't go with the others? You shouldn't stay cooped up inside this house all the time, Red. It isn't good for you."

"Louann hasn't been well. I stayed behind to care for her."

He took the cup she proffered, blowing at the steaming liquid to cool it before taking a sip. "What's the problem? She have too much to eat yesterday?" He shook his head. "I know I did. I probably gained five pounds."

Prudence gazed at his rock-hard midsection, remembered the rippling muscles, and doubted that he'd even gained an ounce. "Louann's been cramping since last night. I fear her symptoms have more to do with the baby than with what she ate yesterday. I'm quite concerned."

"Has Hannah been in to see her? She's quite good at healing."

Prudence wagged her head. "Hannah's still under the weather, and I don't dare expose any of the pregnant women to what she may have, even if it's only a cold."

Brock propped his feet upon the footstool, then studied Prudence while she sipped her coffee thoughtfully. Anyone walking in on them would think this was quite a domestic scene. A man and woman sharing a cup of coffee together, discussing the day's events, passing the time companionably, as husbands and wives often did.

Red would make some man a fine wife. She was smart and had a real good head for business. And caring—the way she looked after those less fortunate than herself proved that. And she was certainly pretty enough. Why, just looking at her set a man's mouth to watering. There was definitely a lot to recommend about Miss Prudence Daniels. If a man was in the market for a wife. And he'd finally come to the realization that maybe he was. Seeing Sam and Christey together last night had set his mind to thinking in terms of settling down.

"Is something wrong, Brock? You have the oddest look on your face."

He felt the heat creep up his neck. "No. I was just thinking about what else had to be done to the bunkhouse."

She signed in annoyance. "I don't know what is so important about finishing that bunkhouse. It is the middle of winter," she pointed out, "and the men seem happy with their present sleeping arrangements."

"Maybe they are, but I'm not too happy with mine." A look of genuine concern crossed her face, and Brock felt lower than a snake crawling on its belly. Why had he blurted out such a thing?

"Is something wrong? I mean, is the bed too short for you? Or perhaps you need an extra blanket?"

He crossed to the other side of the room and sat on the sofa next to Prudence. He reached for her hand, searching for the words to tell her what was in his heart. "The bed is fine, Red, and so is the room. What isn't fine is that you're not in either one. I need you, Red. I . . ."

Her shocked expression kept him from saying what he'd spent all night thinking about. He was in love with Prudence Daniels, from the top of her fiery hair to the tip of her freckled nose, right down to her stiffly starched ways. Prudence had made him yearn for a home again, for evenings by the fire, for pillow talk late into the night.

But he knew that she was scared of anything resembling commitment, having recognized the same fear in himself. He also knew she was scared of men, a lack of trust that stemmed from her sister's death, which had been reinforced daily over the years by the women she cared for.

But he meant to prove to her that he was different. That he wouldn't leave her, now or ever.

Noting the wary look in her eyes, he questioned if his timing in telling her was right. He needed to go slow where Red was concerned; he didn't want to frighten her.

Heat suffused every inch of Prudence's body, and her cheeks turned a bright crimson. "Are you suggesting that I enter into an illicit alliance with you? Sleep with you without the benefit of marriage?" As Billy had convinced Clara to do!

He drew her into his arms. "What I'm suggesting, Red, is that I care a great deal for you. More than I've cared for any woman in a long time."

Prudence's heart blossomed under his words, but the next sentence sent it straight back to wilting.

"I want to make love to you, Red. I want to plant myself deep inside of you, become one with you." Make you my wife.

She drew back, a shocked look on her face. "What you're suggesting is disgusting, not to mention immoral. Just because I was temporarily overcome by your charms does not mean that I care to experience them again."

Her words wounded his pride, and his eyes darkened in anger. And rather than explain that he wasn't suggesting any type of sordid alliance, but a permanent one, Brock let his temper get the best of him. "You, Miss Daniels, are a goddamn liar!"

Prudence rocked back against the cushion, but before she could respond, a loud scream split the air, followed by another. She jumped to her feet, alarmed. "It's Louann. I must go to her."

His anger forgotten, Brock said, "I'll come with you. I want to help."

It took only a moment for her to decide, and then she nodded her approval. Although it was highly improper for a man to be in attendance at a sick woman's bedside—unless of course, it was his wife—she might need assistance, and Brock was all she had at the moment.

The sight that greeted them when they entered Louann's room brought a horrified gasp from Prudence's throat, filling her with fear. Louann was lying in a pool of blood, grasping her abdomen, which looked to be contracting.

"My God!" she cried, rushing toward the bleeding woman. "The baby is trying to come out, and it's weeks too early."

Louann's high-pitched screams sent the hairs crawling on the back of Brock's neck. "What can we do? She looks bad off." God, why hadn't he gone to town? He wanted to be anywhere but in this room.

"There's a blanket chest under the window. Inside of it you'll find clean linens and rags that I use for the birthings. Fetch them, then go down to the kitchen and boil some water and bring lye soap. We'll need to wash our hands thoroughly to prevent infection." Sepsis, caused by the introduction of bacteria from dirty hands and instruments, was the single largest cause of maternal death. Prudence always took extra pains to be scrupulously clean before touching her patients.

Brock's face whitened. "We?" He shook his head. "I . . ."

"You did offer to help," she reminded him. "Now go. We don't have much time. This baby is trying to be born, and if we don't get this bleeding stopped . . ." She left the thought unsaid, but she knew Louann would most likely bleed to death. Just like Clara.

"Louann," she whispered, brushing back the hairs from the pale woman's sweating face, "you must try to help me. Your baby is coming early. As soon as Brock returns with my supplies, we're going to deliver it, you and I, together. But in the meantime, I want you to relax and not push. Take some deep breaths." She demonstrated.

Biting her lower lip, Louann nodded, tears flowing onto her cheeks. "I'll try, but it hurts so bad. It feels like my insides are ripping apart. I'm so scared, Miss Pru."

Fetching a clean nightgown, Prudence stripped off Louann's soiled one and pulled the fresh one over her head. She rolled the white linen material up to Louann's waist, then lifted the lower half of her body, replacing the bloody sheet with a canvas one, then covered the lower half of Louann's body with another clean sheet.

Brock returned momentarily, carrying a large basin of water and a bar of lye soap; he set it on the washstand, then washed his hands as Prudence directed.

"I need to run downstairs to fetch my medical book. You'll have to stay with Louann, try to keep her calm. I don't want her to push. Help her to take deep, even breaths. Like this." She demonstrated, breathing in and out in rhythmic fashion. "Can you do that?"

Brock took a deep breath of his own and nodded. When Prudence had gone, he pulled up a chair and sat down next to Louann's bed. The poor woman was making an effort not to scream, and the sight of her writhing in pain made Brock want to yell at the top of his lungs.

"Try to relax, Louann. Miss Prudence wants you to take deep breaths." And he didn't want that baby coming out while Prudence was gone. He grabbed a wet rag off the nightstand and sponged her face. "You're a very brave girl. I'm proud of you."

She attempted a smile, but it came out more like a grimace. "You're a nice man, Mr. Peters. I wish I had found me a nice man like you. If I had, maybe I wouldn'ta been a whore."

The whiteness of her skin alarmed him, and he prayed for Prudence's swift return. "Ssh . . . You still have time to meet lots of nice men. And you mustn't sell yourself short. Whores serve a very useful service. I bet there're lots of boys who turned into men on account of you. I bet you saved hundreds of lonely cowboys from spending their nights alone and unwanted. You gave brief moments of happiness to a lot of people, and for that you should feel happy. You're a humanitarian."

"I ain't never considered myself *that* before," Louann confessed, not exactly sure what a humanitarian was. "I guess when you look at it the way you do, Mr. Peters, whoring don't sound all that bad. Of course, it don't set well with the townsfolk. Leastways, the women."

"When my wife and son died, I had nowhere else to turn but to the ladies of the evening. They listened with a sympathetic ear and offered a kind word. I'm much obliged to all those women." He'd never confided that to anyone, but he figured Louann needed to hear it now.

Her eyes misted with grateful tears. "No one ever referred to me as a lady before, 'cept of course, Miss Pru. She finds the goodness in everyone."

Prudence entered at that moment, carrying a heavy volume of Samuel Bard's *Theory and Practice of Midwifery*. She set it down on the bedside table.

A quick check of Louann revealed that the baby's head was butting the entrance to the birth canal and that it wouldn't be much longer until it entered the world.

"I need you to push, Louann. Your baby is ready to be born, but he's going to need a big push, dear."

"She," Louann corrected, barely above a whisper.

While Brock sponged the young woman's brow, Louann commenced to push. Her grunts and groans as she struggled to bring forth a new life filled the room.

"Harder, Louann," Prudence coaxed. "Harder . . . That's it. We're almost there." She could see the shoulders emerging.

"I can't," the exhausted woman wailed. "I'm too tired."

"You must try again." Prudence gently grasped the baby's head, trying to assist Louann in its delivery.

With one final push, Louann passed out cold and the baby slid into Prudence's hands. The umbilical cord was wrapped firmly about its neck; the child was stillborn.

"Louann's out cold," Brock said.

Tears filled Prudence's eyes. "It's just as well. Her child is dead."

"But . . ."

Prudence shook her head, cutting off Brock's question. "I need you to fetch me a bucket of snow. Try and make it as clean as possible."

His brow wrinkled in confusion. "Snow? Are you sure?"

She nodded. "Louann is still bleeding badly. We need to stop the hemorrhage. Snow packed into the womb can constrict the blood vessels. It might slow down the hemorrhaging." She didn't say it, but her eyes communicated that it was the only chance Louann had. She'd already lost a great deal of blood; to lose more would mean certain death.

Brock left to do her bidding, and Prudence took the time to wrap the baby in a blanket and set it carefully into the blanket chest. It had been a girl, just as Louann wanted.

As best she could, she set out to clean up the birth

mess. "Please, God, let this woman live. She's already lost her child. Please don't take her life as well."

Louann was still unconscious when Brock returned with the snow. Prudence ministered to her as best as she could, then they both sat down to wait. And as darkness settled over the landscape—an omen of things yet to come—and Louann's bleeding failed to stop, Prudence knew that the young woman was in God's hands.

An hour later Brock entered the lantern-lit room, carrying a tray with sandwiches and milk, and though Prudence thought the gesture was thoughtful, she couldn't eat a thing.

"Has there been any change?"

She shook her head. "She's the same. Sometimes lucid, sometimes not. I haven't told her about the baby."

Gazing at the stricken woman, Brock knew there was no use burdening Louann with news of the child. "I see no need. We can deal with that unpleasantness if she recovers."

Just then Louann opened her eyes, making an effort to focus on the concerned faces before her. "Miss Pru . . ."

Her voice was frail, and Prudence had to bend lower to hear her. "Yes, Louann. Brock and I are still here." Prudence reached for the woman's hand, which felt cold and clammy.

"I know I'm bad off. I can feel my strength slipping away."

"Hush, now. You mustn't speak so."

"My baby . . ."

Prudence gazed over at Brock, her eyes filling with

tears. "She's asleep," she lied, unable to tell the dying woman the truth.

Louann seemed content to take the news at face value. "If anything should happen to me, would you and Mr. Peters take care of her for me? I know you'd make good parents for Betsy."

Prudence took a deep breath, swallowing her tears. "Of course we will. Won't we, Brock?"

"You're not to worry about a thing, Louann," Brock reassured her. "The child will be well taken care of."

Louann smiled gratefully, then closed her eyes, and a serene look passed over her face that told Prudence she had slipped away to a life beyond their reach.

"She's gone." The words were said on a sob, then Prudence covered her face and burst into tears.

Brock came forward, yanking the sheet up to cover Louann's still body, then pulled Prudence into his chest, wrapping his arms about her in a comforting embrace.

"Don't cry, Red. Please don't cry. You did everything humanly possible for Louann and her child."

She shook her head. "It was just like when Clara died. I didn't know enough to save her." She gripped the front of his shirt, drawing comfort from his warmth. "I failed."

He drew her away from the bed, toward the window. A full moon shone, and snow had begun to fall gently again.

"Who's to say why God takes some and not others. It's not for us to decide. We have to trust in the Lord and know that He's doing the right thing." It had taken him a long time to come to grips with that notion after Catherine and Josh died. But after blaming himself for so long, it was that comforting thought that had finally saved his sanity.

"You lost your wife, didn't you?" Prudence asked.

"Yes."

There was pain in his voice, and she reached up to caress his cheek, which was stubbled with beard. "I'm sorry. I didn't mean to dredge up painful memories."

"Someday I'll tell you about her, but not now." Louann's death made him feel too vulnerable, too conscious of his loss. Perhaps in time he'd be able to confide his feelings for his dead family.

Prudence turned to stare out the window. "It's snowing again." Her voice suddenly filled with alarm. "The others. They might not be able to make it home."

"My guess is that they'll remain in town for the night. Moody and Shorty would never jeopardize the women's safety. They'll get rooms at the hotel."

"I guess you're right." She was so weary that she couldn't even think about the impropriety of the situation or the fact that tongues would be wagging in Absolution by morning.

Taking her gently by the hand, Brock led her toward the door. "You look exhausted. I think it's best if you turn in. I'll take care of everything else that needs to be done."

The lamps in the hallway had been lit, and Prudence had yet another thing to be grateful to Brock for. She would never have been able to get through this day without him. He'd been by her side the entire time, his support never wavering. Nor his kindness. They paused before her bedroom door. "I haven't thanked you for all you did today, Brock. I . . ."

He covered her mouth with his fingertips. "You don't have to thank me. I liked Louann. I did no more than anyone in the same circumstance would have done."

"You were very good with Louann. There's a gentleness about you that she responded to." She smiled softly, thinking back to a conversation they'd had once a long time ago. "Maybe you should have been a doctor."

"I was scared, Red. Really scared. I could never have done what you did today. I would have lost my wits— gone to pieces. But you didn't. You were brave in the face of a very difficult situation. I admire you for that. And for many other things." He wanted desperately to tell her that he loved her. But now was not the time.

She shook her head to deny his words, then burst into tears again, and his arms surrounded her in comfort. "Hush, love, don't cry anymore." He patted her back, kissed her hair, wiped at the tears on her cheeks with his fingers.

Prudence looked up at him and felt the barriers around her heart melting away. "Why do you always have to be so nice?" she whispered.

He kissed her then, not in passion but in friendship, then opened the door to her room and bade her good night.

18

*When a woman starts to draggin' a loop,
there's always some man willin' to step in.*

It was a solemn, teary-eyed group that gathered at dusk in the Danielses' cemetery two days later to lay Louann Jones to rest.

Prudence had read scriptures from the Bible, knowing Louann would have preferred that than having the reverend pray over her, as if he would. Baby Betsy was laid alongside her mother, and simple wooden crosses, lovingly fashioned by Joe, marked the spot until more permanent structures could be ordered from the undertaker in town.

"I can't believe she's really gone," Sarah said, sobbing into Moody's chest, and his arm came around to comfort her. "She was so full of life."

"Don't be cryin' over Louann, Sarah," Mary counseled, squeezing Will's hand. "You know she'd have hated for us to do that. Louann always said that if the time ever came, she wanted people to dance on her grave."

"At least Polly was spared Louann's death," Will said almost to himself. "She'd have felt terrible after the way her and Louann were always at each other's throats."

"Death is merely another part of life," Eliza stated, drawing her cloak more tightly about her against the biting wind, grateful for the presence of the man at her side. She looked over at Shorty and was greeted with a soft smile.

Twisting his hat self-consciously between his fingers, Shorty cleared his throat. "I ain't much for public speakin', but I thought I'd say a few words for this departed little girl. Louann was a good sort, even though there was some that considered her a bad woman." He shook his head. "The West is a good country for men and dogs but mighty hard on women and oxen."

There didn't seem much else to say after that, and the small group dispersed, save for Prudence and Brock, who stood staring at each other over Louann's grave. It was Prudence who finally broke the silence.

"Thank you for helping me break the news to the others. I don't think I could have managed it by myself."

"A burden shared is always lighter, Red."

"I was relieved that Laurel stayed inside to care for BJ. I don't think I could have taken her tears today. Not on top of everything else."

Prudence began to sob softly, and Brock walked over to her, drawing her into his chest. "You might not have been able to spare Louann's life, Red, but you gave her more than most. You made her feel like somebody cared. Gave her a sense of identity. Showed her what it felt like to be part of a family. She'll take those gifts with her to her next life, and be all the richer for them."

He bent down to brush her lips lightly, but Prudence grabbed on to him, deepening the kiss. When she released him she looked into his eyes, and the pain he saw reflected there wrenched his soul.

"Stay with me tonight, Brock. Stay with me and make me feel that there's a purpose to life beyond death and destruction."

Her words sent shock waves throughout his body. "You don't know what you're asking, Red. You're tired, defeated. I won't take advantage of you in the state you're in. Even I'm not that big a heel."

Leaning into him, she wrapped her arms about his waist, needing to feel the strength, the solidity, he provided. "I need you, Brock. I need you to make love to me. I need you to make me feel alive."

"Are you sure that's what you want? Really sure?" She was so vulnerable right now. And though he wanted her badly, he wouldn't take advantage of her vulnerability.

Prudence pressed her breasts into his chest and looked up into his face to find it filled with concern. "I've never been more sure about anything in my entire life."

Placing a kiss on her lips, Brock wrapped his arms around Prudence's shoulders, and led her back to the house. It was quiet when they entered, and Brock surmised that everyone, spent by Louann's funeral, had retired for the evening.

He followed Prudence into her room, noting the chill in the air. Hannah was still confined to her bed with a cold, so she had not been over all day, and the fire Prudence had started earlier had burned down to embers. Brock strode to the hearth and began to lay a fire, and in a matter of moments the logs caught and the flames licked at the chimney.

He turned around then to find Prudence standing right inside the door where he'd left her, hands clutched in front of her, uncertain what to do. "You can still change your mind, Red. I'm not going to force you to do anything you're not ready for."

His kind words impelled her forward, and she presented him with her back. "Would you mind undoing my buttons?" she whispered. She lifted the heavy weight of her hair off her shoulders to give him access. "I have a difficult time reaching them."

Brock's fingers trembled as he unfastened the bone buttons. The long length of Prudence's neck drew him like a bee to a flower, and he placed kisses there while continuing to undress her.

"I've never done this before," she confessed, feeling her cheeks redden, grateful her back was to him.

He whirled her around, lowering the bodice of her gown to her waist to gaze at her. The firelight cast her skin all rosy and warm, and he leaned forward to place kisses there. He could feel her heart beating erratically, nervously, and he caressed her cheek as if she were a child.

"I can't deny that I'm happy to be your first, Red. A man sets a real store by that kind of thing."

Especially a husband, Prudence thought. But Brock hadn't offered marriage, only comfort. And it was what she needed right now. She'd worry about the other when it happened . . . if it happened. "I hope I won't disappoint you." She stared at him, then at the bed, biting her lower lip apprehensively.

"Never!" He kissed her tenderly, then swept her off her feet and carried her to the bed, laying her down gently on top of the comforter. When he saw the fear, the uncertainty, in her eyes, he said again, "There's still time to change your mind."

She took a deep breath and shook her head, offering a tentative smile. When he stripped off his shirt, then his pants, her smile wavered slightly. When he stepped out of his underwear to reveal his nakedness, her eyes widened in appreciation, and he grinned. "Your turn, Red."

With crimsoned cheeks, she began to fumble with the ribbons of her chemise, but Brock was too impatient and brushed aside her hands. Leaning over her, he pulled the silk strands with his teeth, unlacing the garment, kissing every inch of the skin he exposed as he removed her underclothing.

"You're truly lovely," he whispered before taking her erect nipple into his mouth.

Prudence stared in fascination as he suckled first one nipple, then the other; for a fleeting moment she wondered what it would be like to have Brock's child at her breast. But all thoughts fled as his lips trailed down her stomach and his hands moved to the nest of curls between her thighs.

Like a coiled spring, she grew taut, intense heat centering between her legs. When his lips touched her moist apex, she thought she would explode with the joy of it. "Please," she pleaded, not recognizing that raspy, wanton voice as her own. "I need . . ." Her head lolled from side to side, and she clutched the material of the comforter between her fingers. "Oh, *God*," she cried out when the first spasms of pleasure overtook her.

Brock eased himself over her, positioning his hardened shaft at the core of her womanhood. "That's it," he encouraged as her hips rose to meet his first thrust. He plunged forward, past her virginal barrier, then stopped, allowing her body time to accommodate the thickness and length of him.

When he was completely sheathed in her velvet warmth, he rocked forward, harder and faster, urging her to meet him stroke for stroke, swallowing her cries with his mouth as she reached for her climax at the same time he released his seed deep within her.

When they were sated he rolled to one side, taking her with him. He pulled the comforter over their sweating bodies, then caressed her cheek, kissing her tenderly.

The firelight played over them, casting strange shadows on the wall. Cradling Prudence to his chest, Brock felt a protective warmth surge over him. Red was truly his now. His to hold, to protect, to love.

He loved her, truly loved her, as he had no other woman since Catherine, and that realization sent a warm, satisfied smile to his mouth as he gazed at her sleeping form.

The morning silence was shattered by the splintering of glass, startling the two lovers into wakefulness.

"What is it? What's wrong?" Prudence bolted upright, her heart pounding in her chest. A chest that was totally bare, she realized, and yanked the comforter up to cover herself.

Brock jumped out of bed, unmindful of his nakedness, and walked to the window. In the early morning daylight he saw two riders galloping away from the ranch; it was then he spied the large rock on the floor beneath the window. Retrieving it, he unwrapped the note that was attached; his eyes darkened as he scanned the contents.

"What is it? What does it say?"

"Great! Just great." He handed her the note, though

he was disinclined to do so, knowing how much it would worry her.

Leave town, you daughters of Satan. Leave before the wrath of God comes down to smite you a mighty blow.

Prudence looked up from the threatening note, horrified. "My God! Who would write such a thing?" But she knew in a town like Absolution, it could be just about anyone, including the fanatical Reverend Entwhistle or one of his many apostles. "I didn't think the reverend would go so far as to damage my property and the lives of innocent women."

Pulling on his pants, Brock shook his head. "It wasn't Entwhistle, Red. I'd bet my last dollar on that. More likely it's from that idiotic neighbor of yours."

Her face paled. "Jacob? But why would he do such a thing?" And then she remembered his ominous warning the day she'd tossed him off the ranch. She shook her head in disbelief. Even Jacob wouldn't have gone so far.

"I'm riding over there to get to the bottom of this."

"No!" she cried. "I forbid you to go."

One eyebrow arched as he buttoned his shirt. "Forbid me? You're not my mother. You can't forbid me to do anything."

Her chin tilted up. "But I am your employer. And as such, I am ordering you not to interfere." She couldn't take the chance that he would be hurt or, worse, killed. Despite her convictions, her vows to the contrary, despite everything she had ever believed in, she cared deeply for this man.

Brock sat down on the edge of the bed, and it was all he could do not to shake some sense into her. Didn't she realize she was in danger? That Morgan would stop at nothing to get whatever it was he wanted? "You hired me as foreman. And as such, it's my duty to protect you and the other people on this ranch."

"Please, Brock." She placed a placating hand on his arm. "I'm asking you not to go after Jacob."

His hand covered hers and he grinned in a lazy, playful way. "Then are you asking me to come back to bed? 'Cause if I don't ride over to Morgan's, that's what I'm bound to do." Last night had been incredibly, totally satisfying. Making love to Red had been all he'd ever dreamed of and more. He couldn't wait to tell her so, to tell her of his love for her.

Prudence's face reddened. "No! I'm not asking you for that. One mistake was enough. I don't think we should compound my foolish behavior with another one."

He reeled back as if slapped, unable to believe what she was saying. "You're calling what we shared last night foolish behavior? A mistake?" He shook his head. "Come on, Red. You don't mean that."

No, she wanted to reassure him, she didn't mean it. But something inside of her—fear—kept her from speaking the truth. "I do mean it," she insisted.

His voice hardened. "I should have known you'd cry foul."

She gasped. "Get out of my room. And stay out. What happened last night was a mistake. And if you are any kind of gentleman, you will not mention it again."

He glared down at her. "You know, if I hadn't heard that heart of yours thumping to beat the band last night, I'd be certain you didn't have one." Without another word, he stalked into his room, slamming the door behind him.

Prudence slumped dejectedly against the pillow. What on earth was wrong with her? She shook her head sadly as she stared at the door. What had happened between them last night had been wonderful, magical. Why was she throwing it all away? Tears slid down her cheeks, and she dabbed at them with the edge of the sheet.

Because she knew, she answered silently. Knew that Brock was a drifter. Knew that someday he'd get tired of her and the ranch and leave. He'd told her from the onset that their arrangement was only temporary, that he didn't like putting down roots.

Well, she might have surrendered her virginity to him, but she wasn't foolish enough to surrender her heart. And if there was a repeat performance of last night, that's just what she was afraid would happen.

Brock pushed his mount faster through the thick new snow that blanketed the ground, trying to rid himself of the demons that possessed him as he rode toward Morgan's ranch.

Damn Red! Damn her to hell for putting him through this torture, he thought, pulling up on the reins to slow his pace. He sucked in huge gulps of frigid air to calm himself, noting that his horse was having as difficult a time breathing as he was.

"Sorry, Willy. I shouldn't have taken my anger out on you." No, but he would take it out on that damn low-life Morgan.

He rode through the gates of the Bar J without incident. Apparently Morgan expected no reprisals for his latest act of villainy. Staring at the ranch house in the distance, he noted a couple of cowboys posted at the entrance and shook his head in disbelief at his folly.

What the hell was he doing here, anyway? He felt like some fool cowpoke out of one of those dime novels.

Most likely he was going to get his blamed fool head shot off. Why the hell didn't he just return to the practice of law, instead of riding about the countryside like some half-crazed vigilante? At least as a lawyer he only had to contend with badgering reluctant witnesses, and they were hardly ever armed.

The cowboys on the porch stood when he reined up in front of the house. "Is Morgan here?" he asked, not bothering to dismount, wishing he'd had the foresight to put on a pair of woolen underwear before riding off half-cocked. He was freezing his goddamn ass off!

"Who wants to know?" asked the scruffy-looking, dark-haired man.

"Tell Morgan that Brock Peters wants a word with him. And if he knows what's good for him, he'll get himself out here on the double."

The shorter of the two men, who wore a patch over his left eye, hurried inside and returned a moment later with Morgan on his heels. The older man glanced up at Peters, a look of disbelief on his face, as if he hadn't quite believed the one-eyed cowboy's claim that Brock had ridden in by himself.

"You got balls, boy. I'll give you that," Morgan stated. "What the hell do you want? You interrupted my breakfast."

Brock leaned over the pommel of his saddle, staring the older man in the eye. "I didn't think threatening innocent young women was your style, Morgan. I guess I was wrong. Usually you take a more direct approach, like slaughtering cattle."

Morgan's face grew red. "I don't know what the hell you're talking about."

"I'm talking about tossing rocks through ladies' bedroom windows. I'm talking about threatening Prudence Daniels."

"You'd best stay out of affairs here in Absolution, Peters. You don't know what you're letting yourself in for."

"I think I have a pretty good idea. I've dealt with scum like you before."

"Help Mr. Peters on his way, boys." The two cowboys stepped forward, but before they could step off the porch, Brock drew his gun, aiming it dead center at Morgan's chest. His trigger finger was so numb, he doubted he could pull it, but Morgan didn't know that.

"I'll leave when I'm damn good and ready. So unless you want a lead plum to go with your eggs this morning, I'd suggest you call off your dogs."

Morgan gave the signal, and the disgruntled cowboys backed up. "Say your piece, then, and get off my land."

"If any harm comes to Prudence Daniels or any of the women in her charge, you'll have to answer to me and the other hands at the R and R. I don't know what you're after, but I aim to find out. And when I do, you'll be sorry you started this mess."

"I'm quaking in my boots," Morgan answered brashly, but Brock could see the concern in his eyes.

"You'll be buried in those boots, Morgan, if you dare show your face on R and R property again. And if any of your cattle find their way across the boundary line, they'll be shot on sight. I'm giving orders to shoot first and ask questions later. You'd better spread the word, or you won't have enough of those hired thugs left to do you any good."

Without giving Morgan a chance to reply, Brock yanked on Willy's reins and rode away, heading back toward the R and R. When he'd ridden a safe distance and was sure a bullet wouldn't be following his back, he slowed his pace and took a deep breath, wiping away the nervous perspiration that now dotted his forehead.

There was a lot more to being a hero in a dime novel than he'd thought, he decided, patting the side of Willy's neck absently. It was a hell of a lot scarier actually doing heroic deeds than it was reading about them! And wasn't the hero supposed to get the girl after he rescued her? Wasn't she supposed to fall in his arms and say "My hero," then ride away with him into the sunset?

"Ha!" Brock said, shaking his head in disgust. That was rich. Obviously no one had told the authors of all those novels about stubborn, opinionated, man-hating spinsters like Prudence Daniels. They wouldn't have written such drivel if they'd been subjected to her acerbic tongue.

One mistake was enough. Prudence's words pricked Brock's pride, and he grimaced. He should have known better than to lay his heart at her feet. She had stomped all over it, just as he'd known she would.

Thank God he hadn't told her that he loved her. She probably would have laughed in his face. It was obvious Red didn't harbor the same feelings for him as he did for her.

One mistake was enough.

"Well, you got that right, Red. And you can be damned sure that I won't be making another mistake anytime soon."

19

*There's a little boy a-sleepin' in many
a grown man you'd call sensible.*

"**This bunkhouse looks** too purty to be sleeping in," Shorty said to Brock upon entering the building. The old man gazed about, inhaling deeply of the fresh pine scent. It sure smelled better than the combination of sweat, dry cow manure, old work boots, and tobacco plugs he was used to. "You sure did make us a comfortable place to hang our hats. Yessiree!"

Brock smiled at the praise and laid down his hammer. He'd spent a lot of time repairing the bunkhouse; he was going to miss it when he left. "I stacked the bunks on either side of the room to make it roomier in here," he explained. "I set the potbellied stove in the center, so it heats the building evenly."

Shorty noticed that the bunks had already been made up. Each cowboy, in order of seniority, would choose which one he preferred. Being the eldest, and the one with the most time on the job, Shorty had first pick. He carried his gear to the bunk on the far wall next to Brock's and it was then he noticed that Brock's bunk was empty of a mattress and blanket. His forehead wrinkled in confusion. "Where're you stowing your gear, Brock? I thought we'd decided to bunk together."

Brock was grateful he and Shorty were alone. He didn't want to face the others right now, especially Will. The boy looked to him as a father figure. Hell! Will had become like another son to him. It was a loss he'd regret for a long time—a lifetime.

"I'm leaving, Shorty. As soon as I can get my things together and give Prudence notice, I'm heading out." He had thought about it long and hard and had finally come to the painful conclusion that it was the only way to keep from getting even more hurt than he was already.

Shorty spit a stream of tobacco juice into the brass spittoon by the stove and frowned. "Well, if that don't beat all. When did you up and decide that? It's the first I'm hearing about it."

Brock sighed, pulled up a chair, and straddled it. "I just decided last night. After Louann's funeral. . . ." He paused and shook his head, unwilling to explain the real reason for his sudden decision to leave. "It's for the best."

"But what about Miss Prudence? I thought you and her . . . well, we all thought you was beginning to cotton to one another."

That's what he'd thought, too. But apparently everyone was incapable of second-guessing Prudence's feelings. "I care for Red, Shorty. Like I haven't cared about another woman in a long time. But I don't think Red has the capacity to love a man. She's gun-shy, afraid of getting too close. Hell, I know what that's like. For years I've avoided getting entangled with anyone."

A gray eyebrow arched. "Until now?"

Brock pushed himself to his feet. "It's time for me to move on. I was wrong to think that there could be anything between Prudence and me. Between the two of us, we've got too much baggage. She's carrying as much as, or more than, me, and she's not about to let it loose."

"If you fall in a cactus patch, you kin expect to pick stickers," Shorty advised. "Miss Pru's as prickly as any cactus, I'll give you that. But there's more beneath that woman's hide than even she knows. There's a heart that beats for you, Brock. I seen the way she looks at you. I tell you she truly cares, whether or not she realizes it herself."

"Maybe she does, and maybe she doesn't," Brock conceded. "But I've had my share of pain in this lifetime, Shorty, and I can't open myself to that kind of hurt again. I'm too old to start over."

Shorty drew his fingers through his mustache. "You love her, don't you?"

Brock shrugged, unwilling to admit his feelings to anyone, even though he'd already admitted them to himself.

The old man chuckled at Brock's evasiveness. "My daddy always told me that surprise is a nearsighted porcupine falling in love with a cactus. I do believe he may have been right."

Grabbing his hat and jacket, Brock made his way to the door. "I can see where you learned your philosophy from, old man. I admit I'm going to miss hearing your sage expressions." Brock strode out the door, letting in a blast of cold air as he exited.

Shorty spat again, shaking his head in disgust. At least he'd given Brock something to think about. Maybe the stubborn fool would come to his senses and realize Prudence really loved him. "Treat mule-headed men the

same way you'd treat a mule you're fixin' to corral.
Don't try to drive 'em in. Jus' leave the gate open a
crack'n let 'em bust in." He smiled. Yup, maybe the boy
just needed that crack to let the light in.

Prudence bit her lower lip in concentration as she
forced the knitting needles through the dark brown
yarn. She hadn't knitted anything in years, especially
not men's socks. Not since her father died. But Christmas was just a few weeks away. And, well . . . she had
someone to knit them for now.

Brock. Her heart always beat a little faster when she
thought of him. And it was beating a cadence that was
just short of a drumroll at the moment. She loved him.
She could finally admit to herself that she loved Brock
Peters. And though her mind had told her she was
crazy—that she was going to be hurt—her heart had
told her different.

Brock wasn't Billy. Brock wasn't like any man she had
ever met. He was kind, caring, considerate. And he cared
about her. Deep in her heart she sensed that he cared about
her.

Maybe he could never love her the way he had loved
his wife. But he'd told her that he needed her, that he
wanted her in his bed. And that would be enough for
now. The other would come later, after they were married, after they shared a child.

Her stomach fluttered at the idea of having Brock's
child—a baby of her own.

The parlor door opened and she looked up to find
the object of her thoughts standing just inside the doorway. She felt her face grow warm. His face, she noticed,
was red from the cold, and he blew into gloveless hands
to warm them up. Quickly she shoved her knitting back

inside the bag. "Brock!" Her voice sounded flustered, even to her own ears. She couldn't imagine what he must be thinking.

What Brock was thinking was that Prudence looked the picture of domestic bliss, with the firelight playing over her cheeks and her head bent in concentration as she plied her knitting needles. Somehow the sight of Prudence with knitting needles didn't seem to fit. A pen and ledger—yes. Or antiseptic and a length of bandage. But not knitting needles. That seemed too mundane for her spirited nature.

"I hope I'm not interrupting, Red, but there's something I need to discuss with you."

The drumroll started again, for somewhere in the tiniest corner of Prudence's heart lay the hope, the uncontrollable desire, that Brock had come to ask for her hand in marriage. She cleared her throat, and her mind, of the foolish notion.

"You're not interrupting. I'm just trying to keep myself busy on such a dreary day." The sun hadn't put in an appearance for days, and with every gray day that passed, it seemed everyone's mood at the ranch grew grayer too. Louann's death had only added to the darkness.

He removed his hat and coat and tossed them on a chair, then took a seat next to her on the sofa. "I've come to tell you that I'll be leaving in a day or two. I know I said that I'd stay on until you could find another foreman, but I've decided that I've overstayed my welcome here. It's time for me to be moving on."

The pain his words evoked was a tangible thing—a pressure bearing down on her chest, digging into her heart.

Leaving! Brock was leaving! *No!* her mind screamed. *Tell him. Tell him you love him.* But pride kept her from telling him what was in her heart.

"You always said you would someday," she said with more courage than she knew she possessed. "I've been expecting it."

"I'm sure you were," he finally said. "After all, you had me figured out all along. And I never disappoint a pretty lady."

"Brock, I—"

At that moment Moody barged into the room, followed by the town's sheriff, Chester M. Peabody. Moody, sensing the tension instantly, cast Brock an apologetic glance. "Miss Prudence, this gentleman would like a word with you. He says it's urgent."

Sheriff Peabody was a reed-thin specimen of a man, who looked as if a good strong wind could probably blow him off his horse. His eyes bulged slightly, and his bulbous nose was always a bright red no matter the weather. He was possibly the homeliest man who ever wore a tin star on his chest, Prudence decided.

The sheriff removed his hat, an embarrassed half-smile on his face, as he stepped farther into the room. "Excuse the intrusion, Miss Daniels." He nodded perfunctorily at Brock. "I have some pressing business to discuss with you."

Something else to discuss? Wonderful. Prudence sighed wearily. How much more bad news could she take in one day? Stiffening her spine, she rose to her feet, noting that Brock followed suit. "What is it, Sheriff Peabody? It certainly must be important. I can never get you to come out here to investigate when rustlers are stealing my cattle."

The sheriff's cheeks reddened, and he cleared his throat nervously. "No need for impertinence, young woman." He reached into the inside front pocket of his jacket, pulling out what appeared to be some type of legal document. He handed it to her. "I'm just doing my job, Miss Daniels."

Casting a quick glance at Brock, then at Moody, Prudence reached into her apron pocket to retrieve her spectacles; she wiped them on the edge of her apron before putting them on and began to read:

"We the undersigned do hereby insist that Miss Prudence Daniels of the Rough and Ready Ranch, Colorado Territory, vacate the premises immediately. We find Miss Daniels to be harboring women of questionable morals and un-Christian-like values. Her own morals are of a suspicious nature, and we feel Miss Daniels is a detriment to the welfare of this community."

She scanned the rest of the page and was not surprised to discover that it was signed by most of the town's inhabitants.

Brock, noting Prudence's pale face, grabbed the paper from her hands and read it quickly. His face turned red with rage. "This is utter nonsense! How dare you bring such a document out here, Sheriff?"

Chester Peabody clutched the brim of his hat nervously in his bony hands. "I'm only doing my job. I'm a servant of the community. The people have spoken."

"This petition isn't worth the paper it's written on. It's not a legal document. A legal summons of this nature has to be issued by a judge."

"The circuit judge will be here day after tomorrow. And how do you know so much about the law? I was told you were the foreman here, Mr. Peters."

"I wasn't always a drifter and a cowboy, Sheriff. At one time, I was a well-respected attorney."

Prudence gasped and sank onto the sofa, staring at Brock in disbelief. An attorney! Brock Peters was a lawyer?

Moody, who was already privy to that bit of information, smiled smugly at the sheriff. "Brock knows what he's about, Peabody. You'd best be on your way."

Chester scratched his thinning head of hair. "But Jacob Morgan said this petition was perfectly legal. He said all I needed do was serve it like a summons."

Brock's lips thinned, even as Prudence bolted from the sofa. "Jacob Morgan put you up to this?" she asked.

The sheriff nodded, and Brock snorted rudely. "I should have known that bastard was behind this."

"Mr. Morgan is only exercising his rights as a concerned citizen, Mr. Peters. And when the circuit judge comes through town, we aim to have this petition made legal. Majority rules in Absolution. Always has. Always will."

Grabbing the sheriff by the scruff of his neck, Brock practically shoved him out of the room, but not before he said, "Tell the narrow-minded citizens of Absolution, and that devious bastard Morgan, that Miss Daniels and the women of this ranch are being represented by legal counsel. If the circuit judge issues a summons to vacate, then we'll be filing an appeal with the court."

Prudence's eyes widened as she turned to face Brock. "But I thought you were leaving."

Moody smiled smugly at the look on Brock's face. "Brock never runs out on a legal battle. He told me so himself."

Prudence's heart sank. Brock was staying because of the legal battle, not because of her. But at least he was staying.

After Moody and the sheriff left the room, Brock turned to face Prudence once again. "I'll be staying on to represent you in this matter, if that meets with your approval."

She nodded. "I'm grateful for your help. But why didn't you tell me you were a lawyer? All along you've let me think you were nothing but a drifting cowboy."

"I am a drifter, Red. I've been drifting for eight years.

The law's a part of my past that I thought was dead and buried."

Prudence sensed by Brock's guarded expression that he didn't want to talk about what drove him from his law career, so she didn't press. "I don't understand what Jacob hopes to gain by forcing me off my land. He already has all the land he could possibly use."

Brock had his own suspicions, but he wouldn't voice them yet. "I'll be moving back into your father's room, Red. With what we now know about Morgan, and what we've experienced in the past, I don't want to be too far away, in case he or his men decide to put in an appearance."

"I'd feel better, too, if you were close by." Ever since that rock had broken her bedroom window, Prudence had been frightened, though she'd done her best to hide it. She couldn't help but wonder what would have happened if it hadn't been a rock, but a bullet, that had sailed through the window.

Picking up his hat and coat, Brock moved toward the door. "You needn't worry that I'll try to press my unwelcome attentions on you, Red."

Prudence sighed as she watched Brock leave, wondering if she could be as certain about her own self-control.

"Did you sign that petition Mr. Morgan has been circulating?" Caroline Townsend asked Arabella over her cup of tea. She reached for a sugar cookie. "I was eager to put my name to it, I can tell you that. Why, that Daniels woman is nothing but trash, harboring those women of ill repute."

Arabella's eyes widened ever so slightly at Caroline's revelation. So Jacob was responsible for circulating a petition against Prudence Daniels. It was the first she'd heard of it. "Why, no! You say Jacob Morgan has been circulating a petition to rid the town of Prudence Daniels? How very curious." Very curious indeed, Arabella thought, wondering what possible motive Jacob had for wanting the attractive spinster gone. Knowing Jacob, there was money involved. His voracious appetite wasn't confined merely to the bed or the dining room.

Margaret Lowery smirked. "I say good riddance to the lot of them. Why, Prudence Daniels brings those *women*"—she said the latter in the most condescending manner—"into town every single Sunday! She parades those trollops right down Main Street. I had to hide my Lulu's eyes last time we went to church. I wouldn't want their wickedness rubbing off on my sweet child."

Having recognized a kindred spirit when she saw one, Arabella knew firsthand that Lulu Lowery was the biggest slut Absolution had ever seen. And she would relish the opportunity to let Margaret know.

Arabella smiled sweetly. "I think it's admirable that Miss Daniels insists that her brood attend church services. After all, the house of the Lord is for saints and sinners alike."

"Arabella!" both women said in unison, clearly appalled.

"Why, I thought surely," Caroline began, "you being of such sound moral convictions, Arabella, that your name would be the first one on that petition. I can hardly believe you haven't signed it."

Arabella waved away the woman's concern with a flick of her wrist. "Mr. Morgan has never asked me. I don't think he likes me at all. He harbored a real dislike for Henry." Hate was more like it. But only because her husband had had the privilege of touching what Jacob coveted: herself.

Margaret leaned over to pat Arabella's hand in what she considered to be a comforting gesture, but Arabella found her attentions annoying. "I'm sure you must be wrong. Mr. Morgan seems the nicest of men. Why, he told me he thought Lulu was filling out very nicely."

Arabella's eyebrows arched even as her lips thinned. "Really? What else did he say?"

Margaret twittered behind her hands. "Oh, just that I should keep my Lulu under lock and key, else all the eligible men in the town would be sniffing around her skirts." She shook her head and leaned forward in a conspiratorial fashion. "I often wondered if Mr. Morgan didn't have designs on my Lulu. Lulu confided to me that he walked her home a time or two."

Arabella's hands clutched the porcelain tea cup so tightly, the fragile china broke in her hands. The tea spilled down the front of her blue velvet gown. "Oh, how clumsy of me," she said, reaching for a napkin. "Look what I've gone and done." She rose to her feet. "I'd best go up and change. If you ladies will excuse me, I believe I must call our little tea party to an end."

She had more pressing things to do at the moment, like waiting for that faithless bastard Jacob Morgan to put in an appearance, like making the conniving womanizer explain about Lulu Lowery and why he suddenly had such an intense desire to rid himself of Prudence Daniels.

Yes. Jacob had a lot of explaining to do.

Sarah eyed herself in Prudence's cheval mirror and couldn't help feeling pleased. The wedding gown Prudence was helping her sew was turning out just beautiful. The material had cost her dearly, and she'd questioned her sanity a time or two at the extravagance. But it was the color that really bothered her. It was white! White velvet. And Sarah couldn't help but think that, of all people, she had the least justification to be wearing white. She stared down at her protruding belly and sighed. A woman who was seven months pregnant should not be wearing white.

"What's wrong?" Prudence asked, gazing up at Sarah from her position on the bedroom floor. She stuck another pin in the hem of the gown, eyeing her handiwork to make sure the hem was even. "Don't you like it?"

"It's beautiful, Pru. A dream come true. But . . ." Sarah shook her head. "It's white, and I'm not a virgin. Far from it, actually."

Prudence pushed herself to her feet, sticking the excess pins into the red cushion on her left wrist. "You have never been married before, is that correct?"

"Well, yes."

"Then you have a perfect right to wear it. Besides, the wedding will be small. Only those of us here at the ranch will be attending."

"But who will we get to perform the ceremony? I can't imagine that Reverend Entwhistle is going to agree to come here. His was the first name on the petition."

"Brock and Moody said to leave that problem to them. I have every confidence that they'll be able to persuade the good reverend to perform his Christian duty." And she wasn't about to ask how. She had the sinking feeling that she wouldn't want to know.

"I still can't believe that I'm getting married. I hope I'm doing the right thing. I love Martin, but I'm not sure it's fair to saddle him with another man's child."

"Honestly, Sarah, you worry too much. It's obvious that Moody thinks the sun rises and sets on you. I've never seen a man so in love."

"Then maybe you're blind, Pru. You haven't taken a close enough look at Brock Peters." She could see she'd made her point; Prudence's face paled considerably, and she turned away to sit on the bed.

"You're imagining things, Sarah," Prudence insisted, running her fingers over the blue counterpane. "Why, Brock was ready to leave the ranch a few days ago. If Sheriff Peabody hadn't arrived with that stupid petition, Brock would be long gone."

Stepping out of the gown, Sarah put on her robe and sat on the bed next to Prudence. "You're thinking with your head, Pru, not your heart. Brock loves you. I know he does. And I think you feel the same way about him."

Prudence made a halfhearted attempt at a laugh, but it sounded strained even to her own ears. "Don't be ridiculous. We're friends, nothing more. I won't allow myself to fall in love with a man who wants no ties to bind him. Brock's content to be a drifter. I want a man I can count on. One who's going to be there for me when the going gets rough."

Sarah couldn't help the sarcasm that edged her words. "Oh, you mean like when the whole town is trying to force you to leave, and Brock steps in to take on your defense? I doubt anything can get any rougher than that."

"I appreciate your concern, really I do. But you just don't understand how it is between me and Brock." How could she expect Sarah to understand their relationship when she didn't understand it herself?

Sarah shook her head sadly. "No, I guess I don't. But I know how it could be between you, if only you'd open your heart and let his love pour into it. Don't throw away your chance at happiness, Pru. You may never get another one."

Brock had proven to be the same as any other man. And that realization had hurt more than anything else. "I'm content to live my life without a man. I've done fine by myself so far."

Sarah released an exasperated sigh. "You know something? Brock was right about one thing: you are too stubborn for your own good. I just hope one day you don't wake up and realize that you made the biggest mistake of your life."

She already had, Prudence decided. She had given Brock Peters her virginity; she had given him her heart. And she had ended up with nothing but bittersweet memories and heartache.

20

*When there's heroin' to be done,
someone has to hold the horses.*

Glancing out the window of the dress shop, Arabella caught sight of Jacob in close conversation with Lulu Lowery. They were standing across the street in front of the hotel, and Lulu's hand was wrapped possessively around Jacob's forearm. Her face was flushed and from the way Jacob was leaning over the young woman, it was obvious he was trying to get a glimpse of her bosom. Eyes narrowing, Arabella hissed like an angry she-cat.

"Mrs. Potts," the milliner called, "we need to finish up with your fitting."

Not taking her eyes off the couple, Arabella replied impatiently, "In a minute, Mrs. Wilkes. I want to see how this material looks in the light of day." She made a great pretense of examining the blue watered silk. "I won't be a minute."

When Jacob leaned over to give Lulu a kiss on her cheek, Arabella's hands balled into fists. "The cheating bastard!" she muttered.

"Did you say something, Mrs. Potts?" Bertha Wilkes asked, not wanting to give Arabella Potts the impression she was ignoring her. After all, Mrs. Potts's purchases kept her little dress shop in business. When Mrs. Potts ordered a certain type of gown, the other women in town tended to follow suit. She was definitely a fashion leader.

"Not yet," Arabella said through clenched teeth. "But I'm going to be saying something very soon."

"Great! Just great," Brock said, walking down the steps of the courthouse, a disgruntled look on his face. Inside the breast pocket of his jacket was the legal order issued by Judge Cooper, ordering Prudence and the rest of the women at the R and R to vacate the premises immediately.

In all his years of practicing law, Brock had never seen such a miscarriage of justice. And though he had pleaded the women's case before the judge, the man had listened with only half an ear. It seemed Judge Cooper was a good friend of Jacob Morgan, and as such he was inclined to respect the contention of an upstanding pillar of the community that the morality of the town was being threatened by the operation of the Rough and Ready Ranch as a home for unwed mothers.

Brock had tried talking sense to him until he was blue in the face, but his efforts had been in vain. If he wanted to take the case to trial before a jury, that was his privilege, the judge had stated; otherwise he would sign the order to vacate immediately. Brock had no alternative but to agree to a trial by jury.

Gathering Willy's reins, he mounted and rode swiftly away from Absolution toward the ranch. He dreaded having to tell Prudence of the judge's unfair ruling. She was so confident in his abilities to defend her. And he hated to let her and the others down.

This case was almost as important to him as it was to them. If he won, it would mean that he could reestablish himself as a lawyer. He'd been away from the courtroom so long, he had doubts that he still had what it took to be a barrister. Winning would give him the confidence he needed to reopen a law office.

Brock realized now, after having put down roots again, that he liked it. He was tired of wandering and wanted to settle down—foolishly, he had thought with Red. But now that was out of the question, and he just wanted to start over somewhere new again. It was time. Time to put Catherine and Josh behind. Time to make a new life for himself.

Absorbed in his thoughts, he didn't see the three riders approach until they were practically on top of him.

"Hold up, Peters. We want to have a little chat with you."

It was Dave Stewart; he recognized Prudence's old foreman immediately, as well as the other two cowboys. They were the same men who'd been at Morgan's a few days back. Great! Just great! So much for heroics, he thought, cursing himself inwardly for not being more observant.

He reined Willy to a halt. Not that he had much choice, he thought, staring down the barrels of three guns. "What is it you want, Stewart? You're blocking my way."

"The boss don't like you interfering in his plans to get rid of Miz Daniels."

Brock's eyebrow arched. "Is that a fact? And did Morgan send you out here to tell me that?"

Stewart shook his head. "Naw. The boss is too soft. He don't hold with killin' and the like. We decided ourselves that we wanted to have a little fun with you and do the boss a favor at the same time. Sort of like killin' two birds with one stone."

Knowing what kind of fun these animals had in mind, Brock's apprehension grew. The one-eyed man was leering at him with a nasty smirk on his face. "What are we going to do with him, Dave? You want I should shoot him?" he asked.

Dave shook his head, and Brock breathed a sigh of relief. "Naw, Patch, the boss wouldn't like that too much. We're just going to teach Mister Fancy-Pants Lawyer here a lesson. Get down off your horse, Peters," he ordered, brandishing his six-shooter at Brock's chest.

Knowing the odds were against him, Brock did as instructed. Even though Stewart had talked against killing him, he remembered what Shorty had said about Buck's demise, and he cringed inwardly.

"Patch, get your rope and tie Peters here up. It's almost Christmas. I'm sure Miz Daniels would like to get a nice, pretty package sent to her." He turned to the other man. "You know what to do, Mason." With the orders given, Stewart rode off, leaving Brock alone with Morgan's two hired hands.

"You boys always do what Stewart says?" Brock said boldly, hoping he could reason with them.

"Shut up," Mason warned. "You talk too much. You made us look stupid in front of the boss the other day. Me and Patch didn't like that."

So much for reason, Brock thought. These men had as much intelligence as a pint of warm owl piss. What made him think that they had any reason?

When Brock's arms and legs were tied securely, Patch stepped forward and punched him in the stomach as hard as he could. Brock struggled against the ropes, but it was no use. He was helpless to resist the punishing blows the two men took turns inflicting, first to his body, then to his face. His lips started bleeding, and he tasted blood. His ears began to ring as the blows to his face grew more vicious.

"Don't go interfering in Mr. Morgan's business again, mister," Patch threatened, landing another punch to Brock's midsection. Brock fell to his knees in the snow, but Patch's knee came up to strike him under the chin. And that was the last thing Brock remembered before he passed out.

"My God! What happened?" Prudence cried, rushing into the hallway from the kitchen as Shorty and Slim carried Brock's unconscious body through the doorway. Her heart constricted at the sight of Brock's badly beaten body, and fear, stark and vivid, glittered in her eyes. Brock's eyes were swollen shut, and there were black-and-blue bruises all over his face.

"We don't rightly know, Miss Pru," Shorty replied. "Me and Slim was riding into town for provisions when we came across Brock's horse. We followed Willy's tracks, and they led us to Brock."

"He's bad off, Miss Pru," Slim said sadly.

Prudence tamped down the hysteria that threatened to consume her and took a deep breath. "Carry him upstairs to my room, boys. Hannah"—she turned toward the Indian woman who had just entered the hallway to see what all the commotion was about—"get boiling water and bandages and bring them upstairs to my room. Mr. Peters has been injured." Hannah nodded, looking more upset than Prudence had ever seen her, and retreated into the kitchen.

When Brock had been placed on the bed, Prudence instructed Shorty to stoke up the fire, then sent Slim to help Hannah with the medicinal supplies.

"I'd like to think Brock's injuries were caused by a fall from his horse," Prudence said, "but even I'm not that naive, Shorty." She began to remove Brock's coat.

"No, ma'am. He's been beaten to a pulp, and that's a fact. I guess I don't have to tell you who I suspect."

Prudence yanked at the coat, and as she did, a thick wad of papers fell out of Brock's pocket. She picked them up and read through them, and her frown deepened. "It looks like Brock went into town to see the judge. It appears he wasn't too successful in convincing him to drop all this eviction nonsense."

Shorty assisted Prudence with stripping off the rest of Brock's clothing. When he saw the contusions to Brock's chest and stomach, a low growl emanated from his throat. "Damn those sons of bitches. They won't get away with this."

Prudence blinked back the tears that rested just behind her lids. "There's plenty of time for revenge, Shorty. Now we've got to concentrate on getting Brock well." But she would get revenge, she vowed. Jacob Morgan would pay for what he'd done to Brock, for bringing grief to her family.

Hannah and Slim returned, carrying basins of hot water, soap, and bandages. The usually stoic Hannah gasped when her eyes fell on the injured man.

"Mr. Morgan a bad man. I will call to the gods to bring evil down upon his head," she said before beginning to bathe Brock's body.

Noting the concern in Shorty's eyes, Prudence patted his arm. "There's nothing else that can be done right now. Why don't you and Slim go down to the kitchen and fetch yourselves something to eat? Hannah saved your supper on the stove. When you're done, ask Colonel Carstairs to come up here. I'd like to talk to him." Though reluctant, the two men nodded and took their leave, and Prudence turned back to the bed.

"Do you think he'll be all right, Hannah?" she asked, wringing her hands nervously. Her usually calm composure was shattered, and she thought it best to let Hannah handle Brock's injuries. Oh, God! What would she do if he didn't pull through? A lump lodged in her throat, and she fought against the rising panic hammering in her chest.

"We make him all right, you and me." She spread out a leather pouch, which Prudence knew held all of Hannah's healing herbs. "Hannah no let anything bad happen to Mr. Peters. He good man. He be your man, Miss Pru."

It was a statement not a question. "Yes, Hannah, he's my man." Prudence sighed. If only that were true.

Hannah smiled knowingly. "You make plenty babies with this man. His seed is strong for sons."

Prudence's eyes were drawn to Brock's member, which lay flaccid against his stomach, and she reddened, leaning over to pull up the sheet, ignoring the Indian woman's soft chuckle. "I don't think we should be discussing such a thing, Hannah. It's hardly proper, especially now."

"You good girl, Miss Prudence, but you foolish woman." Hannah went about her business of tending Brock's wounds, while Prudence stared into the crackling flames of the fire and silently agreed with the Indian woman's opinion.

She was indeed a foolish woman, for more reasons than even Hannah suspected.

Despite Brock's decision to leave, despite everything that had happened between them, she still loved him. And for that, her foolishness knew no bounds.

"Shorty said that you wanted to see me, Miss Pru," Moody said, walking toward the bed. His gaze flew to the injured man, and his lips thinned. "By God, that bastard Morgan will pay for this. How's Brock doing?"

"Hannah thinks he'll be all right. He has a few broken ribs, and he's still unconscious. Fortunately there was no frostbite to his hands or toes." Prudence sighed wearily. "I told her I'd sit with him through the night. The poor woman was exhausted."

"I'd be happy to spell you, Miss Pru, as would Sarah. She said to tell you if there was anything you needed for her to do, all you need do is ask. The others feel the same way."

"Thanks, Moody, but I want to be here when Brock wakes up. I feel so guilty that this happened to him because of me. If he hadn't gone into town to speak to the judge . . ."

"Don't talk nonsense." Moody pulled up a chair next to Prudence and sat down. "You've got nothing to feel guilty about. Brock knew the risks of getting involved." He patted her hand. "None of this is your fault, Prudence."

"Thank you, Moody. I appreciate your telling me that."

"We're all here for you. Just say the word and the boys and I will ride over to Morgan's and—"

"No!" Prudence shook her head, fear lighting her eyes. "I don't want anyone else getting hurt." Her tone softened. "What I do want, Moody, is for you to take charge of the men in Brock's absence. You're a soldier with a lot of experience. I'd like you to use that experience to keep the hands from getting ambushed by Jacob's men." She'd never forgive herself if anything happened to young Will—to any of them, for that matter.

"You mean like military patrols? Guarding the fort from the Indians?" Moody's face grew animated as he warmed to the idea. It had been a long time since he'd been in charge of a military operation.

She nodded. "Yes. Whatever it takes. Do whatever you think is necessary to guard the R and R. I don't want anyone else on this ranch getting hurt."

"It's as good as done, Miss Pru."

She smiled softly. "I knew I could count on you."

"Me and Sarah can postpone our wedding, if you'd like. Perhaps now isn't the best time to be getting hitched."

Prudence shook her head emphatically. "You'll do no such thing. I won't let Morgan interrupt our lives any more than he has already. And I wouldn't disappoint Sarah for anything. There's no postponing Christmas. It'll be here before you know it, so you might as well get ready to get hitched."

A broad smile creased his leathery cheeks. "Yes, ma'am. That's one order I'll gladly follow."

"I confess, Moody, that when I first saw the way it was between you and Sarah, I had my doubts. But you've made her so happy . . . well, I'm quite pleased about your marriage. I wish you both a world of happiness."

"You know I wish the same for you, my dear. You'll have it one day, you'll see."

She shook her head. "It's too late for me. I've made a mess of things. I let my fears overtake me."

Moody leaned down and kissed Prudence on the cheek. "Fear is like that, Prudence. It seeps under your skin, clouding your judgment. It's not always easy to put your fears aside and take a chance. But when it comes to love, sometimes we must, if we're going to be happy. With love, my dear, it's never too late. If there were ever two people who belonged together, it's you and Brock."

Brushing back the lock of dark hair that had fallen over Brock's forehead, Prudence whispered, "I truly hope you're right about that, Moody, for I love Brock with all my heart and soul." But when she looked up, Moody had already gone.

Brock forced open his eyes, and the first thing he saw was Prudence half sitting, half lying next to him on the bed. The lantern on the night table was lit, and he could see, gazing out the bedroom window, that it was still dark outside.

How long had he been unconscious? He remembered nothing after that last punishing blow from Patch's knee. His head hurt like hell, which was no surprise considering how many times the two bastards had tried to crack it open. He sighed deeply, and a stabbing pain centered in the region of his ribs.

Shit! What a mess! He felt as limp and useless as a rag doll. As carefully as he could, he reached out to touch Prudence's hand, but the effort proved too dear and he let out a pained gasp.

Prudence awoke with a start and jerked to a sitting position. Brock's eyes were open, and he was staring at her curiously. Relief rushed through her, and she gave a silent prayer of thanks. "How are you feeling?"

"Like a two-day-old corpse. Got any water? I'm thirsty."

She poured him a glass, then cupped the back of his head in her hand and helped him to take a sip. "Not too much at first," she cautioned, noting how he winced when the glass made contact with his swollen lips.

"I guess I'm a mess," he said, leaning back against the pillows she propped behind his back and head.

"Do you remember what happened?"

"Quite distinctly. And when I get out of this bed, I'm going to make those three bastards sorry they were ever born."

A look of horror crossed her face. "*Three* men did this to you?" My God! No wonder he looked so bad.

He nodded but was sorry for it when the pounding began again. He grabbed the sides of his head. "You don't think just one could have taken me out, do you?"

He seemed clearly annoyed at her assumption, and Prudence couldn't help but smile. "That was rather silly of me, wasn't it?"

"Damned right! They tied me up, or else I would have given them a run for their money. The cowards. One of them was your old foreman."

"Dave Stewart." She should have known. The man had a ruthless streak in him. She should have sensed when Buck died that Stewart wasn't completely blameless. "I'm sorry."

"Don't be, Red." He grasped her hand and squeezed it. "What happened to me wasn't your fault. I had my own run-in with Morgan and his men. This was just their way of saying they didn't appreciate my big mouth."

"But you would never have gone to town to see the judge if it wasn't for me. I can't help but think that everything that's happened is my fault." She turned away from his questioning gaze. Now was not the time for apologies and self-recrimination.

"They haven't won, Red. This is just a minor setback."

"I saw the judge's order, Brock. It fell out of your coat pocket."

"I'm sorry I wasn't able to convince him to drop this whole ridiculous mess. It looks as if we're going to have to have a jury trial."

She gasped, her eyes widening in surprise. "A trial! But why? I don't understand."

"If we leave it to Judge Cooper to decide, he's going to side with Morgan. Apparently they're friends. I had no alternative but to request a trial by jury."

Her shoulders slumped in defeat. "But what good will that do? The men in this town will side with Jacob. Half of them owe him money. I guess I'd better make plans to move."

"Is this the same Prudence Daniels I've come to know?" And love? he wanted to add. "The one with a stubborn streak a mile wide running down her back?" Brock sighed. "I never figured you for a coward, Red. And your attitude doesn't say much about what you think of my legal capabilities."

She had the grace to blush. "I didn't mean to doubt you, Brock. It's just that . . . well, the cards seem to be stacked against us."

"Nobody ever said this was going to be easy. I admit things don't look too good right now. But they'll get better. I still have a few aces up my sleeve."

Prudence's heart melted at the crooked smile Brock attempted. "You're awfully cocky for a man with two broken ribs, two black eyes, and a body that looks like it's been through a cattle stampede."

"You haven't been peekin' at my naked body again, have you, Red?"

Her face flamed. "No, of course not! Hannah was bathing you and said . . ." Her mouth snapped shut. She was not about to reveal what Hannah had said.

"It must have been pretty scandalous to have brought such a blush to your cheeks. I think I'll ask Hannah the next time I see her."

"You'll do no such thing, Brock Peters! Now get to sleep. You'll need plenty of rest if you're going to recover properly from your injuries."

He yanked on her hand. "Only if you'll consent to lie with me until I go to sleep."

Ripples of desire coursed through her, and she was going to object, but then he smiled that crooked smile again and she knew she was lost.

Taking a deep breath, she replied softly, "All right. But you must promise me that you'll go right to sleep." She knew she wouldn't be able to, not with Brock lying right next to her.

He smiled and tried to lift the blankets, but Prudence shook her head. "I will remain on top of the covers."

His smile melted. "Spoilsport," he murmured.

She turned out the lantern and nestled her back into Brock's chest, careful not to hurt him. She smiled into the darkness. *Thank you, God, for giving me a second chance.*

She closed her eyes and went to sleep.

21

*An overpolite man is hidin'
some mighty unpolite ideas.*

"*I can't believe* you have the nerve to show your face here, Jacob. Not after what you've done." Prudence stared daggers at the man standing on her front porch, thinking of the man she loved, lying broken and beaten upstairs in her bed.

"I'm sorry, Miss Pru," Slim said, hurrying after Jacob, a distraught look on his face. "I only was gone from my post for a minute, and he sneaked by me." He thumbed his finger at Morgan.

Prudence patted the cowboy's arm. "That's all right, Slim. You'd best get back to the gate before the colonel finds out you've gone." Moody had taken her instructions to heart and had been a strict disciplinarian these past two days; she doubted he would be as easy on the cowboy once he found out Slim had left his post. "I can handle Mr. Morgan."

The cowboy's look was skeptical, but he beat a hasty retreat, and Prudence turned her attention back to Jacob, who was looking mighty pleased with himself.

"Aren't you going to invite me in, honey?"

Her eyes narrowed into thin slits. "I am not. And if you don't desist in calling me that repulsive nickname, you're going to be looking down the business end of a gun." She patted the derringer in her apron pocket; she'd leave nothing to chance this time.

"Your defenses are rather shabby, Prudence. Putting a dimwit in charge of the main gate wasn't a very bright idea."

"What is it you want, Jacob? I haven't got all day to spend talking to you. I have more important things with which to occupy my time." Brock, for one. And it was nearly time for his afternoon meal.

Morgan grew indignant at her dismissal. "I just wanted you to know that I had nothing to do with Peters's beating. Dave Stewart and two of my hands took it upon themselves to punish him. It was not done on my order."

"And you expect me to believe that? Really, Jacob, I was naive once when it came to you, but not anymore."

He held out his hands beseechingly. "Prudence, I swear I'm telling you the truth. Stewart and the others have been fired. They're no longer working for the Bar J."

"What's the matter? Were you afraid you'd be connected to the crime? But then, why should you be worried, Jacob? You own the sheriff, you own the judge. I doubt you would have been charged with a crime anyway."

His lips thinned in annoyance. "I always took you for a reasonable woman."

"And I always took you for a friend." She chafed her arms against the cold. "I guess we were both wrong."

"You can't win, Prudence. I have the whole town on my side."

Prudence's eyes darkened, and her voice grew as cold as the snow that littered the ground. "Just watch me," she said, and slammed the door in his face.

"Is anything wrong, Miss Pru?" Mary asked, stepping into the hallway with BJ, who broke into a grin at the sight of Prudence.

Prudence took the child into her arms and hugged him to her breast, caressing his downy head with her fingertips. "No, Mary, nothing's wrong. Not anymore."

"Do you think it would be all right if BJ and I go on up to see Mr. Peters? We've been awful worried about him."

"Of course. I'm sure he'd enjoy a visit. Just don't stay too long. And be careful the baby doesn't kick Brock in the ribs."

"No, ma'am. We sure won't."

Handing the child back to his mother, Prudence left to prepare Brock's meal.

Balancing BJ on her hip, Mary knocked softly on the bedroom door, then entered. "Mr. Peters, it's Mary. Miss Pru said it would be all right if BJ and I came to visit you for a spell." She hung back by the door, waiting for an invitation, which was issued a moment later.

"I'm glad you came, Mary." Brock indicated the chair by the bed. "It gets mighty boring lying in this bed." Though if the truth were told, he didn't feel like being anywhere else just yet.

"You look just like my pa did when he drank a whole quart of corn liquor and fell down the stairs at Madam Eva's."

Brock forced a smile. "That bad, huh?"

She nodded and said quite seriously, "One of them whores blackened his eyes before he fell."

Brock's smile didn't have to be forced this time. "How have you been? Has BJ been behaving himself?"

Her voice filled with pride. "Yessir! BJ's done got himself a tooth." She opened the baby's mouth and showed him the singular accomplishment. "Some babies don't get their first tooth 'til their fifth or sixth month, but Miss Pru says BJ's special."

"Very impressive. And how's Will?"

"Madder'n a hornet about what Morgan's men did to you. Shorty and Burt had to talk some sense into him. And the colonel's made him do extra drills just to keep his mind busy."

Brock couldn't help but smile. Moody was certainly in his element, ordering everyone around as though he were still in command of Fort Garland. He just wondered how Shorty and the others were responding to it. Knowing Shorty, it wouldn't be gracefully.

"And how are you, Mary? You haven't been working yourself too hard now, have you?"

"Oh, no, Mr. Peters. Miss Pru would never allow that. She makes each of us rest every afternoon. I tried to tell her that I didn't need to no more, since I weren't in a family way. But she says with BJ being as spirited a baby as he is, I needed the rest more than the others."

"Miss Pru's a smart woman."

The young girl fidgeted nervously with the folds of her dress. "I was wonderin', Mr. Peters, if what Miss Pru told us is true." Her eyes filled with concern. "Are we going to have to move from here? I ain't never had a home as nice as this one."

Brock sighed at the distraught expression on the young girl's face. What could he say? How could he predict the outcome of a trial that hadn't even started yet?

"I'm going to do my best to see that doesn't happen, Mary."

Consoled by his words, Mary smiled in relief and pushed herself to her feet. "In that case, I'll tell the others not to worry. I've got a whole lot of faith in you, Mr. Peters. You rescued me once. I don't doubt you'll be able to do it again. You're a very special man. Everyone thinks so."

Brock's eyebrows arched, and he couldn't help himself from asking, "Everyone? Even Miss Pru?"

"Especially her, Mr. Peters. She's always talking about how brave and smart you are. Why"—Mary blushed to the tips of her toes—"I think she sort of fancies you. Louann told me once that opposites are likely to attract."

Brook frowned. "You're wrong, Mary. Prudence and I attract about as well as oil and vinegar. We just don't seem to mix."

"But when oil and vinegar come together over freshly sliced tomatoes . . . well, I just don't think there's anything better." She gave him a saucy wink as she headed out the door, and Brock's frown deepened.

Oil and vinegar could never mix in a hundred years, he decided stubbornly. And neither could he and Prudence.

"You've certainly got a lot of nerve showing your face here, Jacob, after what you've done!"

The words had a sickening similarity to those Prudence had thrown at him a few hours earlier, and Jacob could only stare slack-jawed as Arabella whirled into the parlor, her nostrils flaring in fury. Stopping in front of him, she drew back her hand and smacked him soundly across the face. The sound seemed to reverberate over the purple-flowered walls.

"If I'd known it was you knocking on my door," she continued, "I would have instructed the maid to turn you away."

Rubbing his cheek, Jacob wondered what the hell he had done to incite the woman's wrath. "Now, honey," he cajoled, holding out his hands in supplication.

"Don't you 'honey' me, you randy old goat!" She punctuated her words with a stabbing finger to his chest. "I saw you and Lulu Lowery in front of the hotel the other day. I saw the way you were drooling over her. I honestly thought you had better taste, Jacob. The girl is nothing but a slut."

He shook his head in denial, a look of innocence on his face. "I was only escorting the silly chit home, Bella. Why would I want her when I have you? She means nothing to me."

"Just like Prudence Daniels meant nothing to you? But you've gone out of your way to rid this town of the poor woman. I'd certainly like to know why." When he flinched, she knew she'd hit close to the mark.

Jacob crossed to the ornately carved cherry cabinet and retrieved a crystal decanter, pouring a snifter of brandy to fortify himself. Damn Bella for her jealousy and her unending curiosity! A man had needs. And business matters to tend to. And he didn't need an interfering woman butting into his activities, not even one as comely as Bella. "You must learn to trust me, honey."

She threw back her head and laughed, and the sound that poured forth was coldly derisive. "That's rich. Trust you? I'd sooner trust a rattlesnake. I mean to find out what's between you and Miss Daniels, and that miserable little hussy, Lulu Lowery. And I won't rest until I do."

Wrapping his arms about her, he drew her into his chest. "I didn't come over here to argue with you, Bella." His hand slid up to cup her breast. "Why waste the afternoon on such ridiculous subjects when we can idle away the hours much more pleasurably?"

She pushed hard against his chest, yelling for her two wolfhounds and smiling in satisfaction at the look of fright on Jacob's face when the two dogs came bounding into the room and made a beeline for his legs.

"Call them off, Bella! They're trying to bite my crotch. Stop it! *Stop it!*" he ordered the dogs, trying to slap them away. They snarled in response, baring large, white teeth.

"Well, isn't that just too darn bad. Maybe if they take a nip out of that miserable piece of unfaithful meat you call a cock, you won't be able to plant it inside Lulu Lowery again."

He backed toward the door, trying to cover his private parts with his hands. "I swear you're the only woman for me, Bella."

"When you're ready to make that permanent, Jacob, when you're willing to offer me your *name,* then maybe I'll listen to your pitiful explanations. But until then I don't want you showing your cheating face here again. No one plays me for a fool, Jacob Morgan. Especially not you!"

She yanked open the front door, and Jacob ran from the house, but he didn't escape totally unscathed. One of the dogs held a large piece of the seat of Jacob's pants in his teeth.

"Good boy, Cletus," she told the dog, and patted him on the head before slamming the door shut. At the liquor cabinet she poured herself a glass of brandy, then sat on the purple brocade sofa.

There was more to this Prudence Daniels business than met the eye, she decided, taking a sip of the liquor, and she aimed to find out just what that was. Perhaps she'd find another way to get even with Jacob.

"Hell hath no fury like a woman scorned, boys."

And she meant to prove that to Jacob Morgan in spades.

A few days later Prudence entered her study to find Brock seated at her desk, his head held dejectedly in his hands, staring down at a piece of paper.

"What is it? What's wrong? And what are you doing out of bed so soon?" He looked up, and she saw the concern in his eyes and knew there was something terribly wrong.

Handing the paper to her, he replied, "Judge Cooper has set a date for the trial. It's to begin in two weeks."

"And you're worried?" She took a seat on the wing chair in front of the desk. "But why?"

"I'm not prepared," he confessed. "If only I had my law books . . . but I left them with my mother in Sacramento. And there's not enough time to get them here." It would be foolhardy to attempt a defense without studying certain legal cases.

"Are they so very important?" Even before she asked the question, she knew they were. She wouldn't be able to function without her medical books and journals.

He sighed. "I'll just have to make do without them."

The light streaming in through the shuttered windows cast a striped pattern across the desk, across Brock's hands, which were folded on top of it. Prudence's gaze lifted to his face, and she felt relieved to see that his bruises were beginning to fade. It would still be weeks till his ribs were completely healed, but he was already much improved.

Suddenly Prudence's voice filled with excitement as she remembered the crates of books that had been delivered to her father years ago. "You might not have to," she told him, adding at his questioning gaze, "Shortly before my father died, his brother, Robert, passed away. Crates of Uncle Robert's books were shipped here from Denver."

"But I fail to see—"

"Uncle Robert was an attorney," she interrupted. "He practiced for years in Denver. The books are probably old and terribly outdated, but they might prove useful."

Brock pushed himself up from his chair, and his step faltered. "Show me."

Her voice filled with concern. "Are you sure you're up to this? You should be resting, not worrying about this trial."

"Didn't you hear what I said? The judge has set the trial to begin in two weeks. I don't have time to lie in bed any longer. I've got to prepare your case."

"But nothing is worth risking your health, Brock." His eyebrows shot up, and she added hastily, "I mean—can't we ask to postpone it for a little while?"

"Judge Cooper is ready to rule against us. He isn't about to grant a continuance. He'd like nothing better than to hear that we can't go to trial."

Prudence sighed, knowing that if they were to save the ranch, Brock would have to proceed, healthy or not. "Follow me. I stored the crates in the spare bedroom across the hall from mine."

They entered the sparsely furnished room, and Prudence wrinkled her nose at the musty smell. She crossed to the window, drew back the drapes, and cracked the window slightly. "I never come in here. I use this as a storage room," she explained.

The three wooden crates marked *Robert Daniels,*

Esq. stood flush against the left wall, and Brock headed straight for them. The first one contained clothing and personal effects, and at the sight a feeling of disappointment swept through him. "Nothing much in this one."

"Try the others," Prudence suggested, kneeling down beside him. She had never looked in the old crates and found her curiosity piqued. Uncle Robert had been a strange old coot, and she wondered if his personal belongings would reflect that.

They lifted the lid together, and inside, much to Prudence's great relief, were books, lots and lots of books. Brock rummaged through the crate, dumping out fiction novels and various leather notebooks.

"These were probably your uncle's case notes," he explained, wishing he had the time to read them. They were quite detailed, and Brock's respect for Prudence's dead uncle grew. The man had been exacting in his work.

Searching further, he finally found what he was looking for and smiled. "Now this is more like it." He yanked at the brown leather volumes, dusting off the first one before thumbing through it. "They're old, but should serve my purpose, at any rate." He continued to scan the legal works, his voice filling with uncertainty when he said, "I just hope I still have it in me to argue your case effectively. It's been a long time, Red."

Prudence placed her hand on his forearm. "I have faith in you."

Staring into her eyes, Brock saw trust, and confidence, and something else he could not fathom. Suddenly he pulled her into his chest, capturing her lips with his own. What started out as an impulsive gesture deepened into much more, and soon Prudence's arms were draped around his neck while his hands made a thorough investigation of her breasts.

His tongue explored the recesses of her mouth, sending her stomach into a frenzy. Tentatively she touched her tongue to his, and heard him moan softly in pleasure. Emboldened by his response, she leaned into him, feeling his male hardness pressing against her leg; she rubbed against it and he groaned aloud, his hands moving down to cup her buttocks, pulling her into him.

Prudence moaned, running her hands through Brock's hair, trailing them down his chest, caressing the hard muscles there. When her hand moved to stray lower, Brock grabbed it and pushed her from him.

Taking a ragged breath, he fought for composure. "I'm sorry, Red. I know I said that this would never happen again, but I was caught up in the moment. I swear it won't happen again."

Disappointment stabbed at her breast. And anger. For she knew she had brought this upon herself. "You needn't apologize. I—"

"If you'll grab an armful, we can take these down to the study," he interrupted, gathering the books in his arms. "I need to get started preparing our strategy."

Prudence swallowed with great difficulty. "You go on. I'll be right down. I want to sort through some of my uncle's belongings," she lied, knowing that what she really wanted to do was have a good cry and plan her own strategy.

She didn't know exactly how she was going to accomplish the impossible, but somehow, some way, she was going to make Brock Peters fall in love with her.

22

Love your enemies, but keep your gun oiled.

"*I can't believe* that Scrooge of a judge has rescheduled the trial for three days before Christmas," Eliza declared, pulling the baking sheet of gingerbread cookies out of the oven. She began to lift them onto a platter with a spatula. "I think it's disgraceful. And I've a mind to tell the old codger so."

Prudence inhaled deeply of the familiar spicy scents of ginger and cinnamon. What should have been a joyous time of year, with Christmas only a week away and Sarah's marriage to Moody about to become a reality, had become as depressing as their present set of circumstances.

As Brock had predicted, Judge Cooper had refused any type of continuance. The trial was set to begin on the twenty-second of the month, and there was nothing Brock could do about it, though he had tried his damnedest. They'd both suspected that the motive behind the move was to throw Brock off balance and deprive him of enough time to prepare a proper defense. Prudence just prayed that the judge's tactics wouldn't prove successful.

"There's nothing we can do, Eliza, except try to make the best of things," Prudence said. She reached for a warm cookie and took a bite. "Mmmm. These are good." She reached for another. "Brock tried to reason with the judge, but apparently the man has no family and could not care less about something as trivial as our Lord's birthday."

"Well, it certainly has put a damper on things, I can tell you that. I don't know how we're going to enjoy Sarah's wedding on Christmas Eve, and have any kind of a celebration the following day, with that trial looming over our heads. Why, it's BJ's first Christmas!" She broke several eggs into a ceramic bowl, which already contained flour and shortening, and began beating the mixture so viciously that it made Prudence smile.

"Have you and Shorty decided on a date for your own wedding?" Prudence asked, almost laughing aloud at the look of mortification that crossed Eliza's face.

"Why, the old fool hasn't even asked me yet," the older woman replied, brandishing the wooden spoon like a weapon. "But I suppose he will. He's already declared himself. Mortimer is slower than molasses in midwinter when it comes to speakin' his mind about such things."

"Well, you must promise to let me help you plan your wedding. I've had such fun with Sarah and Moody's."

"If we're all still together." Tears sprang to Eliza's eyes, and Prudence came around the table to comfort her, wrapping her arm about the woman's thick waist.

"You mustn't speak like that, Eliza. You must have faith in Brock and know that he'll get us out of this mess."

Wiping her face on the edge of her sleeve, Eliza sniffled and shook her head. "I'm sorry. I know you have a lot to deal with at the moment. This is, after all, your home. But I can't help feeling that it's mine, too. I think all of us feel that way."

"Then you must believe in Brock the way I do."

"You love him, don't you?" Without giving Prudence a chance to reply, Eliza added, "Shorty suspected as much, but I wasn't quite as sure. You've always worn your feelings close to your sleeve, Pru."

Prudence sighed. "I do love Brock. But I despair of evoking a similar response in him. Why, he's so caught up in this trial, he hardly knows I exist." Her plan to interest him had certainly gone awry. The passionate kiss they'd shared a week ago was only a distant memory. Brock had been polite and businesslike. Oh, so damned businesslike! The lawyer in him had risen to the forefront, and she couldn't help yearning for the arrogant, footloose cowboy he'd once been.

With a firm hand to Prudence's shoulder, Eliza pushed the young woman onto the ladder-backed chair, then followed suit. "If I had waited for Shorty to make the first move, I'd be spending the rest of my days alone. The man puts a snail to shame."

Prudence's lips twitched, and Eliza added, "You've got to take matters into your own hands, girl. Make the first move. Let Brock know that you're interested."

"I can't do that. You don't understand. I've already wounded Brock's pride, deflated his male ego. I made it quite clear to him some time back that I didn't welcome his advances." Eliza made a disgusted sound, and Prudence looked chagrined. "I know I was stupid. I realize that now. But back then I didn't know I was in love with him."

Eliza tapped her finger against her cheek while she contemplated the situation. "As much as I hate to say this, I think you're going to have to let matters lie until this trial comes to an end. Brock needs to focus all his attention on winning this case. Once he does, he'll be more receptive to your advances. I'm sure of it."

Hope ignited in Prudence's breast. "Then you think I have a chance with him?"

"As my darling Mortimer is so fond of saying, 'There ain't a hoss that cain't be rode. There ain't a man that cain't be throwed.'" Eliza did an excellent imitation of Shorty's cowboy twang. "Well, in my opinion, there ain't a man alive that can't be brought to the altar by a clever woman." She patted Prudence's hand. "And, my dear girl, you're about as bright and clever as they come."

Later that afternoon Brock and Moody burst into the parlor, carrying brown paper-wrapped parcels and wearing huge grins on their faces.

"We've just won a major victory, Red," Brock announced, dropping his packages onto a nearby chair. He and Moody had spent the better part of the morning shopping for Christmas presents.

Prudence cast a quizzical glance at Sarah before putting aside the large red velvet bow she was fashioning for Sarah's wedding. "A victory? I don't understand."

Crossing the short distance to where Prudence and Sarah sat on the floor by the fireplace, Brock held out his hands to haul her to her feet. "It seems the prosecuting attorney, Thomas Reed, doesn't have much love for your friend, Jacob Morgan. Morgan cheated his father out of some property some years back. . . ." He waved the explanation away. "I have requested that women be allowed to serve on the jury, and Reed gave his approval. Judge Cooper was powerless to deny me his compliance, and thus has granted the motion."

"Is that legal?" Sarah asked, her voice filled with uncertainty. "I've never heard of such a thing."

"That's the beauty of it, Sarah," Moody explained, rushing forward to help his fiancée to her feet. "It's never been done before in Colorado Territory. But, Brock, being a clever lawyer, cited that Wyoming, which has already given women the right to vote, has allowed the use of female jurors for quite some time."

Brock smiled smugly. "Judge Cooper is afraid of alienating the women's vote should the territory become a state, as everyone is predicting. It seems the judge has designs on running for governor and, knowing that the women's suffrage movement is strong here, was unwilling to put all his eggs into one basket. He's afraid of losing potential votes."

"And you think that having women on the jury is going to help us?" Prudence's forehead wrinkled in confusion. "I still don't see how. Most of the women in this town are against us. If they serve on the jury, they're sure to vote against us."

Brock led Prudence to the sofa and sat her down, then took the seat next to her. "I've spent the whole day interviewing potential jurors, Red. And I don't mind admitting, I had to scour the countryside to find four women who had not been unduly influenced by Reverend Entwhistle. Two are farm women, one just moved here recently from Denver, and one, I found out after careful questioning, had been forced to marry or suffer the consequences of giving birth out of wedlock. Not everyone in this town is against us, Red. I firmly believe that. And besides, you'll receive a much fairer trial with them on the jury, than solely from men, who are likely to be swayed by Morgan's threats and empty promises."

Skeptical though she was, Prudence digested Brock's reasoning, and the more she thought about it, the easier it went down. Tentatively she covered Brock's hand with her own, staring deeply into his eyes. "I'm very grateful that you consented to represent me in this matter, Brock. I just know that we're going to win."

Moody glanced over at Sarah and winked.

Finding himself drowning in an emerald pool, Brock pulled his gaze from Prudence's and cleared his throat self-consciously. "Yes, well, if I'm going to live up to your praise, I'd best get back to work."

Her hand tightened. "Must you? It's nearly suppertime, and, well . . . Sarah and I were hoping we could talk to you and Moody about the wedding plans." Prudence looked to Sarah for confirmation and found her friend nodding in agreement. She'd spent so little time in Brock's company lately and found she missed their banter, friendly and otherwise. She wasn't ready for him to leave her just yet.

Sarah searched for a topic. "Yes, we need to discuss"—she paused a moment—"the minister. You haven't told us yet how you plan to procure one. And frankly I'm getting a bit worried."

Brock pulled his hand out of Prudence's grasp, as if he'd been scorched, and bolted to his feet. "Moody can put your fears to rest. I've got things to tend to in the study. Don't wait supper for me. I'll most likely work straight through it."

"But, Brock!" Prudence wailed, watching him walk out of the room.

Moody and Sarah shared a disgusted sigh.

As if the devil himself were on his heels, Brock hurried to the study, slamming the door behind him once he'd reached his haven.

Damn Red! Didn't she know what she was doing to

him with those grateful smiles and big green eyes? He wanted her so badly, he could still taste their last kiss on his lips.

But she didn't want him.

She'd made that perfectly clear. And though she was grateful that he was helping her, she didn't want him in her bed. And if he couldn't have all of her, then he wanted no part at all.

Slumping dejectedly onto the swivel chair, he poured himself a stiff glass of brandy, then stared at the amber liquid. "Great! Just great!"

He set the glass back on the desk, though he felt like heaving it across the room. He needed to stay focused. He couldn't dull his senses with liquor and thoughts of bedding Red.

But as his member throbbed painfully, and memories of Red's naked body blurred before his eyes, Brock's determination to stay in control of his faculties wavered, and he picked up the glass, downing the liquor in one gulp.

The sound of pounding shook Brock into wakefulness. Grabbing the sides of his head, he cursed himself inwardly for drinking so much the previous night, then realized that the pounding wasn't coming from his temples, but from down the hall. Just as he was about to rise from his chair, Shorty burst into the room, an agitated look on his face.

"You'd better come quick, Brock. Those damned fool women are up to no good . . . Shit!" Shorty stared at Brock. "You look like the hind end of a mule train."

Following Shorty out the door, Brock decided that he felt about as good as he looked. As they approached the door of the great room, the pounding grew louder; the women's laughter could be heard quite distinctly.

"I'd recognize Eliza's cackle anywhere." Shorty shook his head in disgust. "That woman is going to be the death of me yet."

Brock could certainly identify with that. Opening the door, he found Prudence and the rest of the women hard at work fashioning placards. Mary and Laurel were busy pounding nails, while the rest wielded paintbrushes.

"Might I inquire what you ladies are doing?" Brock asked, his gaze falling on a completed sign that read "Absolution Means Forgiveness." He sighed deeply.

"I should think that would be perfectly obvious," Eliza replied, casting Shorty a disdainful look. "We're making signs. We intend to picket the church services tomorrow."

"I done told you the woman was crazed, Brock," Shorty said, returning her look with an icy one of his own. "You women are plumb loco."

With paintbrush in hand, Prudence turned to face Brock, intending to defend their idea. But rather than the look of condemnation she expected, he was smiling. "I think Eliza's plan has merit, Brock. Don't you?" she asked, hoping that his smile meant approval.

Brock's gaze flitted to the other signs, which read "Justice for ALL Women" and "Save Our Home." He rubbed his chin thoughtfully. "I think I like the one that you're hiding behind your back, Red."

Her cheeks aflame, Prudence pulled the sign forward and listened while he read aloud, "Who Says God Is a Man?" Brock's eyebrows arched. "I don't need to ask who wrote that one, now, do I?"

"It's blasphemy," Shorty said. "Of course God is a man. Why, a woman could never have kept her mouth shut long enough to have created the earth and all the animals. She'da been too busy cacklin'."

Noting the hostility on Eliza's face as she clutched her paintbrush like a sword, Brock grasped Shorty's arm and hurried him out of the room before the older man suffered an injury.

"Shorty, I want you to ride into town for me. I need you to send a telegram."

"A telegram?" Shorty scratched his head as he followed Brock into the study. "Who you going to send a telegram to?"

Brock smiled, pleased that he'd come up with such divine inspiration. "To the *Rocky Mountain News*. I'm sure William Byers would be very interested to hear about what is going on in our quiet little community."

"You mean we's goin' to be in the newspaper?"

"That's exactly what I mean. Never doubt the power of the press and the determination of five stubborn females!"

Armed with their placards, the ladies of the Rough and Ready Ranch for Unwed Mothers descended upon the town of Absolution the following day.

With heavy boots on their feet and fleece-lined jackets to keep them warm against the cold, they paraded in front of Reverend Entwhistle's church, holding up their signs for everyone to read as the parishioners filed by.

"Disgraceful!" said one plump old matron, holding her skirt out of the way so she wouldn't come in contact with the women.

"Sinners, the lot of them!" her hawk-nose companion concluded.

Brock smiled even as he listened to the disparaging remarks, his attention focused on the reporter who stood on the steps of the white clapboard building, taking notes. Apparently word of the trial had already reached

Denver before his telegram arrived, and not one but several newspapers were represented in the town.

Public opinion could be swayed, if the newspapers determined that the women were being treated unfairly. And Brock was going to make certain that they did.

Reverend Entwhistle, who had just been apprised of the situation outside of the church, came hurrying down the steps, shaking his fist at the women. "You had better clear the area," he warned. "I won't have you interfering with my services. We don't want your kind here."

"This is a public sidewalk, Reverend," Prudence informed him without breaking stride. "And I believe we are perfectly within our rights to congregate here. After all, my father did help to construct this church." She smiled sweetly at his indignation, noting that the newspaper reporter was writing fast and furiously.

"I shall summon the sheriff," Entwhistle threatened, his beady eyes narrowing.

"Go ahead," Brock said, standing before the ferret-faced minister. "I'm sure the sheriff will agree with Miss Daniels's position. This is still a free country, Entwhistle, though you and others like you have done your best to make it otherwise."

"This is an outrage! I shall report you to . . . to . . ."

"Mr. Morgan?" Prudence finished for him. "Well, here's your chance, Reverend. I do believe Mr. Morgan is approaching." She turned to glare at Jacob.

Jacob looked fit to be tied, but it wasn't Prudence or Brock at whom he stared, but at the person directly behind Reverend Entwhistle.

"I'm certain the Lord doesn't mind if these ladies want to walk in front of His house, now does He, Reverend Entwhistle?" Arabella Potts inquired. "After all, we are all God's children, are we not?" She patted his arm in a placating fashion, thinking that the little pipsqueak looked too much like her dead husband, Henry, to be likable. "Your congregation is waiting. I think it would be prudent if you went back inside."

Entwhistle looked helplessly at Morgan, who was staring daggers at the woman. Not wishing to offend one of his most generous benefactors, not to mention the loveliest, Ezekiel Entwhistle nodded in agreement, then spun on his heel and headed back inside his church.

Brock and Prudence glanced at each other in confusion, and Brock shrugged, but he smiled inwardly nonetheless.

Not wishing to make a scene, Jacob followed the reverend into the church, leaving Arabella alone with the picketers.

"Thank you for coming to our aid, Mrs. Potts," Prudence said to the dark-haired woman who had come to stand before her. "Though I doubt you'll be looked upon favorably for your actions."

Noting the courage and conviction on the young woman's face, Arabella smiled. Prudence Daniels was someone she could like, she decided. And if helping her meant thwarting Jacob's plans, then so much the better.

"Not everyone in this town is against you and your ranch, Miss Daniels. I, for one, think what you've been doing is splendid. There isn't a woman in this town who hasn't been faced with the prospect of pregnancy, wanted or otherwise. They've just forgotten that fact."

"And do you intend to remind them, Mrs. Potts?" Brock asked, wondering what motivated the attractive widow. If the nasty look that passed between her and Morgan was any indication, he had a pretty good idea.

"Indeed I do, Mr. Peters. I've always been a sucker for lost causes and underdogs. And besides"—she smiled at Prudence—"I happen to agree with Miss

Daniels's sign." With a nod, she lifted the voluminous folds of her skirts and proceeded down the sidewalk.

"Well, what do you make of it?" Prudence asked Brock once Arabella Potts was out of earshot.

"I learned a long time ago, Red, never to look a gift horse in the mouth."

"But I was so certain that Mrs. Potts and Jacob had formed a tenderness for each other. Why, at the dance last autumn they seemed quite enamored of each other."

"Things change," Brock said, and walked away.

Prudence wanted to cry at the iciness she heard in his voice. Things certainly had changed between them. And it hadn't been for the better. But she was bound and determined to rectify that situation immediately.

Upon their return home, Prudence was more determined than ever to set things right with Brock. With yards of red satin ribbon and a large clump of mistletoe clutched behind her back, she paused before the door to the study, where she knew Brock was working on his defense strategy.

Taking a deep breath, she opened the door and entered. He looked up, and immediately she noticed the wariness in his eyes. Ignoring it, she smiled. "I've come to decorate the office for Christmas." She pulled the decorations out in front of her by way of explanation.

"What?" He shook his head. "I'm trying to concentrate, Red. The trial starts tomorrow, and I still haven't figured out my opening statement."

"I won't disturb you. I'm just going to hang some streamers and bows, to brighten up the room."

"See that you don't," he said, knowing quite well that she already had. As soon as she'd entered the room, the scent of lilac had filled his nostrils with longing. Listening to the soft rustle of her skirts as she moved around the room, fastening bows and streamers everywhere, he did his best to concentrate on the papers before him, but he found his eyes following her every movement.

She was in front of the fireplace, standing on tiptoe to tie a ribbon around the brass candlestick holder, and her breasts strained against the soft wool fabric of her gown. Her hair was loose and hung down her back in riotous curls, and he longed to run his fingers through them.

"Damn!" he cursed, trying to get himself under control.

Prudence turned, smiling sweetly. "Did you say something?" She could see by the annoyed expression on his face that he was flustered, and that gave her a small measure of satisfaction. Perhaps he wasn't quite as immune to her charms as he pretended. "I'll only be another minute. I need to hang this mistletoe over the door."

"Mistletoe?" His voice sounded utterly anguished.

"Why, yes. It's traditional, you know." She began to drag the ladder-backed chair beneath the door frame. "I always hang mistletoe at Christmas." She climbed up on the chair and heard another of Brock's vile curses.

"Get down off that chair. You'll hurt yourself."

She laughed. "Don't be silly. I do this every year."

He came up behind her, grasped her about the waist, and lifted her to the floor. She turned in his arms, holding the twig over her head. "I believe you owe me a kiss, for you've caught me under the mistletoe."

"Come on, Red. Quit fooling around. I've work to do."

He tried to back away, but she clung to his waist with her free hand. Much to her disappointment, Brock didn't kiss her but grabbed her hand, removing it from his person.

"You'd best leave, Red, before we both end up doing something we might regret."

"And who says we'll regret it?" she asked.

But before Brock could reply, Prudence had dashed out the door and closed it firmly behind her, leaving Brock to stare at the formidable piece of oak and wonder if he was losing his mind.

"Women!" He snorted in disgust. The most contrary species God had ever set upon this earth. With another muffled curse, he returned to his desk to prepare for tomorrow's trial.

23

Lawyers get you out'n the kind of trouble you'd never get in if there was no lawyers.

"*Hear ye!* Hear ye! The District Court of Absolution, Colorado Territory, is now in session. The Honorable Judge Jonas Cooper presiding."

Prudence listened to the clerk of the court and her hands started to sweat; she wiped them on the skirt of her gown and noticed that Sarah, seated next to her, was doing the same.

Prudence sat in the first row of spectators, directly behind Brock. She'd been spared the humiliation of sitting at the defense table, thanks to Brock, who had arranged it with the judge, citing the pregnant women's condition and her need to be close to them.

Staring at the broad width of Brock's back, she couldn't help but think how terribly handsome he looked in his suit of black superfine, which he'd purchased recently. His white shirt was spotless; a black string tie hung around his neck. And the gold pocket watch, which had once belonged to her father and that she'd given him to use "for luck," hung suspended from his black brocade vest.

She marveled at how different clothes could change a man's appearance. The cowboy was gone, replaced by a highly competent attorney-at-law.

"Are you doing all right, Miss Daniels?" Brock asked, turning about to face her. Though his manner was polite and indifferent, his eyes held a wealth of concern, and she was deeply touched.

Smiling tentatively, Prudence nodded, thinking how odd "Miss Daniels" sounded on his lips now; "Red" was usually all he ever called her. But they'd decided it was best to keep up appearances and use the formality.

Judging by the stern expressions on the four women seated in the jury box, she was going to need every advantage. As far as she was concerned, their eyes already seemed to condemn her. She recognized one of them, though none of their names had appeared on the petition; Brock had made certain of that.

The eight men seated with them looked about as eager to be here as in church. The red-haired man with the wire spectacles kept tugging on his stiffly starched collar, and Prudence recognized him as Mr. Thurgood, the schoolmaster.

Taking a deep breath, she settled back against the hard bench, noting that Thomas Reed, the prosecuting attorney, had stood to begin his opening remarks.

"Ladies and gentlemen of the jury," he began, "as you all know, a petition has been circulated and signed by most of the citizens of this town, asking for the removal of Miss Prudence Daniels and the pregnant women who reside with her from the Rough and Ready Ranch.

"It is the opinion of these concerned citizens that Miss Daniels's continued operation of a ranch which harbors women of questionable moral fiber is detrimental to the Christian values we embrace here in Absolution. We hope to prove to you decent, law-abiding folks that Miss Daniels should be evicted from her property and forced to leave the territory."

Prudence took a deep breath and was grateful when Sarah's hand reached out to grab hers. She drew strength from it and from the fact that Brock was handling her defense.

After Brock's opening remarks, which briefly detailed her reasons for starting the unwed mother ranch, it was no surprise that Reverend Entwhistle was called as the prosecution's first witness.

The reverend went on at great length about how it was his duty to protect his flock from the evils of sin, and Prudence was gratified to see that during his oration, some of the men and women seated in the jury box yawned in boredom. One elderly woman, seated in the back row, had even closed her eyes for several minutes and had to be nudged in the arm by the rotund woman seated next to her. Her behavior wasn't surprising, considering that the reverend usually had the same response from his own congregation at Sunday's church services.

"Does Miss Daniels represent a threat to this town, Reverend Entwhistle?" Mr. Reed inquired. The question suddenly refocused everyone's attention, especially when Brock jumped up from his chair.

"Objection, Your Honor. Mr. Reed is calling for a conclusion of the witness. We're not dealing in opinion here, but in fact."

"Overruled, Mr. Peters. The reverend's opinion is important to this case, since he is the spiritual leader of this community." Judge Cooper turned toward Entwhistle. "You may answer the question, Reverend."

"It is my opinion," the reverend said, his pointed chin notched ever so slightly, a smug smile on his lips, "that Miss Daniels is not setting a good example for the people of this town, especially the younger children, who look to their elders for guidance and counsel. I definitely consider Miss Daniels a threat to the well-being of this town."

Stone-faced, Prudence stared straight ahead, doing her best not to show emotion. Reverend Entwhistle's opinions were not new, and she'd had years to grow used to his narrow-mindedness.

When the reverend was finished and started to leave the witness box, Brock walked up to him. Prudence shivered at the cold-blooded anger she saw in his eyes.

"Not so fast, Reverend. I have a few questions for you."

There were snickers of derisive laughter as the red-faced minister retook his seat, and the judge banged his gavel and called for order in the court.

"Isn't it true, Reverend Entwhistle, that Miss Daniels brought her small flock to church every Sunday to hear your sermon?"

The reverend wiggled nervously on his seat. "Well, yes."

"And by doing so, wouldn't you say that Miss Daniels was setting a good example for her ranch hands and those women who were placed in her care?"

"But they were women of ill repute and sinners."

Sarah stiffened, and it was Prudence's turn to offer comfort by squeezing her hand.

"Doesn't the Bible say, Reverend, 'Let he who is without sin among you cast the first stone'? Are you without sin, Reverend Entwhistle?"

The wiry man began sweating profusely and had to mop his forehead and face several times before answering. "I . . . I am a man of the cloth."

Brock braced his hands on the railing and leaned forward, stabbing the pious man with a pointed look. "True. But are you without sin?"

Brock glanced at the jurors, noting that he had now their undivided attention, even the old lady in the back, who'd been dozing off and on during the proceedings. He also noted that most of the women were scowling deeply at Entwhistle, who had still not answered the question. Guilt by omission was almost as powerful as admission, he decided.

"You may step down, Reverend. I have no more questions at this time."

A buzz of excitement flitted about the room, and the judge's gavel pounded, signaling the end of the first day's session.

Prudence breathed a sigh of relief. She wanted to go home—home to friends and people who cared about her. But she knew that tomorrow she'd be facing more of the same, and she prayed for the strength to survive it.

It was a quiet group who gathered around the table for dinner that evening. Each was immersed in his or her thoughts about the day's events, and it was Moody who finally broke the silence.

"I thought things went well today, Brock. You handled the reverend quite admirably."

"I agree," Sarah stated, nodding. "I watched those ladies in the jury box, and they didn't seem to take too kindly to the reverend's evasiveness."

Brock glanced down the other end of the table at Prudence, whose face had whitened at the mention of the day's session. He wished he could have spared her the humiliation she'd endured today. But tomorrow would only be more of the same, and it was probably going to get worse before it got better.

Thoughtfully he sipped his Bordeaux, then asked, "How are you holding up, Red? You're awfully quiet this evening."

Her smile was tentative. "I'm fine. Just a bit tired. I never realized how draining such a procedure could be. All those people, staring, wondering . . . And the reporters . . ." She shook her head. "I never realized . . ."

"A cowchip is paradise for a fly, Miss Pru," Shorty counseled, picking at a stubborn piece of meat between his teeth with the tip of his knife. "A courtroom ain't no different. Them that are curious swarm about, hoping to hear the least little tidbit of gossip. You just got to shut your ears to it."

"I wish I'd been there today. Me and Will is beginning to feel left out of things," Mary complained.

Brock noted that Will seemed more interested in procuring second helpings of roast beef than in visiting the courthouse. "You'll have your day in court, Mary. I'm planning to have all of you ladies testify before this trial is over."

Prudence gasped and choked on the wine she was sipping. Slim slapped her gently on the back, and she soon recovered enough to say, "Are you insane? You're planning to put all of these women on the stand?"

"Oh, how exciting!" Eliza blurted, clapping her hands. She received a quelling look from Prudence.

"I'll not allow it. Except for Mary, these women are all in various stages of pregnancy. It would not be good for their health. It's out of the question."

"I'm afraid that's not your call to make, Red. As your lawyer, I have to do what I deem best."

"But they'll be crucified!"

He noted the fear in her eyes and was saddened by it. "Then I will leave the ultimate decision to them. If they decide not to testify in their own behalf, I won't force them to."

Prudence breathed a sigh of relief, but it was short-lived. Sarah said, "Of course I'll testify. This is my home. I'm not going to give it up without a fight."

"I quite agree," Eliza said, and Shorty's chest puffed up with pride.

"Well, you can count me in," Mary said. "I ain't got no love for this town, especially that mean-spirited Reverend Entwhistle. And I'd love to tell the old buzzard so."

Seemingly unaware of what was going on around her, Laurel sat folding and refolding the napkin in her lap. When she looked up to find all eyes upon her and realized that she was expected to answer, she jumped up from the table and ran out of the room.

"Now see what you've done," Prudence chastised, hoping the young woman, who was progressing so well, did not suffer a relapse. Before she could get up to follow after her charge, however, Laurel came bounding back into the room. Her eyes lit up with excitement, she handed Brock a piece of paper.

Scanning the note, Brock swallowed the lump in his throat and smiled, giving the woman an affectionate hug. "It says: 'I want to help.'"

All eyes were trained on Prudence, who slumped dejectedly on her seat. "All right," she agreed. "We'll testify."

When the ranch wagon pulled up in front of the courthouse the following morning, Prudence's eyes widened in disbelief while Sarah squealed in delight. Standing in front of the red-brick building, bearing crudely fashioned, painted signs, was Arabella Potts and several of her lady friends.

Prudence could hardly believe that the seamstress Bertha Wilkes was there, as were Caroline Townsend and Margaret Lowery. Why, they were actually protesting on her behalf! And she knew for a fact that Caroline and Margaret had signed the petition to evict her.

Brock chuckled. "Well, well, Mrs. Potts came through. I never would have believed it if I hadn't seen it with my own eyes." He set the brake on the wagon. "Morning, ladies. How are you this fine day?"

Caroline looked mortified, but one glance at Arabella told her to keep on marching with her sign held high. She nodded politely in greeting at the handsome lawyer.

"Good morning, Miss Daniels," Arabella said. "We're here to show our support for your worthy endeavors. Aren't we, ladies?" The trio nodded, and Arabella smiled. "One must provide guidance when necessary, don't you agree, Miss Daniels?" Arabella said with a secretive smile.

"Thank you. You've made me feel so much better."

"Uh, I wouldn't speak too quickly." Arabella's eyes narrowed as she glanced over Prudence's shoulder. "Here comes Jacob Morgan."

Prudence turned and, with a nod of farewell at Arabella, presented Jacob with a frosty stare before following the others into the courthouse.

Hiding his disapproval behind a mask of civility, Jacob tipped his hat to the placard bearers and walked up to Arabella, drawing her aside. "What is the meaning of this, Bella? If your aim is to humiliate me, you have succeeded. Now desist in this childish behavior and call off your disciples. You are making spectacles of yourselves."

"I think not, Jacob. I'm quite enjoying myself. In fact, I haven't enjoyed myself so much in years. I'm seriously considering joining the women's suffrage movement." Her voice rose loudly enough for the others to hear. "Men have ruled the roost too long. Isn't that right, ladies?"

"Amen," came the simultaneous response.

Red-faced, Morgan thrust his balled fists into his coat pockets. "We'll just see about this," he said, and stormed off down Main Street in the direction of the hotel.

Fifteen minutes later, when Jacob arrived with William Townsend and Seth Lowery in tow, Arabella's little group had swelled to five. Muriel Fox, whose husband owned the butcher shop, was now marching, as was Thomas Reed's wife, Amanda, who carried their small child in her arms.

"See"—Jacob pointed—"I told you your wives were behaving outlandishly."

"Caroline!" William's voice boomed, making Caroline flinch. "Put down that sign and come home at once. You've chores to attend to." He glared straight at her.

Taking a deep breath, Caroline, who had never gainsaid her husband anything in her entire life, shook her head and received a shocked gasp from William. "You men have ruled the roost too long, William. It's time we women made a statement." She looked at Arabella for approval and received it in spades.

"You'd best go on home, too, Seth," Margaret Lowery said. "We've got important work to do for women everywhere."

Just then a reporter with a camera came up to the group, tipping his hat at the ladies. "Mind if I take your picture for the *Rocky Mountain News*?"

There was a chorus of giggles, then Muriel Fox said, "Step right up, young man. We want this important event recorded for posterity."

Arabella smiled sweetly at Jacob, whose face had purpled with rage and whose eyes were fairly bulging out of his face at the sight of the cameraman about to take their photograph. Patting her hair, she said, "Do you think I look presentable enough for a photograph, Mr. Morgan?"

Arabella thought she heard Jacob mutter, "Holy cowshit!" before he stalked off, but she couldn't be certain.

Turning his collar up against the chill night air, Brock headed in the direction of the cemetery. Some sixth sense told him he'd find Prudence there.

She'd been sullen since that afternoon's court session, and her mood had not lightened during dinner. But who could blame her? She'd had to endure a vicious attack against her sister, mounted by Reed, Morgan, and the senile doctor they'd dredged up from the bowels of Denver's red-light district. It was the same doctor who had treated Clara so many years ago.

As he neared the graveyard, Brock spotted Prudence kneeling beside her sister's grave. She was weeping into her hands, and the sound of her torment tore into his gut like a jagged-edge knife.

"Red," he called out as he stepped through the gate. But she didn't hear him above the steady roar of the wind, and he called again, louder this time. "Red, are you all right? You'll catch your death of cold out here."

She looked up then, and her tears, like shimmering crystals, pierced his heart. God, how he loved her, wanted to take her pain away, protect her from the harsh realities of the world.

He held out his arms, and she rushed to him, clutching his arms as she buried her face in his coat front.

"I'm so glad you came. I hoped you would."

She gazed up at him, and he brushed away her tears with his thumbs. "What is it, love? Why do you cry?"

Prudence swallowed her sobs and said haltingly, "You heard the awful things they said about Clara. They called her a whore—a sinner. They made her out to be some trollop, not the sweet, caring woman I knew her to be."

He caressed her cheek. "I'm sorry you had to go through that. I knew they would try to cast aspersions on your character, but I never dreamed they would vilify a dead woman."

"The dead cannot defend themselves," she said sadly.

"This is a cruel and unjust world, Red. But it's people like you who'll make it better. You must believe that any pain you endure now will only serve to make you stronger."

And what of the pain in my heart? she wanted to ask. What of the love I bear for you?

"There'll be no session tomorrow. Reed's wife convinced him that he'd better be home on Christmas Eve or else. He in turn convinced Judge Cooper to delay the trial until after the holiday."

Prudence's heart lightened at the news. "I saw Mrs. Reed today when we left the courthouse. She was picketing with the other ladies." She shook her head in disbelief. "I can't believe Mrs. Potts convinced all those women to join her in supporting our cause."

"I think Arabella Potts could charm a snake if she had a mind to," Brock commented.

A stab of jealousy darted through Prudence. "Do you find her attractive?"

"In an earthy sort of way," he answered honestly. "My guess is that Mrs. Potts has been around the block a time or two."

"Oh, you mean she's worldly?"

Brock grinned at what he thought to be Prudence's naiveté. Wrapping his arm about her shoulder, he led her back to the house.

"Men like experienced women, or so I hear," Prudence remarked, wondering if she had displeased Brock in bed. Perhaps that was the reason he no longer wanted her.

"Do they now? And what do you base your conclusion on?"

She shrugged. "The amount of business Madam Eva does, I guess."

Brock threw back his head and laughed, bringing a scarlet stain to Prudence's cheeks. "What's so funny? You told me yourself that men have their needs."

When they reached the porch, Brock paused before the door. "This is an odd conversation for us to be having, isn't it, Red? Especially in light of your feelings on the subject." He opened the door, and she entered without answering.

The house was quiet, and it was apparent that everyone had gone to bed.

"Well, guess I'll head up," Brock said, unbuttoning his jacket and hanging it on the hall tree. "We have a busy day tomorrow with Moody and Sarah's wedding."

He turned toward the stairs, but before he could make good his escape, Prudence blurted, "Please don't go just yet. Stay and share a drink with me."

His mouth fell open, then snapped shut. "A drink? You don't drink, Red. Remember?"

All her stupid rules and misconceptions were coming back to haunt her, Prudence thought. "It's a woman's prerogative to change her mind. And I'll have you know that I do have a glass of sherry on occasion." She moved toward the parlor, hoping he would follow, breathing a sigh of relief when he did.

She fetched a decanter and two glasses, carrying it to the sofa where he was now seated. "I'm out of sherry. I guess we'll have to have brandy instead."

One dark eyebrow arched. "Are you sure? That stuff can go right to your head if you're not used to it."

She filled two glasses, handed him one, then took a seat beside him. The fire crackled cheerfully, casting strange patterns on the walls and lending a warm, cozy feeling to the dimly lit room.

Brock watched in amusement as Prudence took her first sip of brandy and screwed up her face in disgust. "It takes a bit of getting used to," he said.

She took a few more sips and found out he was right: the liqueur went down smooth as satin. "I guess a lot of things take getting used to. I mean"—her face grew warm—"sometimes, at first, we're not too good at things. But after we do them a few times, we get better."

His brow wrinkled in confusion. "You mean like dancing or something?"

Embarrassed, she took another swallow of the brandy. "Or something. Tell me why you stopped being a lawyer. You're so good at it, and yet you gave it up to become a cowboy." She felt relaxed and leaned back against the cushion of the sofa, closing her eyes for a moment, never noticing the pain that crossed Brock's face at her question.

Several minutes of silence followed, then Brock took a deep breath. "I gave up my practice when my wife died. I couldn't stand the loneliness, the memories that surrounded me in Sacramento."

Slowly her eyes opened, and she said softly, "Her name was Catherine, wasn't it?"

He seemed surprised that she knew. "Yes. But how . . . ?"

"That first time at the cemetery. I heard you whisper her name." She had also heard the anguish, the utter desolation, in his voice that day, and she knew he had loved his wife very much. What would it be like, she wondered, to be loved so totally, so completely?

"Catherine died from nursing our son, Josh, who was ill with the cholera. She contracted the disease, and they both died from it."

Prudence touched his hand. "I'm so sorry, Brock. I never knew you had a child."

"It's been eight years, but I had a difficult time putting it behind me, until . . ." He wanted to say "until I met you," but he didn't.

"And that's when you left Sacramento? Closed up your law practice?"

He nodded. "I drifted, did most anything that was legal to make a living. But I'm tired of drifting. I've decided that it's time to put my past behind me and get on with my life."

Hope soared within Prudence's breast, until his next words crushed all belief that they would ever be together. "This trial has made me realize how much I miss the practice of law. Once it's over, I'm going to find a nice town and settle down, set up practice again."

Her throat filled with tears, and she took a large swallow of brandy to wash them away. Brock would never be content to stay at the ranch and continue on as before, she realized that now. He had his future planned, and it didn't include her.

"Thank you for sharing your past with me, Brock. I'm sorry you had so much sorrow to deal with."

Absently he caressed her hand. "I've learned a painful lesson, Red. You can't run away from life. Instead, you've got to face it head on, or you can never be happy."

"And are you happy now?"

Their gazes locked, and he stared at her for what

seemed like an eternity, then he kissed her gently on the lips, saying in a voice that could not conceal the emptiness he felt inside, "No, but I could be. Good night, Red. I'll see you in the morning."

Prudence watched him go, fighting the urge to run after him, wanting him to explain what his enigmatic words meant, wanting to tell him how much she cared.

But she couldn't. She was a coward. She was still afraid to face the possibility that she wasn't the one who could bring him the happiness he sought.

So Miss Prudence Daniels did something she had never before done in her life: she drank herself into blessed oblivion.

24

Drownin' your sorrows only irrigates 'em.

Shorty's eyes widened in disbelief when he stepped into the kitchen the next morning to find Prudence with her head held tightly in her hands. Her eyes were puffed up like two red zinnias, and she looked as if she hadn't slept a wink. He'd never seen skin that particular shade of green before, he thought.

"Can I get you some coffee, Miss Pru?" he offered, taking pity on the poor woman. "You're lookin' a mite poorly this mornin'." She still had on the same dress she'd worn yesterday, and Shorty was fairly certain that she'd slept in it.

Prudence tried to nod, but the effort proved too dear, and she moaned instead.

He set down the hot cup of steaming liquid before her. "If you wake up feelin' halfway 'tween 'Oh, Lord' and 'My God,' you've overdid it, Miss Pru."

Her voice was hoarse when she spoke. "Please don't

breathe a word of this to anyone, Mr. Jenkins. I'd sooner die than have anyone find out I'd been imbibing too freely."

Smoothing down his mustache, Shorty covered his smile and sat at the table beside her. "Your secret's safe with me, ma'am. But iff'n there's something you'd like to get off your chest, I've got me a good ear."

With great difficulty she patted his hand, shook her head, and took another sip of the strong black coffee. "I appreciate your offer, but I've got to work this out by myself." She'd certainly learned one lesson the hard way: liquor provided no insight into a person's problems.

Hannah came in then to start breakfast and began banging the pots and pans around. This elicited another loud moan from Prudence, who grabbed her head, which was pounding like a kettle drum, and rose gingerly to her feet.

"I'd best go up and change," she said, feeling as if she might disgrace herself at any moment. Swallowing the bile that rose thickly in her throat, she excused herself and hurried upstairs to the safety of her room.

Hannah smiled knowingly at Shorty. "Miss Pru got herself a big headache this morning."

At that moment Brock entered the kitchen, looking little better than Prudence. "Mornin', everyone."

Shorty and Hannah stared at him, at each other, then burst out laughing. "Yup!" Shorty agreed. "She surely does."

Sarah paced back and forth across the braided rug of the parlor, the short velvet train of her wedding gown trailing behind her. She stopped at the window to peer out, then looked back at the clock on the mantel.

"It's nearly four o'clock, Prudence. What do you suppose could be keeping Martin and Brock?" She gnawed her lower lip anxiously. "You don't suppose Martin has had a change of heart?"

"Of course not, Sarah! Don't be ridiculous. You know the colonel and Brock went to fetch the reverend. You didn't think that horrid little man was going to come without an argument, did you?" The pain in Prudence's head made her voice shriller than usual, and she pressed the sides of her temples, wishing she had drunk another cup of chamomile tea before coming downstairs. The pounding in her head had subsided to a dull ache, thanks to Hannah's mixture, but it was still an ache nonetheless.

"Lord have mercy!" Eliza called out from the dining room, where she was in the midst of helping Mary and Laurel set out the food for the wedding feast. "I'd heard brides were nervous, but you take the cake, Sarah."

Sarah smiled sheepishly. "I'm sorry to be such a worrywart. I guess I'm just nervous. What if they can't convince the reverend to come?"

At that moment the front door burst open and Moody, Brock, and Shorty entered, hauling Ezekiel Entwhistle into the room by a lead rope. The man's head was covered with a burlap grain sack, and from the sound of his muffled screams, his mouth was bound tighter than Elvira Entwhistle's corset.

Sarah's hands flew to her cheeks, and her eyes widened at the sight. "Merciful heavens!"

Prudence wanted to laugh but refrained from doing so. She couldn't help but feel a small measure of satisfaction at the sight of the pompous minister trussed up neater than tomorrow's Christmas turkey.

"Moody, you'd best run and change your clothes," Brock suggested. Turning, he caught sight of Prudence and his eyes lit with pleasure. She was wearing an emerald velvet gown that nearly matched her eyes; it was trimmed with white satin ribbon, and he couldn't remember seeing anything lovelier. "You're beautiful," he said almost reverently, his eyes lingering on the fullness of her lower lip as the tip of her tongue came out to moisten it. Feeling himself stiffen, he shifted his weight.

Prudence blushed, unaware of the effect she had on him but pleased nonetheless by the admiration she saw in his eyes. "Thank you."

"Well," Shorty remarked, winking at Sarah, "I think the bride looks pretty good, too."

"Indeed she does," Brock agreed, diverting his attention to Sarah, smiling at the nervous woman. "Sarah, why don't you take your place in front of the Christmas tree?" he suggested. "As soon as the colonel returns, we'll untie the reverend and get on with the ceremony."

The large blue spruce stood nearly ten feet high and was decorated gaily with tiny white candles and red velvet bows. Prudence and the others had spent the better part of the day preparing for the afternoon's festivities.

Moody returned, and Shorty removed the reverend's hood and gag but kept the rope tied around his hands.

"This is an outrage!" the reverend sputtered once the gag had been removed. "I shall report all of you to the authorities!"

Shorty drew his gun and pointed it at the back of the reverend's head, which had an instant calming effect on the outraged man. "This is what we're goin' to call a modified shotgun wedding, parson. Now shut your trap and take your place in front of the Christmas tree. These folks is fixin' to marry up, and they don't need to listen to any more of your jawin'. You get my meanin'?"

Fuming with indignation, Entwhistle did as

instructed. "I shall need a Bible, if any of you heathens possess one."

Eliza brought forth hers and handed it to the man. "You'd best watch out who you're calling a heathen, Reverend. My papa was a Baptist minister, and he wouldn't take kindly to hearing another man of the cloth refer to his daughter like that."

Brock and Prudence exchanged amused glances, and the ceremony began.

As quickly as it had begun, it was over. And Prudence breathed a sigh, watching as Reverend Entwhistle was trussed up once again and escorted out the door to his horse.

Burt and Slim, who had shown up minutes before the ceremony got under way, had volunteered to take the reverend home, telling Brock that they had a sure-fire way to insure his silence. Prudence wasn't about to ask what that was, but she hoped it fell short of cutting out the man's tongue, as Shorty had suggested.

"Would you care for a glass of champagne, Red? Moody and I brought some back from town for the occasion."

Fighting the urge to gag, Prudence leaned back heavily against the sofa. "No. No, thank you. I'm still full from that wonderful feast Hannah and the girls prepared. It was delicious."

"Why, you hardly ate a thing, Miss Pru," Mary said, gathering up the dirty glassware. "Will and I had two helpings of the roast goose and cornbread dressing. But you hardly touched yours."

The sight of the greasy goose had almost made her vomit, but Prudence refrained from saying so, not wanting to hurt Mary's feelings. "Everything was just wonderful, Mary. Sarah and Moody were quite pleased."

"Do you really think so? Laurel and I wanted to make it special for them."

She patted the girl's cheek. "I really think so."

Appeased, Mary went off to tell Laurel, and Prudence found herself alone in the parlor with Brock once again. "It was a lovely wedding, don't you think?" she asked.

"I can't deny that I'm glad it's over. Kidnapping is not my usual style."

Her brows knitted together. "Do you think the reverend is going to report us to the authorities?" Her chances of winning the court case would be nonexistent if that happened.

Brock grinned and shook his head. "It seems Burt and Slim caught the reverend in a rather compromising position at Madam Eva's not long ago. They threatened to tell his wife if he so much as breathes a word of this to anyone."

Prudence started to giggle, then threw back her head and laughed; the sound, like the effervescence of bubbly champagne, went straight to Brock's heart. "It's good to hear you laugh again, Red. It's been a long time."

She sighed happily. "There hasn't been much to laugh about lately."

"That's all going to change soon, but until it does . . ." Brock rose from the sofa and crossed to the Christmas tree, kneeling beside it. When he returned to Prudence's side, he was holding a brightly wrapped package. "Merry Christmas, Red," he said, kissing her softly on the lips.

At his touch, a surge of warmth washed through Prudence, and her heart beat an accelerated rhythm. She swallowed with some difficulty. "I don't know what to say."

"Well, aren't you going to open it?"

"But we usually don't open the presents until Christmas morning," she said, toying with the red satin bow, wondering if he'd wrapped the gift all by himself. That thought touched her as intimately as his kiss. "Are you sure you want me to open it now?" She needn't have asked. The eager look on his face, like that of a child with a great secret, told her that he did.

Slowly she untied the bow and removed the wrappings. Her eyes widened in wonder as she stared at the exquisitely carved walnut box on her lap. "It's beautiful."

"Open it," he urged, and when she did she discovered it contained a music box. A miniature carousel whirled round and round to the tinkling strains of "Clair de Lune."

"I ordered if from Denver," he explained. "I hope you like it."

Tears filled her eyes as she stared into his face, for what she saw reflected there was hope. Hope for their future. Hope for a new beginning.

The courtroom was crowded again the following Monday morning. Prudence was more nervous than usual. Brock planned to put the women on the witness stand today. They were all here, even Laurel, who sat very close to Sarah, holding her hand for support.

Outside, Arabella and her group, which numbered close to twenty now, still marched in their behalf. And their chants of, "Save our sisters! Down with inequality!" could be heard every so often when the courthouse door opened.

Prudence had learned, much to her amusement, that several of the ladies' husbands had been forced to take up residence at the hotel. Muriel Fox's husband had complained that he'd received no decent meals for a week. And Thomas Reed's wife had refused to launder his clothing.

Glancing at the rumpled-looking prosecutor, Prudence almost felt sorry for him, he looked so unkempt and miserable. Almost. She had a lot to be grateful for when it came to Arabella Potts.

"I'm nervous, Miss Pru," Mary whispered. "Mr. Peters said not to be, but I can't help it. I saw my pa in the back of courtroom."

Turning, Prudence looked over her shoulder. The sight of Wilbur Winslow filled her with rage. After what he'd attempted to do to his only daughter . . . well, he should have been strung up by his . . . No form of punishment was too cruel to consider, she decided.

"You don't have to do this, Mary," Prudence reminded her. "Neither Mr. Peters nor any of the rest of us will think less of you if you decide not to testify."

"Will says I owe it to BJ. He stayed at home so that I could come say my piece. And, well, I reckon that he's right. I don't have nothing to be ashamed of."

"I don't think I've ever been more proud of anyone than I am of you at this very moment," Prudence told the young woman.

Mary's face lit up with joy, and she squeezed Prudence's hand. "I want to be just like you when I get older, Miss Pru. You're gentle and kind."

Prudence's eyes filled with tears as she remembered back to another girl's dying comments: *You're like a diamond in the rough. Your true beauty is hidden, but it sparkles brighter than anyone else's I know.*

Swallowing her tears, she replied, "You already are, Mary. Don't ever forget it."

Thomas Reed looked vastly uncomfortable as he stared at Sarah, who was seated on the witness chair "Miss Davenport," he began.

"It's Mrs. Carstairs, young man," Sarah answered in her best schoolteacher voice. Obviously unnerved, the man turned various shades of red. Shuffling through the papers on his desk, he said, "My notes tell me that your name is Sarah Davenport."

She smiled at him. "It is. It's Sarah Davenport Carstairs. My husband is a retired army colonel, Mr. Reed."

"But—I was under the impression that you were pregnant and unwed." He looked toward his clerk, who shrugged in bewilderment.

"You are incorrect, Mr. Reed." She held up her hand to show him the gold wedding band. "Colonel Carstairs and I are expecting this child in February."

"I apologize for the confusion, Mrs. Carstairs," he said. "You may step down, if Mr. Peters has no further questions."

Brock stood and approached the jury box. "I just have a couple, Mrs. Carstairs. Do you and the colonel reside at the Rough and Ready Ranch?"

"Indeed, Mr. Peters. Miss Daniels was kind enough to take us in when we were down on our luck."

"And as a former schoolteacher, I presume you would know if anything sordid or sinful was going on under Miss Daniels's roof. Wouldn't you, Mrs. Carstairs?"

Sarah made eye contact with Mr. Thurgood. "Indeed, a schoolteacher must be above reproach." She smiled at the little man, grateful when her smile was returned. "Miss Daniels reads from the Bible every evening. And all of the women share in the chores at the ranch, as well as earn their keep by making leather goods and accessories. Idle hands are the devil's workshop, Mr. Peters. And none who reside at the R and R are ever idle."

After Mrs. Carstairs's testimony, Prosecutor Reed was downright hesitant when he stood to call Eliza Dobbyns to the stand. The older woman, who reminded him of his great-aunt Hattie, a most disagreeable woman, marched by him with her nose held high in the air.

"It's Miss Dobbyns, is that correct?"

"It certainly is not!" she replied, and the prosecutor paled. "I am presently married to a pig of a man named Simon Dobbyns. As soon as my divorce is final, I will be marrying Mortimer Jenkins, my fiancé."

Thomas pulled his handkerchief from his coat pocket and mopped his brow. "Could you tell me, Mrs. Dobbyns, how you came to be at the ranch?"

She stared straight at the jury box. "When I found out I was going to have a child, I rushed home to tell my husband. I found him in bed with his mistress." There were several loud gasps and a very distinct "Tsk, tsk, tsk," before Eliza continued. "I was at my wits' end, I can tell you that. I had very little money, and nowhere to turn." She dabbed at the corner of her eye with a lace handkerchief. "When I heard about Miss Daniels's ranch, I went there. And the blessed woman took me in, no questions asked."

Several people in the back of the room applauded, and Judge Cooper banged his gavel. "Stop that this instant, or I will clear this courtroom. Mr. Reed, do you have any other questions for Mrs. Dobbyns?"

Reed slunk down on his chair, shaking his head. "No, Your Honor. We will not be presenting any other witnesses."

"Now wait just a minute!" Jacob Morgan shouted from his seat behind Reed.

"Mr. Morgan," the judge warned, "you are out of order. If you do not keep quiet, I will hold you in contempt of this court."

Prudence gazed over at Jacob, who was glowering at her, and smiled sweetly.

"Mr. Peters, you may proceed," Judge Cooper directed.

"I have only one witness left, Your Honor. I wish to call Mrs. Laurel Harper to the stand."

Prudence gasped, staring at Brock as if he were crazed.

"Mrs. Harper does not have the facility for speech, Your Honor. If I may be permitted, I would like to read her testimony."

Thomas Reed nodded his approval, and Laurel, wringing her hands nervously, walked up to the front of the courtroom. Brock helped her onto the chair and patted her hand comfortingly. "Don't be frightened, Laurel, no one here will harm you."

She nodded, and he withdrew a sheet of paper from his coat pocket. "This statement is Mrs. Harper's own words." He began to read: "I was married to a wonderful man named Michael Harper. We were newly wedded, coming west to make a home. On our way here, our stagecoach was attacked by a band of outlaws. . . ." Brock paused at the sound of Laurel's weeping, then continued, "My beloved husband was killed by those monsters, and I was violated, over and over again. I found myself to be with child shortly after."

The courtroom was so quiet, you could have heard a pin drop. Only the sounds of Laurel Harper's pitiful sobs could be heard. And then a most terrifying, hideous scream escaped from her mouth, and she shouted, "Michael! Michael!" She covered her face as if to block out the images of that horrible day.

The spectators gasped aloud in unison.

Prudence jumped up from her seat, about to rush toward the young girl, but Brock motioned her back. He retrieved a glass of water from his table and handed it to the distraught woman.

"Tha-thank you," she whispered in a raspy voice, then drank greedily. Her hand went to her throat, and she cleared it several times.

"Are you ready to continue, Mrs. Harper?" Brock waited, hoping that Laurel had finally found her voice and the courage to continue with her testimony.

She nodded. "I will try to answer your questions, Mr. Peters."

"How did you come to reside at the ranch, Mrs. Harper?"

"After the incident, I was brought into town and placed in the home of Reverend Entwhistle. A few weeks later, I discovered I was pregnant. The reverend cursed at me, called me evil, said I was a whore. He told me I was white trash, and that he wouldn't have me living in his house."

An angry roar went up in the courtroom, and all eyes turned to the reverend, who had mysteriously disappeared from his seat.

"Order! Order in the court!" the judge shouted.

"Miss Pru, that's what we call Miss Daniels, she was asked to take me in." Laurel's gaze sought out Prudence, and she smiled at her. "I love her. She's been like a mother and sister to me, all rolled into one. Sometimes she can be strict, especially if anyone is caught drinking liquor. Miss Pru don't abide with liquor. But she's always kind, even if she's a mite put out with you."

Prudence had the grace to blush at the mention of the alcohol, thinking that if these people knew how she'd indulged herself with brandy, they would ride her out of town on a rail.

"What will you do, Mrs. Harper, if the Rough and Ready Ranch is forced to close?"

Laurel started crying again, shaking her head. "I don't know. It's the only home I've got."

"Thank you, Mrs. Harper." Brock turned toward the jury. Several of the women had tears in their eyes, and Mr. Thurgood was wiping his nose with his handkerchief.

"Ladies and gentlemen of the jury, we rest our case."

25

Do not desire what you can't acquire.

The jury deliberated exactly forty-six and one-half minutes. And during that time Prudence sat stiff-backed on her seat, alternating between wringing her hands and biting her fingernails.

When the four women and eight men finally reentered the courtroom, their faces gave not a clue as to how they had voted.

"This is it, Red," Brock turned to whisper as Judge Cooper came back into the courtroom to take his seat on the dais.

Prudence nodded, licking her lips nervously, and reached out to clasp Sarah's hand for support. Each woman in turn, Sarah, Laurel, Mary, and Eliza, followed suit, grasping each other's hands, presenting a united front as they stood to hear the verdict.

"Foreman of the jury, have you reached a verdict?" the judge asked.

Lester Thurgood stepped forward, his head bobbing up and down like a cork floating in a river. "Yes, we have, Your Honor."

Prudence shut her eyes, praying silently as Mr. Thurgood announced, "We, the jury, find in favor of Prudence Daniels and the Rough and Ready Ranch."

A roar of approval rose up from the gallery of spectators, followed by a round of applause and a shriek of joy from Eliza Dobbyns.

Prudence let out the breath she was holding and hugged each woman in turn to her breast. When her eyes met Brock's, she held out her hands to him. "Thank you. We wouldn't have won if it weren't for you." Her eyes filled with tears. "I don't know how I can ever repay you."

I can think of at least a dozen ways right off the top of my head, Brock wanted to say but instead replied, "Since I'm close to starving, you can repay me by letting me take you and the other ladies to dinner at the Blue Willow."

Prudence's smile was radiant. "An excellent idea. However, it is we who will take you. Isn't that right, ladies?"

The group nodded enthusiastically, and Laurel and Mary began to giggle uncontrollably, prompting Shorty to snort in disgust. "Are we goin' to stand here jawin' all day? Or are we goin' to eat? I'm hungry enough to eat a stinkbug off a dead skunk."

Brock laughed. "Shorty's got a point, Red." He stepped through the gate to take her arm, but before they had gone five steps, Thomas Reed approached, holding out his hand in a congratulatory gesture.

"Good job, Peters. I can't say that I'm sorry to have lost. This was one case I had no stomach for. I'm sorry, Miss Daniels, for putting you and your ladies through the wringer."

Studying the numerous wrinkles on Mr. Reed's shirt, the stains on his necktie, Prudence felt that it was the young lawyer who'd been wrung out, but she refrained from saying so. "Thank you, Mr. Reed. And I hope that Mrs. Reed will consent to do your laundry again now that the trial is over." Prudence heard Brock's chuckle, and it was all she could do not to laugh at the mortification on Thomas Reed's face. The poor man was doing an excellent imitation of a ripe, red cherry.

"Yes, well, Amanda has indicated that the household chores need to be divided up a little more evenly," he muttered, then made farewells and hurried out the door.

From his position at the back of courtroom, Jacob Morgan glared at the triumphant couple as they made their way outside. The cheers that greeted them as they stepped into the street made the pulse in his neck throb violently, and he clutched his hands into fists.

"That fancy-pants lawyer hasn't heard the last from me," he vowed, his lips thinning into a vindictive line. "Brock Peters may have won the battle, but he hasn't won the war."

It was obvious Peters would have to be eliminated— and soon.

"There's something I need to do before joining you at the café," Prudence told Brock once the crowd had dispersed. Arabella Potts had been nowhere in sight, and Prudence wanted desperately to thank the courageous woman for her help.

Brock pointed down the street toward the pink Victorian-style house. "Arabella Potts lives in that pink house yonder."

A delicate eyebrow arched. "Are you a mind reader as well as a magician, Mr. Peters?"

He tweaked her nose. "We'll wait for you at the café, Red. But don't take too long, I'm starving." The excuse sounded plausible, but it was not the real reason he wanted Prudence to hurry. He feared for her safety now that the court battle had been won. Morgan wasn't the type of man who'd take losing graciously; he just might decide to take out his frustration on Prudence.

She patted his arm. "Go ahead and order. I'll just be a minute."

She hurried over to the pink house and stepped onto the porch, gazing in wonder at the ornate brass knocker that graced the front door. It was shaped like a serpent with two green eyes that glowed like emeralds. And she wondered if they were, in fact, the precious stones. Her knock was answered a moment later by a lovely Oriental woman.

"Is Mrs. Potts at home?" she asked. "I'm Prudence Daniels."

The dark eyes brightened with recognition. "Yes, miss, come in. Mrs. Potts is in the front parlor. I will show you."

Prudence entered the lovely lavender room to find Arabella regally ensconced on the sofa, reading a Beadle's dime novel entitled *Mountain Kate*. She smiled inwardly, for it was hardly the type of literature one would associate with the reigning queen of Absolution society.

"Mrs. Potts?"

Arabella looked up and her eyes widened. She closed the book and stuffed it beneath the cushion of the sofa. "Come in, Miss Daniels. This is a pleasant surprise."

"I can only stay a minute. We're having a victory party, of sorts, over at the café."

"Congratulations, dear. I heard you had won."

Prudence took a seat on the sofa. "I wanted to thank

you and the other ladies for all you did to help our cause. I don't believe we would have won without your support."

Arabella blushed slightly. "I must confess, Miss Daniels, that my motives were partially self-serving. You see, I have a personal grudge against Jacob Morgan. Although I was happy that I was able to help you, I was even more delighted to thwart Jacob's plans." Whatever they were. She had never really found out why he wanted to rid the town and himself of Prudence Daniels.

Prudence noted the way Arabella's face softened when she spoke of Jacob. "You're in love with Jacob, aren't you?"

"Of course! Just the way you are in love with Mr. Peters." At Prudence's blush, Arabella patted her hand. "When it comes to snagging a man, dear, we have to do whatever is necessary."

Her brow wrinkling in confusion, Prudence asked, "But I don't understand how making Jacob mad at you is going to help you win him over. I know he's got to be furious with you for helping me defeat him. I've known Jacob Morgan a long time. He's not a man to accept defeat easily." And that one aspect of his personality had her worried. Especially since Brock had been the means of that defeat.

Arabella laughed, and the tinkling sound floated around the room, stealing back Prudence's attention. Arabella dismissed Prudence's fears with a wave of her hand. "Jacob is a silly old fool who loves money and power. What he hasn't come to realize yet is that he loves me more. I pity the man when he wakes up to that fact."

"But how can you be so sure?" If only she were as positive about Brock's feelings, everything would be perfect.

"Dear me, you do have a lot to learn about men."

Prudence sighed in resignation and nodded.

"It's a fallacy that the way to a man's heart is through his stomach, dear. Jacob's appetite leans to the carnal side of his nature, as I'm sure most men's do. I've learned to feed that appetite. Like a starving man at a banquet, Jacob absolutely craves me. When he gets hungry enough, he'll come back to satisfy his craving."

Prudence swallowed hard at the images Arabella depicted and felt her cheeks glowing. "I wish you much success, Mrs. Potts," she said, rising.

"Men are really such simple creatures," Arabella continued, following Prudence to the door. "They think with a part of their anatomy that is way below their brain. Try to remember that. It's the key to attaining your goal."

"I . . . I will. And thank you again for everything."

Prudence hurried down the street toward the café, thinking of all Mrs. Potts's advice. According to the experienced woman, the key to winning Brock's heart meant taking him to her bed again.

Her heart began to pound as her steps quickened.

What might once have been an easy task now seemed downright formidable. Brock didn't seem the least bit interested in being seduced. Her one miserable attempt at seduction had failed miserably. She thought of the mistletoe incident and cringed inwardly.

Of course that was during the trial, when he was preoccupied with her defense. Maybe now his defenses would be down. Maybe now she'd be able to show him how much she loved him, and he would never want to leave her or the ranch.

Spying the Blue Willow up ahead, she stopped. Stuff and thunderation! This outrageous idea required a lot more thinking, a lot more planning. One didn't just walk into a restaurant and begin seducing a man.

Brock cared deeply for her, she knew that. He would

never have given her the music box if he didn't. There had to be a way to show him that she loved him. And if taking him to her bed, as Arabella intimated, was the only way, then so be it.

Arabella was right about one thing: she had an awful lot to learn about men. What she knew couldn't fill a thimble. Fortunately, she thought, smiling confidently, she was a quick learner.

The two men hunkered down by the bunkhouse, waiting for their intended prey to put in an appearance. The wind howled unmercifully, and the scar-faced man shivered within the confines of his heavy deerskin jacket.

"Are you sure Peters is going to come out of that building tonight, Jack? I'm freezing my ass off, and if he doesn't show soon, there ain't going to be enough of it left to use at Madam Eva's tonight."

Jack Adams knocked his companion's arm. "Shut up, Beevis! Do you want to give away our position? You won't have to worry about freezing your ass off if they shoot it full of lead."

"But what if he don't show? Morgan ain't paying me enough to get myself killed."

"He'll show. I've been watching this place for over a week. Peters comes out every night and walks up to the cemetery. He's as regular as clockwork. Once he shows, we'll nab him and make him disappear, just like Mr. Morgan wants."

"Why don't we just shoot him and get it over with? It seems an awful lot of trouble to abduct a full-grown man, especially one who's packin' iron."

Nate Beevis wasn't known for his smarts, Jack thought, but he sure as hell never figured him for a coward. "If you don't shut up, I'm going to shoot you myself. Then you won't have to worry about Peters killing you."

"There ain't no call to be surly, Jack. I was just—"

"Ssh! I hear something." The bunkhouse door slammed shut, and a lone figure emerged from the building.

"There he is! Let's grab him."

The two men burst forth from their hiding place, and just as the man leaned over to pull on his boot, they threw a heavy woolen blanket over his head.

Panic and instinct made Will Fletcher rise up. Flailing his arms about wildly, he surprised the two men with his strength, snatching the blanket off his head before screaming at the top of his lungs.

"Shit! This ain't Peters," Nate cried. "Let's get the hell outta here!"

Jack took off at a sprint after Nate, thinking that for once in his life Nate was right: Morgan wasn't paying them enough to get themselves killed. That thought occurred just as the first bullet whizzed by his ear.

Shorty and Slim, guns drawn and firing, took off after the two men, disappearing into the night.

"Are you all right, Will?" Brock asked, looking the boy over from top to bottom. Fear, stark and vivid, had coursed through him at the sound of Will's shouts. He'd already seen one son die; he couldn't bear to lose Will, too.

Will, who had come outside to relieve himself, shivered in his underwear, rubbing his arms against the cold as his head bobbed up and down. "Yes, sir, Mr. Peters. I'm fine. Just a mite cold. I never did get my boots pulled on all the way."

Brock hustled the boy back into the bunkhouse, pushing him onto a chair by the wood stove while he poured him a cup of hot coffee. "Drink this. It'll warm you up."

"They wanted you, Mr. Peters. Those men were after

you. I heard them say so." Will stared wide-eyed at Brock.

Morgan again, Brock thought. But how did they know that he'd moved back into the bunkhouse after the trial? Obviously they'd been watching him for a while.

He'd moved back to the bunkhouse the same night the trial had ended. Though Prudence had protested vehemently, he couldn't take living in the same house with her. If he had stayed in the house one more night, there was no telling what he might have done.

Brock knew it was time to move on. His need for Prudence had become a palpable thing. Every smile, every innocent touch, burned through him like a red-hot branding iron. She'd seared his soul, his heart, and it was pure torture sleeping in such close proximity.

"You sure look funny, Mr. Peters. Are you scared about something?"

Brock patted Will on the shoulder and nodded. "Terrified, Will. Absolutely terrified."

At that moment Prudence and Moody burst through the doorway, each carrying a rifle. They were dressed in nightclothes covered by heavy wool coats.

"Is everything all right?" she asked. "We heard gunshots."

"Some men tried to kidnap me thinking I was Mr. Peters," Will offered. Prudence blanched and looked at Brock for confirmation.

"That bastard Morgan is not going to give up, is he, Brock?" Moody asked.

"It appears Morgan hired a couple of thugs to abduct me. Shorty and Slim took out after them."

"Well, I won't sleep a wink knowing that you're out here where Jacob can get his hands on you," Prudence said. "I want you to come back to the house with me."

Brock shook his head. "That's not a good idea."

"Why not? There's plenty of room."

Brock looked over at Moody, who stared back at him sympathetically.

"You said you were terrified, Mr. Peters," Will reminded Brock. "Maybe Miss Pru is right. Maybe you'd feel better if you were living in the house."

Moody covered his laugh with a cough, and Brock ruffled the boy's hair. "I told you I was terrified, Will. But I didn't say of whom."

"What's that supposed to mean?" Prudence asked, her back stiffening in indignation. Why on earth would Brock be frightened of her? She hadn't even had a chance to plan a proper seduction before he'd hauled himself off to his precious bunkhouse.

Brock grinned. "Why, Morgan, of course. Who else? Come on, Red," Brock said, grabbing her arm. "Let's hie ourselves off to bed."

Will coughed in embarrassment, and Moody chuckled. But Prudence, who now realized that Brock was trying to get her goat, only smiled and patted his cheek tenderly. "If you think you're terrified now, Brock Peters, just you wait." With that, she twisted out of his grasp and hurried toward the door.

"Hey," Brock called out after her, "what's that supposed to mean?"

But the only answer he got was the sound of her seductive laughter. And it sent chills running down his spine and all the way down the front of his pants.

Prudence knocked softly on the bedroom door, then entered, pleased to find Laurel alone.

"May I come in, Laurel? I'd like to talk to you, if I may."

Laurel seemed apprehensive, wringing her hands

nervously as if she were expecting some type of punishment. Eliza had informed Prudence last night of the girl's odd behavior since the trial, and Prudence felt it was time to get to the bottom of it.

Taking a seat on the edge of Laurel's bed, Prudence held out her hand to the young woman. "I'm sorry we haven't had much time to talk since the trial. I've been preoccupied trying to fill that last order of boots for Mr. Willis." And she'd also been preoccupied trying to figure out a way to lure Brock into her bed. Convincing him to move back into the house last night was a start. But where did she go from here? she wondered.

Slowly Laurel approached, taking the seat next to Prudence, grasping her hand. "Is that why you've come up here? To talk to me?"

Prudence smiled. "Why, yes. Did you think there was some other reason? You seem awfully on edge. You've been feeling all right, haven't you?"

Laurel inclined her head. "Yes, ma'am. It's just that . . . well, now that the trial's over, I wasn't sure if I was supposed to continue living on here as before. I know you took me in when I was mute and pregnant, but now that I'm able to talk, I thought you might be asking me to leave."

Noting the fear in the young woman's eyes, Prudence wrapped an arm about her thin shoulders. "I wouldn't think of asking you to leave. You've had a traumatic experience. I want you to take all the time you need, and when you feel the time is right to leave, then that's when you must do it. Besides," Prudence added, tweaking the young girl's nose, "just because you've gotten back your ability to speak doesn't alter the fact that you're still pregnant."

Laurel breathed a sigh of relief. "I'm scared, Miss Pru. I feel so alone. Sometimes I don't think I'll ever be able to go out and face the world again."

"I felt that way for a long time after my sister died," Prudence admitted. "But Mr. Peters made me realize that we can't always hide from our past. Sometimes it's better to meet our problems head on. It's taken me a long time to come to that realization. Someday, when you're stronger, you'll feel that way, too. But in the meantime you're to consider this your home, just as you've always done."

"Thank you, Miss Pru. What I said the other day in the courtroom was true: you've been like a sister and mother to me, and I'll never be able to thank you for everything you've done. I didn't have the words before to tell you how I felt. But I do now, and I want to say that I love you, Miss Pru."

Prudence blinked back the tears that came quickly to her eyes and hugged the young woman to her breast. God may have taken Clara away, but He'd given back tenfold the love and friendship, with these women whom He'd placed in her care.

She had always thought of how much she'd lost. But she could see now how much she had gained. And she thanked the Almighty for that.

"What did you say we were looking for in these old books?" Moody shook his head as he thumbed through the yellowed pages of Robert Daniels's private journals. "Don't seem all that interesting to me. I'd much rather be taking a nap with my wife."

Brock looked up from the case book he studied and smiled. "I must admit, sleeping with a beautiful woman does beat the hell out of studying these old journals, but I can't help feeling there's something important to be found within the pages of these books."

"What makes you so sure that what we're looking for is in these books? We've already spent the better part of the morning reading, and so far we haven't come up with a thing. It's going to take us a week to read all those books." He pointed to the stack on the floor beneath the window. "And I don't even know what it is I'm looking for."

"Call it intuition, Moody, call it a hunch, but I'm certain that the answer to why Jacob Morgan wants to get his hands on this ranch lies within the pages of these journals. Robert Daniels was Prudence's father's lawyer. As such, he would have kept a record of all Cody Daniels's business transactions.

"Morgan's gone to a lot of trouble to get rid of Prudence. We know it's not because his moral sensibilities were threatened. That bastard doesn't have any. So there has to be a more practical reason."

"You sure are going to a lot of trouble for a woman you profess only friendship for," Moody pointed out. "I'm just wondering why that's so. Especially since you were so intent on leaving this place a few weeks ago."

Brock stiffened on his seat. "I thought winning the court case would get Morgan off Prudence's back. But after last night, and the attempt to abduct me, I can see now that he has no intention of letting up. I can't leave knowing that Prudence and the women aren't safe."

"I'm sure that me, Shorty, and the others can protect the ladies from Morgan. You shouldn't feel it's your sole responsibility, Brock. After all, you were saying only last night that it's time for you to be moving on." Moody hoped that by pressing Brock, he could get the stubborn man to admit his feelings. Noting the angry flush on Brock's face, he smiled inwardly. His probing questions were starting to nettle.

Moody's suspicions were confirmed a moment later when Brock slammed shut the book in front of him. "Why the hell is everyone so concerned about when I leave? Shorty can't stand not butting into my business, and now you. I'm going to leave when I'm goddamn good and ready and not before."

Ignoring the outburst, Moody leaned forward and turned up the lamp on the desk to compensate for the lack of sunlight. He waited until Brock had settled down on his chair again, then said, "Just seems peculiar to me that a man would stay where he says he isn't wanted. You've made it clear to Shorty and the rest of us that you think Prudence doesn't want you. Just seems peculiar, that's all."

Brock wasn't about to admit that he hadn't been able to bring himself to leave. That the thought of never seeing Prudence again tore into his gut like splintered glass.

But he knew once he'd settled matters with Morgan, he'd have no more reasons for staying. His time at the R and R was at an end: he'd have to move on.

Prudence checked her reflection in the mirror and gasped aloud. The nightgown she wore was practically transparent. How could Clara have ever worn such an outrageous thing? she wondered. She'd found the garment among her sister's belongings in the bottom of the blanket chest, deciding it was just what she needed to provoke some type of response from Brock. Only now, looking at herself in it, she wasn't sure she could go through with her plan to seduce him.

Knowing it was now or never, she took a deep breath and crossed to the connecting door that separated their rooms. Before she had a chance to change her mind, she knocked softly two times and entered.

Brock was seated on the big leather chair by the fire, staring into the flames. "Brock," she said softly, "do you mind if I come in?"

At the sound of Prudence's voice, Brock turned to look over his shoulder. The glass of brandy he held slipped out of his fingers and crashed to the floor. His eyes rounded like saucers. "Jesus!" he whispered, drinking in the sight of Prudence's near nakedness. Her breasts were clearly visible through her nightgown; he could see the dark circles of her nipples and the patch of dark hair between her legs. "Jesus!" he said again, rising to his feet. He shook his head as if to clear the vision.

"I hope I'm not disturbing you," she said, "but I couldn't sleep, and I thought you might like to talk."

Talk! Was she kidding? How could he talk? He was goddamn speechless. Swallowing with a great deal of difficulty, he said, "Are you insane, coming into my room dressed like that?"

Prudence shrugged, doing her best to appear nonchalant, and she noticed how his eyes followed the rise and fall of her bosom. "It's not as if you haven't seen me undressed before. I don't know what you're so upset about."

"You don't know . . ." He practically choked on his words. "I suggest you turn around and march right back into your room, Miss Daniels."

"But I thought . . ."

He grabbed her none too gently by the arm and escorted her to the door. "I know what you thought: you thought to tease me, to test your womanly wiles on me, once again. Well, it worked. Are you satisfied? I'm aroused." He grabbed her hand, placing it on his throbbing manhood. "Satisfied? But I'm not going to fall for your fickle-natured tricks again. I'm not going to have you ask me to make love to you, then have you throw it all back in my face the next morning."

She shook her head, begging him to understand. "It wouldn't be like that. I—"

Whatever Prudence was about to admit was muffled by the sound of the door slamming shut as she was propelled forward into her room.

She stared at the door in disbelief and promptly burst into tears. Her attempt at seduction had been a miserable failure.

Brock didn't want her.

26

Play your hand close to your belly.

"This is it!" Brock declared the next afternoon, smiling in satisfaction, slapping the pages in front of him with his fist. "I knew it. I knew we'd find what we were looking for if we kept at it long enough."

Moody yawned and stretched his legs out before him, dropping the leather journal he held on to the floor. "Hallelujah!" he retorted with no small amount of sarcasm. "Does this mean I can rejoin my wife?"

Brock pushed himself to his feet. "I'm riding to Morgan's immediately. That bastard is going to rue the day he tangled with me and mine."

Moody's eyebrows shot up in disbelief. "It's nearly suppertime. Why don't you wait till morning? I'll be happy to go with you then."

Shaking his head, Brock grabbed his hat and coat off the chair. "Nope. I'm going now. This can't wait till morning. Tell Hannah not to wait supper for me. I don't know how long I'll be."

Moody shook his head in disgust. "For Christ's sake, Brock! You can't ride over to Morgan's by yourself. Are you purposely asking for trouble? Or are you just dumber'n a stump?"

Patting Moody on the shoulder, Brock said, his tone suddenly serious, "Thanks for all your help, Moody. If something should happen and I don't return, I know I can count on you to look after the others."

Moody bolted to his feet. "Jesus! You're scarin' the hell out of me, boy. I'm coming with you."

"No! You've got a wife and child to consider. I'm going alone. I've got a score or two to settle with Morgan, and I relish the chance to do it alone."

"Aren't you going to tell Prudence?"

The mention of Prudence's name brought a frown to Brock's lips. What the hell had gotten into the woman last night? Had she been tippling at the brandy decanter? She'd certainly acted out of character. He shook his head. Damn irritating woman! Who could figure her out? One time she burned so hot, he scorched his fingers on her flesh. Then the next she was so cold, he was afraid of getting frostbite.

"Prudence is going to have my hide when she finds out I let you ride out alone."

Brock redirected his attention to Moody and grinned. "Yep. And isn't that your just reward for butting into my business."

Moody watched Brock go and swallowed nervously at the idea of having to face Prudence when she found out where Brock had gone. Christ! He'd sooner face the wrath of God.

*   *   *

Prudence's shriek of anger was much louder and stronger than anything Moody could have imagined. He shrank back against the kitchen door, wishing the floor would somehow swallow him up. He'd faced cutthroats and hostile Indians in his lifetime, but they were nothing compared to the furious woman standing before him.

"I can't believe you allowed such a thing! Brock will surely be killed. You know how much Jacob hates him."

"Now calm down," Sarah said, coming forward to force the hysterical woman onto a chair. "Martin explained that Brock was determined to go alone. You know how stubborn he can be when his mind is made up. It wasn't Martin's fault that he couldn't persuade him to stay."

A determined glint lit the green eyes. "I want the men rounded up, Moody," Prudence ordered. "We're going after Brock."

"We can't do that, Miss Pru. We might put him in more danger if Morgan sees a show of force. We have to trust that Brock knows what he's doing."

"But what if he's killed? What if he doesn't come back?" Prudence asked on a sob, starting to cry in earnest.

Sarah looked at Moody, then at Hannah, who only shrugged and shook her head. "You put your life and everyone else's into Brock's hands once before, Pru. You've got to trust that he knows what he's doing. Martin says Brock was positive he could end the trouble with Morgan over the ranch."

Wiping her face with her apron, she stared at her two friends, wanting them to understand, needing them to understand. "But don't you see? The ranch—my life—it means nothing without Brock."

Kneeling by the distraught woman's chair, Moody took Prudence's hands in his. His voice was gentle when he spoke. "My dear, maybe it's time you told Brock how you feel. Just because he's a man doesn't mean he doesn't share the same insecurities as a woman."

Brock insecure? Her eyes widened at the notion. Brock was the most self-assured person she'd ever met. It didn't seem possible that he would be vulnerable about anything, especially a woman.

"Brock doesn't want me," she confessed, her voice etched with the pain of last night's rejection.

"That's a pile of horse—"

"Martin!" Sarah scolded.

Moody heaved a disgusted sigh. "I know Brock wants you, Prudence. I see it in his face every time he looks at you."

A flicker of hope ignited in her breast. "Do you really think so?" She wanted so much to believe it, needed to believe it. But after last night . . .

He nodded, patting her hand. "Yes. I'm positive. Now, are you feeling better?"

"Yes," she replied softly. "And I'm sorry I behaved so badly."

"And you'll think about what I said concerning Brock?"

She nodded, unable to find her voice, hoping upon hope that Brock would return unharmed and she'd be given the chance to tell him just how much she loved him.

It was pitch black out by the time Brock arrived at the Bar J. The front yard was deserted, and Brock guessed that most of the hands were in the bunkhouse having dinner. He couldn't help but envy them that. He was near to starving himself. His stomach growled, attesting to the fact that he hadn't had a bite to eat since breakfast.

Tying Willy to the hitching post, Brock knocked on the door, waiting but a moment for his summons to be answered, surprised when Morgan answered the door.

The older man's eyes widened in shock, then he glared at Brock, his face purpling in rage. "What the hell do you want, Peters? You're like a bad penny that keeps showing up, over and over again."

Brock came right to the point. "I know about the arrangement you made with Cody Daniels, Morgan. I know that this property you call the Bar J isn't really yours."

Morgan blanched, then shook his head. "You're crazy! I don't know what you're talking about." But even as Morgan turned to walk into the parlor, Brock detected a slight shudder of his shoulders.

Slamming the door behind him, Brock followed Morgan into the front room. "I've been doing a bit of investigating, Morgan. That episode with your hired thugs made me curious to know why you wanted me out of the way, and why you were so eager to get your hands on Prudence's ranch."

Without a word, Morgan headed for the whiskey decanter on the side table and poured himself a drink. "You'll have a tough time proving anything in court," he finally said, gulping down the contents of his glass. "Cody's dead, and there's no proof about anything concerning the Bar J. As far as anyone in this valley is concerned, this is my ranch."

Brock was suddenly grateful that he hadn't brought along the ledger book that held the vital information about Prudence's property. "I'm sure you know by now, Morgan, that I don't leave things to chance. I'm too good a lawyer for that. I know that Cody's brother, Robert, did all of his legal transactions for him. It was all detailed in black and white, meticulously spelled out in the ledger I read."

Morgan's face paled, but Brock continued, "I know that you were leasing this land. That this property you call the Bar J legally belongs to Prudence Daniels."

Morgan slumped down on the leather wing chair, a look of defeat and resignation on his face. "I figured after old Cody died that no one would be the wiser. I used to send my yearly payments to Robert Daniels in Denver."

"And after Cody died, you ceased making payments at all."

"Prudence didn't know about the arrangement," Morgan explained. "Cody never told her, out of respect to me. And anyway, she didn't have need for all this land. I've made the Bar J what it is today: the largest cattle ranch this side of the Rockies."

"And you did it by stealing, lying, and cheating."

Morgan hung his head, a look of regret passing over his face. "I never wanted to be dishonest in my dealings with Prudence. I truly cared for her. But the chance to keep the land without paying for it was too tempting. And I needed to get my hands on her land. I don't have enough water to run all the cattle I want, while Prudence has more than she needs."

"Did you ever think to ask her if you could share her water? Maybe offer to pay her for the use?"

Morgan looked so old and defeated at the moment, Brock almost felt sorry for him. He was beaten and he knew it. Perhaps that was revenge enough, Brock thought. For a man with as much pride as Morgan, defeat was synonymous with failure. And Brock doubted that Jacob Morgan had ever failed at anything in his entire life.

"What do you intend to do?" Jacob asked. "I guess Prudence will be wanting her property back."

"Could you blame her if she did, after everything

you've put her through? The woman has a heart as big as Texas, and you've done your best to trample it."

"I'd make it up to her, if I could. Her daddy was my best friend."

"And wouldn't Cody Daniels be rolling over in his grave to see how you've been treating his daughter?"

Morgan nodded. "Cody would have put a bullet in my brain. He was that kind of man."

"It's a tempting idea, Morgan, but a little drastic for my taste. I think I'd settle for a complete written confession, and a written promise that you'll never harass or do injury to Prudence Daniels, or any of the people at the Rough and Ready Ranch."

"Does this mean you're not going to turn me over to the law?" There was a wealth of hope in the question.

"I don't see as how putting you in jail would serve much purpose. Greed rides heavy on every man's back. It's just that most of us know how to buck it off before it does us any harm. If you're agreeable, I think I can come up with a more preferable form of punishment."

"Anything. Anything you want. Just name it."

"In addition to the written statements, you must make complete restitution to Prudence for the monies owed for back rent on the land." Morgan's face turned a sickly shade of green, and Brock figured he was mentally calculating the loss. "There will be a substantial increase in future rents, of course."

Morgan grimaced. "Of course."

"And the R and R cattle that mysteriously disappeared, or were killed during your fence-cutting shenanigans, will have to be replaced."

"Done."

"And the last stipulation, which you may find more painful than all the others put together"—Brock paused, letting Morgan stew in his own juices momentarily—"is that you must propose marriage to Mrs. Arabella Potts and wed her within six months' time."

Jacob gasped, clutching his chest as if his heart had just failed him. "You want me to marry Bella? But why?"

"Because she's a woman, not unlike Prudence. A woman who has guts and gumption. A woman with a lot of class, who puts her money where her mouth is when the going gets tough. And she's a woman who has the ultimate misfortune of being in love with you."

When Morgan looked as if he were about to protest, Brock held up his hand. "Take it or leave it, Morgan. It's the whole package or none. Jail or marriage. Either way you'll be bound for life."

"I'll have the statements written, and the monies owed, to you by tomorrow morning. Will that be satisfactory?"

Brock's eyebrow arched expectantly. "And Mrs. Potts?"

Morgan shook his head, his voice heavy with disgust. "She's not even talking to me. That might take a little more time."

"Owing to how difficult women can be, I'll give you till day after tomorrow on that one."

"But what if she says no?" Jacob asked, following Brock to the door.

"If I were you, I'd get down on my knees, real humblelike, and beg the little lady. For if she says no, you'll be spending the remainder of your days in prison. Good night, Morgan."

Brock tipped his hat and walked out into the night. And the grin that split his face was wide enough to give the Grand Canyon some serious competition.

*   *   *

Everyone was gathered in the great room, awaiting Brock's return. Slim and Burt were engaged in a friendly game of checkers; Shorty had Eliza's knitting yarn wrapped around both hands, much to his mortification—he'd already threatened Slim and Burt with their lives if they so much as breathed a word of it to anyone; Mary, Will, and Laurel were on the floor in front of the stone fireplace, playing with BJ; Moody and Sarah sat at the table, going over plans for the house they planned to build; and Prudence had her eyes glued to the window, watching and listening intently for the sight and sound of a horse and rider.

A few minutes later the front door slammed open, followed by the sound of boots hitting the wooden planks of the floor as Brock made his way down the hall to the great room.

"Praise the Lord!" said Eliza when Brock entered the room. "Another five minutes and Prudence's nose would have been frozen to the window."

Brock grinned. "Is that a fact?" He walked up to Prudence, who still stood by the window, seemingly frozen in her spot. "I'm home, Red."

Prudence was so relieved by the sight of him, she didn't know whether to slap him silly or throw her arms about his neck. She opted for the latter. "I thought for sure you were dead."

Brock's composure shattered instantly. The feel of Prudence's arms about his neck was creating havoc in the pit of his belly, and lower. He tried to make light of the moment. "I hope I didn't disappoint you."

Unwilling to let him see how his words had hurt, Prudence withdrew her arms from around his neck to take a seat on the rocker by the hearth. Brock had disappointed her greatly, but not for the reason he cited.

"Me and the boys were madder'n a sore-titted bitch when we'd heard you rode for Morgan's by yourself," Shorty remarked, removing the yarn from around his hands impatiently. "You ain't got the sense the good Lord done gave you, boy, ridin' off alone like that."

"Really, Mortimer!" Eliza chastised, clucking her tongue in disapproval. "Such language, and in front of the ladies, too."

Shorty had the grace to blush, but mostly at the fact that Eliza had called him "Mortimer" again.

"We were all worried about you, Mr. Peters," Will said, and Mary nodded in agreement. "Why, Miss Pru really let the colonel have it when she found out you were gone."

"That'll be enough, Will!" Prudence remarked, hoping the bright stains on her cheeks would be attributed to the heat of the fire.

With an apologetic look at Moody, Brock took a seat at the table. "If you'll all give me a moment to explain, I think you'll be happy with what I have to say."

"Nothing you can say will compensate for the worry and aggravation you have put us through this evening," Prudence said.

"Not even if I tell you that Jacob Morgan has agreed to stop his harassment of this ranch and make restitution for the stolen cattle?"

Prudence jumped to her feet, her eyes widening in astonishment. "I don't believe it! Jacob's never run from a fight in his life."

In great detail, Brock explained everything to Prudence and the others, relating the discoveries he had made in the journal and the subsequent discussion and agreements he had made with Morgan. After he was finished, Prudence could only stare at him, her mouth agape.

"So you see," Brock said, "there is nothing more to worry about. Jacob Morgan will never bother you again."

Prudence finally snapped her mouth closed and smiled. "You really convinced him to propose to Arabella Potts?" Her smile widened. "I wish I could be a fly on the wall when that event happens." Arabella Potts might be in love with Jacob Morgan, but there would be hell to pay first before she accepted his proposal. And that thought pleased Prudence no end.

"It's entirely possible that Mrs. Potts will swat him like a fly when he gets done proposing," Sarah remarked.

Eliza tapped Shorty on the shoulder. "Speaking of proposing, Mortimer," she said, "you have not done me the formal honor of asking for my hand in marriage. You do intend to marry me, do you not?"

Turning various shades of red, Shorty gazed about the room at all the expectant faces. At last he shrugged, indicating that he knew he'd be bested by the honey-tongued woman. Going down on one knee in front of Eliza, he held both hands over his heart. "My darlin' Eliza, would you do me the honor of becoming my wife?"

Wrapping her arms about Shorty's neck, Eliza squealed in delight, nearly knocking him to the floor. "I'd be more than honored, Mr. Jenkins."

"Well, now, this calls for a little celebration," Moody said, smiling happily. "Sarah and I will go into the kitchen and fetch some cider from the pantry."

Her spirits and self-confidence buoyed by all that was going on around her, Prudence stepped closer to Brock, holding out her hand. "I'd like to talk to you for a minute, if I could."

Brock's eyebrow arched, but he swallowed her small hand in his larger one, fighting the urge to pull her into his arms and kiss her, as he'd been wanting to for weeks. "What about, Red? You're not going to yell at me again, are you?"

Her heart was hammering so loudly in her chest, Prudence was positive everyone in the room could hear it; it certainly sounded like a roaring freight train to her ears. Taking a deep breath, she shook her head. "No. It's sort of personal."

His interest piqued, Brock allowed her to lead him to the window, out of earshot of the others. "I'm all yours, Red."

She hoped so, Prudence thought. She hoped that after what she had to tell him, Brock would be hers forever. Licking her lower lip nervously, she searched for the right words. "Brock, this may not be the appropriate time to tell you this, but—"

"Brock!" Shorty shouted from across the room. "I almost forgot . . ."

Prudence heaved a frustrated sigh as Shorty approached, waving a piece of paper at Brock.

"Sorry, Red. This should only take a minute," Brock said, an apologetic smile on his lips.

"This telegram came for you today, Brock. I think it might be the answer to that lawyerin' job you was inquiring after."

Prudence's stomach dropped to the floor, and she fought against the tears that suddenly flooded her eyes.

No! This can't be. Not now, Lord. Not now.

Swallowing with great difficulty, she said in a voice that was little more than a whisper, "If you'll excuse me, I don't feel very well. I'm going upstairs to bed." Hurrying out of the room, she shook her head mutely as she passed Sarah and Moody in the hallway.

Brock watched her go, and a great emptiness welled up inside of him as he stared down at the paper Shorty handed him. The law firm of Banks and Biddle wanted him to join their practice in Prescott, Arizona. Why had he answered that damned advertisement in the *Rocky Mountain News*?

"Whatever is wrong with Prudence?" Sarah asked, setting the tray of glasses on the table, her voice filled with concern at the raw pain she had seen on her friend's face.

Eliza shook her head in disgust. "Mortimer, the insensitive clod, told Brock about a telegram he'd received. Apparently Brock's applied for a job somewhere else."

Sarah's face whitened, and she sat down heavily on the ladder-backed chair, looking across the room at Brock, who was staring at the missive. For a man who'd just received news of employment, he didn't look pleased at all. Turning toward Moody, she asked, "Why can't everyone be as happy as we are, darling? I was so sure those two would get together."

Moody sighed in frustration. He'd had such high hopes for Prudence and Brock. He'd been so sure that they would recognize their love for each other and come together as he and Sarah had.

"Perhaps we were wrong, my dear," he said, patting his wife's hand. "Perhaps it was just wishful thinking on our part to want the same happiness for Brock and Prudence that we have with each other."

"But, Moody," Sarah protested, "you know that those two belong together."

He nodded, and a great sadness filled his voice. "I know it. And you know it. The trouble is, Brock and Prudence don't seem to know it."

27

*No matter how hard the winter,
spring always comes.*

"*You've been moping* around this house for days, Prudence Daniels, and I don't mind telling you that I'm greatly disappointed in you."

Sarah set down her section of the wedding ring quilt they were fashioning for Eliza's trousseau to stare at the young woman seated across the worktable from her. "Your pretty eyes are smudged purple from lack of sleep, and your skin looks as pale as a bowl of clotted cream. Why, I've seen turtles basking in the sun who have more energy than you've had lately."

Prudence drew a deep sigh, but she didn't take offense at Sarah's words, for she knew the older woman's heart was in the right place. Anyway, Sarah's remarks were similar to those she'd heard from Eliza last night when they were cleaning up the dishes after supper.

"Mercy me, Prudence!" Eliza had said. "You're going to end up a spinster if you don't take matters into your own hands and hog-tie that man to make him stay. A true southern lady goes after what she wants. She doesn't wait for it to come to her. Didn't I do that with Mortimer? Didn't I have that man down on his knees, begging for my hand?"

Prudence had done her best to point out that she was neither southern nor much of a lady, but Eliza had only snorted her disgust and ignored her for the remainder of the evening.

Trying to hide her misery, Prudence answered in a voice deceptively calm and full of control. "I don't know what it is you all expect me to do, Sarah. Brock has made his decision to leave tomorrow, and we must honor his wishes. I can't very well get down on my hands and knees and beg him to stay."

"Why ever not? I certainly would, if the man I loved was going to ride out of my life and never return. Honestly, Pru, I thought you had more gumption. You've taken up for others all your life. Don't you think it's time you took up for yourself?"

"But Brock doesn't love me! If he did, he wouldn't be leaving." She had told herself that over and over again, trying to ease the pain of his defection. But it hadn't worked. She was heartsick and miserable. And she wasn't sure she would ever get over the loss of Brock Peters.

"Maybe he doesn't think he's got a reason to stay."

Prudence shook her head in denial. "Brock's a man who craves his independence. I won't be a ball and chain around his neck, begging him to remain and live a life he's ill-suited for. He's a lawyer. He wants to practice his profession. He would grow to hate and resent me if I deprived him of what he loved most."

Plying the needle in and out of the cotton material, Sarah wished she could puncture Prudence's hard-shelled convictions as easily. She tried another tack. "Well, this town could certainly use another lawyer. Until Brock came along, there was no one to take up for the rights of the underdog. He championed our cause. He could do the same for others. Have you even suggested such a thing to him?"

"No. I haven't spoken to him since . . ." Since the night he'd received the telegram—the night she was going to confess her love. She'd remained in her room when Brock had come into the house for his meals. It was too painful to see him, so instead she'd hid like a frightened rabbit, licking her wounds like an animal, waiting for the day he would leave and their good-byes could be said quickly and unemotionally.

Prudence supposed Brock had felt the same way; he'd made no effort to see her or talk to her.

The door to the great room opened, and Hannah entered. "What type of cake do you want I bake for tonight's party, Miss Pru?"

At the question, tears slid down Prudence's cheeks, her throat tightening so, she couldn't speak. Shaking her head, she flung herself from the chair and ran out of the room.

Sarah's eyes misted with tears, and she shook her head sadly. "I never thought I'd see the day when Prudence would run from a fight, Hannah."

The Indian woman smiled thoughtfully. "Miss Pru's battles have always been for others, never for herself. Give her time, Miss Sarah. Miss Pru's got more courage than many fierce warriors I have known. She will find the way."

"I hope you're right. Brock's farewell party is tonight, and Prudence doesn't have much time left. If she's going to find her way, she's going to have to find it soon."

A shadow passed in front of the window, and Hannah crossed to the portal to look out. What she saw filled her with pride and satisfaction. Prudence was headed in the direction of her and Joe's cabin.

From the time she was a small girl, Prudence had always gone to Joe when she was troubled.

At last, Hannah thought, Miss Pru was on the right path.

Shorty stared at Brock in disgust, spitting a stream of tobacco juice into the tarnished brass spittoon. "I feel like this is some sort of dream I keep havin', watchin' you pack up your gear again." His eyes were dimmed with sadness. "The boy's been down in the mouth since he heard you was leaving, Brock. And the others . . . Well, Slim and Burt can't hardly believe it."

Brock sighed, rolling his dress suit into a compact size to fit into his saddlebag. He guessed he'd need the damn thing in Arizona.

"I can hardly believe it myself, Shorty. But I'm going this time for sure. I've made up my mind." Prudence had made her feelings for him quite clear; she hadn't even wanted to be in his company the last few days, claiming she was ill. But Will had told him she'd been down to eat every night after he'd returned to the bunkhouse.

Women! Who could figure them?

"I've been around the pot after the handle longer than you, so I guess my age gives me permission to talk some sense into that stubborn head of yours," Shorty said, ignoring the way Brock's eyes rolled toward the ceiling. "Women have a way of makin' a man run around like a cockroach in a hot skillet. You never know which way their mind is a-goin' to work. They are downright confusing creatures. But mark my words, Brock, Miss Pru is in love with you. And if you leave, you're gonna break her heart."

The sunlight streaming in through the window revealed the disgust on Brock's face. "I've heard that kind of talk before—from you, from Moody, even from little Mary. But I've never heard, never was given, one sign from Prudence that she felt that way. It's too late for what might have been. I'm going. My mind's made up."

Shorty spat again, and this time he came dangerously close to hitting Brock's boot. "Well, you ain't never told her neither how you felt. And don't go tryin' to deny that you love that little gal. My head ain't full of stump water. Don't be pissin' down my back and tellin' me it's rainin', 'cause I ain't gonna fall for it. You love Miss Daniels, and iff'n you leave without telling her so, then you are one sorry sonofabitch."

With one last disgusted look at Brock, Shorty shrugged into his jacket and slammed out the door.

"Great. Just great!" Brock cursed, throwing the tin cup from his bedroll across the room. His last day at the ranch, and even that had to be spoiled by Prudence.

Well, he was determined to go to that damned party tonight and act as if everything were honky-dory. Then he'd fetch his things, saddle Willy, and ride into town. Maybe even find himself a whore to bed down with. Lord knew, it had been a while since he'd had any female companionship.

No one would ever be the wiser that he was dying on the inside. Not Shorty, not Moody, and most especially not Red.

He shut his eyes and felt unwelcome moisture burning behind his lids. "Damn it, Red!" he whispered. "Why did you have to be the one?"

*　　*　　*

The mood was somber as the cold, dark January night, for those who sat in the great room knew that this would be Brock's last night at the ranch.

No one was more melancholy than Brock as he gazed about the room, committing to memory each face, each gesture, wanting to store all the treasured times in his mind and heart so he would never forget the time he'd spent at the ranch.

As if he'd be able to. He looked at Prudence, who was seated on the rocker, holding BJ on her lap, kissing the baby's head, talking soothingly to him as she rocked him to sleep; the sight brought a heaviness to his chest. He would miss the child, his namesake. He would never see BJ take his first step, never hear him utter his first word.

And he would miss Red.

Would she miss him? he wondered. Would she ever think about him? Wonder where he'd gone? Or would he just become another fragment of her life—one that didn't fit into her well-ordered scheme of things?

"Would you like another piece of cake, Mr. Peters?" Mary asked, jarring Brock from his misery.

Patting his stomach, he forced a smile to his lips. "No, thanks, Mary. I've already had two, and that was on top of Hannah's delicious chicken'n dumplings." The Indian woman had prepared his favorite meal, and the gesture had touched him more than words could say.

Moody stood, clearing his throat. He had once again donned his uniform and looked resplendent in his blues. "I've been appointed the official spokesman," he informed Brock. "Shorty's been around Eliza too long and has gotten a bit long-winded, so the boys wanted me to speak on their behalf."

"Why, I declare!" Eliza's lips pursed in indignation.

"Now, sugarplum," Shorty cajoled, kissing Eliza on the cheek. "You know it takes a minimum of ten sentences for you to say what someone else could say in one."

"Hmph!" was all Eliza replied, crossing her arms over her chest in a gesture that Shorty knew spelled trouble.

Brock smiled at the older couple. "Don't let that old goat fool you, Eliza. He told me once that he loved hearing you talk. Said your voice was like sweet maple syrup."

"Oh, Mortimer." The woman's cheeks blossomed prettily while Shorty's turned florid.

Moody cleared his throat and motioned for Sarah to bring forward the package. "The boys and I went together and bought this for you, Brock. We hope it'll come in handy, and that you'll think of us when you use it." Moody dropped the heavy bundle on Brock's lap and stepped back, adding, "Although we hope that you won't have to use it too often."

Brock stared in astonishment at the silver-handled Colt .45 revolver. He swallowed his surprise and thanked everyone. He certainly hadn't been expecting presents, and never anything so fine as this gun.

Mary stood next, walking toward him with a gaily wrapped package in her hands. "This is from me and BJ, Mr. Peters. We wanted to say thank you for everything you done for us. And . . ." She started to cry, and Will came forward to wrap his arm about her.

"Mary's a bit emotional, Mr. Peters. Women, you know." There were tears in the young man's eyes as well, but Brock pretended not to notice and nodded in understanding.

Unwrapping the gift, Brock found a handsomely

tooled leather holster with his initials on it. Silver conchas lined the belt, and he knew Mary had spent many hours working on it. "It's beautiful, Mary. I've never had anything so beautiful." The young woman beamed, her sadness forgotten for the moment.

Prudence watched Laurel approach Brock shyly. She knew the young woman had worked many hours on her gift, and she hoped Brock would be understanding when he saw that it wasn't quite perfect. The pair of warm woolen socks were hopelessly uneven, but Brock's enthusiasm for Laurel's offering was just as great as it had been for the others. Somehow Prudence had known it would be.

"I'm just learning to knit," Laurel explained, "so they might not be as fine as what you're used to, Mr. Peters. But I know they'll keep your feet warm."

Brock kissed the young woman's cheek and thanked her and Prudence felt her eyes well with tears.

Please God. Let him like my gift equally as well.

Sarah presented her gift of a finely stitched linen shirt, and Eliza handed over the leather satchel she had fashioned. "For your court papers," she explained.

After the last gift had been opened and the last farewell had been said, everyone filed out of the room, leaving Prudence and Brock alone for the first time in days. Prudence's hands started to sweat when she heard the door bang shut. Brock was gathering his gifts, making ready to depart, and she knew that the time had come for her to present the last remaining gift: her own.

"It was a fine party, Red. I'll remember it for a long time to come." Brock attempted to keep his voice light, though his eyes mirrored the sadness he felt.

Stepping forward, Prudence dragged her gift behind her, fearful she would drop it, she was shaking so uncontrollably. "I have something for you, Brock," she said. "Something I hope you'll want and will learn to cherish."

He was surprised but pleased by the gesture. "You shouldn't have bought me anything. The party was enough."

"I . . . I didn't buy it. Indian Joe helped me make it." She brought the heavy package forward. "I've never been very good at putting my feelings into words."

He grinned. "Oh, I don't know about that, Red. You've taken me to task a time or two."

Brock took the gift from Prudence's hands, and Prudence's heart immediately jumped into her throat as she watched him open it. Confusion wrinkled his forehead as he stared at the large wooden sign, his eyes widening in disbelief, his mouth dropping open when he read the inscription: *The Rough and Ready Ranch for Unwed Mothers. Brock Peters, Esquire. Prudence Peters, Manager.*

Prudence *Peters!* He glanced up, and the look of hope and love on her face made his eyes fill with tears. He swallowed the lump in his throat. "This sign says Prudence Peters."

Her words came out in a rush. "I . . . I know that you want to leave here to set up a law practice. But . . . well, I thought if you wanted to stay, you could set up your practice right here. There are plenty of young women who'll be needing your legal advice and expertise. And, well . . ." She burst into tears. "I don't want you to leave. I love you, Brock. Please stay."

Astonishment touched his face, and he stood staring at her for what seemed the longest time. When she couldn't stand his silence one more moment, she blurted, "Well, are you going to stay or not?"

"You sure do know how to take a man by surprise, Red," he said, setting down the sign and drawing her into his arms. "I've never had a woman propose to me before."

She caressed his cheek tenderly. "I love you, Brock. I have for a long time. And although you may not feel the same way about me . . . well, sometimes love can grow. And you'd be half owner of the ranch. And—"

He smothered her persuasions with his mouth, kissing her long and hard until she was breathless. "Woman! If you don't think that I'm already crazy in love with you, then you're positively deaf and blind. I have loved you since that first moment I stepped through your door." He grinned at her bewilderment. "Actually it was before that. It was when Hank Brewster down at the livery told me that you were the meanest spinster this side of the Rockies."

"He said that?"

Brock's grin widened as he swept Prudence off her feet and into his arms. "I figured any spinster that mean had to have a whole lot of passion stored up inside of her. And I was right, Red. And I'm going to prove it to you right now."

Prudence gasped. "Right now? You mean, right this very moment?"

"Love, I doubt these pants are going to hold in a minute longer what's been straining to come out for months. If we don't get on up the stairs this very instant, I'm going to have to take you right here on the floor."

Wrapping her arms tight about him, Prudence snuggled her nose into his neck. "You'd better hurry, Brock," she whispered. "I think I hear your buttons popping."

The room was pitch black, save for the glow of the fire in the hearth. But Brock didn't need the light to see the perfection of Prudence's body.

Reverently he moved his hands over every exquisite, naked inch of her, tracing the lushness of her mounds, the length of her legs, the soft moistness of the curls between her thighs, then followed the path of his hands with his tongue.

"Brock, Brock, you're torturing me," Prudence said, moaning in pleasure, clutching the rigid muscles of his back, his head, as it dipped lower into her most secret of places.

"It's sweet torture, love. Such sweet torture," he whispered, taking an erect nipple between his lips and sucking on it.

Prudence reached down to grasp Brock's hard, silken shaft and heard his sharp intake of breath. It pulsed in her hand as she stroked its length, and she guided it to the apex of her thighs.

"Tell me what you want," he coaxed.

"I'll show you instead," she said brazenly, wrapping her legs about his waist while impaling herself on his rigid member.

"Oh, God!" Brock cried, thrusting into her over and over, murmuring love words and sex words, declaring his love for her just as they reached the pinnacle of their fulfillment and became one.

Later, when they were sated and wrapped in the glow of their lovemaking and each other's arms, Prudence snuggled into Brock's chest, tracing the soft hairs with her finger.

"Was I all right? Did I please you?" she asked, wanting to please Brock in every way that she could. To show him each and every day of their life how much his love meant to her. And she would.

Brock heaved a sigh of pure peace and contentment, hugging Prudence close to his heart.

"Red," he said, kissing her cheek, "you were great! Just great!"

Epilogue

For better or for worse means for good.

December 24, 1876

"I declare!" Eliza stated, banging the front door shut with her behind. "It's snowing to beat the band out there. I wasn't sure I'd be able to make it across the yard with my pies."

Prudence rushed forward to help the woman whose hands were full of pie tins, setting the delicious-smelling concoctions on the entry hall table. "Where's Shorty? I can't believe he let you come out in that storm all by yourself." Eliza and Shorty's cabin sat right next to Hannah and Joe's, near the bunkhouse; and though it wasn't far from the main house, in a snowstorm the trek across the slippery ground could be treacherous.

Prudence smiled to herself. Since their marriage in January, Shorty had turned into a regular mother hen where Eliza and nine-month-old James Mortimer Jenkins were concerned. Brock claimed that if Shorty's chest puffed out any farther, he was likely to explode.

Eliza snorted, removing her coat and hanging it on the hall tree. "The old fool wasn't done wrapping his Christmas presents. And I told him that we were going to miss all the festivities if we didn't come over right away." She unwrapped the scarf from her head, shaking the snow onto the floor. "Honestly, the man is more trouble than little Jimmy. Speaking of which, how is my darling baby boy?" Her eyes lit with joy.

"Jimmy's upstairs asleep in the nursery. Laurel arrived from town a couple of hours ago, and she's tending to all the babies." The poor woman definitely had her hands full. In addition to Eliza's baby, which had been born last March, the R and R now boasted three new babies, including her and Brock's own two-month-old little girl, Clara Anne. With Mary's son, BJ, that brought the total number of children to five.

Eliza made a beeline for the fire, holding out her hands to the flames. "I suppose Laurel closed up the mercantile early because of this storm." Harper's Mercantile was the newest addition to Absolution's growing business community.

Prudence nodded, crossing to the large fir tree to continue with her decorations. "Laurel works too hard as it is. I'm just grateful Slim was able to talk some sense into her by convincing her to close early." Slim and Laurel had been keeping company of late, and everyone was hoping theirs would be the next wedding to take place.

"The tree looks just lovely," Eliza said. "I think this is going to be our finest Christmas celebration ever. It certainly will be an improvement over last year's. Remember how worried we all were about that trial?"

How could she ever forget? Prudence wondered. But then, some good had come of it. She and Brock had finally gotten together, Laurel had regained her speech, and the jury's favorable verdict had forced Reverend Entwhistle to leave town.

Absolution now had a new minister. Reverend Silas Morley, a rotund, jowly-cheeked, joyfully kind man who epitomized everything good about religion and was the exact opposite of Ezekiel Entwhistle. He had married Prudence and Brock last February.

"Things always seem to work out for the best," Prudence finally said, her cheeks blushing softly as she thought of how happy she was to be a wife and new mother.

Just then Brock entered, carrying Clara in his arms. The baby was dressed in a lovely little red velvet dress that her aunt Sarah had made her for the occasion. "Laurel said to tell you that Clara's getting fussy. It's time for her to eat."

By the fullness in her chest, Prudence had already guessed it was getting close to the baby's feeding time. She crossed over to Brock, giving him a tender kiss on the lips before taking the baby from him. "Will Sarah and Moody be much longer? Hannah says we're going to eat promptly at eight this evening. And she's made a cake, so we can celebrate their one-year anniversary."

"Sarah's showing Mary how to operate that new Singer sewing machine Moody bought her for Christmas. And Will's trapped Moody into telling him another one of those Indian stories. The boy's got a penchant for gore." Though Brock knew Moody loved the retelling of his army adventures.

"I hate putting the colonel and Mortimer in the same room together. It's hard to say who can spin the talles tale," Eliza quipped, rising. "I'm going to lend a hand in the kitchen. I'm certain Hannah could use some help 'long about now." The older woman disappeared out the door, and Brock took a seat beside Prudence on the sofa.

He watched in awe as Clara sucked contentedly at Prudence's breast, marveling once again at the wonder of birth. He'd never thought to have another child of his own and felt damn lucky that things had worked out between him and Red. He reached out to toy with a stray curl that rested against Prudence's cheek. "You're even more beautiful now that you've had a child, Red."

Prudence smiled tenderly, turning her head to kiss his hand. "I love you, Brock Peters. I've never been happier in my life. I wonder if all married women feel the same way I do." She sighed in contentment.

Brock chuckled. "Speaking of married women, I ran into Arabella this afternoon when I went into town to pick Laurel up. She's got Jacob on an awfully short rope these days. He was following behind her, carrying an armload of packages. I think now that she's Mrs. Jacob Morgan, Arabella is enjoying the heck out of spending all his money."

"I've invited them to Christmas dinner tomorrow. I hope that meets with your approval." She searched his face anxiously, hoping he would concur with her decision. Though Brock had decided to let bygones be bygones, he still hadn't forgiven Jacob completely. But that would take time.

"That's fine. After all, if it wasn't for Jacob, you and I might never have gotten together."

"Oh, yes, we would," Prudence argued. "I'm a strong believer in fate. And fate's what brought you to this ranch."

"Not to mention Mary. Which brings to mind: Did you get the new arrival settled? Miss Oliver looked scared witless when she showed up on our doorstep yesterday."

"Kelly will be fine. She's upstairs resting."

"I don't know how you do it, Red. Everyone's always coming to you with their problems. I'm the lawyer, but you seem to be the one who knows how to give the best advice."

"Don't sell yourself short, Mr. Peters. You're the best damn lawyer that this town has ever seen. Why, there's talk of running you for mayor, now that statehood's been achieved."

"Great! Just great! That's just what I need." Brock shook his head. "I've got no interest in politics, Red. I'm content to be a husband, father, and lawyer, in that order."

"And I love all three of you," she whispered, leaning over to kiss him.

"Do you think we'll have time to sneak upstairs before the rest of the folks show up this evening?" He grinned lewdly at her. "Save some of that for me." He gestured toward her breasts. "It isn't fair for Clara to get all of it."

"You're shameful!" she replied, laughing.

"Shamefully in love with you, Mrs. Peters."

"And I you, Mr. Peters. And I you."

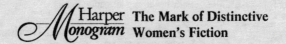

COMING NEXT MONTH

HIGHLAND LOVE SONG by Constance O'Banyon
From the bestselling author of *Forever My Love* comes a sweeping and mesmerizing continuation of the DeWinter legacy begun in *Song of the Nightingale*. In this story, set against the splendor of nineteenth-century Scotland, innocent Lady Arrian DeWinter is abducted by Lord Warrick Glencarin, laird of Clan Drummond—the man of her dreams and the deadly enemy of her fiancé.

MY OWN TRUE LOVE by Susan Sizemore
A captivating time-travel romance from the author of *Wings of the Storm*. When Sara Dayny received a silver ring set with a citrine stone, she had no idea that it was magical. But by some quirk of fate she was transferred to early nineteenth-century London and found a brooding and bitter man who needed her love.

ANOTHER LIFE by Doreen Owens Malek
Award-winning author Doreen Owens Malek takes a steamy look behind the scenes of daytime television in this fast-paced romantic thriller. Budding young attorney Juliet Mason is frustrated with her job and pressured by a boyfriend she doesn't want to marry. Then she gets assigned to defend handsome leading actor Tim Canfield, who may be the most wonderful man she's ever met—or the most dangerous.

SHADOWS IN THE WIND by Carolyn Lampman
The enthralling story of the Cantrell family continues in Book II of the Cheyenne Trilogy. When Stephanie awakened on Cole Cantrell's ranch, she had no idea who she was. The only clues to her identity were a mysterious note and an intricate gold wedding band. Feeling responsible for her, Cole insisted she stay with him until her memory returned. But as love blossomed between them, could they escape the shadows of the past?

DIAMOND by Sharon Sala
Book I of the Gambler's Daughters Trilogy. Diamond Houston has always dreamed of becoming a country and western singer. After her father's death, she follows her heart and her instincts to Nashville with legendary country star, Jesse Eagle. There she learns that even for a life of show biz, she must gamble with her soul.

KILEY'S STORM by Suzanne Elizabeth
Daniella "Dannie" Storm thought she had enough trouble on her hands when her father found gold in the local creek and everyone in Shady Gulch, Colorado began to fight over it. But when Marshal Jake Kiley rode into town to settle the matter, she realized that her problems had only just begun—especially her strong attraction to him.

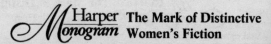